A Story from Many True Stories
A South Point Rickey Suspense Novel

NO EXIT FOR THE innocent

by Robert M. Granafei

ISBN: 978-1-09831-983-0 (print)
ISBN: 978-1-09831-984-7 (eBook)

No Exit For The Innocent

This coming of age suspense novel centers on nineteen year old Richard Wilson Osgood, aka South Point Rickey, a handsome, Southern Californian surfer who through no fault of his own becomes entangled in the chaos of the '60's.

After high school Rickey's interests extended no further than surfing, hanging with his buddies, his dog, Rusty, and exploring romance. But all that changes when he saves a famous actress from getting beaten by the police at an antiwar demonstration. Now he is being watched by people who are exploiting the antiwar movement for their own political ends.

His situation becomes complex when he loses his student deferment and is ordered to report for induction into the US Army.

It then becomes deadly when he witnesses the killing of Bobby Kennedy and knows the lone gunman theory is a lie. Now he has both the government and the mob after him.

What choice does he have but to flee to Canada and try to start a new life for himself?

And now they are closing in on him.

1

Rickey leaned against the building as the November morning air gently blew his longish sun-bleached hair from his face. A face which was tanned by many hours on the sea waiting for the swell to form and the right wave to catch. His green eyes seemed to have a secret source of light behind them as they appeared to sparkle under the fine arch of his eyebrows. Yet, this morning, there was a narrowing of his eyes and a slight tightening around his jaw-line. He stood five feet eleven inches and carried a middle weight's frame on long powerful legs. He moved with grace and the quickness of a feline without haste or wasted motion. He never seemed hurried or anxious, all the while maintaining a poise much older than his eighteen years. He was an attractive man in the full flower of his youth, as he gazed across the quiet street to the large grey building with the ominous sign towering over the entry: WELCOME US ARMY INDUCTION CENTER.

A stranger watching him would have seen a young man standing quietly alone, smoking a cigarette, casually watching the other young men across the street sort themselves into an orderly line under the barking orders of a man in a drab green uniform. The stranger would not have seen the conflict and turmoil raging through Rickey as he stood there trying to decide whether to join the line or walk back to his van and flee.

The clamminess of his hands and dead sweat under his arms arose not from the warmth of the morning sun but from the fear which gripped him. The fear he felt since reading the note left in his van earlier that morning was something new and strange. He had experienced physical fear many times before, but not this dread; not this paralyzing chill which radiated through his body causing his hands to tremble and his breathing to be quick and shallow. This was all new and frightened him to his core.

The sense of despair overwhelmed his choices. To flee meant an opportunity to live, but never to see his parents again. To join meant there was a real chance he would be killed which he knew would destroy their lives. The anger he felt was deep and hard as he asked himself, *Why do I have to make this choice? Who is to blame for this?* But he knew there were no answers to these and the countless other questions that flooded his brain both night and day. It was what it was.

It was like a wave was forming and coming at him; he had to decide to catch it or let it pass. It was steep, and to catch it meant risking getting wiped out on the coral reef below. To let it pass meant being alone as darkness fell, knowing his buddies on shore could not rescue him when the next set rolled in. He was alone with the decision, and it was his alone to make. And, he had to make it soon.

He again fingered the edge of the single sheet of paper tucked inside the belly pocket of his poncho. He didn't need to remove it to know what it said. In simple third-grade English that even his slowest classmates could understand, it was an order from the President of the United States telling him to report to the Induction Center across the street at 0900 hours...which in his world was 9:00 AM - this morning. His failure to report would result in his being arrested and in federal prison.

He'd only received the notice a few days before, along with a large stack of mail which had accumulated on his mother's entryway table while he had been surfing in Mexico. Welcome home, Rickey

He knew it was coming ever since he dropped out of City College to chase waves in Mexico. But that didn't lessen the impact when he saw the envelope labeled Selective Service in bold black letters peeking out from his magazines with their glossy waves peeling back in perfect shape. The contrast couldn't have been more stark. He understood selecting a wave but didn't understand what Selective Service meant. He can't select. They selected him and everyone else he knew from school. Didn't seem very selective to him if they took everybody. No, it wasn't *selective* at all. But, whatever they called it, it was calling him this morning in the late Fall of 1968.

The sun was warmer on his face now as he glanced at his watch: a *Seiko* his father had given him as a graduation present from high school. Seven thirty-five. Less than an hour and a half to decide how his life was going to go. He had only two choices: walk into the Induction Center and place his fate in the hands of the US government, or flee into uncertainty.

He walked further into the shadows and pulling cigarettes out of his pocket. He quickly drew one from the pack and tapped it slowly against his *Zippo* lighter to pack the end. A small burst of flame, a short draw of breath and the *Lucky* filled his lungs with that warm calming air which he recognized as something known and familiar. It was comforting on a morning filled with the strange and unfamiliar.

Instinctively he fingered the notice again. The name on it was Richard Wilson Osgood. No one called him that. His mother called him Rickey and his father called him Rich but most people called him South Point Rickey or South Point or SP, but no one called him Richard.

Another deep draw on the *Lucky* and he remembered the chilly winter morning at Rincon when he first heard it. He grew up in Long Beach, and while the city lived up to its name, the long beach had nothing for waves. Any surf it once had was killed back in the '30's when the city fathers built a huge jetty of rock and stone about two miles out from the beach making Long Beach one giant pond: great for shipping but poor for surfing. So Rickey and his crew had to travel down the coast to Huntington or Laguna or north to Redondo and Malibu to find waves with the shape and power to satisfy their desire for freshness and speed. But sometimes, when the rumor mills spilled sights of even better waves further north or south, they would pile their boards on top of their cars and head out in the blackness of four in the morning to be at the right spot by daybreak.

That December morning the spot was Rincon just south of Santa Barbara, a small beach protected by a long point. That point, when the sea had some north in it, caused a wave that broke right to left in the sweetest arch known to boy or man, never ending as it spilled its aqua-green and emerald curl southward, splashing reflected sunlight in its crest and covering its foam in white effervescence.

It was magic that morning: so fresh and clean, calling to him with a quiet whisper. He rode wave after wave all morning long, catching some for so long it felt they would never end. Never had he had such rides. But by mid-morning the on-shore breeze came up and blew the tops off the waves destroying their shape and ending the day. As he walked back up the beach to meet his friends he heard a voice speaking about him. "Hell, man! He's a south point." His friend heard it too, and from then on, he was South Point Rickey. They called him that although he rode with a regular stance, his left foot forward, his was extreme. His left foot was almost to the tip of the board. They called him South Point that morning and it's been South Point Rickey ever since.

He turned back toward the street and took a final drag on the *Lucky*, the sunlight cutting across his face. The safety of the shadows gone. He doubted they would call him South Point in the Army.

It's not like he didn't know about the war. He had already lost a childhood friend late last year. Randy had always been a flaky kid, in and out of trouble. Once he stole all the silverware out of the junior high school cafeteria and then dumped it into a garbage bin behind a strip mall across from the school. When asked why he did it, his simple answer was, "Their food sucks!" This and other behavior convinced his father, a man of strict moral values but of limited intellect, to pressure him into joining the Marines at eighteen. "They will make a man out of you," his father had said, clapping him on the shoulder as he departed for boot camp. Randy liked the uniform and the idea of getting away from his father.

He was on point with a patrol just outside Da Nang when he was caught in a cross-fire and killed by the hail of bullets. Others say he was sitting just inside the camp's perimeter smoking a joint when an RPG landed, cutting him in half. Others still, say he died of an overdose using heroin for the first time. No one really knew the truth of how Randy died but he was the first of Rickey's surfing buddies to die in Vietnam.

There were others too, and yet, they were only eighteen, just months out of high school. Gone. Cut down before they could buy a drink legally. Some he guessed, had never even been laid, unless it was in the whore house in Tijuana on one of their treks south to find surf and cheap beer.

He felt a metallic taste in the back of his throat and for a moment thought he might toss up the coffee he had before leaving the house. He paused and stepped back into the shadows which he quickly realized weren't as deep as before and now had an acute angle to them. A panic wave rushed over him. He glanced again at his watch and was relieved to see it was just 7:50: still an hour to decide. He lit another *Lucky* and watched the smoke drift away. Oh how he wished his problems would drift away as easily as the smoke.

He must have wandered off in thought as suddenly his fingertips were burning. The *Lucky* was nothing but ash and a red hot ember stuck to his index finger and it hurt like hell. He quickly snapped his fingers and the ember flew off leaving a nasty burn mark. He sucked on the finger to ease the pain and in that moment, a memory flashed on him with all the power of yesterday brought into the moment with such total clarity, the memory seemed more real than the experience itself had been.

That was how he had met Marsha. He had cut his hand on a broken bottle hidden in the sand at old Tin Can Beach; not an unusual occurrence at the beach which was more dump than playground. He was sitting there trying to get the bleeding to stop by pushing his tee shirt into the gaping hole in his right palm. He looked up and she was standing there with an amused grin on her face. She laughed slightly and said, "Silly, that won't work. Here, let me help you." With that, she reached into her purse and withdrew a per-fectly folded handkerchief; snow-white with dark blue initials which read MLM. She pushed his hand away and placed the handkerchief directly on the cut and squeezed his hand between hers so tightly he thought she would break his fingers. *Wow!* he thought to himself, *this girl has some strength*, and as that thought passed through his mind, another one quickly followed. *Whoa! she is really beautiful.* He felt his heartbeat quicken and an unknown feeling surge through his chest as his head spun for just a moment. *What is this? This feels like the first drop on a 20 foot wave but I am sitting here in the sand.* Confused, he started to pull away his hand but she resisted saying, "No, you must keep pressure on it." He tried to think of something clever to say but instead mumbled, "Hi, I'm South Point Rickey." She laughed and said, "What a funny name, but it's cute and seems to fit you. I'm Marsha."

They spent the rest of the Summer together. That amazing carefree time between high school and college, or for some, between high school and 45 years of work. Basically 90 days to be a kid but with a license to be an adult. But like any vacation, there is an ending which is rarely fun.``Even with good endings, there is a sense of loss, of leaving something behind that you will never recapture.

2

As he watched the other young men across the street continue to organize themselves, he walked up the alleyway out of the shadows and into the sunlight. Quickly he felt the warmth of the sun replace the chill which had attached to him while in the shadows. The sun's radiance relaxed him and the slight nausea which had nagged him all morning disappeared. He felt stronger and more like himself, and yet fear still surged through him like a relentless stream.

He wondered if the young men across the street felt the same way as he did. *No, they couldn't because they haven't been through what I've been through. They don't know what I know, and I wish to God I didn't.*

He stepped back into the shadows as if seeking shelter, but his mind continued to race across the landscape of his past. Relentlessly his thoughts tumbled back across the months since he left high school and all that had happened. He began to remember all that he'd had and all that he'd lost.

*　*　*　*　*

Before that night in June he had struggled with thoughts of the draft and the idea of going to Vietnam to kill or be killed. The freedom in refusing to go weighed against the practicality of joining. But now the choice was to live or to die. He knew in his heart that to cross the street and line up with the others would probably mean the men in suits who had been looking for him, would have him and take him away. He knew something they wanted no one else to know.

The warmth of the sunlight did little to wash away the harsh images cluttering his mind of the blood seeping from Bobby Kennedy's skull. Why, oh why had he been trapped, standing there just behind the Senator and next to the gunman who had shot him? The world thought Sirhan Sirhan alone had shot him but Rickey knew otherwise. He could not erase his images of that navy blue sleeve, the white cuff and the gold links which contrasted so starkly with the steel grey gun; the long white fingers which wrapped around the grip and pulled the trigger. First the pop, which made him turn toward the shooter, then the second pop which made him realize this was a gun and it was real. And finally, the third pop. Oh! That sickening third pop which thrust the Senator's head forward, causing blood to flow out from his hair and down into his collar. He watched as the Senator sunk to the floor, and there in front of him under a pile of men was Sirhan Sirhan and Rickey knew in an instant that he had not acted alone.

In that moment, Rickey did not realize that all he held dear to him was instantly taken from him, to be replaced only by his will to survive. Though even this morning, he'd naively believed they would do nothing more than question him; until he discovered the note. And, the note had been quite clear. Cross the street and you risk dying.

His mind, nearly breaking from the stress of having to choose, slipped quickly into the past and surfed his memories as to how he wound up standing in this concrete maze, confused and alone. A twilight haze enveloped him as his thoughts churned backwards.

*   *   *   *   *

The warmest water for surfing is in September and October, and Rickey could feel it on the soles of his feet as they were unprotected by his wetsuit. As he sat off of Sunset Beach waiting for some small shore break to form, he couldn't help wondering at the beauty of the azure sea and the heavenly blue sky. The sun was streaming down in shifting patterns of light, as the cloud cover moved out to sea. The greens and greys mixed flawlessly with the yellow and gold shafts that crept into the shadows.

He was at peace, but he felt an undercurrent of doubt at the edges of his consciousness. It was mid-September and he knew that Marsha would be leaving soon for Berkeley. Only 400 miles away, but it felt like 5,000. He had read about the place, and it seemed to him a far and different land, filled with people of passion and rage, people of many colors and customs, people who preferred to read books than surf waves, as if from different tribes. His Marsha would soon leave the warmth of their tent on the beach for the stillness of a dorm room. He knew it, but had difficulty accepting it. But accept it he had to, for like the effect of the full moon on the tide, it was happening with or without him.

Later that afternoon, he was surprised by a phone call when she asked to meet down by the Seal Beach pier, at a small taco joint where they would often go to share chips and that green salsa that had just enough bite to leave your tongue a little numb around the edges. As he drove down Coast Highway past the old white building that always looked like it would fall over from the weight of the large sign atop it which pronounced LIVE BAIT SOLD HERE, past the cricket pumps pulling the black crude out of the ground and leaving the air with a slight acidic smell, past the small boat marina filled with dreams both broken and realized, past the hamburger stand that was always encircled with cars, and finally past the mud flats with their sweet smell of decay. He felt at home. This was his town. There, waiting for the signal to change, he was lighting up a *Lucky* it struck him: she was meeting him to tell him good-bye.

The thought struck him like a body blow, causing his foot to slip off the clutch. He felt his heart sink at the same time the cars behind began to honk as the signal had changed. He fumbled for the key, and only after turning it he remembered the old *Ford* had a button starter on the floor. Flushed and confused, he pressed the starter, heard the engine roar, released the clutch and hip-hopped his way through the intersection feeling both victimized and humiliated.

He parked down by the old Bay Movie Theater, giving himself a few blocks to walk and think before he reached the taco shop and Marsha. As he glanced at the window displays of the shops and stores, he began to talk himself out of his premonition. She wasn't scheduled to leave for another eight days. There was no need to say good-bye now. There was still a week together. A week to talk and decide if he would go up to Berkeley with her, or go up to Santa Cruz where he could surf but still be only a short drive away, or, his fondest hope, that she would stay and live with her parents and go to the local college. Yes, there was time, plenty of time and he had been foolish to think that she would say good-bye over chips with so much time together still left.

As he crossed the abandoned railroad right of way that the city had turned into a green belt, his confidence was back and he secretly hoped that perhaps they could go up the road to the Golden Sails Inn for a little time together. *Yes, this could be a great afternoon*, he thought to himself as he pushed open the front door to the taco shop and heard the jingle of bells announcing his entrance. She sat in the back, under the stuffed hawk hung to look like he was ready to land. A half-filled glass sat on the table in front of her and Rickey could tell by the multiple rings of water on the tabletop, she had been there awhile. He smiled at her, and opened his arms, anticipating her standing to embrace him as she always did. Instead she sat there and looked up and under at him from the grey felt derby, her blue eyes rimmed in red and her pink lips drawn tightly across her mouth. He paused, feeling his knees weaken, and his left leg began to shake for no reason. "Mars, what's the matter? Are you OK?" As he spoke he could feel the bile rising in his throat, and the sense of unknown anxiety surge through him.

She shook her head from side to side and bent forward almost touching the tabletop. Rickey could see her shoulders heaving under the dark blue pea coat yet while sensing them, he could not hear her sobs. Rickey stood there frozen, confused as to what he should do. Finally, he reached out and placed his hand at the base of her neck, feeling her fine, soft hair and the tenderness of her skin, then slowly, turning her to face him. The black mascara tracks against her pale skin gave her a comical look but the burning red eyes and heavy sobbing meant this was no laughing matter. Rickey felt his stomach heave and he momentarily lost his balance. Grabbing the back of one of the cane chairs he almost knocked it over but he caught his balance and lifted it off the floor.

Rickey sat across from Marsha and reached out and took her hand. "Honey, what is wrong? Please talk to me." He saw the waitress approaching, walking in a casual style while chewing gum, giving off the impression of not having a care in the world. Yet, a few feet away, his world was collapsing. *How could she not see this*, Rickey wondered. With his hand, he tried to wave her off, but to no avail. She came up to the far side of the table, and said in a voice loud enough to be heard across the small room, "Manager sezs you gotta order somethin' or leave. Me, I don't care, but he's kinda a prick." As she spoke, she was running the tip of a pencil around the inside of her ear. While Rickey was taken aback by what she was saying, he almost laughed at the sight of a grown woman probing for earwax while telling customers they had to order food. After that display, the last thing Rickey wanted was food from that kitchen.

"We will leave, thank you." He put a dollar bill down on the table, not knowing if Marsha had paid for her *Coke* and stood up. At the same time he reached under Marsha's arm, feeling the warmth of her body, and lifted her up. "Come on, honey, let's go walk the pier."

There was a strong on-shore afternoon breeze which they walked into as they made their way to the pier. It had been built back in the '30's and immediately upon stepping onto it, you felt a time shift. The old telephone poles which had been driven into the sand by steam engines still smelled of creosote, the rough planks which formed the walkways still bore the markings of the railroad tracks. The waves crashing into the supporting poles made it move slightly, giving one the feeling of being afloat.

As Rickey and Marsha walked past the fishermen lining both rails, neither said a word. No words were needed as Rickey understood that this was good-bye. The why it was today no longer mattered; all that mattered was these were their last moments together. Arms intertwined they slowly walked toward the end of the pier where the great expanse of the Pacific greeted them. The seemingly never-ending vista of blue-grey water stretching as far as you could see, then marrying itself to the blue sky far out in the distance. Marsha held his arm tightly as if the stiff breeze would blow her away, and at the same time conveying to him that she loved him and leaving him was the hardest thing she ever had to do. He felt it and understood it, but his heart screamed, *why?*

They stopped at the end of the pier. Through the late afternoon haze and glare, could see the thin outline of Catalina Island against the blue-grey sky. *Not quite an island but more a promise of an island*, Rickey thought as he watched portions fade away then slowly return as the afternoon light shifted. She hugged his arm again, and as she buried her face into his chest, he felt the joy of the love he had for her, the anger at her for leaving, the fear that they would never feel this way again, the unfocused rage of uncertainty. But most of all, the aloneness of being just Rickey again. Baffled and beaten, he sagged against the railing and fought back his tears.

Marsha raised her face from his chest, reached up and pulled him down to her and kissed him gently on the lips. Then for the first time she spoke, "Rickey, I am so sorry." Then she slipped away and started walking back to shore. Rickey stood there stunned, squeezing the rail until his knuckles almost burst, unable to move or say a thing. She turned once and gave him a small wave then disappeared into a group of school children.

He looked out at the sea and saw the waves of four feet forming nicely until the wind tore the tops off them making them unrideable. *A lot like relationships*, he thought, as he started to make his way back to shore.

3

Months passed, bringing with them the cold and chill of Winter, and the sparkling lights and goodwill of the Christmas season. While never forgetting Marsha, she wasn't in his mind as often and he was beginning to feel whole again. He always liked the time between Thanksgiving and the New Year. It was filled with friends and family dinners, a break from the tedium of school, as well as the promise of a fresh start. Other than Summer, it was his favorite time of year. He thought she might come home for the holidays but he vowed to himself he would not call her. So he was both surprised and pleased when the phone rang a few days before Christmas and heard her say, "Can we meet?" She said it as if he would say no, and if he did, she would understand. She knew she had broken his heart, but what he needed to know was that she had broken her own as well.

"Of course. What's good for you?"

"How about the Hof's down in the marina?"

"Fine. When?"

"Oh, let's say around six. Is that OK?"

"Perfect. See you then. And, ah, Mars, thanks for calling."

"Oh, Rickey, of course I would call. I wouldn't come home without seeing you."

"Ah, yeah, well, see ya at six." With that, he hung up and realized he had a huge smile on his face.

At first he barely recognized her. Gone was the preppy ivy league look she had sported all through high school. Now she wore tight denim jeans tucked into knee-high boots with a belt of violet crimson which at first glance, looked like a curtain tie. She sported a large floppy black hat and a leather jacket with fringe that bounced and swayed as she walked. Under the jacket was a thin tee shirt of multiple colors which hardly concealed her breasts; he could tell immediately she wasn't wearing a bra. This was a very different Marsha.

She slipped into the booth across from him and flashed him that brilliant smile as she whipped the hat off and reached into her purse to pull out a pack of cigarettes. "Boy, can I use a smoke and some coffee. An afternoon with the folks is just too much. You look good, but then, you always did. What are you up to?"

But the small talk didn't last long.

"This war is wrong. It's wrong on so many levels. I can't believe you can sit here and say the government knows best. They don't. And they lie to you. Over and over again. Please listen to me, honey. I don't want you to die."

Rickey knew people died in war. But somehow that was not real to him; that was not part of his life. Here in this warm booth, sipping coffee, eating pie, dying seemed too abstract, too remote for him to grasp. He shook his head. "Look, this thing will end soon. How can a little country like that stand up to the United States? Besides, they can't make me go."

The glare out of Marsha's eyes was something he had never seen before. Those blue eyes, like small robin's eggs, were now a dark hue of cobalt and had a razor's edge of anger which pierced his calm.

"How fucking dumb are you? I know you spend all your days in salt water but has it filled your head? They can't make you? What? You think this is high school and they have to have your parents' permission? Christ, Rickey! Don't you remember that form you filled out the last week of school? The one that said in big bold letters: DRAFT REGISTRATION. Or were you too loaded to know what you were signing?"

"Hey! Back off! I came here to see you and have some pie. Not for you to rag all over me. Yeah, I remember that form but I thought that was just so they would know where I lived now that I was out of high school. Ya know... so they could contact me." He paused, reached across the table and took the lighter out of her hand. He hoped a little skin to skin contact would calm her down a bit. He lit his cigarette and waved at the waitress for more coffee. There was a prolonged silence between them broken only by his, "Thank you," to the waitress. Finally he said, "You're right. I knew that signing that letter thing had something to do with the Army and that maybe that meant I would have to go talk to them if they called. But I didn't know it meant they could send me to Vietnam if I didn't want to go. I thought I had to agree. I mean, maybe to Germany or something like that, but not to Vietnam. Really?"

"Yes, really. And you have no say so whatsoever where they send you or what they ask you to do." She reached over and held his hand in hers and smiled softly. "Please. We may not still be together but I care for you. Come with me and talk to some of my friends. They will explain the situation to you and why you do not want the government to get their hands on you. Here, come with me tonight and we will spend some time trying to understand what this mess is all about." With that, she stood up and turned towards the door.

He stood and followed. *What was there to lose?* At least he would still be with her and maybe old times could be revisited.

They walked out into the chilled, thick sea air, hand in hand, toward her car.

"Come get in. We're just going over to Seal Beach by the pier. A place called Cosmos. Ever been?"

"Ah, no. I don't think so. What's there?"

"Most nights folk music. Do you like folk music?"

"Yeah, I guess. Not really sure what you mean. Like Dylan? Baez?"

"Yeah, like that. But these guys aren't famous or anything. They play to play and, ya know, maybe someday someone will know them."

"So we're going to listen to music?"

"Yes and no. Music will be playing but I am hoping my friend, Bobby, will be there. He hangs out there a lot when he is down South."

"Who's Bobby?"

"Bobby is a friend of mine from Berkeley. He is very much into the anti-war movement. He's been in a lot of demonstrations. Closed down a few draft boards. He's been on television a few times. He knows this shit, Rickey. Listen to him. I am not asking you to burn your draft card tonight. But just listen to him. And ask yourself if what he is saying makes sense. Later check it out on your own. But please listen. OK?"

"Yeah, sure."

She parked across from the Bay Theater right in front of Harbor Surfboards. Rickey glanced at the boards suspended from the ceiling and the familiar scene relaxed him.

They walked through the damp, clinging air and stopped in front of a simple red door. "Cosmos" was written sideways across it and beneath the name was a simple, "Welcome."

4

The club was dark, the only light dimly coming from the bar and a single spotlight shining down on an empty stool. Rickey tried to adjust his eyes to the darkness but kicked a chair causing him to stumble. He felt out of place and wanted to leave. But Marsha held his hand tightly and that gave him both reassurance and the hope that maybe later they could do more than hold hands.

She guided him through the darkness toward the back of the room where larger tables had been set up; like they'd had a meeting there earlier but now all that was left were the empty cups and the cigarette butts which littered the floor.

Back behind the last table was a small booth where two men sat smoking and watching them as they approached. "Marsha," one called out as he stood up. "Over here. Good to see you. And who is your friend?"

"Bobby, this is Rickey, my friend from high school." She turned and said to the other man, "Hi, I am Marsha, this is Rickey," and she extended her hand. He took it and in a voice so soft that Rickey could barely hear it said, "Hello, I'm Tom Hayden." Then turning to speak to Bobby, said, "I've got to go. Let's talk further about Century City." And with that, he was gone.

Rickey hadn't felt so out of place since the senior prom. He felt inadequate, his life's story a mere comic interlude to the serious work these people did. And yet, he didn't even know what they did.

He looked around and now could clearly see the bandstand with the bar behind it across the room. Suddenly the place seemed to be filling up with people. *What's this about? Some protest rally?* he wondered. *Christ, I don't need a bunch of true believers drilling my head.*

Bobby motioned them to sit down and Rickey took the chair which faced both the door and the bandstand. There was a low-level panic going on just south of his belt line and he knew he had to hold it together. Marsha pulled a chair between them and slid an ashtray in front of her. It acted like a DMZ between Bobby and Rickey. Marsha wasn't sure where the tension was coming from. But she had a guess. She figured that Rickey was upset because he thought she had slept with Bobby and Bobby was upset to be confronted with her former lover; especially one so handsome. She sighed, knowing nothing she could say would make the situation better. Yes, she had slept with Bobby and yes, Rickey had been her lover. *Fucking men!* she thought to herself, *So childish. What's an afternoon of making love more than that? That's the now of love-making. It happens then it's gone. Why do they cling to such foolish notions as just one, always and forever. What is this, the 50's?*

Bobby felt the tension, too, and saw that space between her eyebrows tense radiating anger and concern. He knew the moment wasn't right for much of anything but some light banter and a few drinks. He wasn't much good at the former but damn good at the latter. *Reprieve!* The waitress was standing next to their table and seemed impatient, and perhaps, *rightfully so,* Bobby thought, as he had been traveling faraway in his mind. He coughed. That's what he always did to buy a few seconds to get himself together. "Hey," he turned toward the waitress, "Hoyt up next?"

"Yes, now can I get you something?"

"Sure, a carafe of house red and three glasses." He glanced at Marsha and Rickey, both numbly nodded an OK.

Rickey was confused. He was eighteen as was Marsha. You needed to be 21 to drink in the great State of California but apparently here in the great state of Cosmos, eighteen was game. Suddenly he felt more relaxed and thought, *all this might be OK.*

5

The waitress set the wine down in the middle of the table. She paused, and asked, "Anything else?"

"Not just now, thank you." Bobby replied.

"Well, it looks like it's going to be a packed house tonight and if you need a second round just wave at me, I won't be offended."

Bobby looked around the table and said, "You know what? Just bring another one over when you get a chance."

"Sure, no problem." And with that, she turned and walked away, leaving the three of them in an awkward silence. But just then there was a rustle on stage, causing Rickey to turn to his left for a better view. There stood a large man with a guitar slung across his belly and a mug of beer in his right hand. He took a long pull on the beer, putting the half empty glass down on the stool next to him. Turning to the crowd, he said, "Howdy, I'm Hoyt Axton, so let's get to it."

With that he started to sing a song Rickey had heard before but couldn't recall by whom. He remembered the phrase, "I am just a good loving rambling man..." but little else. But it was a good song and the way Axton did it made Rickey believe that old Hoyt was a good ramblin' man. He sat back, sipped his wine and felt relaxed for the first time that evening.

When Hoyt took a break, the houselights came up and the cozy womb-like atmosphere evaporated, leaving behind only a smoky haze and the smell of too many people in too small of a place. Rickey looked around and everywhere he looked, there were people, mostly young but with a few older folks here and there. *Christ,* he thought, *at 50 cents a beer and a dollar a glass for wine this place must bust it. Good bread,* and he thought, *good vibes.* No sense of the potential of violence that was in every bar he had been in in Mexico. That sense, that at any moment, a fight could break out. That underlying tension that you accept as part of the deal. He thought all bars were like that and was pleased he could just relax. But not fully, as he caught Bobby looking at him, and as he did, Bobby looked quickly away. *What's with this guy?* Rickey thought. *Either he's jealous or paranoid; or a little of both.* Suddenly, Rickey was ready to leave but knew he had to find a way to placate Marsha and not offend Bobby. He still wanted to hear what Bobby had to say.

He sat up straighter, reached for the last bit of wine in his glass and started to speak. But before words could come out, Bobby over-spoke him. "Listen, it's late and it's the holidays. I should go and say good night to my folks. Rickey, I want to talk to you about the war, if you really want to and aren't just here to make Marsha happy."

Surprising himself, Rickey blurted out, "NO, man! I want to. I need to know this shit and Marsha says you are the man. So when you can, then let's do it. Just call Mars and tell her the where and when. I'm cool with it anytime."

"Glad to hear it. But before we do that, I would like you to do some-thing for me. Read Robert Sheer's piece in last month's *Ramparts* magazine. He lays it all out. It will give you a basic understanding of what is really going on. When we meet we will talk about what it means and what it means to you. OK?"

"Yeah, sure. I guess that newsstand down on Main should have it. I'll get it and read it. Meanwhile, thanks for taking the time; I appreciate it."

"No man, thank you for being willing to listen. So many aren't. Look, I gotta go. I'll pay the tab for the wine on my way out. If you could leave her a tip, that would be cool."

"Yeah, sure thing. Thanks, man."

With that Bobby turned, kissed Marsha on the cheek and walked into the smoky haze.

"Pretty cool guy," Rickey said as he watched Bobby disappear into the darkness.

"Yes and no. He is super smart and knows a shitload about the war but there is something a little off about him. He's hard to get close to. It seems that there is a piece of him that is held in reserve; sitting, watching, judging, and perhaps telling him how to react. I don't know, it's just an odd feeling. But the guy's got some balls, he's not afraid to put it out there."

"Yeah, how so?" As he spoke, he was reluctant to hear the supposed virtues of one Bobby, half fearing she would say how great he was in bed.

"Well, you know, he has been in a lot of demonstrations, gone to jail a few times. Got beaten in a march last year in Berkeley; they had 35,000 people in that one. He met Jerry Rubin there. Rubin hooked him up with Hayden who you met tonight. But I think his best statement so far was 4th of July. He grew up in Bel Air. His folks have a lot of money and his father knows a lot of people.

"So, on the 4th when everyone is 'Oh, so patriotic,' he flies the Viet Cong flag off the porch of his apartment. He was interviewed by the local papers, was on TV; I think there was even a piece of it on the *Today Show*. Man, he knew he was going to catch hell, but he just shrugged it off…like no big deal. But it was. Some red-neck Congressman called for him to be tried for treason. Some others wanted his immediate arrest. He just laughed and said, 'It's all just a hot air exchange. Who cares?.'"

Rickey looked at the empty wine glasses and felt a heaviness he had never known. Not even buried under tons of white water when one of the 20 foot monsters crushed him against the coral bottom off the north shore in Hawaii had he felt so tired, so spent, so exhausted. Her praise of Bobby left him feeling like a loser.

"I gotta go." He stood up and just walked out without looking back. It was only when the night air hit him did he realize he had no car; she had driven. He had two choices: wait for her and prolong the evening, or walk. In spite of a lingering desire to be with her, he turned toward Coast Highway and started walking back to his car. Feeling more alone than ever.

6

He awoke in the morning with Rusty by his side. It was a reassuring feeling to feel Rusty's warmth along his right leg and his weight slightly pressing down the bed on the window side. A feeling of normalcy.

Rickey's dad got Rusty when Rickey was six years old and they had been best friends now for 12 years. Every night Rusty slept beside Rickey and when he was gone, Rusty would sleep in the bed alone but always staying on his side.

Rickey remembered the day his dad brought Rusty home...just a little bundle of fur and energy with large paws that he hadn't grown into, and soft orange tinted fur that shined just so when the light was right. His tail wiggled nonstop and his big brown eyes begged Rickey for a smile. His dad sat him down and told him how the pup was his dog and how it was his job to take care of it. If he didn't want the responsibility that was fine as he was sure he could find a good home for him.

Rickey was aghast. Take his dog? No way! He reached out and grabbed the dog from his father's hand and squeezed it to his chest. "No, no dad. I'll take care of it. I will, I promise!"

"Fine, but your first job is to give it a name." For a six year old, that was an overwhelming task, but Rickey quickly responded, "Can we call him Rusty?"

"Of course, but why that?"

"Well, see that streak on his belly? It looks like the rusty cans down on that beach we go to sometimes."

"Good choice. From now on, he's Rusty."

His mother, Maggie, had sat by quietly as he and his father had their exchange. That was so much like her; to sit in the background and watch, not saying much but understanding everything, never missing a thing. Rickey found out later, by chance, it was his mother who had found the dog and brought it home but thought it best if Bailey gave it to his son.

Rickey pulled the covers back and started to sit up when the memory of the night before came to mind. The thought of Vietnam and the choice he had to make struck him like a right-cross and he fell back among the tangled sheets and pillows. As he lay there, he flashed back to his dad sitting there on the floor with him holding the little fur-ball in his elbow while the dog licked his shirt. His mother sitting on the sofa with that soft look in her eyes. They were her world; her husband and her son. Nothing else seemed to matter to Maggie. She had friends and people she knew at the church and a sister back in Vermont. But all of Rickey's life, he knew that what mattered to her was him and his dad. As the only child, he had the advantage of all of their attention. As the only child, he had the disadvantage of all of their attention.

Christ, he thought, *they can make me go to Vietnam and kill people.* A chill swept through him at the thought of killing someone. *But yes, what about if I get killed? Mom would never be the same.* Tears formed in the corners of his eyes and he blinked them away.

He reached over and patted Rusty. "Come on boy, time to get up."

His eyes searched the room, scanning side to side as he did every morning, as this was his "new" room and ever since he moved in, about nine years ago, he felt a little disoriented first thing in the morning. He needed to adjust himself to the surroundings.

His first room was a small bedroom just off the hall and a few feet from his parents' room; small but workable for a young boy. What he liked most about it was a window seat that he could crawl onto and look out through the trees and watch what was passing on the street. It was also a good place to hole up and read a book. He always felt safe there.

His new room was an addition his parents had built on the back side of the house. It was much larger than his old room and had the great advantage of having a bathroom. It opened out onto the backyard through a sliding door which was something very modern in the older neighborhood where he lived. The large glass door filled the room with light and he had views of the fruit trees in the back yard. It was nice, but it never truly felt like home. It was always, "the addition."

Years later, he found out the reason his parents built it was because his mother was pregnant and the baby would move into his old room and he would have the new room or, the suite, as his father liked to call it. But his new brother or sister never came and his parents never spoke about it. Instead, they turned his old room into a guest room; but guests rarely came.

The house was empty as his parents had both gone off to the office. For a number of years now, his mother worked in his father's office downtown; he thought it started when he was about ready to go to junior high school, six or seven years ago. At first it was odd not having her there when he came home from school. But soon it became the norm and he liked the freedom that came with her being absent. But it also came with some new responsibilities. Before she went to work, she shopped for the groceries, made the meals, and did all the clean up. Now, every afternoon when he got home, he checked the note pinned to the cork board in the service porch and got his instructions as to what foods to pull from the refrigerator or freezer to let defrost in the sink, what type of salad to make, and always a reminder to set the table. Why she reminded him of that everyday never failed to amuse him. He liked doing these tasks; they made him feel like he was doing something for them.

As he wandered into the kitchen the phone on the wall rang. "Hello, the Osgood's."

"Hey man! It's Sticks. Junior just called me and it's breaking tubes down at Rosie's. Billy, Jacks and I are heading down there. Wanna come?"

"Hell yes. When are you going?"

"Jacks is driving and he can't go until he finishes work at 4:30. So around five or so."

"OK, that's cool. I need to put in some time at Taco Time so that works. Jacks taking the Beast?"

"Yeah. So bring some dough 'cause that sucker drinks gas."

"No shit. A five should cut it?"

"Oh yeah, that's plenty. But bring some beer and girl money and we'll stop in TJ."

"I figured ya would. See you at five behind Bob's Big Boy on Bellflower."

"Cool."

Rickey hung up the phone and with it all thoughts of *Ramparts* magazine, Bobby, the war and last night were quickly forgotten. *They're breaking at Rosie's, fuckin' great!* he thought. Which board to bring was now his only concern.

7

The flames in the hand-dug fire pit were getting low, hardly taking the chill out of the Mexican night air. They had been south of the border for four days and both the beer and their groceries were in short supply. They were much further south than they had planned, in fact, about 400 miles down the Baja Peninsula at a wide spot in the road calling itself San Quentin.

To get to it they'd had to leave the main road and bounce down a dirt pathway which caused the Beast to moan and groan like a dying animal. And every time it happened, Jacks would grunt, "Mother fucker." He hardly had time to sip his beer between grunts. The rest just passed around a joint and tried to act like, *hey, no big thing, stuck in the heart of Mexico with the banditos and drug runners, we cool.* All were praying to their own God to keep the Beast alive and well at least back to San Diego.

That was two days ago, and they faced the return trip in the morning. They'd wound up in San Quentin because the waves at Rosie's weren't tubes at all but sloppy soup which weren't ride-able. As usual, another member of the band of surf brothers came by, saying he was up from down south and they were breaking sweet just this side of Cedros. He hadn't been lying, they had.

Rickey reached for another beer from the cooler they'd fashioned from an old refrigerator they found abandoned on the way to the beach. They had laid it on its back with the door pointing at the sky, then filled it full of ice and beer. It worked perfectly even though the door was a bit heavy to open. A local saw them using it and asked if he could have it when they left. It would help him save his fish from day to day. "Of course," they said, and the next day he brought them a 15 pound snapper that was still dancing on the line. They had just finished their meal of snapper, fire roasted corn and mangos and were now slipping into the post-meal dazed, beer-hazed consciousness which mellowed you out nearly to the point of sleep; but not quite.

Rickey looked around at his friends, their features softened by the light of the dying fire and saw three very different individuals but all bound by a love of the sea and the thrill of the waves. They were all eighteen or nineteen, maybe Jacks was twenty, as he seemed older. Rickey suddenly realized they faced the same dilemma as he did: the draft. *Or did they?* he wondered.

He looked around the group again, took a long pull on the *Tecate*, and asked, "What're you doing about the draft? 'Cause I sure as hell haven't figured it out."

Sticks spoke up first and quickly, as if he was blurting something nasty and wanted it over fast. "Nothin'. You might have noticed my leg is fucked up. They won't take me."

"Yeah, we noticed...that's why we call you Sticks, ya dumb shit. Wha'da ya mean, they won't take you? I thought they took everybody." As Junior said this, he turned and mugged a face to Jacks, like Sticks was dumb as a post.

"You're the dumb one," Jacks replied. "They have a system. That's why they call it the Selective Service. The way it works is, everyone our age...let's say eighteen to twenty-six or so is fair game. You're theirs. But if there is something wrong with you or if you fit one of their special categories then you get a pass. Sometimes forever, sometimes just a bit...depends."

"Yeah, well they ain't gonna take me, my doc says so," Sticks said while rolling a reefer while there was still enough light from the fire to see by.

"Good for you. But it ain't that easy. Their doc has to agree. So you gotta go down to what they call the Induction Center and see their doc and then they decide."

Rickey leaned forward now, trying to grasp the details of what Jacks was saying. "So, you go down there to this center and they talk to you? You tell them what's wrong with you or that you don't want to go to Vietnam and they listen?"

"Well, it ain't that simple. What I understand and now remember, I'm getting most of this from the Lad; you remember the Lad - guy who looked 25 in junior high school? Well, he told me over beers one night at the 49'er that he got his notice but didn't show up on time 'cause he was up in Alaska catching crab but when he went down there they didn't seem too upset that he was two weeks late. They just told him to get in line with the other guys whose last name started with an R. So he did. It was no big thing, he said. Stood around for hours, filled out some forms, dropped your shorts for a doc who asks you a few questions. Then it's over. They give you a piece of paper and the one they gave him said you will hear from us. I guess other guys got cards telling them to report on such-and-such date. He said there was one guy who was taken away in a van. But he didn't know why. Said the whole thing was no big deal."

"How long ago was that?" Rickey asked.

"About three months ago. Yeah, right around the start of football season."

"So what happened to the Lad? They get him?"

"Well, yes and no. What I heard is, it often works out like this. Guy gets right up to being drafted, knows he'll be an Army goof for two years and sure as hell will go to Vietnam, and then decides to enlist in the Navy for three years or the Air Force. Hell, it's another year, but the odds of getting killed are a lot less; in fact, in the Navy, only a small force is in Vietnam. You're on a ship with decent food, a dry bunk, a shower…man, it's not so bad. I mean, think about being in the jungle having to sleep under a tree with the Cong all around trying to kill ya. Same clothes for weeks on end. Fuck that! This here is about as rustic as I ever want to get."

"So, just because you show up doesn't mean they will ship you off to Vietnam?" Rickey asked.

"Hell no! Even those with orders to report go to a place for boot camp… like, that's where they train you. Then you get to leave to see your family or whatever, then you report for what they call deployment. That's when they send you to wherever. But what they say is, every guy who gets drafted has to do 13 months in Nam."

"So what happened to the Lad?" asked Junior "He in Nam?"

"Don't think so. He went the Navy route and I heard they were sending him to diesel school, you know, to work on engines."

"So no Nam?"

"Junior, who the fuck knows what they will do, but right now the Lad is in school somewhere."

Rickey sat back and took a drag on the reefer Sticks had rolled. *Well it's not as bad as Mars made it sound.* He looked out to sea and saw a small freighter moving north; its green light dancing on the water. *Time to go home,* he thought; *wonder if Mars is still in town.*

8

By the time they got back, 1967 was just a few hours away. Rickey pulled his board from the top of his car and headed down the driveway to the garage where he would stow it along with the five others up in the rafters out of the way. His father still parked his beloved *Buick* inside every night and Rickey did not want to interfere with Bailey's ritual. So he quickly slid the side-to-side door open, always feeling how old-timey it was, and stepped on the overturned ammo box in order to reach the canvas straps hanging from the roof. He slid the smallest board in place and stepped down. He glanced up, admiring his collection and remembering that each board had a story to tell. But not that night. It was New Year's Eve and he had a party to attend; actually, a few parties.

"God, you are tan! Who the hell is tan in December?" He knew she was kidding him and was so grateful she was still in town. He would have felt that a door between them had closed forever if she had left without saying good-bye. But with her being here, he still had a chance to win her back.

"Been south for a few days with the boys. Went down to San Quentin on the Baja, had some great waves. And the people were so nice; but damn, they were poor...but still so nice."

"So what did you think of the piece Bobby asked you to read? You know, the one in *Ramparts*?"

Rickey froze. He had totally forgotten about the article. He stammered, looked at the ceiling, anywhere but at her. Marsha didn't say a word. She just took tiny sips from her wine glass and looked at him; he guessed it was the same look she would give a misbehaving dog. Finally he turned to face her full on, cocked his head to one side and said, "I didn't read the damn thing. Yet. But I will. Look, this trip came up at the last minute and I really wanted to bust some waves before the semester starts. You get that, right?" his voice was pleading.

She placed her hand on his forearm and could feel the sun's radiance still coming off him. But she could also hear in his voice the pleading for forgiveness and the chance to try again. "Look, I just want what's good for you. I know surfing is good for you. I just don't know if the US Army would be." She didn't want to lecture him, not tonight, of all nights. "How about this? I'll get a copy and send it to you. You read it and if you want to talk with Bobby, great. If not, that's cool. It's your decision. No one is trying to force you to do anything. OK?"

"Yeah, but how about we read it together. Talk about it before I see Bobby."

"Rickey, I can't. I have to be back in school in three days and tomorrow I have to go with my folks to Pasadena for the parade and the game. USC is playing and you know how my dad wouldn't miss it for the world."

"OK, yeah. I get it. No problem. Well, send it to me and I will read it. I promise."

Just then Bobby walked up, nodded at Rickey and said to Marsha, "There is someone I want you to meet. It's about Century City." With that, he took her by the arm, turned her and walked toward a small group in an alcove across the room.

Rickey wouldn't see her again for six months.

9

He knew it would come as Marsha always followed through on what she said she was going to do. Neatly wrapped in a brown envelope with his name in her distinctive handwriting, it signaled to him that she still cared. He knew that already but there was something about getting that envelope which took away part of the sting of watching her walk off with Bobby at New Year's. If not lovers, at least close friends.

He opened the envelope and was surprised to find a slick, full-color magazine, not unlike *Time* or *Newsweek*. He thought it would be poorly printed on "rag" paper and look like the freebies they handed out at the college, protesting this or that.

He thumbed it open and found the article quickly. He scanned the opening lines and realized that this wasn't going to be some rant by some zealot but more like reading one of the history texts he had been assigned by Professor Clarke. "This is serious shit," he told himself. Maybe he'd read it later after school and some time at work. But he found himself drawn in and continued reading. He wandered into the kitchen, sat down at the table and continued to read.

"Holy shit!" he said to Rusty, after he had finished. "Even if half this is true, then the war has nothing to do with protecting America but is just a way for a lot of big companies to make a ton of money."

Rusty looked at him with his big brown eyes which seemed to say he understood.

Rickey got up from the table feeling his knees crack; he had been sitting for too long. He glanced at the clock and was surprised it was quarter to two already. *Well, so much for English 101,* he thought to himself, as he headed across the kitchen to the back door. He needed a smoke and to do that he had to go outside. His mother did not allow smoking in the house and even when she wasn't there, he would always honor her wishes.

As he stood among the fruit trees, he watched a hummingbird hover above a flower, pecking at it with a rapid jerking motion yet maintaining its perfect position. He struggled with the idea that corporations could be so cold as to care about profits more than people. But he was young and what did he truly know about the world. His world had been for eighteen years, his mom and dad, a few friends, the comfortable life in Belmont Heights, an affluent part of Long Beach, and surfing.

He didn't know hunger, pain, business, or what government really meant. He didn't know how corporations ran or what it meant to make a profit or suffer a loss. The more he thought about this, the more he realized how little he did know.

He lit another cigarette and reached down and patted Rusty across the back of his neck and along the top of his head. "Christ, boy! I've got a lot to learn." And none of it sounded good to him.

He turned and headed back into the house, call Marsha and tell her he'd read the article and wanted to talk to Bobby.

10

As he stood at the fryer, his head was a confusion of facts, figures, arguments and why this war was just wrong. Although confused, he felt a sense of peace thinking about these things while he went through the motions of frying the shells.

He liked his job at Taco Time. The best thing about it was that the hours weren't fixed. Mr. Pierce, his boss, was a good guy and let him come in when he wanted as long as there were plenty of crispy shells in the racks. The money was OK too. He got 50 cents a rack and a rack held 25 shells. The raw tortillas came in stacks of 50. His job was to count them out as he spread them out onto the stainless steel tabletop next to the fryer. He kept the tabletop lightly dusted with flour to prevent the tortillas from sticking. Once he had 50 laid out, he would load a rack which required him to half-fold the shell and insert it into a slot which held it while it cooked. The key to getting the shells just right was hot oil and clean oil. The oil needed to be at about 400 degrees to start, as once he dipped the entire rack into the vat, the temperature dropped to about 380 degrees which was near perfect. Ninety seconds was it; anything more and they got soggy or over-cooked which made them tough and chewy. Out of the fryer and onto the cooling tray which had a drip catcher; it was amazing, but after doing about 500 shells, there might be a quart of reusable oil.

Rickey had a method. Two racks then wait two minutes for the oil to recover its heat. While he waited, he laid out another 50 tortillas. Then every ten racks, he drained the oil and replaced it. He drained the oil into a large vat that had multiple layers of screens to filter out the pieces of shells and the fat which had hardened. When the vat was full, they let it sit for two days then drained off the upper two-thirds and reused it. This meant that the 20 gallons of oil that came in each box could be stretched to about 50. Because he had it down to such a routine, he could let his mind wander and think about all sorts of things without ever interrupting his work. Normally his wandering took him to far off surf spots or the just-remembered smile of a girl on the bus the other day or even sometimes, his school work. But not today; today it was the war.

11

Rickey settled into a booth in the front of the restaurant so he had a clear view of the street. He wanted to see what Bobby drove and how he carried himself just out and about. They were to meet at eight but now it was quarter after and Rickey was starting to think Bobby had blown him off or was just damned rude.

Just then he saw a flash of ice-blue speed by and recognized Bobby behind the wheel of an *Austin Healey*. Rickey wasn't a car guy like a lot of his friends but he knew that a *Healey* was a cool car and damned fun to drive.

Bobby flipped a U-turn and slid into a parking spot across the street. He quickly stepped out and checked traffic both ways before half-jogging across the street. With the top down, his hair was a mess and he ran his fingers through it to give it a quick comb.

He came into the restaurant like a whirlwind but paused when he saw Rickey.

"Sorry man, to be late. But I got off the freeway on the wrong exit and after that I was all screwed up."

"Hey, no worries. I appreciate you taking the time to talk to me."

"That's cool. How's the food?"

"It's not bad. Breakfast is their specialty. The ham and eggs are pretty good. Cool car. Not exactly what I thought a revolutionary would drive. "

Bobby looked up from the menu with a cold glare in his eyes. "Let's get one thing straight, right up front. I am against the war. I am not against America or capitalism. I am not a bomb thrower or so closed-minded that I can't see the other's side of the argument. I was brought up to respect America and value her traditions and laws. And I do."

"Ah, sorry. I didn't mean any offense by it. It's just that I thought you were for Ho and against us and he is a Commie."

"They're Commies because they had no choice. But before we get into the history let me say one thing. I am the end product of the American system. My grandfather came to America at the turn of the century; came in right through Ellis Island. A few dollars in his pocket, spoke nothing but German and had no relatives here to help him out. He got a job with a blacksmith and learned that trade. When my father was born, my grandfather swore he would sit in an office and not before a hearth.

At 14, my father got a job in a law office, cleaning up and taking messages around the courthouse and doing anything else they asked of him. At 17, he started his studies and sat for the bar five years later. At 24, he moved west to LA to be near the movie business. Soon he was representing movie stars, directors, whatever came in the door. He's rich now and he and my mother live very well up in Bel Air and because of him I live damn well too. And why? Because the system we have in America works. It works for the rich and the poor. You can be anything in this country you want to be. You just need to get off your ass and try. So don't confuse me with the hippies who are always looking for a free lunch or the Commies who think Lenin was a great man or peace-nicks who think all war is wrong. War is basically a failure of governance; and often, not only wrong but unnecessary. But sometimes it is necessary and to think otherwise is to be naive."

The waitress had been standing there for a piece of Bobby's monologue with her mouth agape, "Well now, honey, now that you got that off your chest, you want to order?"

Bobby looked sheepishly down at the menu and said, "I'll try the ham and eggs. I hear they're good here."

They spent the next two hours talking. Bobby did most of the talking with Rickey asking a question now and then or making an observation. Bobby started at what he felt was the beginning; the bleak field from which all else grew. Explaining that the Allies had promised the Vietnamese that if they fought against the Japanese and helped the Allies then after the war, the United States and Britain would see that France gave up its colonial claim on Vietnam and it would be an independent nation. The war ended and the US and Britain reneged on their promise; so the Vietnamese revolted and tried to drive France out of their country. In spite of the US siding with France, the Vietnamese won and the French effectively surrendered in 1954. There were Peace Accords but no sooner than they were signed, the US started a covert war against the government of Vietnam. By 1963, the US had thousands of advisors in Vietnam and the numbers were growing each year. However, President Kennedy decided this was the wrong course and signed an Executive Order to begin the draw-down of American troops. This was to start after the 1964 elections.

Shortly thereafter he was assassinated.

Bobby, by now, had finished his breakfast and was working on his third cup of coffee. He nodded at Rickey and asked, "Know what happened next?"

Rickey, having read the article and remembering most of it said, "Johnson started the war big time."

"That's right. Two days after getting sworn in, Johnson signs an Executive Order which repealed Kennedy's and signs two huge contracts with Brown & Root to build, among other things, several large Air Force bases. This all happened within 48 hours of the President's death. You can't tell me this wasn't pre-planned."

Rickey was stunned. "You think Kennedy wasn't killed by Oswald but by somebody who wanted the war to go on?"

"When it comes to that, I am not sure what to think. But I'll bet 40 to 50 years from now, few people will believe that Oswald acted alone. But I do know that once Johnson became President, the war took off. Just look at the numbers: starting in '64, the number of people killed just goes up and up. More killed last year than all the previous years combined."

"And look at the phony excuse they made up to get Congress to authorize the war."

"What was that?" asked Rickey.

"In August of 1964, the President presented to the Congress, an intelligence report that stated the naval vessel, USS Maddox, had been shot at by Vietnamese gunboats in the Token Gulf. It was paramount to 'Remember the Maine,' another phony story to cover America's desire to escalate a conflict. In both cases, Congress believed the story and authorized war. Turns out, the Maine exploded either due to improper stowage of gun powder or was set afire deliberately by its crew. Here, the Maddox wasn't even where they said it was and when the crew was interviewed, they knew nothing about being fired upon."

"Wow! And they got away with that bullshit?"

"That and more. Look, I've gotta go. There's a lot more out there. But this war is wrong. Our brothers are dying for no good reason. Don't let them make you a part of it."

And with that, they stood up and shook hands. Bobby quickly moved out the door and into the street but Rickey had to pull his windbreaker out from the fold in the seat and that took a moment. He glanced at the table and while he had paid for breakfast, he saw that Bobby had left a ten dollar tip for the waitress. *Yeah*, Rickey thought to himself, *he's living just fine on daddy's money.*

12

Rickey came into the house from work and immediately knew something was wrong. His mother was crying and his father was standing there stiff, holding a drink in his hand. His father rarely drank.

The TV was off and the room was totally quiet except for his mother's sobs. Rusty was curled up on the ottoman and barely stirred when Rickey came in; he looked at Rickey with big, sad eyes.

"What's wrong?" Rickey asked; speaking to his father but looking at his mother. He had never seen her like this. Seated on the edge of the big leather chair, bent at the waist, her head nearly at her knees one moment then raised up the next, her sobbing so violent it shook her whole body. All the while, a soft moan of, "Why, why, oh Dear God, why?"

Rickey tossed his windbreaker over the back of the nearest chair and started for his mother. But he caught a glimpse of his father slowly shaking his head, which stopped him in stride.

His father said softly, "Billy Bland is dead. Killed in Vietnam. We just heard at the office and had to come home. Just terrible. So young. His parents are torn up; you know how they tried to talk him into staying in school."

Rickey remembered. It was their senior year and a Marine recruiter had visited their high school wearing that sporty uniform, standing so erect, looking so fit and talking about all the benefits the Marines could give you. Sounded good until he got to the part about a four year commitment. Rickey had taken some of the literature to be polite but had no intention of joining up; then or later.

Some heard the siren song of glory, free education, seeing exotic lands, but more than anything, they felt the surge of patriotism through their hearts as the recruiter spoke of duty, honor, country. Billy was one of those.

They had a special program. Enlist now while you were still in high school and when you completed boot camp, you would get a two thousand dollar bonus and be given a choice of assignments from which you could choose what you wanted to do. What he failed to mention, was that boot camp started two weeks after graduation; there would be no Summer of fun for those who signed up.

Rickey and Billy weren't close in high school even though when they were younger, Billy had spent a lot of time at their house as Maggie watched Billy after school while Billy's mom was at work. They were friends but not buddies as Billy didn't surf.

Still, it hurt to know he was gone. Rickey flashed back to the last time he saw Billy. It was at the Bob's Big Boy over on Bellflower. It was about four months after high school was over and Billy was standing outside having a smoke. He looked striking in his uniform with its dark blue jacket with the red piping and the white belt pulled tight around his small waist and the extended shoulders which gave him an appearance of a large V atop long, strong legs encased in tan slacks with a ribbon of dark blue down each side. No wonder there were several girls hovering around him; all hoping to get this wonder man's attention. Now he was dead. Rickey wondered if those girls would even remember him.

The room got quiet as Maggie's sobs slowly ebbed. She looked up at him through red-rimmed eyes and started to cry again. This time he moved to her and put his arms around her. He said nothing as there was nothing to say. Grief has its own language.

He held her for awhile longer, then she raised her head and kissed him on the forehead. He leaned back and through the tears and the grief, he saw her great love for him. It was hard for him to hold back his own tears. She clutched him tightly and whispered, "Stay in school and let this horrible war pass."

"I will, mom, I promise."

In less than a year, he would break that promise.

13

They were just south of the Seal Beach pier, the sun was just starting to spread its glow over the water. It was flat this morning but still they sat there in a small semi-circle, sitting erect on their boards, feet dangling in the water, clad in their wetsuits, looking like black seals with their backs arched and their heads held high. Each of them knowing there wouldn't be any rideable waves that morning, but better to be together, sitting in the sea, waiting for the possibility of a ride, than to be in the classroom drowning in boredom.

"Billy Bland is dead. Killed last week in Nam." Sticks said it like it was news but each of them had known for awhile yet none of them had mentioned it until now.

"Yeah, I know," said Rickey. "My mom was really torn up over it. His service is tomorrow. Any of you guys going?"

"Nah, that shit creeps me out, " replied Sticks. "Besides, what's the point? He's dead; he don't give a shit."

Jacks couldn't believe his ears. "What's the point? The point is respect... respect for a friend, respect for his parents, respect for the fact that he was fighting for our country. That's the fucking point, you dumb shit! Hell yes I'm going. Christ, what an idiot." With that, Jacks paddled away from the group and took a position about 20 yards away.

"What the fuck was that?" Sticks muttered. "That dude's gotten weird lately."

"Yeah, well, we'll see how you do when you get called up. He got his Induction Notice three weeks ago and has to report next Monday," Junior replied in a flat and even tone.

"Fuck! I didn't know that. What's he gonna do?"

"Hell if I know," Junior replied, "but he better make up his mind pretty damn soon."

Rickey shook his head in disbelief. "What happened to his 2S? I saw him at school just the other day."

"Yeah...well, they fucked him. He needed 15 units a semester to keep the 2S. Last semester he got an incomplete in art history 'cause he got his paper in late. The teacher was a prick and wouldn't give him the credit until this semester so he was short of credits. So they drafted him. He asked for an appeal and they denied it. 'Short was short,' they said. He kept coming to class hoping they would reconsider. But no, and now he's fucked. And that's not all. Mary Ann thinks she's pregnant. And even if he marries her that won't get him out because they already called him."

"Jesus Christ!" Rickey was overwhelmed. Jacks was going to be the first of their clan to go. For the first time the reality of being forced to go struck Rickey. "Holy shit!"

"You said it, brother," Junior said, while turning his board toward the beach. "I'm outta here."

They sat in the sand, much like they sat in the water; in a small semi-circle facing the sea. They were quiet as they passed the joint around, each taking a hit, then passing to the next guy. They continued the ritual until there was nothing left but burning ash. Finally, Rickey broke the silence. "OK, Jacks, so what are you going to do? And what can we do to help you?"

"Marry Mary Ann," which caused the whole group to laugh. "Man, I don't know. I guess the best thing is to go down to the Navy office there on Atlantic and see if I can enlist. I do not want to be in the Army even if it's just 21 months versus 36 or even 48. I was thinking I'd go down there later this morning. I was hoping for one last good set before I go but it looks like this shit will be here until the wind comes up."

"Well, you want me to go with you? We could go to both the Navy and the Air Force; see who is offering what. Kinda like shopping for a car. Kick the tires, see what they say. Besides, if I'm there, they can't pressure you into signing anything. I won't let 'em."

"Hey, thanks, Junior, very cool of ya. Yeah, let's go after lunch and see what they say."

With that, the group broke up with Rickey heading back into the water with Sticks and Junior and Jacks heading up to the parking lot.

14

The next time Rickey saw Jacks was in the Spring of 1968. He had come home after his initial training but Rickey had been in Mexico and had missed him. He heard from Junior that Jacks would be in town later in the week. Coming to good old Long Beach aboard the naval vessel USS McCaffery. The Big Mac, a destroyer that was coming into the naval ship-yard for some outfitting before going to Vietnam.

Rickey checked the *IPT*, the local paper, which had a section called Shipping News, that listed the comings and goings of all ships through the port; both commercial and naval. He thought he would surprise Jacks and meet him when he came off the ship. But Rickey was quickly disappointed. MP's stopped him at the gates and told him the shipyard was off limits. He explained he just wanted to meet his buddy who was aboard the McCaffery and take him out for some beers.

"Sorry, sir, I can't let you into the yard; but you can sit there and wait for your friend."

"Thanks." Rickey quietly moved over to the bench. Just about when he had given up hope, an old grey bus sped by and he heard Jacks' booming voice, "Hey, Rickey. Stop this son-of-a-bitch and let me off." Dust clouds exploded from the bus' rear wheels and the bus quivered to a stop. Jacks came bouncing out the door. "South Point, you old bastard, you! What the fuck are you doing here?"

"Came to get your sorry ass wasted at the Niner and hear all your bull-shit war stories."

They embraced quickly, before the other guys on the bus started hol-lering and yelling "faggots" and other friendly jibes.

Rickey took stock of his friend as they walked back to his car. Jacks had always been tall and thick through the shoulders but with a soft belly and some baby fat still in his face. But Rickey noticed the belly was flat where his blue denim shirt tucked into his blue pants; not a hint of bulge where his belt bit into his waist. The baby fat was gone, replaced by a long, strong jaw-line. Jacks looked like a man ready to face his fate.

Rickey slapped him on the shoulder as they split apart to enter the car. "Damn, man, good to see you. How is life in the Navy?"

Jacks opened the door of the *Ford*, looked across the roof-line at Rickey and winked. "Damn good, amigo!" And ducked down inside.

Rickey rolled down the window as Jacks did the same. The morning was starting to warm up but the car was still comfortable. "Still got the old *Ford*. Shit man, by now I thought you'd have one of those fancy British sports cars or maybe even a *Porsche*."

"Yeah right, on a Taco Time salary."

"Christ, you still working there? I guess not much has changed since I left."

"Well dude, it's only been a few months or so and not all of us are off to see the world. Truthfully, how is it?"

Jacks took a moment before he replied, "Ya know, South Point, it ain't anything like I imagined. I like it. I like the order, the routine, knowing what the rules are and what you can and can't do. Hell, I even like the food. The crew is a bunch of great guys and the officers aren't half bad. Sure, I miss you guys and I sure as shit miss my wave time, but overall it's OK."

Rickey wasn't surprised. Jacks was always the most easy going of their group. A guy who knew how to bend, rather than break. And Jacks was smart. He had done pretty well in high school, won some award in chemistry and had even thought about going to UCLA for awhile but decided to live at home for the first two years and save some money. Rickey patted his breast pocket as he always did before reaching for a smoke. He pulled the pack of *Lucky's* from his pocket and offered it to Jacks.

"Nah, man. Stopping smoking, at least those things," he said with a slight chuckle.

"Good for you. And how is Maryanne?"

"OK, I guess. Wasn't knocked up, thank God. But once I left, she seemed to lose all interest in our relationship. Hear she's dating some rich guy."

"Oh, I'm sorry, man."

"Why? I'm not. One thing I've learned in the Navy. It's a big world out there. Filled with beautiful women."

Rickey shrugged, and said, "Niner?"

"Hell yes, the Niner! Let's go pick up some college girls."

With that Rickey started the *Ford*, made a big turn around the front of the gate, flashed a peace sign at the guards and headed for the bridge that would take them downtown then over to the college.

15

Throughout the late Spring and early Summer, Bobby, Marsha and a small army of volunteers planned for a massive demonstration in Century City, California, for June. There had been important anti-war demonstrations across the country since Christmas.

Martin Luther King at the Riverside Church in early April had given the most pointed anti-war speech by any prominent political figure to date. It was more than just a speech against the war. It was a repudiation of American foreign policy worldwide and a challenge to the Johnson administration to explain why Americans and Vietnamese had to die when even if Ho and his forces won, they didn't pose any threat to the United States.

A few weeks after "The Riverside Speech," as it came to be known, there were massive anti-war rallies in San Francisco and New York. The *Washington Post* estimated that more than 350,000 had turned out between the two cities.

Those who wanted to end the fight also wanted to make it personal to Johnson. To tag him forever with the war, and let everyone know that the blood that was let was on his hands. This required a confrontation with Johnson so the line could be clearly drawn.

Bobby and his small group of organizers thought the best way to do that was to face Johnson down. Pick a place where he couldn't ignore or dismiss their demonstration. But it had to be big, and best if it was on the West Coast so live TV coverage would be in primetime nationwide. Late last year, they heard that Johnson was going to commit to a Democratic fund raiser at the Century Plaza Hotel. It was a $1,000 a plate and every important Democrat in the State of California would be there. Once he committed, there would be no turning back.

Bobby got the call from his former prep school roommate who now had a job as a Democratic congressman's staffer. "Johnson will be in Century City on June 23rd; the invitations are being printed."

Bobby slammed down the phone into its cradle and shouted to an empty room, "We're on, God damn it! We are on!"

He quickly dialed his inner circle and spread the news. Century City was in six weeks.

It was a massive undertaking. And to ensure a large turnout, they asked Muhammad Ali to be their keynote speaker. He agreed. And the energy level sky rocketed and everyone reached out to everyone they knew. Please come! Be heard! Let them know we are against this insanity.

Marsha, of course, reached out to Rickey.

16

Rickey always liked the month of May; not only was it his birth month, but it also signaled the coming end to the school year. This May was extra sweet as he was turning 19; the year he got the money his grandmother had left him. It was an informal but binding agreement with his parents. Grandma Jennings had left him $10,000 when she died a few years ago. She put no stipulation on it as to when he could receive the money or how it was to be used. His parents wanted him to hold it in a simple trust until he was twenty-one, he argued for eighteen as that was California's legal age for consent. They had agreed to nineteen; and now he was nineteen. He had promised his parents that he wouldn't "piss it away," a term his father used which always caused his mother to rebuke him; but ever so slightly.

Now that he could spend it, or some of it, he knew exactly what he wanted: a new *Volkswagen* camper bus with the sleeping bunk and a small galley. A place for his boards, his food and all the other stuff he wanted to take on his long-planned sojourn south. Way south, perhaps to Costa Rica, where he heard the waves break in perfect shape, there's fruit hanging in the trees just waiting to be picked, and there were pretty dusty-brown girls with the whitest, brightest smiles, and eyes that just drank you in.

"Now, Rich," his father started in, "you don't need to spend all of your money on a car."

"I'm not, dad. Not even a third of it. The van I want costs $2,150 plus about $40 for the coco mats. Tax will be about $88 and I asked mom and she said the insurance would be about $65. So, less than $2,400, and it's brand new." Rickey, at this point, hadn't told his parents about his planned trip south of the border. One step at a time. Get the bus first, then start the persuasion campaign. "The rest I am going to save. I promise."

"OK, I am glad you thought about this. I will withdraw $2,500 from the bank. You'll need some gas money."

Rickey was so excited. Finally, he could get rid of the *Ford*. "Thanks, dad." And, glancing toward heaven, "Thank you, grandma."

When Rickey and Junior walked into Circle *VW/Porsche*, the salesman barely looked up from his newspaper. He had seen the type before; surfers. Grown men with nothing better to do all day than sit in the ocean waiting for a wave to ride for ten seconds. *Christ, they should all get drafted and have the Army make real men out of them.* He glanced over the top of the newspaper again and snorted. *Not wasting my time on those kids*, he thought.

Julie Ann was the owner's niece and working at the "store," as her uncle called it. It was a good summer job when she was out of school. She saw Rodney reading the paper and not speaking to the two boys looking at the new *Kombi* bus. She walked over to him and asked, "Rod, I know you are up, but if you don't want to deal with them, mind if I do?"

"Knock yourself out. They ain't got no money, honey, but have at it. Oh, and thanks for asking."

Rickey was sitting behind the wheel getting the feel of its position and the nearness of the windshield when she approached and said, "Good morning, can I help you?" She expected a "No thank you, we're just looking," in reply, but got, "I want this in the aqua-blue and tan. Can you get it that way?"

"Of course. We can check the other dealers to see if they have any, but if not, we can have it made in Germany just for you."

"Oh, yeah, I want a real refrigerator, not just a cooler."

"Planning a long trip, 'eh?"

"Yeah, maybe. Wanna come?" he said, half kidding and half hoping.

"Well, it will take about six weeks and I need half down; let's say, $1,400. The rest you will pay when we deliver it."

"OK, cool." Rickey pulled out twenty-five one hundred dollar bills and started to count out fourteen of them. He smiled at her as he did it, feeling very sure of himself.

17

"Look, you have to understand. This is a big deal for me. I've planned this trip for months. I'm gonna leave on the 15th. It's set. Junior's going with me for the first bit, and I don't want to change everything for some silly demonstration."

He could hear Marsha breathing heavily over the phone. She was pissed. At him mostly, he guessed, but also at his priorities. Surfing over confronting the President over a bloody and misbegotten war; but she was controlled. In a calm and rational voice, she said, "Rickey, do you really think if you leave on the 15th rather than the 25th, your life will be better? Because I can tell you, if you stay, and march with us, for the rest of your life, you will feel that even if you couldn't change the course of the war, at least you tried. Trust me, Honey, thirty years from now, everyone, and I mean everyone, will know this war was wrong. What are you going to say to your children when they ask you about it? 'Daddy, what did you do during the Vietnam war?' What are you going to say, Rickey, 'I surfed?'' Is that how you want your children to see you? People were dying, people were getting beat up by the cops for speaking their minds, boys were coming home blown apart and you were surfing?"

There was a long silence on the line and he thought maybe she had hung up. "Marsha? Marsha?"

"Yes, Rickey, I am still here. But I am worn out. Will you meet me or not?"

He could tell from the tone in her voice she was at the end of the line. And he was drained. How could he say no to her when this was the most important thing she had ever undertaken; this defined her. How could he deny her, when in his heart, he knew he still loved her. Would always love her; or at least the memory of her that summer.

"OK, I will meet you. I will come to the demonstration but only because I know how important it is to you. I don't think those fucking things do any good and are just a waste of time. But for you, I will be there."

"Thank you, Rickey. I will let you know where we will meet. Try and bring some friends."

"I'll see what I can do," but as he spoke the words, he knew he would never ask any of his friends to join him; why bother? To them, the world was made up of the rich who ran things, the slobs who follow along, and surfers. Nothing was going to change. But surfers don't care about that. All they want are some tasty tubes, a clean beach and decent reefer. You can march until your legs fall off and nothing will change. Rickey hated the idea but knew it was true. On top of a 20-footer waiting for the drop or moving through life, it's all up to you; no one else. But he could see where a massive movement by the people could influence the money boys; but only because they were afraid to lose it.

He should call Junior and tell him of the change of plans. He'd better come up with a damn good reason. Telling his friends that he wasn't going to go on a surf safari just to please Marsha would doom him to the land of the pussy-whipped forever. No, he would have to come up with something.

18

Bobby was standing in a small, bland office in a small professional building in Culver City. It was the local operating office of the Peace Action Council, the coordinating group for the demonstration. Bobby doubted this was really their office, but rather, something borrowed for the day from some local CPA or attorney who was supporting the cause. "Bobby, meet Irving," Don said. "Irving, this is Bobby, the guy I spoke to you about with the connections who got Spock and Ali to attend."

"Very impressive and, just how, might I ask, did you do that?"

"My father is a big-time Hollywood lawyer. He knows people, he made a few calls, opened some doors for me."

"Well, thank him for us. Having them at the park should guarantee a big turn out."

"Let's hope, but the police are saying only about 500 are expected." Bobby said, but more like an implied question. Testing what they would reveal to him.

"Yes, we heard that and aren't about to challenge it now. It could affect our parade permit. But we are confident that it will be much larger. Much larger." Don replied, while looking at a map of the area and how they would proceed. "Where are you going to have Spock and Ali and who is the third guy?"

"H. Rap Brown, the current head of SNCC. We got a trailer from one of the studios and have arranged to have it parked on a side street. They will walk into the park from the east side and go directly to the stage."

"Separately or together?"

"Together. Spock will speak first. Then Brown will introduce Ali. All together, they should speak for about 30 minutes, then the march starts with them leading it. The idea is they will break off after a few blocks. We don't want them exposed if there is trouble but we want the photo op of them leading the march."

"Slick. Now, Don, what's the word on Johnson's arrival?"

"My sources in the LAPD all confirm he will be coming in by helicopter, landing at 4:45 on the pad on the roof of the Century Plaza."

"OK, so we need to have as many people in front of the hotel by 4:30 as we can. Any problem with that?"

"Not that I can see, if the march leaves the park by 3:30. I've told Ali's people to have him here by 2:00 but I know he won't show up until five of three, Spock won't be a problem nor will Brown. We should have the bulk of the people there before Johnson arrives."

"Great. Don and I appreciate all the work you and your group has done." With that, Bobby knew he was being dismissed and made his good-byes.

*　*　*　*　*

Marsha was to meet Rickey at Ship's coffee shop about a half-mile from Rancho Park where the rally would start. But first she had to meet Bobby there to finalize their plans. She was just thinking he was late when he walked in the door. He always had that look about him of being somewhere else and a bit frazzled. No matter how much money he spent on clothes, they never seemed to fit him properly, further contributing to the hassled professor look he seemed to project. But she still thought he was cute.

"How'd it go?"

"Fine. Everything seems to be falling into place. Oh, you got me tea, thanks." He reached over and patted her on her arm and smiled gently at her. "We are almost there."

"Looks like it. I think this thing is going to be much bigger than they think. I don't know what numbers they are talking about but my guess is it's going to be tens of thousands. I hear people are coming down from the Bay Area, over from Arizona, up from San Diego. This is going to be big."

"Well, if it is," he said, looking her squarely in the eye, "then there will be trouble. They will tolerate 500 or so 'hippies,' as they see them, but if thousands show up, there will be trouble. I just got a sense of what could be a problem. They want a big crowd in front of the hotel when Johnson lands.

They say 4:45, but if he is late, how will they have the numbers if the crowd has to keep moving? Remember, the permit is for a march and states there can be no stopping or sitting down. It's a parade permit, which means, it has to keep moving. My guess is, if it slows down, like to a crawl, or stops and the people get backed up, then they will pull the permit and declare it an unlawful assembly and start arresting people."

"Where are you going to be?"

"With the three all-stars. The idea is to get them in the front of the march as it leaves the park; there will be plenty of news cameras there, but once they reach Pico, they peel off and we take them back to the trailer. There won't be any problems there. If there is a problem, it will be in front of the hotel."

"Well, let's hope there is no violence. It's kinda counter to our message."

"If there is, it will be the cops who will start it. Look, I gotta go. It's one o'clock already and I still need to get the trailer stocked. Bye. Be safe." He stood up, reached down and kissed her on the cheek as he turned to leave.

She muttered, "I will."

19

Rickey waited a week before picking up his new van from the dealer: the longest week of his life. He needed a cover story for Junior and the best one he could come up with was the factory delayed shipping it. He hated lying to Junior but he hated the idea of his buds thinking he was under Marsha's thumb.

He had it now and turned up the on ramp to the 405 north for what should be a quick trip to Culver City to meet Marsha. As he crested the ramp, the 405 looked like a parking lot. *What the fuck,* he thought. *It's one o'clock on a Friday; why so much traffic?*

Nothing he could do; just drive. As he drove, his mind wandered, with many different subjects crisscrossing one another in his mind. Damn, was he glad to be out of school. Finished with a strong C plus GPA and enough units to keep his 2S; pleasing both his mom and Marsha. He'd worked out a deal with Mr. Pierce to hold his job open for when he got back in September and his parents had agreed to his southern adventure with the provision he call them at least once a week. So things were looking pretty good. Just go do this thing for Marsha and grab Junior in the morning and we will be surfing San Onofre tomorrow at this time. He always liked surfing there although the long walk in was a bummer. The surf was generally good but what made it special was the super warm water from the generating plant. As good as it felt, he always had a nagging doubt about getting radiated from the atomic pellets that drove the reactor. But, hey, he had been doing it for almost ten years without any noticeable effects, so it must be safe.

By the time he reached Hermosa Beach, the traffic had thinned and he was able to slip up into third gear and get the van moving over 50. It rode nicely. The air-cooled engine made a lot of noise and, after awhile, it was just in the background and part of the ride.

Marsha was staring out the window when he entered the coffee shop. The afternoon sun struck her face harshly. For the first time, he noticed the drag lines around her mouth from the cigarettes she smoked by the carton, the small lines creeping out from her eyes and a general sense of weariness she seemed to radiate. Yet, realized again, for the thousandth time, just how beautiful she was. But he recognized it wasn't the same as before. Before, when he looked at her, he could actually feel his heart soar, his pulse increase, and warm emotion flood through him. Now, he recognized her beauty as one would a piece of fine art or a sunset. He knew he had deep permanent feelings for her, but no longer did he desire her with that wanton feeling he carried for so long. Somehow it was gone, replaced with a fond memory. *Perhaps that is the difference between loving someone and being in love,* he thought.

He deliberately bumped the table as he slid into the booth, jarring her out of her daydream and causing her to jump back a bit. "Rickey!" she blurted out.

"Yep, that's what they call me, and South Point, some just say SP, but you have always called me Rickey."

She smiled at him and said, "Yeah, South Point Rickey, surfer dude, now war protester. Thanks for coming. It means a lot to me."

"Hey, no worries. So, we eating first or do we have to go?"

She lifted her eyes up and smiling, said, "No, we have time."

He turned, looking for a waitress.

20

Rickey stood at the crest of Pico Boulevard and looked east and all he could see were people. Like a multi-colored sea gently rolling westward, there were people of a single mind and of a single voice. Some young, some old, some in the middle. Mostly whites but a few black and brown faces that stood out in the crowd. Many held signs proclaiming their opposition to the war. Some pushed small children in front of them in strollers, others carried their off-spring in backpacks slung across their bellies so the baby was always looking back into its parent's shirt, and still others simply held a small hand as the child followed behind. It was a peaceful scene despite the constant chanting of, "Hey, hey, LBJ, how many children did you kill today?" after they grew weary of that one, they would start with, "Hell no, we won't go," and kept at it until it reverberated down the avenue and floated up to the hotel's upper floors.

Rickey stood in the park with Marsha while the speakers made their pleas. Spock for peace generally and Ali for not going.

"Christ," he whispered half out loud, "to give up the heavyweight championship, to lose your career, to face going to jail all because of your beliefs." *I doubt I could do that.*

Rickey heard what both of them said, and while it wasn't new, it was good to hear it again.

Marsha had left a few minutes ago to meet up with Bobby and get the speakers back into the trailer and safety. She said she would meet him back in the park in about 40 minutes and then they could leave. Rickey saw no point to walking to the Century Plaza Hotel and chanting mindlessly at the wall of closed windows. He would rather just take the scene in, absorb its energy and remember the moment. Peaceful Protest. The First Amendment in action, something to be proud of. He thought of his father and the war he fought to make this possible and realized he still had that lingering doubt that maybe, just maybe, the government knew more than he knew; or these people knew, or Ali knew. Hell, it was the government.

He turned back toward the park and searched the sea of faces for Marsha but couldn't find her. He stopped to light a smoke and as he did, he felt a rush of people; a panic was in the air that he could taste. He dropped the cigarette and pushed off from the tree he had been leaning against. He thought he saw Marsha and started for her, but the crowd pushed him back and spun him around; in doing so, he was pushed out of the stream of the crowd and into a small clearing.

There he saw what was causing the panic. A wall of police, holding body shields at arm's length using them as rams; knocking people to the ground and pummeling them with long black batons as they were falling. He saw one officer kick a slightly built young man in the head as he laid on the ground defenseless; blood started squirting from his head quickly covering the ground around him. Rickey felt the bile rise in his gut, and for a moment, thought he would throw up. But then the panic hit him; the fear pulsing through his blood made him regain his focus. Just like that weightless drop off a large wave; nothing but air under you. Knowing you misjudged the angle and now it was a free-fall to the bottom. "Survive," is all your brain is screaming and so you take counter measures.

He slipped back behind the tree to gain some cover and avoid the motion of the crowd. He had a moment's reprieve before, in horror, he saw a cop standing no more than three feet away with his baton raised, ready to bring it crashing down on the stomach of a woman curled at his feet. Rickey saw the arm raising and as it did, the cop's head arched back and the white flesh of his neck was exposed between his helmet and his body armor.

Rickey felt the crash of his right forearm against the soft flesh and felt the cop's body collapse to the ground. The cop's feet were tangled between the legs of the fallen woman and Rickey could feel him twitching as his body tried to regain consciousness. He had hit the carotid artery just right; hopefully just pinching it, not crushing it. But, at that moment, he didn't care. *Fucking asshole, hit a defenseless woman!*

Rickey backed up a step and found her under the officer's legs, sobbing uncontrollably. He reached down to help her up and saw immediately why she was so upset. Her belly arched out, telling the world that she was a mother and her child would be here any day now.

"Look, we gotta go. Can you walk?" Rickey asked in a low, calming voice. "We need to get out of here."

She nodded, but the sobs continued. Her eyes were wide with fear and she began to shake. Rickey was afraid that shock would set in and he had no idea how that would affect the baby. He steered her off to the side of the park thinking that maybe the trailer would still be on the side street behind the east entrance. He started walking toward it when she spoke for the first time.

"Why would he do that? I was just standing there waiting for my husband." She looked at Rickey as if he knew the answer.

"I don't know. Sorry. I'm South Point... Ah, Rickey. I think there is a trailer around the corner where you will be safe." He knew she looked familiar but couldn't place her. "Have we met before?"

"I doubt it but people always ask me that. I'm Rita Rains."

"Of course, the actress. I really liked "Fail Safe." You were great."

"Well, thank you."

They walked the rest of the way in silence.

21

Remy was what they called a "hanger-on," an outsider, a hustler. Remy called himself a freelancer. A freelance photojournalist who roamed LA looking for situations to photograph when the people in them didn't want to be photographed. His specialty was catching husbands with someone other than their wives in what the polite press call a compromising position. He called them the Fuck Shot. He also called it his bread and butter.

He always offered the picture and its negative to the people in the shot before offering it to the *Hollywood Star* or *LA's Backdoor*, publications that even in Remy's opinion were nothing but sleaze. But, it paid the bills.

One studio executive handed him $1,000 and a nod which said, "don't fuck with me again!" A prominent attorney, one of those lawyers to the stars type, gave Remy $800 just for a shot of him getting out of a car with a younger woman. Of course, it was four o'clock in the morning and out in Malibu, about 30 miles from where he lived with his wife of 25 years. But then there was a time a guy promised to pay him $500 for a shot of him in bed with some hooker. When he handed the photo and negative to the guy, he was hit so hard his head ached for three days. The guy was a lefty and Remy never saw it coming.

Today he had headed down to the anti-war march hoping to get a frame or two of some people whose employer didn't want their political views known. He knew it was a long shot because the world was changing and people didn't give a damn what other people thought and right now being against the war was a popular thing; at least in LA. But he had nothing better to do on a Friday afternoon and besides, Ali was going to be there and maybe he could get a good shot and sell it to *AP* or *UPI*. He did that on occasion but generally it was by accident.

When he got home from the park, he ran his film through the developer process. He would lay the strips in their sleeves out across the light box at the far end of the table. He would take a close look at each frame to see if there was anything usable. Today, he was especially interested in the last shots on the roll. He was getting ready to go. Ali had left the park and there wasn't much going on until he heard some yelling which seemed close by. He ran toward the yelling and saw a huge crowd charging at him, looking like Satan himself was chasing them. To keep from getting run over, he stepped behind some hedges and braced himself against the retaining wall.

What he had always had was what they call in the business, a quick eye. Even his photo editor at the *LA Times* would say, "Remy, you got the eye." Of course then he would ream him out for missing deadlines and field assignments like covering City Council meetings. He wasn't long for the *Times*

He saw a police officer arched back with his baton in the air, ready to strike at someone or something at his feet; Remy couldn't see the whole scene. But he knew the composition was good and the distance was close enough that his *Leica* would capture it. He had the automatic shutter on at the end of the day; simply by holding his thumb down, the camera would shoot picture after picture until the film ran out.

Now in the closet-sized service porch which served as his office, darkroom and storage facility, he bent over the light board to see what he had. Ten frames had fired off, four of which were of the sky. Of the six, two were good and four were killers. The first showed the cop almost at full extension; his right arm raised high with the baton ready to come crashing down. The next was a whirl of motion. A white tee shirt stretched across a large back that was hunched partly down but looked to be turning at the same time. Hard to see really what was happening. The third frame had the officer falling backwards and the body in front of him turning to the left. The fourth frame showed the officer flat on the ground while the other guy was reaching down extending a hand to someone. The fifth frame showed a young woman, who looked very pregnant, starting to stand up. The last frame showed the man and the woman turning right in his direction while they stepped over the police officer.

"Shit howdy!" Remy swore under his breath. "That's a great sequence. Who the hell are those people and where did that guy come from?"

He took the frames, reorganized them in glass holders, and placed them on the light board for a better look. After a few minutes, he removed the last frame and placed it in the enlarger. He turned its powerful light on and adjusted the focus. Even with the image upside down, he recognized the woman. "That's Rita Rains!" he almost shouted out. "Hell, I might have something here." *But what?* Rita Rains was known for her liberal views and her anti-war sentiment so neither her agent nor the studio would care that she was at the rally. She was obviously the victim so what was there to gain by going down that path.

And did he really want to take on the LAPD? Even if he sold it on the QT to *LA's Back Door*, sooner or later the cops would find out it was him; hell, there were only about six of them that did this on a regular basis and his style was distinctive. They would find him and kick his ass. Forget that.

But still he was curious. So he took the first frame out and started working the enlarger to see if he could make out a name or somehow identify the cop. It might just be worth something to him someday.

He was shooting on a 35mm format with 400 speed film which when blown up tended to degrade the image detail and prevented clarity. Still he worked on, taking smaller and smaller sections, blowing them up to where the grain of the silver started to breakdown the image and then stopping right on the edge. Printing it and then bathing it in various chemicals to enhance the clarity and hopefully, to pull an image which would ID the officer.

It was nine o'clock at night when he pulled from the developer tray a single piece of paper which focused on the officer's upper left chest. There was a long narrow nameplate which read, LOGAN, H.

The Hollywood cowboys. He didn't recognize the face but he had this year's division yearbook which he took down from the shelf above the combo washer/dryer and flipped the pages to the L's. He glanced at the roster and at the name LOGAN, Herman, 28, (8-17-40) Class of '64, Glendale High School 1958, U.S. Marines 1959-'62.

"Well, hello Herman."

He was tired and hungry and decided to go out and grab some dinner down the hill at the Pantry. *Always open and always good, hearty food*, he thought; already tasting the pork chops with the side of sauerkraut and that mustard which always brought tears to his eyes.

He was pleased with himself; but not sure why.

22

Rickey walked away from the trailer in a semi-daze. *What the fuck just happened? Christ Almighty, how did I get caught up in this shit?*

He realized he was walking the wrong way back to the van, and spun around nearly losing his balance. As his right food dug into the street and his hips flipped the other way reversing his balance, the memories flashed on him. The endless foot drills with Mr. Lee at the House of Judo. "Plant and turn. Plant and turn," Mr. Lee would say over and over again as he had him spin from position to position always with the follow up reminder, "Plant again and attack. Attack." The hours he spent on the mat doing nothing but planting one foot, then the next, then launching himself into his imaginary opponent. But what Mr. Lee was teaching wasn't planting and spinning, but balance; the balance of the inner-self with the physical-self, a harmony of being which gives you the balance to survive your opponent's attack.

Judo was made up of several techniques, one of which was *Atemi*; the art of striking your opponent either *persuasively* or with what Mr. Lee called, *soft power*. The former was to stop your opponent immediately but almost always was a gamble in that if you misjudged your blow you left yourself open to an *Atemi* by your opponent. Whereas, *soft power* was to move your opponent into a position for a take-down and hopefully defeat.

He shook his head and mused, *that was one persuasive Atemi you hit that guy with. Where did that come from?* he wondered. *Hell, one second, I was trying to get out of the way of a mob and the next, I was lifting that girl off the ground. Fucking weird.*

OK, dude, it's over. Head home and forget this whole thing. Nobody knows it was you - just let it slide.

He swung himself up into the van, turned the key and drove away, leaving the anti-war march for others. *If this is what happens at these things, then I don't want any part of 'em. What was accomplished? Jack shit. Johnson doesn't give a damn. Marsha and her gang are just kidding themselves. Maybe it makes them feel good but it doesn't do a damn thing.*

Traffic was light on the freeway and the van swayed slightly as he sped south heading home. He needed some shelter and his parents' house was the best he had ever known.

As he walked in the door, he heard the TV on which meant his parents were home early; not unusual for a Friday. He walked into the living room where his mother was sitting on the edge of the sofa and his father was seated on the ottoman hunched over staring intently at the screen. George Putnam was on commentating on the riot at the Century Plaza Hotel where thousands of demonstrators had turned on the police, throwing bricks, bottles and whatever else was handy, causing the police to retreat before re-grouping and then moving them away from the hotel. George Putnam was *KTLA*'s lead anchorman and for him to be on this early meant this was a big story. He was also pro-war and super conservative in his social views. He had a large following in LA and was considered a legitimate newsman unlike Joe Pine who was considered more of a right wing provocateur.

Rickey sat down and watched the story about all the police and how they were attacked until they cut to a live feed from the Beverly Wilshire Hotel. There was a female reporter saying that in a few moments the actress Rita Rains was going to give a statement about the events at the Century Plaza. After a commercial break the reporter was back and then there was a stirring behind her as Rita Rains walked up to the podium, which was fashioned with a large array of microphones with various station's call signs prominently displayed. Finally, in a soft and quiet voice she said, "Good evening. I was at Rancho Park this afternoon and I saw and experienced what really happened. What happened was the police rioted." She paused for effect and Rickey thought how pretty she was and how unlike the girl he had lifted off the ground sobbing.

> "Yes, that's right, the police rioted. I was standing alone waiting for my husband when I saw at least 20 officers in full riot gear charging down on a group of people who doing nothing but standing there talking amongst themselves. I saw police officers hit women with their batons, I saw them kick people in the head who were lying on the ground defenseless, I saw them

use their shields as battering rams, slamming into men, women and in one case, even a child, knocking them to the ground. I was attacked. An officer knocked me to the ground, and then raised his baton to strike me while I was there helpless at his feet. By the Grace of God, a young man knocked the officer over before he could hit me, he helped me up and then led me away. I don't know the young man's name. I must have been in shock; I was so afraid for my baby. I have never known that kind of fear before; I pray I never feel it again. To that young man out there, whoever you are, thank you and may God go with you through life. Thank you very much." With that, she turned and walked back inside the hotel.

"Oh, how awful," his mother said, "that poor woman."

"Well, I'm not so sure. Her views on the war are pretty well known. She's no Jane Fonda, but darned close. Those people will lie to make the government look bad just because they don't understand why we are fighting in Vietnam." His father spoke with a firmness and an edge of anger Rickey rarely heard.

"She's not lying," he blurted out.

"Oh, really. Well, how do you know?"

"I was there. I was the young man who stopped the cop from hitting her."

23

"Hey, Herm, you were in that mess over at the hotel, weren't you?"

Herman Logan looked over to his watch commander, "No, sir. I was assigned to the park."

"That's what I thought. Assistant Chief Davis wants you over at Parker ASAP."

"Fuck," Herm swore under his breath but casually asked, "What's this about, you know?"

"Christ, you are a Jar Head Logan, it's about Rita Rains, the fucking actress. Didn't you see her all over the TV last night? Chief Redden is a friend of hers and he is pissed. Not so much about the way the break-up of the rally was handled but how she was treated. He assigned Davis to investigate and Davis is pissed about everything. I heard when he came back from San Diego yesterday he read out everybody, including the Chief, on how it went down. He's looking to hang somebody's ass. Be straight with him, Herm. The man can smell bullshit a thousand yards off."

"Yeah? Yeah, thanks Sarge. I'll get right over there. Sixth floor, right?"

"That's where the brass lives."

As he drove down the freeway, he could smell himself: fear sweat coming from his armpits. *Holy shit! What should I say? Man, I can't cop to it, they'll toss me in jail just to shut up the press. Even if they don't do that, they'll kick me off the force. I'll lose what little pension I got built-up and it will just be a shit show. Hell, Julie might even leave me.*

I can't tell what the others did either but shit, they could tell on me...Nah! they won't. Hell, I don't think they can, no one saw me. They were on the other side of the park. I got separated when I went after the kid with the "Fuck the LAPD" shirt on. What a dumb shit, what did he think we would do...kiss his ass?

He got off the freeway and made his way across town on surface streets. He parked in the patrol car lot behind the Center and opened the trunk. He fished out a fresh shirt and slapped on some aftershave, he felt like he was going on a date; a date with the hangman.

He cleared in with the desk man who told him to go right up. Davis was waiting for him. Davis had been a Divisional Commander when Herm joined the force and the word was he was a hard ass, a stickler for detail, and followed the book. Herm knew nowhere in the book did it authorize beating a pregnant woman...especially a movie star friend of the Chief's.

As he rode the elevator up to the sixth floor, he still had no idea what he would say. *Play it as it lays*, he thought.

"Officer Logan, welcome, I am Ed Davis and the Chief has asked me to look into what happened yesterday over at Rancho Park. I understand you were there. Is that right?"

"Yes sir, that 's where I was assigned." He said it like it was someone else's idea and he couldn't be blamed for what happened.

"Tell me what you saw."

"Well, at first, it was all peaceful and calm, you know. Those guys spoke, you know Ali and them other guys, then people started walking over to the far end of the park to march up to the hotel to give Johnson shit."

"Oh, is that what they were doing?" His glare at Herman Logan looked like a laser. "Look, Officer Logan, I understand you were a Marine, I guess you lost some friends over there. Probably still have some there. I served in the Navy during World War II, I left the Department to do so. A lot of men did. It was a different war; everyone knew why we were fighting and supported it. This war isn't the same and a lot of people don't like it. And under our laws, they have the right to go out into the streets and in a peaceable manner, let their government know that they are unhappy. That's the way it is and that's the way it should be. Now, what I am trying to find out is if the people in the park were acting peaceable or not yesterday."

"Yes, sir."

"Well, Logan, were they?"

"Ah, well, sir, yes, at first. But I guess there was some problem because Sergeant Lewis told us to clear the park; so we did."

"What type of force did he tell you to use?"

"Ah, you know, I don't think I was told that, sir. You kinda understand it from what is happening around you."

"Well, did you see anyone using what you consider excessive force?"

"Ah, no, sir."

"OK. Did you see anyone using their batons?"

"Yes, sir, to nudge people along out of the park."

"See any officer strike anyone with his baton? Or his shield?"

"No, sir."

"How about kicking someone?"

"No, sir."

"Do you know anything about what the actress, Rita Rains, is claiming; that someone knocked her to the ground with his shield then was going to club her while she was on the ground? Know anything about that, Officer Logan?"

Fuck, he knows! How could he? He's bluffing, seeing how I'll react. Just stay cool, Herm. "No, sir, I don't know anything about that. Just heard about it on the tube last night. That's all I know. She says it happened, but I don't know if it did or not."

"OK, Officer. Thanks for coming in. Please report back to your division."

"Thank you, sir." He wasn't sure to salute or not, so he turned and walked toward the door, feeling the sweat running down his back.

The afternoon light was pouring in through the ceiling-to-floor windows which formed the west side of AC Davis' office. As he crossed the room to his desk, he looked out and saw the endless sprawl which constituted Los Angeles, the City of Angels. He wondered where they were hiding.

He looked at the photographs on his desk, several of which contained clear images of the police, his men, charging a group of unarmed men and women, in full riot gear with their batons raised. The sign in the background read Rancho Park, and he could tell the officer on the far right was Logan. He was a liar. But what to do about it?

24

"That was you?" his father asked with a great deal of doubt in his tone.

Rickey was on one of the dining room chairs but had it facing backwards so he was straddling it, with his arms hanging off the top of the chair's back, leaning forward, his body taught with tension. "Yes, that was me."

"Why were you there?" his mother asked from her perch on the sofa.

"Number of reasons. To see what it was about, to hear Ali speak, to support Marsha and listen to what the anti-war folks are saying. "

"Oh, Marsha," his mother sighed, "I knew she would get you into trouble."

"Mom, Marsha had nothing to do with it. It was the cops. They just ran wild. Beating people, kicking people, slamming them with those shields, knocking them to the ground. And, nobody was doing a damn thing to cause it."

"Rich, watch your language around your mother."

The room was silent for awhile, the only sound, Rusty licking himself. Finally, his father spoke up.

"So, why did you have to hit a police officer? Where did you hit him? In the neck? By the artery? Don't you know you could have killed him?" His voice getting louder and louder with each question.

"Why, *why*? The guy was about to unload on a pregnant woman and it looked to me he was aiming at her stomach. What kind of animal knocks a pregnant woman to the ground and then stands over her ready to beat the shit out of her? Just because he wears a uniform doesn't mean he gets to do what he wants."

This was new territory for them. Unlike many of Rickey's friends, he and his dad always had a great relationship. Now raising their voices to one another felt both odd and wrong. But he was upset. How could his father be

66

so blind? How could he cling to the idea that all cops were always good all the time? Was he really that naive? Or did he just want to believe in an America where that was true?

Rickey stood up and looked at his father. "I was there. I saw peaceful people with their children who came out to tell the President that this war is wrong. And they were trampled, kicked, beaten, and had their rights violated. You may not like it. It may not fit your idea of what America should be. But, I am sorry to tell you, Dad, it's what America has become."

He turned and headed for the door. "I need some peace and quiet. I'll be at the beach."

His mother and father looked at each other, each looking to the other for answers. Finally, his mother said, "Our boy is growing up." Bailey nodded in agreement.

25

Bobby sat with Irving and Don in a booth in the bar of Valentino's out in Santa Monica. Lawyers and accountants and other business-types started to filter in as the hour wore on past five o'clock.

"I'd say to a job well done, sir," Don said, as he tipped his glass toward Bobby.

"I'd second that," Irving said, and he too tipped his glass in Bobby's direction.

"Getting Spock and Ali there was such good work. And that piece with Rita Rains...how did you arrange that? No, maybe I don't want to know."

"Well, I do," interjected Don. "How did all that happen?"

Bobby shifted in his seat; he wasn't sure just how much he should tell and how much he should keep to himself.

"Well, Rita's an old friend. A client of my father, and I asked her to attend and to bring some of her friends. I told her it would be a big protest and would get a lot of coverage but if we had some stars there, it would be even bigger. And, I promised her she would meet Ali. I don't think she really cared but her husband is a big fan of Ali's so she came."

"Yeah, but that's not the whole story is it? Of the tens of thousands of people there that cop just happened to pick out a famous movie star to hit? Come on, Bobby! That whole thing was staged like a Busby Berkeley musical."

"No, Don, it wasn't that. It was just good luck."

"Bullshit! You're telling me that a group of cops, who were far from where the marchers were sitting down blocking the parade just on their own decided to kick some ass? And one of them just happened to pick out Rita Rains? Bullshit! Hey, I think it was brilliant, and if you don't want to take credit for it, fine. But it's thinking like that we need more of. We have to push this stuff not only onto the front pages but further back into the Home Section and where the entertainment shit is...hell, half the people don't even read the front page. They turn to the Sports Section or the stock market or whatever their interest is; it's there we have to get them. And this, whatever you want to call it, did just that. This will be in the paper for days and will lead the nightly news for a week. We need to find a way to find the kid who saved her. Hell, if we did, we could put him on the cover of *Life Magazine*. You know who he is?"

"No, I have no idea," Bobby replied, telling the first of many lies to many people regarding the "Riot at Rancho" as the press had begun to call it.

Don signaled the waitress for another round by spinning his finger in the air. He would press Bobby more as the night and the booze wore on. He thought, *This kid is hiding something.*

26

Marsha called Rickey's house but his mother would only say he wasn't there. Something was off as Mrs. Osgood had always been friendly to her. Her guess was his parents found out he went to the march and blamed her for it.

He must be at the beach. He has that new van and he can sleep in it, so now it's just a question of which beach. Sunset, she said to herself. *That's where we first made love. Out on the cool sand next to a fire pit Rickey had dug out with his hands.* She remembered the blackness of the sky, the texture of his skin, and the warmth he radiated under that thin blanket which kept the damp air off and gave them a sense of privacy. Oh, she remembered it well. It was her first real experience with making love; unlike those rush jobs with her old boyfriend. Shaking her head, she thought, *Whatever did I see in him?* She caught herself asking herself the same question about Bobby. Where was he today when the shit went down? Where he always seemed to be: on the sidelines, just off the playing field, just out of reach, always calculating the odds. A thought struck her with frightening clarity: *Did he know the police would attack? Did he let it happen? Did he cause it to happen?* She nearly ran the red light crossing PCH, so distracted was she by these thoughts.

Not now, she thought. *I need to find Rickey and make sure he's all right.*

She saw the aqua *VW* parked just off 6th where the street ended at the sand; a light dimly glowed from inside.

She approached the van slowly listening for voices. She didn't want to find him with another woman and embarrass them both. But all was quiet and she knocked softly.

He pulled back the curtain which covered the window in the door and said, "Yeah?"

"It's me, Rickey. Marsha."

He opened the door and she stepped up into the van. The odor of reefer hung in the air mixing with the smell of tacos.

"Taco Time?" she asked.

"Damn straight! Best 15 cent tacos around."

"But not the best tacos," she parried.

"No, the best are down in Mexico, hand-made on stone by little old ladies with claw-like hands." He paused and looked down, feeling a bit ashamed at having left the march without making sure she was OK. Somewhat defensively he said, "Look, sorry about leaving you but I need to put some distance between me and anti-war rallies. Mars, you've gotta understand, that's not my world. And it's a world I don't want any part of. I let you guilt me into going by asking me what will I tell my kids about my role in Vietnam. You know what I am going to tell them? I surfed. That's right. I lived my life, my way, on the beach or on a wave but not on some asphalt street chanting some mindless mantra to a bunch of people who don't give a shit because they are making so much money off it they will never give it up."

"I just feel I have to try."

"That's good for you and this is good for me."

"So, what are you going to do?"

"Tomorrow I am driving my brand new *VW* van south with my friend Junior and we are going to surf every God damned beach from the border to Cabo San Lucas. That's what I'm going to do. And when I am done doing that, I will come here, go to City College, take some courses I couldn't care less about and try to ride this fucking war out. What else can I do?"

She moved closer across the pad which made the back seat a bed and reached for him. She gently stroked his face while saying, "Honey, there is nothing else you can do." In a few minutes they were locked in a deep embrace and the van swayed slightly from their love-making.

27

Remy was sitting at one of the back tables at Philippe's eating their famous French dip roast beef sandwiches and washing it down with their nickel coffee. Here it was 1967 and Philippe's was charging the same for coffee that they had during the Depression. Remy liked this place with its constant motion and the noise from the shuffling of feet as the people stood in line, and the voices from the counter yelling orders back into the kitchen and the impersonal feeling of the whole place. White on white and we don't give a damn. Eat and go, and please don't linger. Not a place for a first date Remy thought; hell not for any date until long after you were married.

Remy had been married for six years. But one night he came home and she was gone. Just a note that said, "sorry." He didn't understand exactly what she meant until he went to the bank a few days later to deposit his check and found the account had been closed. About $3,200 gone. He had been saving to buy a bigger house. One out in the new suburbs with their nicely cut lawns and trimmed hedges. For some reason, he really liked trimmed hedges. But that was now gone, along with Betty, so he would just stay in the house in Highland Park where he had grown up. *A man could do worse*, he thought to himself, unaware of the large fellow sitting down next to him.

"You Remy?"

"Yeah, who's asking?"

"Oh, sorry, I'm Colin O'Connell. Mostly they call me Irish," and he held out his hand. Remy took it and they shook briefly but neither understanding why. *Habit*, Remy thought, *and being polite.*

"Look," Irish said, "I don't want to be rude, especially when a man is eating his lunch but it's kind of important."

"Lunch is done. Just finishing the coffee and I don't need that."

"Great, let's walk."

They both got up and Remy was surprised how tall Irish was, not to mention, broad. This was a fellow they sent when they wanted answers; and answers now, not later.

They left Philippe's and started up the small hill to Union Station. As they walked, they both pulled cigarette packs from their pockets and lit a` smoke from a wind-proof lighter.

"So, how can I help you, Irish?"

"Well, the word on the street is you have some pictures from that mix-up over in Rancho Park. I have some friends who would like to buy them and I understand you are in the business of selling photos, so I thought we could, you know, do a little exchange."

"Who are your friends?"

"Well, see, that's the sticky part. They prefer, you know, to stay in the background."

"Well, tell me this. Will they use the photos to hurt anybody?"

"Nah, I don't think they will hurt anyone who doesn't deserve it," he paused, then followed up.

"Well, I don't see why they would want to hurt the girl or the guy that helped her. They already know who the girl is, Rita Rains, hell, she told them herself. And why would they want to hurt him - Kid Galahad?"

Remy took a long drag on the *Camel* and looked at Irish. He wasn't a cop but he didn't have that air about him that criminals carry. "So, what's your story, Irish? What's in this for you?"

Irish dug into the upper pocket of his shirt and pressed a business card into Remy's hand. Nice card made of heavy stock and engraved, not printed, with his given name in clear, crisp letters, a phone number in the left hand corner with a Fairfax prefix and the simple word "Collector" in the right hand corner. "You see, when somebody needs something, they send me out to collect it. I carry a private dick license but I don't do all that sleazy stuff. I don't peer into windows or tap peoples' phones. I just know a lot of folks in this town and know who to talk to to get what someone wants. Right now, I want those photos, so how much?"

"Exclusive or not?"

"Good question. Let's say exclusive."

"Well, it's a set of six and each picture generally goes for a few hundred."

"Look, my guys, they run things here. You do them a solid and they will remember it. I can give you $500 but that's it."

"Yeah, how would they know me if I needed a little something?"

"You've got my card. You call me and I will speak to them. Besides, I would consider this a personal favor and then maybe I could help, too."

"OK, $500 it is, and two favors," and Remy held out his hand, which Irish took and shook. Both of them now fully understanding why they were shaking.

"How about Musso & Franks tonight at seven? I'll have them for you."

"You got good taste. See you at seven."

They parted ways with Remy walking up toward the *Times* building and Irish heading down to Union Station, wherein he tried to fit himself into a phone booth but to no avail, so he stood half in, half out and dialed the number. "'Parker Center," answered the operator in her cheery voice.

"Ed Davis, please."

"Can I ask who is calling?"

"Just say Irish."

28

Remy figured, what the hell. Those prints were worth more than $500 but he was in no mood to argue with a fellow like Irish. At least, not that afternoon.

He hustled back to his house in Highland Park and checked that no one was following him. He opened the front door and everything looked normal; well normal with Betty gone, like the *new* normal. He quickly walked through the small cottage-like house and opened up the in-wall ironing board. He dropped it down, exposing a small latch which he pushed. Bingo! The panel opened up and there was the safe where he kept the special negatives; sometimes they were duplicates of the, "Yes, that's the only one there is," negatives he had sold to clients. *A boy always needed a little back-up*, he chuckled to himself; *back-up is always good*. He withdrew the white envelope with the single black line running through it. Rancho Park, it said to him.

He hardly stopped to think about what he was doing. He swiftly printed the six pictures and then printed the smaller one identifying Logan as the bully with the stick. Then he printed a second copy. He placed all the prints in the big drying book which lived in a slot between the washer/dryer combo unit. They would take about half an hour to dry, he figured.

He pulled the Hollywood Division roster booklet off the shelf and found the Division's phone number. He wrote it down on a piece of scrap paper and headed out the door. Better to make this call from a public phone and there was one down at the corner in the gas station.

He fingered a dime from his pocket and dialed the number. An operator broke in and told him it was a toll call and he needed to deposit another 20 cents. He listened as the two dimes ran down the slot, making a tinny clicking sound when they reached bottom. "Thank you," and she was gone and there was a ringing sound which seemed to come from faraway. A rich, full voice answered with a single word, "Hollywood."

"Yes, Herman Logan, please."

"What is this about?"

"It's personal."

"This division doesn't allow personal calls. You will have to catch him off duty."

Remy quickly added, before the voice on the other end could hang up, "It's about Rancho Park."

There was a pause, then a gruff, "OK," then silence. Remy worried that the call had been disconnected, however, after a few minutes, a voice said, "Logan."

"Officer Logan, I have something for you from Rancho Park."

"What could you have but a bad memory? Fuck off!"

"I have pictures of you getting ready to strike Rita Rains before that kid kicked your ass. That's what I have. I was going to give you a chance to buy them but I think I'll just take them to the *Times*."

"Whoa! Hang on there. What makes you think it was me? All of us were wearing the same shirt."

"How do you think, dumb fuck. Your nameplate shows in one of the shots."

"Holy crap!" he heard Logan bellow. "Look man, I need this job. You can't take them to the *Times*. I will buy them from you. How much?"

Remy had been thinking $500 might be hard for a cop but this guy was an asshole and besides, it was known that the Hollywood boys made a bunch on the side; both legit and not so legit.

"A grand. This afternoon before five or I will get my money elsewhere."

"Fuck, a grand. Oh, no, that's fine. I can get that real quick. Where do we meet?"

"We don't. You know the dive bar over on Iverson, Slims?"

"I can find it."

"OK. Walk in a few minutes before five and go to the bar and order a *Pabst Blue Ribbon*. Say it just like that. Drink a bit of it, then go to the men's room. There is just one crapper and on the wall of the stall there is one of those things that has paper to put over the toilet seat when you sit down. Put the money in there. I suggest in hundreds and in an envelope. Then go back and finish the *Pabst*. Wait five minutes. Not four or three, but five, and go back into the head. The photos will be in the same place where you left the money."

"How do I know you won't just take the money and split?"

"OK, I'll tell you what I'll do. I will leave the shot of you on the ground and the one with your name showing. I'll do that before you get there. That's fair, not that I give a shit as to what you think. OK?"

"OK."

Just then, the operator was asking for another 20 cents. He hung up quickly and left the phone booth dripping sweat.

Chump! Didn't even ask me if it was the only set. Christ, they get dumber and dumber with each new class.

It was nearly three o'clock, he needed a shower and to do a few things before heading out.

$1500 for one day's work. Not bad, Remy, not bad at all.

29

Remy walked into Slims at 4:40 and saw Jake behind the bar. "Shit, Jake, you must live here. You're always here."

"Seems like it. What can I do for you, Remy?"

"First, get me a *Four Roses* neat in a clean glass."

"All my glasses are clean. Well most of 'em, most of the time." He sat the whiskey down and asked, "OK, why are you really here?"

Remy leaned over the bar and motioned Jake to come closer. He held a 20 dollar bill between his fingers and said, "Look, I need a little favor. I need to do an exchange but I don't want the guy to see me. He will come in here just before five and order a *Pabst Blue Ribbon*. He will say it just like that. I want you to let me into your storage room down the hall. After a few minutes he will go to the head and then come out. Once he's back here, you come down to the storage room, grab a bottle or something and go back to the bar. In about five minutes the guy will go back to the head. When he comes back he should just walk on out the door. Can you do that?"

"Yeah, sure, no problem. But not for a twenty. Gimme fifty and you've got a deal."

Remy pulled another twenty and a ten from his wallet and handed them to Jake. "Thanks."

"Oh, and a buck and a half for the *Roses*."

By 5:30, Remy was heading across town to Musso & Franks. The wad of hundreds rested comfortably against his hip. He knew the next exchange would be even easier.

He was right.

30

Herman Logan exited Slims into the late afternoon sun. The glare of it off the windshields of the parked cars along Iverson gave him one of the flash headaches he experienced now and then. His eyes lost focus and there was a ringing in his ears. *This is more than the normal migraine,* he thought, adding yet another layer of anxiety to his overwrought system.

He slid behind the driver's seat of his patrol car, hit the mike switch and told dispatch that he was back from his break. She 10-4'd that, and he let out a long sigh. Well, at least he didn't get jammed up over picking up the evidence, which if true, would totally jam him up. He had an hour to go to end of shift but would not open the envelope until he was in a secure place. He flipped the glove box and tossed the photos in. Hidden, but not forgotten.

Later, Logan stood in the mess, as the officers called it, changing into his street clothes. He half expected someone to walk in and tell him Davis wanted to see him again. So he dressed quickly, placing the envelope inside his shirt so no one would see him carrying it. As he walked out, Branson called out to him, "Hey, Herm, we're heading over to Lucy's for a bit. Wanna come?"

"Thanks, man, but not tonight."

"Hot date, eh?" Logan didn't reply but thought, *If you only knew.*

He hadn't been able to hold out the last hour of his shift before giving in to the overwhelming impulse to open the envelope and see exactly what they had on him. If it was as bad as the voice on the phone had said, he was fucked, and hell, maybe worse. There he was, all six feet three of him, arched over the woman with his night stick ready to crash down on her. *What was he thinking about?*

What he always was thinking about: the money. Between the house, Julie's spending, just the expense of living, he always felt broke. The nickels and dimes he picked up for doing favors for some of the hustlers and drug dealers on his beat only seemed to disappear as soon as he got them. This had been a shot at some real money: three thousand dollars cash in his hand all at one time. Christ, that was nearly half of his annual salary. He started at $623 a month and now, three years later, he was getting $666 and he knew that was fair for police work; but he was always broke.

He had made the phone call from the pay phone at the liquor store down the street from the division. A number he had been told to call only in an emergency; he thought this qualified. The female voice answered by repeating the number he had just dialed. "Tell Bobby, Hollywood will be at the Tam tonight." With that, he hung up.

Now Herman was driving over to Los Feliz to the Tam O'Shanter restaurant; an old-school eatery with a dark and private bar. He was worried that maybe Bobby wouldn't get the message and wouldn't come. He worried that Bobby would get the message and still not come. He worried that Bobby would come and tell him to fuck off. He worried that Bobby would send some goons and he would wind up in Griffith Park, beaten or worse. He worried that Julie would yell at him for coming home late again. Hell, he worried that he wouldn't find a parking spot.

Easing into a bar stool at the far end of the bar he caught the bartender's eye. He thought about a *Pabst* but decided he needed something stronger. "Whiskey sour on the rocks." The bartender nodded and came back with the drink, setting it on a dark green napkin with Tam O'Shanter across the bottom. "Bobby says the first two are on him. He'll be here by 6:30." Logan nodded and took a sip off the top of the sour. He felt himself relax.

*   *   *   *   *

Bobby placed his hand on Herman's large muscular shoulder and said, "So what rates the Tam?"

Herman jerked around and glanced at the wall clock behind the bar: 7:15. "Fuck, where you been? We got some problems."

"OK, I've arranged dinner in one of the private dining rooms. Let's go and see what all the bumpiness is all about."

After dinner, Bobby looked Herm straight in the eye and said, "OK, you got unlucky and someone took some pictures. It's not the end of the world. Get yourself together and look at the big picture. You don't know that the Department has the photos, right? And even if they do, what do they show? You standing over a woman; that's it."

"That's it, my ass! She's a famous actress, who is pregnant and I look like I'm about to club her. And they will say in the belly; killing the kid. They will make me out to be a baby killer. Oh, Jesus, what am I going to do?"

The gentle approach was not working, so Bobby shifted gears as he had seen his father do with reluctant clients. He slammed his opened palm on the table causing the dishes to jump and one water glass to tip over. "You stupid piece of shit! The first thing you will do is stop drinking. Here, have some coffee. The second thing you will do is get a grip on yourself. The situation is just not that bad. Even if they get the photos, even if they confront you with them, they got shit. You never hit her! Your story is, she was mouthing off, calling you 'PIG' and you stepped closer to her and she stepped toward you at the same time and your feet got tangled together and she fell down. You twisted your back after you too lost your balance and what looks like you arching your back is really you trying to stretch the 'charlie horse' out of your back. The angle in the photo just distorts what was really happening. You never hit her; that's the key."

"Yeah, what's she gonna say? She'll say I knocked her to the ground with my shield."

"Why did you do that? The plan was just for her to get in your face and for you to arrest her. Where did this other shit come from? Ah, never mind; it doesn't matter. She is not going to say anything. She's my father's client and she's up for a big part over at Paramount. He'll let her know that all she can say is that it's you in the photo; she doesn't remember the rest of the incident."

"Why does she have to say that? Why can't she say it's not me or she can't tell or something?"

"Because, knucklehead, the photos clearly show it's you. Your name tag is right there for the world to see. If she identifies you then she has credibility. If she refuses to or says she can't tell then her value as a witness is destroyed. We want people to believe her because she will say that she never thought you were going to hit her. And that is true because she never looked up. Anyway, that's our story. Got it?"

"Yeah, I got it."

"Here, I was told to give you this and for you to remain calm and strong. You can do that, right?"

"Herman took the small package in hand; could tell it was money; a large stack of money. "Yeah, calm and strong."

Bobby turned and said over his shoulder, "I'll clear the tab out front."

Herman looked at the cigarette butts piled up in the ashtray in front of him and felt dirty and used. He knew tonight was not the end of it.

31

Rickey woke before dawn and reached up and turned the little overhead light on. Its dim light cast a yellow hue over the bunk where Marsha lay. Her blonde hair spilling down over the dark blue sheet seemed to glow in the dim light. She was asleep and he hated to wake her but he had to get going. He was to meet up with Junior at 6:00 and he still had to go back to the house and get his boards and his other stuff for the trip.

He shook her gently and said, "Mars, wake up, honey. I have to go."

Slowly she stirred and upon opening her eyes and seeing him, a huge smile broke across her face. "Hey, pretty boy, wanna spend the day with me?"

"Can't, unless you want to go south surfing."

"Oh, that's right, the big trip is today." As she sat up, the sheet fell away exposing her breasts but she didn't seem to notice or perhaps just didn't care. She reached over and grabbed her purse looking for a cigarette. "If you gotta go, then go."

"I am, but I'll be back by September. Back in school. Back to follow all the rules. Back to the boredom which feels like it's eating my brain; I know it's eating my soul."

She reached over and kissed him on the cheek. "Yes, but you will be alive. Now take me to breakfast before you go."

32

Ed Davis sat at his desk, his face flushed with anger.

"That motherfucker sat right here and lied to me. God damn it! I will take his gun, his badge, I will strip him down to his shorts and then cut off his dick."

"Yes sir," his aide said, "But we have one problem. The Association, sir, they will fight us on this tooth and nail. First, they may already know, if not, they will soon enough that Chief Redden authorized the use of force Level 3 to clear the crowd. As you know, sir, Level 3 warrants the use of extreme force if necessary and..."

He was cut off by Davis, "Hitting a pregnant woman. Where in the God damn book does it say that's OK?"

"Well, see sir, that's the problem...he never hit her. And he may well have some explanation of why he was standing over her like that. Or why she is on the ground. We have to tread lightly or we will have the whole blue line pissed at the brass, and we just can't afford that, sir."

He looked out onto the unchanged scene of sprawl spilling from downtown, past the rail yards and down to the beach. "Miles and miles of territory to patrol and keep quiet and they had to do it with 25 percent of the number of officers New York City has. And in a town where every fifth person is a movie star and everyone seems to have a camera. Christ, what a mess.

"Tim, you give good counsel. Measured and thoughtful. They must be teaching you something over there at Southwestern. You thinking of practicing law after you graduate or stay here and ride my coat-tails into the big office?"

"Not sure yet, sir. I still have two years to go and a lot can happen."

"Yes it can. So what do I do with this Logan character besides give him freeway punishment. Where does he live?"

"Simi Valley, sir."

"Of course he does. Everyone after the class of '55 lives in Simi Valley. So, we send him to South Central, that's a good two hours each way. The Sheriff's Department will look good after a month of that."

"Well, that's an option, sir, but I think before we get there, we need to have a sit down with him. Let him know what we got, that he lied to you, which itself can justify termination, we got the photos, and we know he didn't act alone. We need to scare the piss out of him, then offer him his old life back, and all he has to do is tell us who was in on it with him and why."

"Logan's an idiot. He will never know the why. And we don't know if he was part of some group or what happened except he knocked down a famous actress. That's what we know."

"But he doesn't know that. He will be scared shitless. We'll just call him in for a follow-up to his last interview. In fact, we tell him we have a written summary of that interview that needs his signature before it's sent as part of the file up to the Chief. All very routine. Shouldn't even trigger a call to his Rep. Make it sound like he can come in anytime he wants. Just a signature is all we need. You know the line boys think all we do is shuffle paper from one desk to another. This is just part of that same game. Then once we have him in here, we pounce. My guess is he would give up his mother in the first 15 minutes."

"All right, set it up. But you need to be here because I just want to pound his face in."

"Yes, sir. And one other thing, sir, I think we should talk to Rita Rains before we call him in. She may be able to give us something to use against Logan."

"Good thinking. Again. Thanks, Tim."

He reached for the phone, signaling an end to their meeting.

33

Rita Rains opened the front door to her Beverly Hills home herself. "Gentlemen, please come in."

"Good day, Miss Rains. I am Edward Shapiro, Assistant to Chief Ed Davis, Chief of Staff, and this fine looking fellow is Officer Roland, of our office. Thank you for having us and I trust we won't be long."

"What a lovely home you have here," said Officer Roland, trying to appear as more than just a bag carrier.

"It was Cary Grant's. That was before he married Barbara Hutton. It's very comfortable. Please come this way into the morning room. Would you like some coffee or something else?"

"No thank you, we're fine," said Ed, speaking for both of them as they followed her across the entryway and into a room big enough to hold his living room, kitchen and den.

"Please have a seat. How can I help you gentlemen?"

Officer Roland unsnapped the latches on his *Samsonite* briefcase and pulled out the photos. He spread them out on the coffee table and then said, "I don't want to upset you Miss Rains, but we have some pictures from Rancho Park and were hoping you could give us some details about what is depicted in them. Each one is numbered and if you would refer to them by their proper number, it will make the record clearer. Do you mind if I tape record this?"

"Certainly, Officer. Now, let's see here. In photo one, there is a man standing over me as I am on the ground after having fallen down."

"You fell down?"

"Well, not exactly. This Officer was yelling at me to leave the park and I was yelling back that I wouldn't leave without my husband. It got rather heated and we both stepped forward at the same time, and I guess our feet got tangled up and I fell down."

"So he never hit you?"

"No."

"Miss Rains, I don't want to offend you, but I saw you on TV saying this man hit you with his shield and knocked you to the ground and was ready to beat you with his baton. You said that, right?"

She gave him that up from under look that only beautiful women can master and in the softest voice said, "Yes, Officer, you are right. I said that. But I was very upset. I did see the police beat, kick and stomp innocent people who were doing nothing more than standing around." Her voice firmed up as she was saying this, but she never took her eyes off of Officer Roland. This made him feel special and so wanting to believe her.

"I can understand you being upset Miss Rains, but why make up the part about you being hit? I don't get that," Ed interjected.

Without her eyes leaving Officer Roland, she said, "It's poetic license. By making it personal to me, it has more of an impact on my audience. Other people they think about in an abstract way, but me, they feel they know. They sit in theaters and watch twenty foot images of me shining down on them; they care for me. Look, at the time I was very angry with your department. People came out to protest what they believe is a wrong war fought in the wrong way, they want peace. And your department gave them violence; brutal violence. Why? So I over-stated my case. I'm an actress and I'm emotional and I'm pregnant on top of it. I'm sorry but your department has a lot to be sorry about, too."

The room went very still, the only sound was that of a tennis ball being struck back and forth some distance away. The three sat there for awhile until Officer Roland said, "Well, I guess that does it. Just so we are clear Miss Rains, this Officer never struck you or hit you in any way?"

"That's correct."

"When you were on the ground were you afraid he was going to strike you?"

"No, but then, I never looked up."

"OK, one final thing. Do you know the name of the man that intervened? The one in photos two through six?"

"Well, I'm not sure. He walked me around the corner, out of the park. He said his name was South Point or something like that. Then he said 'Rickey.' I remember that because he said it clearly, 'Rickey.'"

"OK, we are done here. Thank you Miss Rains, hopefully we won't have to bother you again." Officer Roland offered her a broad smile and shook her hand. Ed meanwhile was clearing the table of the photos and closing up the briefcase which he handed to Roland. "Ah, thank you Miss Rains. Good-bye."

Driving down Wilshire heading back to Parker Center, Eddie said, "Someone got to her."

"Ya think? Christ, some women think if they just smile at you, you will believe anything."

"Yeah, but with what she says, we can't go at Logan. If we do and later this lawyer finds out we had this testimony and didn't tell him before we questioned him, we would be so screwed. I'll tell Ed. He will be pissed. But he understands how this game is played better than anyone. Someone up the food chain wanted this sealed off. So we will seal it off. I'll bet Logan gets freeway punishment though."

"Yeah, probably."

34

Fall was turning into Winter and Herman Logan was feeling much better about his life.

The money he got from Bobby had gone a long way in removing his feelings of being constantly broke. Three grand up front and then that last kiss of five thousand, boy, that had really helped. Yeah, he had to give the slob a grand, but still, seven grand was a shitload.

He'd paid his bookie the $800 he owed, paid off about $400 of credit card debt, spent $300 on taking Julie to Vegas first class, and he still had over $5,000 stashed in his toolbox in the garage. Just knowing it was there always made him feel better.

Julie had been much more loving lately. Especially after the fling in Vegas; she just loved Wayne Newton. She was actually getting to be a better cook and seemed to be settling down.

Life seemed pretty damn good and he was looking forward to 1968.

But the best thing was, he never heard from AC Ed Davis again. It had been nearly six months and nothing. He would ask around from time to time about Rancho Park but that was old news; no one gave a damn. Fine by him, he thought. *Let's let sleeping dogs lie.*

He found it tucked into the handle of his locker. It was simple and straight-forward: You are to report to your new Area Bureau commencing December 17, 1967. You are to report to South Bureau, Harbor Command. You are assigned there until further notice.

"Fuck me!" he screamed, and a few of the men in the mess turned to look but none spoke a word. They knew all too well what the pale blue envelope tucked into your locker meant. You had pissed off one of the brass and you were going to pay for it; they called it *freeway punishment*.

When they just moved you for personnel reasons, the Watch Commander always called you into his office. When they moved you due to a promotion, they made a show of it. But when they cut your dick off, they did it silently.

Herman stood there feeling all alone. Over 80 miles one-way through some of the toughest traffic in the county. Well, fuck it! He wasn't going to the Sheriff's Department and spend two years doing the jail thing. No God damn way.

He just hoped he could convince Julie to move to Long Beach.

35

Bobby stood while his father sat behind his large oak desk which he claimed was similar to the one in the Oval Office. It was certainly large and impressive, as was the rest of the office with its vanity wall showing Raymond Taylor McKnight in literally hundreds of photos with Presidents, Governors, Senators, starlets, heads of studios, and basically anyone of power or fame in America during the last decade.

Bobby smiled as he looked at the wall and remembered his father's first office with only his degrees on the wall. Now the degrees were nowhere to be seen. Education had taken a back seat to celebrity.

"So is that Rancho Park mess handled?"

"Yes, dad. Davis understands he can't go any further but he says he will still reach out and punish Logan at some point. He filed his final report with Redden and it's a done deal. I can get a copy of it, if you want."

"Not necessary. As long as everything is sealed off and our friends aren't exposed then let's just forget it and move on. Logan getting some slap is fair. He broke script and made the situation much worse than it had to be."

"True enough. But we got great exposure from it. Now talking about moving on, I think our next big opportunity is coming in October. SDS is organizing a march on Washington. They think they can get 100,000 to show up."

"How can we help?"

"Well, if we had a famous person there, I don't know, in a reporting role or something, it would give it a special boost. I mean, hell, if they get 100,000 it will be a huge story anyway. If we could do another Rita Rains bit but classier then I think we could have a great side bar story. And when we get some celebrity to step up then the talk shows all fall in line. They aren't pissing off their right wing viewers by covering those Commie protests but rather they are having America's sweetheart in for a chat and the protest just gets mentioned."

"Yes, that's a great ploy even if the march doesn't draw what they hope it will, we still have a story but it's more important in context."

"Got any ideas who we can use?"

"A few. We have some time. Let me think about it and make a few calls. OK, anything else?"

"No, not really. Oh yeah, the money from, ah, our sponsors, what should I do with it?"

"Put it in the Caymans and use the Freedmen Trust."

"OK, done."

"Oh, one more thing before you leave. Rains is under control, Logan is dead meat but what about the kid that stepped in? Are we looking at any blow back from him?"

"Rickey? Hell no. He hasn't a clue. To him it was over the moment Logan hit the ground. Look, Dad, this guy is a nice guy who isn't real bright and spends his days chasing waves and smoking weed. I've spoken to him and he is mildly anti-war but hardly involved. At best, all he cares about is not going to Nam. My guess is by now he can hardly remember Rancho Park and even if he does, he doesn't give a damn about what happened there. Marsha told me he thinks the whole protest movement is a waste of time. Don't worry about him, Dad."

"Bobby, you will learn, that is what they pay you for. To worry and deal with the stuff no one else sees. Everyone thought the family dog was just oh so cute until it bit the baby. Your job is to look past what everyone else sees and see the killer in the puppy. What's this kid's name?"

"Rickey. But everyone calls him South Point or SP."

"What is his real God damn name?"

"I don't know. I just know him as South Point Rickey."

"Well, find out and let me know," saying it in such a manner that Bobby knew his father was disappointed with him, and the meeting was over.

As he closed his father's office door behind him, he could hear him ask his secretary for Norman Mailer's number. "Christ, that man moves fast," he muttered to himself as he descended the stairs to the ground floor.

36

It was Christmastime again and the bright lights twinkling, the made up shop windows were the only real reminder in Southern California that it wasn't September or March. The air was cool but not cold and the days were sunny and bright. Typical Southern California weather; the reason thousands moved into the area every week.

Rickey was meeting Marsha at the Hof's in the marina. He hadn't seen her since their night together in the van. He was anxious to hear how her life was going and to share some of his adventures south of the border.

She breezed in wearing a black beret, a red turtleneck under a navy blue pea coat, jeans tucked into knee-high boots. Boots October to April, sandals in between; that seemed to Rickey to be her fashion statement.

"Hi ya," she said. "Seems deja vu. Ya know?"

The look on Rickey's face told her he had no idea what deja vu meant. "You know, like we've been here before."

"We have. Many times."

"No, silly, like we have lived this moment before."

"Oh. Well we were here last Christmas and you ragged me out about the war."

"Well, I wouldn't put it that way. So, how are you doing? How was the trip south?"

They slipped into the easy chatter old friends seeing each other again after a long hiatus seemed to do. Like they have a special chemistry which causes them to bond differently than with other folks. And so it was with Rickey and Marsha that late afternoon in Hof's. They talked for hours. Marsha about her studies, the events at Berkeley, the anti-war movement, new foods she had tried and the difficulty of competing with really smart people. "It's not like high school where you do the work and 'bingo' you get an A. I am busting my ass and just getting B's. Every class I am in, there are several people who you just know are going on to Fulbright's and Rhodes' scholarships; they are just so smart. They see things I don't see. It makes me wonder if I should continue studying psychology or transfer to something else."

"Like what? Mars, you're smart. You're the smartest person I know. Hang in there. But the bigger question is, do you like it? If you aren't loving it at this stage, my guess is you'll not be happy doing it ten years from now."

"Gee, thanks. Smarter than Sticks, Junior and Jacks. BFD. Jacks went and joined. Real smart."

"Hey, get off your high horse. Jacks is doing fine. I saw him awhile ago and he was actually enjoying it. Said it made him feel steady. Like he knew what was expected of him. He was on some destroyer in for repairs then they were going to Hawaii."

"Well, I ran into his sister yesterday shopping at Buffums and she said he had been sent to Vietnam and now was on a gun boat patrolling some river. He was sent there to replace a guy who was killed."

Rickey stared into his coffee cup not knowing what to say. Finally, he said, "He'll be all right. Jacks is a strong guy." But as he said it, tears welled up in his eyes, and he tried to hide them from her but couldn't.

She reached over and took his hand, giving it a small squeeze and said, "I know he will be, Honey. You're right, he's a strong guy."

She left the table for awhile and he thought about Jacks and his own situation. He was reading the newspaper more now that he had gotten back and had ordered a subscription to the *LA Times* as the local paper his folks got didn't seem to carry much about the anti-war movement or have articles critical of the war itself. He knew 1968 was going to be an important year and only hoped that he could hang on to his 2S until this craziness ended.

Marsha came back to the table but didn't sit. "Let's take a walk and look at the decorated houses over in Naples. They are so pretty this time of year."

"Sure, why not."

They drove over the bridge and Rickey said, "Turn left here. I know an empty lot where we can park; just there on Naples Plaza. She saw the lot and the small cottage house next to it. *From the '20's and*, she thought, *just waiting to be torn down.*

As they walked, they talked and sometimes held hands. It was Christmas here next to the sea, among the most wealthy of their city. There were parties going on in some of the houses and in others, just a few couples sharing the evening and cocktails. Rickey hadn't felt so content since that last good ride at 38 Clicks on the day before they came back. *This is nice*, he thought to himself, and held Marsha's hand a bit tighter.

But, he knew it wouldn't last.

37

It sat there on the entry table like a butterfly among the weeds. Bright pink with Marsha's beautiful handwriting spelling out his name and address. It had been about two months since he had last seen her but they had spoken a few times on the phone. But this was different. A love note? A Valentine? He picked it up slowly and carried it into his room closing the door behind him. Even though no one was home, he felt the need for privacy.

He slit the envelope open with the small penknife he kept in his pocket. He unfolded the sheet and began to read:

> *My Dearest Rickey,*
>
> *Since the day we met on that funky old beach, I knew you were someone special. That Summer we spent together was magical. We had so much fun and I thought we would be together forever.*
>
> *But things changed. I came up to Cal and you stayed there. I often thought it might have been better if I had stayed there, too. But I didn't. And the time and distance changed us. I started caring about things I didn't even know existed a year ago, and you continued to care about that which you are so passionate. I wish I could feel that way, but I haven't yet. Maybe someday.*
>
> *I met somebody. His name is Charles. He is older and already has his PhD. He recently got a teaching post at the University of Vermont and has asked me to go with him. I am going. Do I love him? I don't know. But he cares for me. We share so much in common, both in interests and outlooks. I know he is a good man and I need to leave Berkeley, it's just too much here. Protests day and night. Crazy preachers on the corners shouting about Doomsday while on the other corner someone is*

*telling you you're a slut and a whore because you don't
wear a bra. And behind them, someone shouting out
about prisoners' rights. Everyone has a cause and I
guess that's OK but it is wearing me out. I want some
peace and quiet and Vermont sounds like it will offer
that.*

*So, dear one, please know that you will always be
my first love and I will carry you in my heart wherever
I go.*

Love, Mars

Rickey's hands trembled as he put the letter down on the corner of the bed. He knew long ago that their feelings for each other had changed, but that night walking through Naples it all seemed so natural to be with her; she fit. She was the one. And since then, he had thought again and again about that night and what it had meant. But, now he knew it hadn't meant for her what it had meant for him.

He hit himself on the leg and swore silently to himself, *Fucking asshole. Why didn't you drive up there, find her and tell her how you felt? Now you never can. What a loser! Too busy making tacos or riding another two-footer off the Seal Beach pier. She was a once-in-a-lifetime woman and you let her go. Why? Afraid she won't feel the same way. So what? You would be embarrassed. Who the hell would know? When you feel strongly about something you have to move on it. Waiting never did anything but waste time.*

He stood up and walked to the window and looked out onto the yard. He took a deep breath and knew he had to move on. But he could hear her words in his head from long ago, *Everything in life is because of Yes. Nothing ever happens because of No.*

She had said Yes and he understood why.

He picked up the letter off the bed and went to put it into the envelope. He noticed another folded paper inside. He flattened it out and read:

Rickey,
*If Bobby comes around, be careful. I don't trust him.
Something is off there. M*

He paused for a moment and thought, *Bobby, who the hell is that? Oh, yeah, the guy with the Healey; the anti-war guy. Why would he come around?*

38

Rickey and Sticks sat in the early morning calm just off the Huntington cliffs waiting for a wave. The pink light of morning was just creeping over the eastern horizon and backlit the ocean in front of them. Alone, sitting quietly, they could hear the squeaking of the oil rigs across PCH. The endless up and down of the jack leg as it pulled oil out of the ground. There were hundreds of them on the lowland between the cliffs and sub-division to the east. In the early morning light, they were shadows of black and grey, looking like some weird insect humping away above an unseen lover.

Neither spoke for some time, then Rickey, looking around, said, "Where's Junior? He usually joins us on Thursdays."

"He won't be joining us again for awhile, bro. He's gone."

"Gone. Gone where?"

"He went and joined up. I saw him up at the Niner the other night and after a few beers, he told me. After he came back from that Mexico gig with you, he felt uneasy, he said. Like he was doing something wrong. How he explained it to me was like everyone else was working the farm and all he was doing was eating the food. "

"What the hell does that mean?"

"Well, what I understood was he felt all the guys were going into the service to fight and he was just sitting here surfing and wasting time at City College. He said it didn't seem right. He said why should that kid he played summer ball with from over the other side of town have to go just 'cuz his auntie couldn't afford for him to go to City and he gets out because his dad has a few bucks. Didn't think it was right."

"Jesus. I remember that kid. They called him Frenchie 'cuz he loved French fries. Man, that guy had a fast ball."

"Yeah, but he couldn't find home plate if you walked him to it."

"True enough. But what caused Junior to think about Frenchie, I mean that was like the summer after tenth grade?"

"Well, it seems, and I don't know about this shit as I don't read the papers or watch the news, but some stuff in Vietnam's been going on since early in the year. Something called Tet; the Tet Offensive. And I guess they have been kicking the shit out of our guys. Like bad, man, real bad. Frenchie got killed at some place called 'K-Song' or something like that."

"Khe Sahn. It's called Khe Sahn and yeah, I read about it; over two thousand Americans were killed there during the first two months of this year. The fighting is still going on. Westmoreland was just on the tube the other night saying how the Viet Cong couldn't win. But Walter Cronkite said we couldn't win either and the best we could hope for was a tie. So Frenchie got killed there? That sucks. But I still don't understand why Junior had to go and enlist. Who did he join?"

"That's what really blows man, the fucking Marines."

"The Marines? Aw, Christ."

Suddenly Rickey lost all interest in the waves that were just beginning to form. He felt sick to his stomach and upset. Upset at Junior for joining the Marines, for not talking to him first, for just joining to make himself feel better. But Rickey knew that feeling wouldn't last long. Upset for Frenchie dying. Upset at the fucking Generals who keep lying about victory when no victory could be won from this mess. Upset at the newspapers that don't show the American people the horror of this war. And, upset with himself for sitting here on a silly board waiting for waves while guys he went to school with were dying. *What kind of piece of shit, I must be,* he thought. But, God damn it, he wasn't going to go and kill people he had no quarrel with. He didn't have a dog in that fight.

He turned and paddled back to shore, mumbling a good-bye to Sticks. The oil wells pumped relentlessly in front of him; *like the war*, he thought, *never ending.*

39

It was a normal Thursday for Rickey that day. He had met Sticks at the pier at Seal Beach around 6:30 after stopping at Donut City for some coffee and some of their famous double-dipped glazed donuts. He balanced the coffee in one hand and the bag of donuts in the other as he carried his nine foot board under his arm. It would be all he would need that day as the surf was running only two to three feet with short tubes and not much length.

Sticks greeted with a "Hey, bro," and reached for the bag of donuts. "Ah, still warm, righteous." They sat on the small cement wall which separated the sandy beach from the concrete boardwalk. They looked out at the surf with the critical eye of someone who has taken its measure many times; much like a tailor can say with certainty this customer is a 42 Regular or a 40 Short at a glance.

After a few minutes they turned to each other and spoke at the same time. "In about twenty, it will fill in." And so they sat on the wall eating donuts, drinking coffee and smoking cigarettes until the sun had risen enough to erase the dew off the windshields of the cars parked behind them. They nodded to one another, picked up their boards, and headed for the water.

There were a few others out that early April morning but not enough to make it crowded and/or tense. One young rider caught Rickey's eye right away. He was riding a very short board and rather than seeking the tube and riding the face just in front of the break for as long as he could, he was breaking off the wave, cutting back into the break, then spinning around, moving up and down the face as fast as he could. Rickey looked at Sticks, nodded in the direction of the younger surfer, and said, "Looks more like dancing than surfing."

"Yeah, those new super short boards are designed for what they call ripping or carving the wave up. They say it's the future and us long-boarders will go by the way of the gooney bird. You should try it."

Rickey looked at him and frowned.

After a few hours passed, Rickey hauled himself out of the water. "I gotta go. I've got class at ten and it's nine now. You staying?"

"For awhile, yeah," Sticks said as he pulled on a fresh joint he had just rolled. "Think I'll hang and see what washes up on shore. I got the drift you weren't too keen on that new style."

"You're right, I'm not. What I have always loved about surfing was being part of that wave. Getting into that section and feeling its power, and joining with it to glide along the face like one being. To feel the break just behind you and the smooth, silk-like face out in front of you and to get into the rhythm of the wave. I swear I feel God in those waves sometimes. That shit that kid was doing has to do with how cute he is, not how beautiful the wave is. If that's the future then they can have it. See ya later. You get the donuts and coffee next Thursday."

Both classes that day were extra boring, and Rickey had a hard time staying awake. Really, who gives a damn about what happened a thousand years ago on the other side of the world. Why don't they talk about what is going on here, today? The war, the civil rights movement, the push for women to be treated as equals with men. That seemed to Rickey to be a hell of a lot more important than who was King of England in 1750 and who came after him. This wasn't education, memorizing lists of names and dates of dead kings of other countries. He couldn't have cared less. At least he could understand it. But this literature class he had to take, Christ, who could make heads or tails out of that guy Joyce; and why would you want to? What a waste of time. But he knew he had to do it and somehow get at least a C so he could keep that precious 2S.

After two crushing hours in the classroom, he would find the work at Taco Time refreshing. Stack the racks, fill the racks, fry the shells, drain the shells, stack the racks. Maybe it was repetitive and mindless, but it had a purpose. More than he could say for his classes.

Yes, just another normal day in the life of South Point Rickey.

Until he got home.

40

He knew something was wrong when he saw the *Buick* parked in the driveway. Then again, it was only four o'clock, maybe one of his parents had just popped home for a minute, he explained to himself, the anxiousness easing a bit.

But it came right back as he crossed the porch and could see his father sitting on the edge of the sofa with a drink in his hand. Rickey had seen his father with a drink only on rare occasions. The last time was when Billy Bland had died.

He kicked off his huaraches, pulled open the screen door and saw his mother sitting quietly in the big over-stuffed chair, wringing a handkerchief in her hands and sobbing so softly you could barely hear her. Her knuckles were white, while her eyes were rimmed in red. She looked as spent as a defendant who had just heard the jury read a guilty verdict.

He paused and could feel grief in the air like a bad odor. He quietly closed the screen door and asked, "What's wrong?"

No one answered although Rusty raised his head as if he wanted to speak, but then quickly lowered it as if it would be sacrilegious. Rickey crossed the room and sat on the arm of the sofa and looked at the small TV screen. There he saw an image of three black men pointing at a rooftop while a fourth black man slumped at their feet. There was a header at the bottom of the screen with the words: MARTIN LUTHER KING JUNIOR SHOT IN MEMPHIS.

Rickey could feel himself rock back as if the news had reached out and struck him in the chest. He held out one hand to steady himself. "What the fuck," he muttered under his breath but apparently loud enough to cause his father to throw a serious reprimanding glance his way.

"What happened?"

"They killed Dr. King," his father said in a flat, toneless voice. "He's dead."

At that, his mother started sobbing louder and gave out a plaintive little wail, "Dear God, no. No. Why, dear Lord, tell me why."

Rickey and his father exchanged glances as neither held Maggie's belief in the Almighty and the power of the Methodist Church.

The picture of the three men came off the screen and was replaced by a serious looking reporter holding his microphone like a club, standing before a run-down motel with the name "Lorraine" in script. His father quickly stood and took two strides across the small room and turned the sound on, "And we are told that Dr. King was shot about an hour ago as he stood on the balcony of this motel with his advisors. We have just been informed by *UP* that Dr. King has died." The reporter turned his face away from the camera for a moment to try and gain composure. When he returned, he waved at the cameraman signaling no more; he was done.

Bailey's drink had disappeared and he walked into the kitchen to get a new one. He called out to Rickey, "Want anything?"

"Ah, no, no thanks."

As Bailey came out of the kitchen, he looked at Rickey and tossed him a beer. "Here, have this; we will all need something tonight. Mother, anything?"

She moved her head ever so slightly indicating that she was fine.

Rickey's father went across the room and this time turned the volume down so the next reporter could barely be heard.

"Next, they're going to feed us some happy horseshit about how he was some lone gunman, some whack-job, acting alone. Just like the Kennedy killing. Christ, how dumb do they think we are? Lone gunman, my ass."

Rickey was actually stunned to hear his father speak like that. His dad said things like "Gall darn it" or "Peaches and Cream" when he was upset. Once years ago, he heard his father call the man down the street an asshole but that was really rare. For him to use that type of language, he had to be really upset.

Bailey was a quiet man who sold insurance by day and read books by night. Rickey wasn't even sure what kind of books as it seemed he had many interests. He remembered a huge set of books that filled the small cabinet at the head of their bed.

They were history by someone named Churchill; and he remembered a bunch of books on the assassination of President Kennedy. In the last few years, there were fewer books and more newsletters and soft covered books. One, Rickey recalled, was from some guy named John Birch. But his father rarely talked about what he read, and Rickey always assumed he just did it for his own enjoyment. But perhaps there was something more to it.

"A year to the day. A year to the day. Christ, they must think we are stupid."

"What do you mean, dad? What happened a year ago?"

"Today is April 4th, exactly one year ago today, April 4th, 1967, King gave the most important speech of his life. Maybe in this century. It's known as "The Riverside Speech." What was important about that speech is King was stepping outside the Establishment for the first time. Since he started, the whole pitch to the Negroes was work within the system; the system will change if we force it to change. And the war was part and parcel of the Establishment. With Riverside not only did he denounce the war, but all of American foreign policy of spreading its will all over the globe. Do you know how much money is made by the military industrial companies selling stuff to the military? Billions. Billions every year."

He paused, took a sip from his drink, looked at Rickey with a seriousness in his eyes Rickey hadn't seen since the fourth grade when he got into a fight with Billy Richmond.

"You see, it's one thing if Malcolm X says it. Or some other outsider, even if they are popular like Jane Fonda. But when King came out with that, it rattled windows in high places. He has huge followings; part of which are church-going mothers. If momma says don't go to war, many of her children won't go. Do you know how dependent the US Army is on recruiting negros? They make up about twenty percent of our population but about 40 percent of the Army. Stopping that flow of fresh blood would really hurt the Army's staffing. They might even have to get rid of the 2S for the white kids to make up the difference." He paused and took another sip of his drink then continued.

"But it was more than just that. With Riverside, an American icon was saying it's OK to be against this war. It's OK to be against American plots to overthrow governments around the world. It's OK not to believe what the government is telling you. Riverside made it respectable, in some places, even fashionable.

"But don't kid yourself. This wasn't just about the war and some speech. There are many people in this country that just don't want to see negroes being treated fairly. Oh, you can be sure that whoever they get to take the fall for this will be some stupid red-neck with a long history of hating negroes."

Rickey was speechless. That was more words than he had heard from his father in the last six months put together. When he finally spoke, his voice broke and he struggled to get the words out.

"Dad, how do you know all this? What you are saying is that the government is lying to us. Not just about the war, which I kinda already figured out, but about President Kennedy and now Dr. King. How do you know all this stuff?"

Bailey paused and sat down, realizing he had been perhaps too forceful before.

"Well, son. Two reasons really. One, I read a lot and most of what I read is about American history and government affairs. But, two, I was in a branch of the service during World War II that's now called the CIA. Yes, yes, I know I told you, and everyone else I served aboard an aircraft carrier out in the Pacific; and that's how it started. But I was recruited for a special assignment and it turned out to be serving with a special group that did secret things; gathering intelligence for sure, but other things as well. And one thing I learned was in a political operation a message had to be left so the powers that be on the other side clearly understood what our intent was. That, in this case means, the two dates are not a coincidence; it's a message. But what it also means to me is that it was done by someone with similar training and experience as mine."

Rickey couldn't say a word. His father was a spy, an assassin, some James Bond-type moving through the dark alleys seeking his prey. Jesus! He had always thought of his father as a Casper Milk Toast kind of guy; quiet, boring really, but a nice man all the same.

"The riots will start next," his father said. "America will be in flames for weeks because of this. They are willing to threaten the stability of our country, to cause thousands to be killed or injured and millions of dollars in property lost due to fires and looting. What kind of people are these?"

"Evil," said his mother. "Just evil."

Bailey was right. The riots started that night and continued for weeks. Rickey was less sure about his place in America than ever before. He had questions and some doubt. Now he felt disconnected and fearful of his own country.

41

Bobby didn't want to call Marsha and ask about Rickey. Their last meeting had not gone well and he thought perhaps she sensed that his anti-war commitment was not quite what it seemed.

Damn, there must be a thousand Rickey's who surf in Southern California. Tracking him down wouldn't be easy. But he could narrow the field. That place where they met that time. *What was that called?* he said to himself as he struggled with his memory. *Panhandle, no, Pots, no, The Towel Rack, no. Come on, think. Why not look in the Yellow Pages,* a voice in the back of his head whispered.

His father's office which had a huge library; part of which was every phone book for California, Arizona and Nevada. He found the Long Beach volume and quickly turned to restaurants. He skimmed the list and saw nothing that triggered his memory so he flipped to Breakfast and there it was; the listing for the Potholder on Fourth Street. He glanced at the clock: 10:45. Perfect. Traffic should be light.

He was right and 45 minutes later, he was talking to a red-haired waitress with a gap between her front teeth as well as her blouse. Annie, read the name tag on her uniform.

He held a twenty wrapped about the middle finger of his left hand but made sure the two and the zero showed. "So, you don't know anyone named Rickey or Rick who's a surfer?"

"No sir, and I would really like to help you, but I don't know anyone like that," she said, eyeing the twenty.

"Well, would you look at a picture for me and tell me if you know him or have seen him around?"

"Yeah, sure."

And with that, Bobby pulled out the best shot of Rickey with Rita Rains and said to the girl, "Do you recognize anyone?"

Annie looked at the photo briefly and said, "Well, yeah, that's Rita Rains."

Bobby sighed and said, "I know, but how about the guy?"

"Oh, yeah, I've seen him in here. They call him South Point."

"Do you know his last name?"

"No, but do I still get the twenty?"

"Do you know where he goes to school?"

"Not now, but he used to go to Wilson. Hey, Bonnie, come over here. You know this South Point guy?" pointing at the photo.

Bonnie cast a long glance at Bobby and immediately saw he had some money. "Nice jacket," she purred at him.

"Thanks, I'll give it to you if you can tell me where I can find this guy. They call him South Point Rickey or Rickey South Point or some such shit." Bobby was starting to lose his cool. *This is all unnecessary, my father is a paranoid asshole*, he thought, as he handed the photo to Bonnie.

"Yeah, I know this guy. Sits in the back of the history class over at City. He's cute."

"When does this class meet?"

"Ten o'clock Tuesday and Thursday," she replied. "Why, you wanna go?"

"Not really." He thanked the girls and gave the twenty to Annie, telling her to give half to Bonnie, and he turned and headed for the door, hearing over his shoulder, "Hey, what about the jacket?" He kept walking.

He would have to come back Tuesday and hope Rickey didn't skip class.

Bobby had heard from Marsha about Rickey's new surf van; aqua as he remembered it. And sure enough, next Tuesday morning, there it was. He walked over and peered through the driver side window and on the steering post in its little holder was the registration. Under the new California law, you didn't need it on display, just in the car, but it was Bobby's good luck that Rickey had done it the old fashioned way.

He started to try to slide the window then thought, *why not try the door?* It opened right up. He pulled the holder off the steering post and said, "Well, hello there, Richard W. Osgood...yeah, I call myself South Point, too."

He quickly copied the information down and refastened the holder in place. Closing the door and walking away without anyone shouting, "Hey, Stop!" he felt like Bond, James Bond. He chuckled to himself in amusement and walked toward the *Healey*. His dad would be pleased.

42

Bailey was right. The riots started that night. But it wasn't the Doomsday he predicted. It was limited to mostly eastern cities with Chicago and Detroit, the biggest cities hit. The unrest lasted for only a few days and after that, the country went back to its normal ebb and flow.

Rickey had worried about LA going up in flames. But there really wasn't much to talk about as it stayed pretty peaceful. Maybe it was because the news broke when it was still daylight and the police had a few hours to organize a response, or maybe it was that the community leaders immediately went out to the negro neighborhoods and convinced the people that it would dishonor Dr. King's name if they rioted because of him, or maybe it was because LA had had its big riot just eighteen months before and the memory of the destruction was still fresh in people's minds. Or maybe it was because the LA Lakers were making a run on an NBA championship and the city was distracted. Who could say for certain, but Rickey was happy that the fear he felt during the Watts Riots didn't happen again.

As April became May, Rickey's routine never changed. Surf a bit each morning, waves permitting, attend class, do school assignments in the afternoon or put some time in at Taco Time so he could refill his travel account, which was a shoebox under his bed. Every paycheck he got, he took to the bank, signed the check and handed it to the teller. She would then count out his earnings for the last two weeks. Then he would dump the change into his pocket and walk over to the tall desks with the envelopes and deposit slips. Taking one of the envelopes, he would write the date and the amount, which was always half of what he collected, and then seal it with a lick. Back home, he would stash it into the shoebox and carefully push it back under his bed. Knowing it was there always gave him a feeling of the future; some adventure somewhere.

But in early May his routine was broken as quickly as a falling glass hits the floor. It was another Tuesday in a long line of Tuesdays and he was walking across what they called the quad, which was really a large open landscaped area right in the center of campus. There were tables and benches for people to sit and gather, and apparently to dance on.

She wasn't dancing, but twirling, spinning about time after time. She had on a candy-cane striped skirt which threw off a rainbow of colors, a creamy, soft, white blouse which buttoned up the front and had short capped sleeves which exposed her pale arms. The moment he looked at her, Rickey was smacked. Her high forehead made her green eyes stand out even more. And mountains and mountains of thick light brown hair. She smiled at him when she stopped spinning, giggling said, "Like what you see?"

"Ah, very much. I'm Rickey," he said, extending his hand because he didn't know what else to do.

She took his hand in both of hers and held it like an egg; so soft and gentle. Her green eyes locked on his and he actually felt his heart jump. "I know. South Point Rickey. I'm Linda. Just Linda."

"Have we met before?"

"No."

"Did you go to Wilson?"

"No."

"Well, how do you know my name?"

"I asked someone. I've been watching you walk by every Tuesday morning for two months and I could never catch your eye. So this morning I decided to be a little bold and do something you might notice."

"Well, I'm glad you did. Should we go get some coffee and talk?"

"Don't you have class?"

"Well, yeah, but I'd rather talk with you."

She smiled so bright and said, "Well then, let's go."

And just like that, Rickey's world went from ho-hum to being in the barrel of a twenty foot tube; full of life, energy, excitement and anticipation.

And like some rides: disappointing.

43

Bobby was back in the great man's office. He was gone, some meeting or something somewhere. Bobby noticed his father had a lot of afternoon meetings. He followed him once all the way into the Polo Lounge of the Beverly Hills Hotel, where he was warmly greeted by a stunning blonde about Bobby's age. *Could have been a client*, Bobby thought, as he walked away, not wanting to know more.

Bobby checked his father's desk calendar and didn't see anything written in it for this afternoon's date. He smiled to himself and thought, *Ah, yes, another potential client interview. He'll be gone awhile.*

With that, he slowly started searching his father's desk. He had no idea what he was looking for but knew he would know it if he found it. His father always told him information is power, the more you know about someone, the greater the chance you can get them to do what you want. And what Bobby wanted was a bit of leverage with his father. The Kingmaker's act was getting a bit worn: do this, do that, how stupid are you, do you really want to be a lawyer, Christ, start thinking. He was sick of it. But the old man did hold the purse strings and unless he wanted to wait tables at Hamburger Hamlet, he'd stay quiet.

What the fuck? was his first reaction when he lifted and the handwritten letter to someone named Carlos Zimmerman. It said simply, "Zimmy, here's the info on the guy we spoke about. See it gets to the right people. Thanks".

Attached with a paper clip was a single sheet of paper with Rickey's given name and his home address, along with his Selective Service number. So old dad did some investigative work on his own, did he? He wondered how he got the Selective Service number but then stopped. What did it matter? His old man knew everyone in the city and half of them owed him favors. Generally, one phone call and he had what he needed.

He wondered what the note meant, but he understood it wasn't meant to help Rickey out in any way.

He leaned over the desk, pulled the large *Rolodex* over to him. He flipped to the Z's but no Carlos was to be found. So he flipped back to the C's and again found nothing. So he went to the back of the roll, to that area where his father stored information not by name but by areas of service. There it was: Lt. Col. Carlos Zimmerman, Fort Lewis.

So he was turning Rickey's information over to the US Army. But why? They already had it, if they wanted to draft him. It must be for another reason.

Barry Smalls was the kind of guy who seemed to know everyone. He knew the starting linemen on the football team on a first name basis. He knew members of the Black Panthers, and had had dinner at Bobby Seale's house. He could call up the Regent's secretary and talk to her like her brother might. Safe to say, if you want to meet anyone in the Bay Area, Smalls was the dude to see.

"Well Bobby, you're asking a lot. I know people. I put people together with people who want to be put together. I don't trade on information. If I did, I would lose all my friends."

"I get that and I'm not asking you to snitch out a friend, unless this Carlos man is a friend of yours. What I am simply asking is if you can find out who he is and what he does. That's all. Pretty simple."

"Well if it was so simple you wouldn't be coming to me, would you?"

He let that hang in the air for a moment before saying, "I'll ask around. Normally, I do my thing for free. But this is outside my comfort zone so give me something to make me comfortable. OK?"

"Yeah, sure. No problem. Here's my card. Call me if you get something."

"If you don't hear from me in four days, then you won't. Talk to ya later. Oh, by the way, nice jacket."

His apartment was warm that late May morning when the phone rang, jarring him out of a post-breakfast stupor. "Bobby here, speak to me."

"God you are a jackass," Barry Smalls said half laughing.

"Yeah, I know. What did you get for me?"

"A little something. Cost you $300. OK?"

"Fine. What is it?"

"Not over the phone. Meet me at the Pacific Dining Car at noon. The reservation will be under Smalls."

"OK, I'll be there."

The Pacific Dining Car was popular at lunch for LA's downtown power boys. Lots of lawyers from the big firms on expense accounts trying to convince their clients that they were the lucky ones to have them fighting their battles for them. Politicians flooded the place but rarely paid for a meal. There were accountants, insurance executives, bankers and an occasional tourist. Because they were in old railway dining cars, the place was crowded, loud, filled with smoke and that bravado of people who are trying hard to be winners in the endless race of who has more.

Bobby walked past the line of people who hadn't made reservations and said to the host, "Smalls."

"Please follow me." And Bobby was glad the host was leading the way as they meandered through one car after another, turning this way and that, until they entered a small room, no bigger than a Pullman stateroom, which it probably had been at one time. There at the table sat someone Bobby had never seen before. He turned to speak to the host to tell him this was the wrong party, but he was gone. The man at the table said simply, "Bobby have a seat. Would you like a drink?"

He was tall, and dark skinned but in a way that some Italians are colored; a tan the Hollywood crowd is always chasing. He had on a light summer-weight suit of pale grey, which was offset by the brightness of his white shirt and the black knit tie. He had a $50 haircut and a pinky ring with a diamond the size of an almond. Everything about him said Mob.

Bobby was too stunned to do anything but sit down and nod while the man poured some white wine.

"I'm Raul. Of course my name isn't Raul but that's what you can call me. I'm here at our mutual friends' request to…ah, let's say, enlighten you on certain things. Some of these things are not very pleasant, but then sometimes life isn't pleasant. No?"

He raised his glass, nodded at Bobby, and smiled as he said, "Cheers." Bobby repeated the gesture but the last thing he felt was cheerful. He was afraid he was traveling into some dark territory. Territory his father helped landscape and he wanted no part of it. But here he was and he would try to make the best of it.

After they ordered, Raul looked at Bobby and said with a flat tone in his voice: "This is for you and you only. I'm here to prevent you from getting hurt. Your father is worried that sometimes your curiosity outruns your judgment. He asked me to convey this thought to you. Before you take a step, make sure the bridge will support your weight. Bobby, it's pretty clear that before you start poking around in matters unknown to you, you need to step back and see what the blow-back might be. Your father has authorized me to tell you the complete story. It's a horrible story of misfeasance, corruption, blatant law-breaking, and even possibly murder at the highest levels of government. He wants you to know how close you came to stepping into a large vat of shit; one you wouldn't have gotten out of. I guess what he wants, Bobby, is for you to grow up and start looking at the consequences of your actions, not just the effects."

The waiter set their lunches in front of them; sirloin steak with pommes frites for Raul and a seafood pasta for Bobby. They ate in silence until Raul, who finished his meal while Bobby was less than half done, dropped his knife and fork on the plate, making a clanging sound that said, "OK, meal's over." Bobby stopped eating and looked up.

Raul, smiling, poured more wine into his glass and said, "OK, kid, here's the drift. No questions. Just listen.

"Some folks at the top feel these peace marches or whatever you want to call them are out of hand. But much worse are the university buildings getting occupied and worse still, the draft boards that are getting shut down. Hell, we had one in Salt Lake, of all places, get burned down last week. To try to restore some law and order they are targeting some of the leaders. In the open there will be excuses to arrest them and charge them with various crimes. I mean, how can they let this shit go on when we are at war?

"That singer, what's her name, coming into the White House and telling the President at lunch the war should be stopped. Who the hell is she to tell the President anything? Last October over 100,000 marched through the streets of our nation's capital demanding an end, no really, a surrender, to the war. Do you know how that affects our enemies? And the crap going on right now at Columbia. A handful of students preventing the rest of the student body from getting their education and getting on with their lives. During the 'Stop the Draft' week there were people cheering while so called protesters burned their draft cards alongside the American flag.

He paused, took a sip of wine, and smiled slyly. Bobby sat there without saying a word, trying hard to keep his knees from knocking the underside of the table.

"No, this shit has to stop. So along with some arrests they developed an alternative proposal. Anyone who is a major leader of one of these groups, or who shuts down a draft board or burns his draft card will be immediately ordered to report for induction. If they refuse, they will be arrested, tried and sent to Leavenworth. But if they report, they will be inducted just like the next guy. However, they won't go to boot camp, they won't get leave to see their mommies. Hell no, they will be sent to the nearest Air Force base for transport to Vietnam. They will be assigned to a platoon and placed on a search and destroy mission as early as their Commander can justify one."

"Holy shit!" Bobby blurted out. "That's like a death sentence."

"Yes and no. They had one guy last two weeks. But, yeah, you're right. One patrol is generally it. Sometimes by friendly fire, but often not."

Bobby was ready to puke up his lunch. This was horrifying. *How could they justify this shit. Oh! Christ! What have I gotten myself into?*

Bobby grabbed his napkin and wiped the sweat off his face. Raul continued to smile and placed his napkin alongside his plate.

"Yeah, I know. Grim, isn't it? And you're asking yourself how can they do this? Bobby, look at me, Bobby, right here. They justify this program and other similar programs because we are at War," his voice rising strongly on the word 'war.' God damn, don't you fuckers know the meaning of that? Kill or be killed. It's that simple. We can't have any weak sisters. Look what happened to McNamara last October. He whispered a doubt about the war, Bang! LBJ canned his ass. And Mac was a trusted friend and advisor to Johnson. So what do you think is going to happen when you get right in their faces?"

"OK, but what does that have to do with Rickey?"

"Who the fuck is Rickey?"

44

This was odd. She wasn't like Marsha at all but Rickey had the strongest attraction to her. This both baffled and concerned him. *How*, he thought, *could he be so attracted to such different women? Was it just because each in her own was really pretty?* He didn't think so because he'd known a lot of pretty girls but didn't feel this way about them. It was like he was so comfortable with her; so relaxed. They seemed to move together feeling the same Earth forces in their limbs. It had been the same way with Marsha. They understood each other's thoughts even before they thought them. It was weird. Such closeness, such intimacy with two women so very different.

Rickey learned that Linda, in spite of her little display that Tuesday morning, was very shy and conservative; both in her dress and her emotional make-up. Unlike Marsha who always was ready with a quick-witted comment or a flash reply, Linda was quiet, and when she spoke, even as she spoke, there was a hesitant quality to her voice. She was very soft both in her speech and the way she dressed. Marsha was all about color and contrast, whereas Linda was all about pastels and the soft blending of color and fabric. Whereas Marsha was the first to toss her bra aside when the times permitted it, Linda would never discard it. Even with him, she was reluctant to remove it while he watched. She was very private, whereas Marsha was more out-going.

How could he love two people who were so different?

It was the first day of June and Rickey was looking forward to getting out of school in two weeks. *Christ, just two more weeks of that bullshit*, he thought as he drove over to Linda's house back behind the high school. It was a pleasant home that Linda shared with her parents and brother. Rickey preferred to visit her there when they weren't there. He didn't think her father liked him much, but then again, Marsha's dad hadn't either. *Maybe it's just a dad thing*, he thought.

As he knocked on the door, he could feel the stillness in the house so he was a bit taken aback when she opened the door. "What, didn't think I was home?" she giggled; she tended to giggle a lot. He liked it, but wasn't sure why. "Ah, no, it was just so quiet."

"Well, I was just finishing setting up. Come in."

This wasn't his first visit to her home, but it was the first time she trusted him to listen to her play. She had spoken about her harp lessons, her instructor and about some of the difficulties with playing the harp, like its size and weight. They walked in what must have been an addition to the original house and now was used as a family room. The harp was in the far back corner but looked as if it had been pulled away from the wall so she could play.

"Here, please sit here. I'm going to bring you a *Coke* and then I just want you to listen, just listen. At first, I will be just doing chords and some random plucking to warm up. Then today I will work on a piece by a Welsh composer, William Mathis, *Harp Concerto, Opus 50*. He is a modern composer, which is a bit unusual, as so many harp pieces were written hundreds of years ago. Hope you like it."

Rickey leaned back into the sofa and flung his long legs out along its length. His feet were bare and the tan showed from out of the bottom of his jeans. Wearing his faded yellow Harbor Surfboard tee shirt and his shark tooth necklace, he hardly looked like your typical concert-goer; but there he was, an audience of one.

At first the music didn't mean much to him, but then he remembered she had said that was just warming up, and like batting practice before the game, didn't count. He laid back and wanted to close his eyes but was afraid if he did he would fall asleep and insult her, the last thing he wanted to do. So he stared at the ceiling with his mind drifting over the waves he had caught and those he was going to catch. He caught himself in mid-cross over on a nicely shaped tube down at Tumblers when he realized how beautiful the music was. All thoughts of the sea and surf left him and he was wrapped up in a tube of a different sort. The music was amazing, and the effect on him even more so. He was thrilled and pacified at the same time. He could feel the music move through him, and relax him. *It is almost spiritual*, he thought.

He realized the music stopped and he turned his head toward where she had been playing. She stood over him, smiling. "That was amazing. I've never heard music like that in my life."

"Really, I thought you fell asleep."

"No, not at all. That last bit where you went up really fast, then paused, then down again but even faster. That sounds how I feel when I catch the face just right on a bigger wave. You just zoom through it, the only sound is the breaking of the wave. But that was the feeling, the same feeling."

"Well, I doubt if Mathis surfed much."

"Nah, I bet he did," he said jokingly as he reached out for her and pulled her close. But as their lips were about to meet her, she turned her head. "No, not here. My brother might be home soon."

This wasn't the first time she had turned away when he wanted to kiss her, but he had come to understand the depth of her need for privacy, and his need to be patient with her. Still, it put an edge on his feelings and some doubt about how long they could be together.

He kissed her quickly on the cheek and pulled himself upright. "It's OK, Honey, I understand. Hey, look what time it is. I need to get to work." With that he stood up, pulling her along with him. They embraced and exchanged a long soulful hug and then he left.

Hells, bells, he thought as he walked to the van. *Am I ever going to sleep with her?*

45

As he walked across the lawn, he thought, *Ahhh, to hell with it. Just go to Taco Time; they can always use more shells.*

As he drove down Broadway heading into the shore he thought about Marsha and Linda and himself. What did he want in a woman; but more importantly, what did he need? Even at twenty, Rickey knew certain things about himself. He wasn't going to take over his father's insurance business. He didn't really want to work indoors. He loved the ocean and his freedom. He wanted to be able to shape his own existence. Joining the post office and putting in forty years for a pension and a "thank you" did not interest him. He could own a surf shop but he had seen his friend Greg go from being an avid rider to an avid businessman. *Good for him*, Rickey thought, *but I don't want a bunch of people looking at me for their paychecks.*

It was confusing and he knew he couldn't stay at his folks' house forever. They were cool, in fact, no one could ask for better parents, but, hey, sometime soon it's time to be independent. And that takes bucks which means working which means less freedom. *Man, this shit can be hard*, he thought as he wheeled into Taco Time.

Later that evening as he drove home he thought about the music Linda played and he thought about how they were close but still had not slept together. That one time, at the Golden Sands when he spent $20 on a room, he thought it was going to happen. She looked so beautiful that night. He would never forget how she looked as she paused just outside the bathroom door. The main room was dark but there was light shining out of the small crack where the door hadn't been fully closed. It bathed her in light and her pale skin glowed. The shadows created deep canyons on one side of her body while the other side was bathed in light. She stood half leaning on the doorway, her head cocked to one side, with a smile breaking across her lips. Lying in the bed naked across the room, Rickey felt his body stiffen as he gazed at her. He'd seen her in art books. That same beauty, that same sexiness but wrapped in purity, not tartness. He took in her breasts, which appeared much larger than they did in her show-nothing clothes. "My God," he had gasped, "you are beautiful."

She had walked slowly across the room to him and turned the cover back so she could slide in. He could feel her long smooth body next to his and the feeling was exquisite. They kissed. They kissed again. He moved his hand from her hip along her back slowly, gently. He felt her stiffen and break away.

"Sorry, Rickey, I can't. I am not ready yet. Please give me more time."

Deflated, he said only what he could say, "I understand. We have plenty of time. Let's just take it slow so we have no regrets later. OK?" And with that, he kissed the top of her head and held her close.

But they were running out of time.

The nation was, too.

46

"So, on this Long Beach State thing, we got anything going on," his dad asked, more like a command than a question.

"Ah, no," Bobby replied. "We thought the political thing was going to overshadow any protest. Besides, it's a friendly crowd. There will be plenty of anti-war signs and speakers."

"Who is speaking besides Senator Kennedy?"

"Well, there's David Harris, Joan Baez's husband. And she will sing, of course. Then some guy from the college. No one is going to listen to shit until Bobby speaks."

"He has sure come on strong, hasn't he. Just steam-rolling the Frog. And old Gene will go nowhere. Too nice. Kennedy will gut him. He'll get the nomination then it will be 1960 all over again. But Nixon will be better pre-pared. I understand that he is going after the Southern vote. Spending a ton of money down there."

"But that's Democratic territory forever. I doubt if he will pick up much there."

"Oh, Bobby, sometimes I wonder why I spent all that money on those private schools. What did they teach you down there? Christ, man, open your eyes. The Democrats, LBJ a Southerner, jammed the '64 Civil Rights Bill down their throats. And now they are choking on it. Telling seven year olds they have to climb onto a bus and ride for an hour when their own school is a five minute walk down the block. They will turn on the Dems in a New York minute. Son, south of the Mason-Dixon line, it's all about race and the Bible. Nixon will sweep the South and I got a good bottle of *Pinch* eighteen year old to bet if you think I'm wrong."

"Well maybe you aren't wrong but their combined Electoral College vote is less than California. And Nixon won't win California; they dumped him as Governor a few years back."

"True but times have changed. I just said he would win the South, I didn't say shit about winning the whole thing."

"Well who do you like?"

"Hell, I don't know."

"Well what about Kennedy?"

The old man grew quiet and finally said, "I wouldn't put much money on him. So nothing for Long Beach?"

"No. Dad, can I ask you something?"

"Sure."

"A few days ago I had lunch with a guy who called himself Raul at the Pacific Dining Car in LA. It was very hush-hush and kinda creepy. We were way back in a little alcove of a room with no one around us, which at the Dining Car is impossible. Anyhow, he tells me, that you told him to explain to me about this program the government has to deal with high profile anti-war people. Like send them to jail or worse, over to Nam to die the minute they get there. What is this all about? And what does it have to do with that surfer guy, Rickey?"

"Son, I am sorry you had to hear about that. I am sure it caused a lot of questions and a lot of them were about our government and how it operates. Look, my purpose was to expose you to something so extraordinary that it would change the way you look at things. You look at things like your mother, sweet woman she is, she doesn't have a clue about the real world and how it operates. All she sees is the surface and thinks everyone is a swell guy because they have a membership in the right club. All that stuff is meaningless, Bobby. Everyone you encounter has an agenda; something they want for themselves. And often they will not even hint at it; you have to draw the lines, connect the dots, to see what they really want. I've been trying over and over with you, to get you to see the dots and connect them, but, hell, you don't even see the dots."

He paused and took stock of his son. The late afternoon sun poured in the side windows bathing Bobby in soft light. But he was feeling anything but soft. He felt ravaged. His father could see this, and it made him smile inside. *He was never going to cut it. Oh, he will be OK over at Merrill-Lynch moving third rate stocks for pension funds and old ladies. But he is never going to sit here; behind this desk. They would eat him alive. I better start preparing another path for him. He's a good kid, and he'll probably be a good father but what he won't be is a mover; no he will stand on the sidelines thinking he is part of the game because he's part of the team, but he will never have any effect on the score.*

Finish this up quickly, he said to himself. *It's like tossing good seeds on the sidewalk.*

"OK, I get it. I shouldn't have looked through your desk. Once I found your note, I should have just forgotten about it. And I never should have mentioned it to anyone. Forget the family angle; you can't walk on ground that you can't trust. And you can't trust any ground that you've walked over before; and even then you need to test it. Times change and everything changes with them. OK, dad, I learned my lesson and I will be much more circumspect in the future. But let me ask one last question. Raul said that program was for high profile anti-war people like Hayden, Harris, Rubin, Stokely, and guys like that. Rickey had never been to a demonstration before and I'll bet he hasn't been to one since. So why give his name to Fort Lewis?"

"As usual, you've got it wrong, Bobby. Guys like the guys you named, they won't get touched by this program; they're too famous. Oh, sure, if some DA or USAG wants to go after them, fine. But the military won't touch them; too high profile. But they have people who aren't famous who carry out the day-to-day shit that makes everything happen. They are the ones the military will take a look at, because without them, those other guys are just hot air on the talk shows. And this Rickey you are so worried about, he's just a loose end. They have his name, that's all. If he becomes a problem then they might decide something. Don't forget, Bobby, you are dealing with the military and it takes eight guys and 14 memos for one guy to make a pot of coffee. So don't worry about it. He'll probably surf forever. Now, get out of here. I need to make some calls."

Bobby left feeling better. He knew the work had to be done but he didn't like seeing people get hurt because of it. Especially if they hadn't done anything.

He wondered if that waitress, Annie, still worked at the breakfast place in Long Beach. Maybe he should stop by on Monday when he was down there to see Bobby Kennedy in action. He liked the gap.

47

Lunch was spread out on the plaid blanket under the shade of a large elm tree in a quiet part of El Dorado Park. The park had been created back in the late '50's when local residents, watching as acre after acre of orange groves disappeared, demanded that the developers save some land for a park. After the typical tug of war, a large tract of land was set aside as a park. It took years of pushing the City Council to spend the money to landscape the raw dirt which had been left when all the trees had been uprooted. Now in early June of 1968, the park was fully formed and a delightful place to spend a Sunday.

Rickey would of course rather have been at the beach, but he had learned recently that Linda didn't like the beach. It wasn't so much the beach she didn't like, it was the sand. She said it made her feel dirty.

Rickey had read that compromise was the oil that makes relationships work, so the park it would be. He didn't really care where they were as long as they were together. He really liked being with her and the more time they spent together, the more he wanted to be with her. He was like a junkie, always on the prowl for his next fix.

The small portable radio was tuned to a local jazz station, *KBCA*, and they were listening to the Chuck Niles show, which often featured the straight-headed jazz of the '40's and '50's. But Linda said his Sunday show was more mellow and had players like Miles Davis, John Coltrane teamed up with Johnny Hartman, and many others who played that cool jazz sound which called up visions of smoky rooms, empty beds with tossed sheets, half drunk cocktails with the ice melted and the undercurrent of sex and romance all mixed together in a way Rickey had never heard before.

That was one of the things he loved about Linda; she opened new doors for him. They would spend hours turning the pages of over-sized art books, rarely reading a word but studying the pictures intently. So many different things she had shown him: the harp and its beautiful sound, this amazing music, Thai food and real French cooking. All these were new worlds for him and he realized she had a lot more to show him.

There was time enough for the beach on his own.

"Isn't this a marvelous day?" she asked while handing him a small sandwich. He ate it in one bite, then said, "Wow, that was good. What was it?"

"Pate and chevre."

"And that's like 'what'?"

"Well, pate is a finely ground liver paste. It can come from different animals but this is duck pate. And chevre is goat cheese."

"Goat's make cheese?"

"No, silly, people make cheese. They use the goat's milk to make it."

"Really, goats make milk, like cows? I didn't know that."

And that is what he loved about being with her. Every time he was with her, damned if she didn't teach him something. Today, so far two things and they'd only been there an hour. *Should be a great day*, he thought to himself.

They spent the next few hours chatting, nibbling, drinking some white wine that Rickey had gotten from his buddy who worked at Morrie's Liquor down on the shore. Listening to the jazz put them both in a romantic mood, perhaps with a little help from the wine. But Rickey knew it wouldn't go beyond the kissing stage and even though he could feel her breasts pressing against his chest, he never moved a hand toward them.

Looking over the park, Rickey made the random comment, "You know they still haven't caught the guy who killed Martin Luther King. Don't you think that's odd?"

"I don't know what to think, but Rickey, you know I don't like talking about that kind of stuff. Politics, the war, President Kennedy's assassination, all that stuff just doesn't interest me. Besides, there's nothing you can do about it."

"I'm not sure that's true. Look what is happening right now. People took to the streets to protest the war, and soon guys like Senator McCarthy are challenging the war, the President decides he can't win because of the war so he bails, and now Bobby Kennedy has joined the fight. I think you can make a difference."

He paused, "Look, come with me tomorrow over to Long Beach State. He will be there. It's like his last speech before the election on Tuesday. It will be interesting."

"No, I can't. My father would kick me out of the house if he knew I went to a protest rally. He has really strong feelings about all that stuff. Burning the flag and draft cards; shutting down universities. No, he would be really upset with me."

"Oh, OK. But it isn't an anti-war rally or demonstration. This is a speech by a guy running to be the President; how can he object to that?"

Linda stared off, looking to the large trees which swayed in the afternoon breeze. *Christ*, she thought to herself, *I have to tell him. I don't want to, but this is wrong.* But still she was unsure. It was so pleasant with him. He was so understanding and so gentle; and yet so sure of himself. You never felt with Rickey he was trying to be someone else; you just got the unvarnished Rickey. And it was good. How could she do this? Why had she let it go so long? Her guilt ran at cross currents, the affection she felt for Rickey and the promise she made to Robby. Between the two, she felt cut in half; lost and alone, and it was all her own doing.

Rickey saw the puzzlement on her face and the whites of her knuckles as she squeezed the hem of her skirt. Something was going on. He pressed her.

"I don't believe you. Your dad is a newspaper man. I've met him, and he may not like me but he's a smart guy. He's not going to get pissed if you go see Bobby Kennedy. What's going on?" His tone was harsher than he wanted it to be, but he could feel in his gut that something bad was about to happen.

She looked at him and all the guilt and mixed feelings came rushing to her; she felt overwhelmed by emotion. She started to cry.

Normally, Rickey's natural reaction would have been to reach out to her, and comfort her. But not this time; not now. Instead he just sat there motionless, not saying a word.

After the sobbing ebbed and she was able to utter a few words, she said, "Oh, Rickey, I am so sorry. I've been so confused and now everything is shit."

Rickey had never heard her swear before and he was more surprised than concerned. But then she went on in a calm and evenly-paced voice, "Before I met you, long, long before, I was involved with another guy. Robby Rollins, he went to Millikan. We started dating in tenth grade; well, really the summer after tenth grade. He was the only boy I knew until I met you. Well, about two years ago, he joined the Army. His brother was in the Army and they promised to put them together. And they did; for about three weeks. Then they shipped Robby to Vietnam while his brother stayed in Germany. He's written me a lot and once about a year ago, I met him in Hawaii when he was on R&R."

She paused and looked around. "Any wine left?" Rickey pulled the bottle from the cooler and handed it to her without saying a word. She drank straight from the bottle, then handed it back to him.

"Then I met you. And fell in love. That's what makes this so damned hard - it's that I love you but I have to be with him."

Rickey spoke for the first time in a while, "Why?"

A sound like, "Arrrggg" came from her, then she was sobbing again. Hugging herself with her arms around her chest, rocking back and forth, sobbing uncontrollably, stopping every once in awhile to gasp air, then starting in again. Finally, spent, her eyes bloodshot and dimmed in red, her mascara running down her face in long narrow streams, all of her poise and refinement washed out of her, she turned to Rickey and said, "He was shot a few weeks ago. I just learned of it yesterday. It looks like he will live and he is going to Honolulu for recovery. I have to go. I have to take care of him. Before he left I promised him I would wait for him. We promised each other that when he came back we would get married. And the note I got from him reminded me of that but said I didn't have to if I didn't want to marry a one-legged man. I can't not go there, you understand, don't you? I was going to tell him about you. I tried several times in letters but I never mailed them. I just couldn't, not with him out on the battlefield. I just couldn't." She stopped and picked at the pattern of the blanket, and then looked up and said, "I'm sorry."

Rickey felt queasy and disoriented. His emotions were mixed: pissed at her for lying to him and sad for her dilemma she had created for herself. Like the swell hitting the shore, in and out, his feelings changed by the moment. Finally, he blurted out, "You mean Rolls Rollins, that guy who rides that ugly yellow board? The fat guy?" Once it was out of his mouth, he regretted it, but there it was, and he couldn't take it back.

She nodded. And somehow with that nod, all the affection and close-ness he had felt for her vanished. He could feel it leave him like his breath when pounded under by a big wave.

He stood up and began to put the picnic away.

The radio was playing a soulful version of *Blue Monday*.

48

Rickey awoke to the sound of rain on the awning covering the porch off his room. He liked the sound of the rain but didn't like the gustiness of the wind behind it. He could hear the trees bending to the breeze and rattling off the half-opened window in the bathroom. "No surfing today," he muttered to Rusty who was lying with his head on a pillow but with most of his face hidden by it; a single eye searched for Rickey behind a long black nose. "Yeah, boy, no riding today." He sat up quickly, perhaps too quickly as the room began to wobble, tilting some this way, some that. He fell back into the bed, thinking, *What the hell?* then it hit him; a cold wave of reality.

The last he could remember of last night was having some Delta Delta Delta sorority girl sitting on his lap in the back of Diver's Cove, a half cool, half dumpy bar in Naples. She was pulling on his necklace and saying, "You didn't really tear this tooth from a shark's head with just your bare hands, did you?" He could remember her comfortable weight on his lap, and the smell of some expensive perfume. That went with the territory; Tri-Deltas had money, or at least their daddies did. She was cute, but damned if he could remember her name or what they did together.

He remembered leaving the park with Linda and dropping her off at her parents' house. He remembered how cold he felt and all of her words and tears could not, would not, change that. He felt he had been fooled; but that he could live with. It was the great hollow spot inside his chest that he knew was going to be a problem. He felt as if his 'being' had been torn violently from him. Only an emptiness and anger lingered inside what, just yesterday, was an endless feeling of affection, love and desire. He felt empty inside.

He got up and checked the clock as he walked to the shower. 8:40. *Christ, so much for Geography 101.* But if he was going to miss a class, then that was a good one as Professor Stone, as he liked to be called, didn't care about attendance; he liked to say, "This is college, not high school. I don't give a hoot in hell if you show up or not. Just do the work." And Rickey did do the work. The mindless drawing of the outlines of countries and filling in their major cities and capitals. As if that taught you anything about the country, its people, how they lived, how they dealt with 20th Century life, which was disrupting long-held traditions and changing the very way they had lived for centuries. Nope, none of that mattered to Professor Stone, who was rumored to be an ex-Nazi. Draw the outline, fill in the blanks and when you are done, place it next to the last country you did from that region. *Christ, what a waste*, Rickey thought, as he stepped into the hot shower.

This morning he let it pound his head and shoulders, hoping to wash the remaining booze out of his brain and the cigarette smell out of his hair. He could still taste the *Lucky*s on his tongue and through the roof of his mouth. A fine film of staleness coated everything, making him wish he never had had a cigarette in his life.

He looked at himself in the half steamed up mirror and saw the redness in his eyes and the shadow of his beard starting to cover his face, his hair was a madhouse of tangles but that would settle down with a good combing. He ached a bit and the hollow feeling from his belly reminded him that he hadn't eaten since yesterday in the park. *God, that seemed so long ago*, he thought, although knowing it was just a matter of hours. But his life had changed, and the road he thought he was on was now a dead end. He knew he needed to find a new pathway and also knew Tri-Deltas and oceans of beer wasn't the way to go.

Rusty barked that quiet little bark of his, saying to Rickey, "Hey, time to feed me," and Rickey smiled to himself and right back, "OK, then. But me, too."

After he fed Rusty, Rickey opened the refrigerator and saw there was no milk for cereal and no eggs to fry. *Ah, Shit! I need a big breakfast to soak up all that booze from last night. Guess it's the Potholder. Their Trucker's Special and about a gallon of coffee should do the trick*, he thought, as he looked for his keys

As he walked to the van, he watched the wind blowing the rain off the leaves of the big oak in their front yard. He tried to dodge the bigger drops as he half walked, half jogged to the van which was parked around the corner for some reason. Oh, yeah, I got lucky last night just making it back. He half expected the van to have a banged up fender or some other evidence of his foolishness, but a quick survey showed everything as it should be. He climbed in behind the wheel and noticed how the streets were covered in rainbow ribbons of color left behind by the oil and gas cars discharged as they made their way to their next destination. *All that will flow down into the sea*, he thought, *turning the waters close to shore brown for the next few days, and no one seems to worry about it.*

He turned the key and headed the van to breakfast.

49

Rickey pulled the door open to the Potholder and was surprised to see Bobby sitting in a window booth quietly stirring his coffee. Rickey approached Bobby as Bobby waved him over to sit down. They sat chatting the twenty minutes that it took Rickey to get his breakfast and eat it. While they were cordial, there was still an underlying tension between them.

"Well, I gotta go over to Taco Time to make some money. Good luck with that waitress."

"Perhaps I'll see ya over at the Kennedy thing this afternoon," Bobby answered.

"Yeah, cool. Later."

Even though Rickey had arrived long after Bobby had, it was clear Bobby was planning to stay even longer. Annie had been their waitress, and Rickey knew Bobby had some ideas about her. *Good for him*, he thought to himself. *But, beware, women can tear your heart out.*

He had a couple of hours before the events over at the college started so he decided to spend them at Taco Time trying to re-fund his travel kit.

The familiar surroundings and the routine, which he quickly swung into, brought comfort to him. Something simple, something known, something he could rely on. He wondered if he could ever completely trust a woman again. Could he ever just give himself like he gave himself to her? Why would he want to, knowing the possibility of the pain he might have to pay? She had scarred him, and what hurt even more was knowing she loved him and was ruining them for some false idea of duty. Rolls Rollins did not deserve her and she would eventually find out he was the kind of guy who hogged waves, would park so as to take two spots even in the crowded lot off of 3rd Street in Seal Beach. And he was the kind of guy who would lie to his girlfriend. Rickey himself had seen him with other girls during their last year in high school. He wondered how many of them had promised to wait for him. Linda would learn, in time. But it still grated on him and he couldn't shake the feeling all afternoon.

He looked up at the big Taco Time clock hung in the kitchen which said it was 1:30 and time for him to go. He had done eight racks and thought, *Let's make it an even ten.* He was comfortable and feeling in the swing of things and didn't want to break the vibe he had going. Who knew when it would come back? He could be late, no one was waiting for him.

As he crossed the slight rolling hills which formed the lower section of Long Beach State College, he saw a large crowd forming around a platform which looked like it had just been built. People were milling about and no one seemed to be in charge. A free-form bank of students, activists, old folks and news people were moving about with no set design or plan. That all changed in a moment when a large round faced man stepped up to the microphone and announced that Joan Baez was going to sing a few songs before husband, David Harris, spoke.

Rickey of course had heard of her, and perhaps knew a song or two she had done, but he was totally unprepared for this raven long-haired woman to transport him with her voice. It was so clear, so pure, so full of meaning and you could tell every word she sang came from her heart. He stood transfixed until she waved her husband forward to speak.

David Harris had a simple message: do not cooperate with the draft. Don't register, don't report for induction, if arrested, fight it and if you lose, appeal. The message had a certain appeal to many as it was simple. The real message though was delay.

Push the clock back, try to restart the game, invoke any claim or defense as long as it pushed the final decision down the line. It was a good strategy in numerous ways. First, it forced the government to spend money and manpower which they claimed was limited. Second, they knew that sooner or later the American people would tire of this war and force the government to end it. Third, it gave them time to get out their message; and that was exactly what Harris was doing today.

Harris spoke for about twenty minutes before taking questions. The first person to speak was polite to Harris but challenged his patriotism. The second wasn't as polite, calling Harris a Commie and telling him to go back to where he came from, to which Harris replied, "Fresno. I'm from Fresno," which got a nice laugh from the crowd.

The third person to approach the mike was a slightly built man of about twenty who seemed comfortable speaking before a large group. After a few minutes, it became clear that he had been trained in debate. His message was not so different than Harris' but revolved around an important distinction. He raised his voice as to emphasize his point. "Don't let them have your body. Don't let them control you. Remember this: The government is corrupt. They lie. They make up facts to support their position. They will do anything to keep their war going. Why? First, it makes money; huge amounts of money for so many people. Second, vanity. LBJ refuses to be the first American president to lose a war. But his vanity is no reason for thousands to die and tens of thousands to suffer."

He paused and looked out at the crowd which stood silent until someone yelled, "Right on!" And a cheer arose from the crowd as if from a single person.

He stood quietly until the crowd settled down before he began to speak again.

"When they have locked you up, not only do they have you, but they have all those outside who are scared shitless of being locked up. When you are roaming free, be it in Canada, elsewhere, or underground, you are giving hope to those who still need to make their decision. Really," he said, "it's pretty simple. The choice is living free or living the life they determine for you. I choose freedom. I choose life."

He stopped, apologized for taking so long and stepped back. The spell was broken and the crowd reacted with cheers. Harris nodded and said, "I still believe in the system and that we can make a change within the system." But he was hardly heard.

Rickey looked at the crowd and realized more than half were women who didn't have to make the choice. He looked closer and saw that many of the people were too old to be put at risk. He saw that maybe only twenty percent of the crowd that day had the decision to make; he was one of them.

Of course, the bulk of the crowd was there to hear Bobby Kennedy and as his motorcade approached the crowd tripled in size. He remembered telling Linda that this was not an anti-war protest but a rally for Bobby Kennedy; he had been right. But the memory of their conversation pulled him into a place of sadness and regret; he would be pulled there many times in the near future.

50

"You what?" his father's voice trembled in both rage and fear. Rickey could tell the moment he walked in the door that Bailey was upset. More upset than Rickey had ever seen him. More upset than the night of Dr. King's killing.

"I was there, dad. I saw it."

His father slowly recoiled having been right up close to Rickey, pushing against his chest. Now he stepped back, opening space between them, and yet at the same time creating an intimacy that was absent before. He seemed to calm down and sat on the arm of the sofa and said, "Tell me about it. Start at the beginning and tell me everything."

"Where is mom?"

"She's in the bedroom. We were sleeping, then I got up to get some water and I saw the light on in the Brandt's house which is unusual for that hour. So I flipped on the TV and heard what had happened. She got up, and well, you can imagine. I think she took one of those pills to get back to sleep. So tell me."

Rickey wasn't sure where to begin, but Bailey said to start at the beginning, and that was yesterday at the college.

He was standing, feeling awkward, so he moved across the room and sat on the ottoman with his hands dangling between his legs. He shot a glance at his father, who had now moved off the arm of the sofa and was sitting in his chair under the reading light. The light bathed him in a pale yellow light and made the whole scene seem even more surreal.

"Well, I guess it started yesterday at the college. I went to hear him speak and was surprised by how moving it was. There seemed to be something special about him. He just seemed more real than most politicians. It's hard to describe. But his message was like we are all in this together and we have to make it better for everyone. Make it more fair. He talked about the war and said he didn't know why we were there and why so many Americans had to die. He said it was unfair that negros were forced to fight a war and then come home and not be able to attend the school of their choice or to eat where they wanted. A lot of the things he said made sense."

Rickey paused realizing he was thirsty and he was still upset from what he had seen. He excused himself and went into the kitchen and got a beer from the door of the refrigerator. Walking back into the room he saw his father sitting in his chair like he had seen him so many times before. But this time he looked different; defeated, as if life had been sucked out of him. He was sitting there, hunched over, shaking his head side to side and whispering something under his breath which Rickey couldn't hear.

Taking his seat again, Rickey coughed to try to get his father's attention, and it worked. Bailey sat up a bit straighter and shifted his eyes toward Rickey.

He started again. "So this morning I was sitting there down at the Cliffs waiting for a wave and thinking about what he had said, and about what the others had said. See the first guy was saying to protest the war you need to not cooperate with the government. You need to change the system from within. And you need to use, I guess stuff that is legal, even if you are breaking the law you are still respecting the system of law. Kennedy was saying something similar. The system just needs *US* to make it right. But there was this other guy who said the system is rigged because the people who run the show can change the rules whenever they want, and once you let them have your body, well you're screwed.

"As I sat out there this morning I was kinda replaying all the things they said in my head so I decided to go up to LA to hear him speak again. See if I could understand better."

"You go alone?"

"Yeah, I asked Sticks if he wanted to go. He asked if there were going to be many girls there and when I said I didn't know, he said he would pass. Sticks thinks his bent leg will keep him out so he just doesn't think about this stuff at all. So, yeah, I went by myself."

He took a long sip on the beer and continued when his dad didn't say anything.

"So it was kind of exciting. There were a lot of people. Big TV's all over the place with the election results blasting out of them, music playing over the loudspeakers, and all these people talking. There was just this feeling that you were part of something. It was cool. Then when around, oh, I don't know, nine or ten, they say Kennedy has won. All hell breaks loose. It was something, really. Then he came out and spoke and said something about Chicago and everyone cheered.

"But I had been drinking a few beers and really had to go. So I start looking around for a bathroom and there are just so many people I decide I will get out of the ballroom and find something on another floor. Well, I finally found a restroom but when I came out I was lost. I wandered around for awhile then I ran into this really pretty girl. She says to follow her, she knew a short-cut to the parking lot. So I did. Next thing I know I'm down in the kitchen and there are all these people pushing their way toward me. I turn around and the girl is gone, and I am getting crushed up against this big table. So I duck under it and come up on the other side, and then cross over to the other end."

Rickey's breathing had gotten more rapid and he was speaking very quickly, and he heard the anxiousness in his voice. So he paused and took another sip of beer. He wanted to get this right. He was trying to tell it, just the way he replayed it in his head.

"When I do, I realize that Senator Kennedy is right in front of me. I am looking at his back but I know it's him. Everyone is pushing around him, and it's a mess of people.

"Then someone pushes me from behind and I fall forward and catch myself on the edge of the table. This kinda knocks the wind out of me, but that's when I hear the popping sounds. *Pop, Pop, Pop, Pop*. I don't know what it is, then I hear screaming. But when I look up I see blood coming from the back of his head. I remember because the hole was very small but the blood was squirting out, and it was very red. But then he was gone; he must have fallen down."

He paused again trying to remember clearly so his father had the right picture of what he was doing. How all this happened.

"What happened next?' his dad asked in a level and calm voice.

"Ah, I stood up and I saw a small man with kinda dark skin standing there with a gun in his hand. And like in a second this huge guy, I mean huge guy, jumps on him and bam just like that, it's over. People are still yelling and screaming but the guy with the gun is under the big guy totally, and I see the gun being taken from his hand. Soon the cops are all over the place and I just bailed. I saw a sign that said exit and I just headed for it."

"Tell you what. Why don't we talk about this more in the morning. It's really late and you look shot."

"Yeah, fine. Hey, dad, do you think this is like before?"

"You mean King?"

"Yeah, like that and the President."

"I don't know just now. Let's see what the story is tomorrow."

51

Rickey awoke in a few hours, still tired and confused. He laid in the bed for awhile, gently stroking Rusty and thinking about the last few days. He started to cry.

He didn't know where it came from but there was a deep ache inside of him and a vile taste in his throat. As he cried, he realized he was so confused. He felt sad, he felt angry, he felt abandoned, he felt lost, he felt a rage stronger than he had ever felt; but most of all, he felt alone, and scared.

In a while he heard someone in the kitchen and decided to get up. A quick shower and a quicker combing of his hair, he walked into the kitchen trying to appear like himself on a normal day. But today was no normal day.

His father glanced over his shoulder at him as he hovered over the coffeepot. Rickey saw his dad had had only one cup which meant that his mother was not up yet. His father understood his look and said, "She'll be awhile."

Rickey poured himself a cup and added some cream from the little pitcher that looked like a cow. He and his father sat there in silence for nearly an hour before his father said, "Guess I better get to the office."

"People are working today?"

"Some I guess. I just want to get out of the house for awhile. I'll put up a sign saying we are closed. I'll be back in a few hours. If your mother gets up, tell her for me."

"Yeah, sure thing."

Rickey thought about heading to the beach, but decided he should wait for his mother to get up. She might need some help. Or just want to talk. So he sat there, staring out the window at the fruit trees in the back yard, his thoughts ricocheting off each other, crisscrossing his brain in one fluid motion and yet in fragments colliding with one another until it was all one giant foamy wave with neither a face nor a break. He was confused.

"Honey, you OK?" His mother's voice brought him back from his wanderings, and he was thankful that she had.

"Oh, hi Mom. How are you doing? Dad said you were upset last night." Once he said it, he thought, *you idiot, why would you say that?* But before he could say anything else to try and cover it, she spoke.

"Quite upset. Honey, I don't understand what is going on and it scares me. And not so much for me or your father, but for you. Your dad and I, we grew up during the Depression and it was scary for a lot of people. But we always knew that there was a solution. Get people jobs and they will work and they will spend the money they earn and that will make more jobs and so on and so on. Jobs. A single-word solution. And we had had jobs before and knew that they would come back. So while there was fear, and trust me, a lot of people were very afraid, there was always hope. I don't see any hope with what is going on today, and it scares me. This war, I don't understand it. I don't know why we are there, and I haven't heard anyone give me a good reason why we should stay. It's clear it's tearing the country apart. And these killings. Three major figures in our country killed in less than five years. And the questions just swirl out of each one of them, and never get answered. It just doesn't seem that the government is telling us the whole story: but maybe they can't.

"And this thing last night..." And her voice just trailed off.

Rickey didn't know what to say. His mom, while quiet, always had this sense of strength about her. When her sister, Mabel, was killed in that car crash a few years back, leaving three children without a mother and a father who was so distraught that he couldn't get out of bed, it was Maggie who went back East and took charge. Got the kids to school, ran her sister's bookkeeping business until she could find a buyer for it, helped Ralph get back on his feet and back to work. She did it, and did it without a second thought. And now, she is scared. *Christ, what can I say?*

He couldn't tell her he had been there. It would upset her too much and he just felt he couldn't tell the story again. In fact, he hoped he would never have to tell anyone again what he saw last night. But what if they wanted to know? What if the cops wanted to know?

He got up and hugged his mother and rocked her slowly in his arms. After a few moments she said, "You better get along to school, it's getting late."

Rather than say anything, he gave her a final squeeze and walked away. *She understood how he felt.*

52

Rickey didn't feel like himself. He was adrift on a seamless ocean of doubt and confusion. The next week drifted by and he had no recollection of what he did. Specific things, he could recall: *Yeah, sure I went to Taco Time yesterday, right? Or was that the day before? Better call Tom and see if they need more shells,* and before that thought was complete, a cross-thought would come over it, about something unrelated. He remembered sitting in front of the TV watching them bury Bobby Kennedy but couldn't remember anything else about it. He remembered his dad talking about the assassinations but could not recall a specific detail. He knew he had gone surfing but could not remember when or where. Most of the last week was a blur; a fuzzy foam of mixed thoughts and memories which may or may not have happened. He could recall in detail a conversation with Marsha where he told her everything, even things he hadn't told his father, about how Bobby Kennedy was killed. But the conversations took place face to face in an old hang out that had been torn down years ago; and he knew for certain Marsha was still in Vermont.

The burden of what he had seen and what he feared was happening was overwhelming. His father was right. A few days after Kennedy was murdered, by yet again another lone gunman, the government announced that they had captured King's killer. Of course he acted alone, and was a crazy racist low-life of no visible means, who confessed. As did Kennedy's killer.

What they were saying was not hard to miss. We've got it covered; we are in control. Nothing more to see here folks, please get back to your lives, back to your routine, go shopping, catch a ballgame, take the kids to school, go see the newest movie. Just don't ask any questions.

He didn't want to ask questions, for he already knew their response. What he wanted to ask was: WHY? But he had no one to ask. And so he drifted for days in a fog of confusion.

It was a week to the day that Rickey awoke fresh, clear-headed and feeling like himself. He thought, *God, I hope that shit is over. Let's go finish up that map and write that essay on King George the Fifth and close the door on this semester.* He jumped out of bed, full of energy and life.

He laid the map down on the pile with the outline of Austria and all of its major cities highlighted in red. He sighed and felt relief of having completed a task that he disliked so much.

"Ah, Mr. Osgood," at first Rickey didn't realize Professor Stone was speaking to him, but once it struck him, he turned quickly to face his instructor.

"Ah, yes, sir. Good morning."

"Yes it is," Professor Stone said, with a smug look spreading across his face. "For them perhaps, but not for you," he said, waiving in the general direction of the other students.

Rickey was puzzled, *What was he saying?* "And why not for me?"

"Because this map you just submitted...I can tell by looking at it that it's done in one to 250 scale and the assignment was to do it in one to 200 scale. This isn't what I asked for. It doesn't satisfy the required criteria; I can't grade it."

"What are you saying?" Rickey replied, the anxiety growing by the minute.

"I think I made myself clear, Mr. Osgood. That map is not acceptable. I won't grade it because it's not what the assignment called for. It's that simple. And all maps had to be turned in today by twelve o'clock noon. I doubt you can do another one, a correct one, in twenty minutes. So, you are short one map and I can only give you an incomplete for the semester. But the good news is, you can make it up over the Summer."

"What, over the Summer? Do that map over and then you give me my grade. I can do it tonight and get it in tomorrow. Can we do that?"

"It doesn't work that way. The semester's work was to be done by noon today. You've known since January your assignments but you waited until the last day to do yours. I know they were laid out one a week but there was no reason you couldn't have done some early just to prevent this situation from happening. And no. In order to get a grade and the units, you must complete the course work for the course you take. This Summer's course is on Asia not Europe so re-doing that map is a waste of time."

"You mean to tell me, that I will get an incomplete and need to retake the entire fucking course?" Rickey could feel the rage coming on, all the emotions from the last week were boiling to the surface. Stone's face was just a hazy blur in front of him. The entire scene was so bright as to be blinding and was made more confusing by the flashes of red and yellow around its edge.

"Is that what you are fucking telling me?"

"Yes, exactly."

"Well, fuck you, fuck the units and you can take those maps and shove them up your ass, you cock-sucking Nazi!" Rickey wanted to smash that smug face into a thousand pieces but instead he turned and walked out. He looked over the classroom and saw a few of his fellow students giving him the "thumbs up;" but discreetly, as they couldn't afford Stone's ire.

As he walked across the quad, his feet were unsteady and his hands were shaking. As he sat behind the wheel, he tried to steady himself, but collapsed in tears and curses.

53

Rickey rarely went to his parents' office. He didn't like to interrupt them and besides, he always felt so confined in the small space they used. It was really a single office with a small work area out front. It was on the ground floor of an older building in the downtown section of Long Beach. His dad moved in after returning from the war and Rickey thought he had painted just once since he moved in. The office opened off a front porch and there was a similar door to theirs on the opposite side, and in-between was a stairwell leading to two upper offices.

As he opened the door off the porch, he walked right into where his mother was sitting, and she gave a bit of a shout, "Rickey, what are you doing here?"

"Ah, I've got a problem. I need to talk to dad. And you too, of course."

"Well dad just went to the bank and he should be back in a few minutes. We could start if you want."

"No, I need dad to hear this, all of this," he replied, his voice a bit weak and wavy.

"OK, fine, dear. Well, why don't you go into his office and wait, he won't be long."

Rickey followed her suggestion and walked into the clutter of papers, folders, books, newspapers and boxes that his father called his office. His desk was as clean as an aircraft carrier's flight deck but the surrounding office looked as if a bomb had gone off. Rickey looked for a place to sit but every flat surface, including the client chair in front of the desk, was covered with the detritus of the insurance world.

Christ, thought Rickey, *save me from this life*. But as he said it, he knew that his parents' squeezing out their living in this office is what made his life possible; and now he had gone and fucked it all up.

"OK, let me make sure I have this right," his father said after Rickey had given a blow-by-blow with Professor Stone this morning and its effect on his future. "This guy, Stone, is rejecting your map because it was in the wrong scale. Correct?"

"Yeah, that's right."

"Now is there any question about it being the wrong scale?"

"No sir. I did it in 250 and the assignment was in 200. I checked. I fucked up."

"OK. And, he won't accept it in the wrong scale?"

"Right?"

"So you flunk this course and have to take it again?"

"Well, not flunk but incomplete."

"Same stuff, right?"

"Well as far as the draft goes, yes. See, if he had given me a D, I would still get the unit credit but with the incomplete, I get zip...like I never took it. That's what is so hard. I hated that fucking class but I did it, but now it's like I didn't and they will take my 2S."

"Well, let's not go there yet. From what you tell me, this Stone guy is a real stiff and won't budge. So, all you can do is go to Summer school and make it up."

"Why? The Army requires fifteen units a semester and I only have twelve. That's all they care about. They won't add the Summer to the Spring term to come up with the fifteen. This is exactly what they did to Jacks, Dad."

"Oh, so what you're so upset about is the possibility of losing the 2S," he said it like an indictment; like Rickey's concerns were misplaced.

"Sorry, Dad, but yes. To tell you the truth, I would not be going to college if it weren't to get to the 2S. It's not for me. It's boring and virtually nothing I have taken has a damned thing about the real world. The world we live in. Like those stupid maps. What was I going to learn about Austria by drawing it in 200 scale rather than 250? They are just throwing up hurdles to see how many make it over. At the end of the race they give you a piece of paper saying you are educated. What bullshit! All they are doing is seeing how much crap you will eat. Their whole plan is to make good little obedient citizens who will do what they are told. Well screw it! I'm not interested."

"OK, fine. I can see your point. Maggie, do you agree?"

She had sat in silence, which was her nature, during their back and forth. She looked at her husband then turned to Rickey, "You get one life to live. That's all God is going to give you. And he can take it away anytime He chooses. But until He does, you have to make decisions not just for today but for tomorrow, too. You have a long life in front of you and what you do today will affect it; be sure of that. But you can't forego today just for tomorrow. A lot of people do; and that is their choice. You have your choices to make. You will make good and bad choices, we all do. The trick is to make the bad ones about little things that don't count much."

She paused and the room remained silent except for the soft thump of the air conditioner. "It seems to me you are being treated unfairly. But it also seems to me that he is not picking on you. He has his rules, and those are his rules and everyone can get hit by them. So, I say, forget about the maps and all that nonsense, and take a look at what you really want. You're twenty, still very young; but the times we live in are making you mature fast. Honey, take some time, cool off, and think about what you want. I know you love to surf but can you make a living from it? If you can, then go for it; if not, then what would you like to do instead?"

Bailey cut in when his wife paused, "She is right, Rich. You have a long road ahead of you. Whether it's a sweet passage or a rough one depends a lot on how you make a living. Do you choose it or do you let it choose you? Do you think when I was growing up I dreamed about selling insurance? Of course not. But after the war, I came here, I found a job that paid OK and took it. I never intended to do this for twenty-some years but I have. Do I love it? No, but I don't hate it either. So the trick, buddy-boy, is for you to find something you love doing, so every day you look forward to doing it, and do it."

He stopped for a moment and looked at his wife as if getting permission to continue. "A few years ago I would have recommended that you go into the service for a few years and mature and get a taste of the real world. But not now. But I don't know how to advise you. If you lose the 2S, you will be drafted. If you don't report, you will be arrested, if they can find you, and sent to prison. If you go, then you have to decide which branch; and for how long. It's a hard decision. My decision was easy. My country was attacked, we were fighting for our way of life; there was no question. And for me, because of your Uncle Bill's stories, the Navy was my only choice. But your choice will be far more difficult. But you don't need to decide right now; you have some time and I want to do some research first."

They sat silently for awhile, then Rickey spoke, "Thanks. Thanks for being so, ah, understanding." He didn't even try to hide the tears that were welling up in his eyes.

54

Rickey was standing by the sink washing out his coffee cup when he saw a figure move across the back yard. It startled him, and his imagination went into overdrive. *So soon? I've only been out of school a month. I didn't even get a notice. Oh, shoot, maybe it's not the Army, maybe it's someone looking for me because of Kennedy.* He could feel his blood actually go cold as his hands started to shake, and the bile rise up from his gut. "Oh, shit!" speaking only to Rusty who was laying quietly under the kitchen table and raised his head slightly at the sound of Rickey's voice but quickly put it back down like he couldn't be bothered.

Rickey did a double-take at Rusty and thought, *Why isn't he barking his ass off? Because he knows who it is, you dumb-ass.*

When Rickey moved over to the window and peered out, feeling foolish, he called out to Mr. Riley, "Morning, up and at 'em."

"Sure am, Rickey, and it's going to be a beautiful day."

"I'm sure you're right." Just then the phone rang and Rickey turned to get it, leaving the window and Mr. Riley behind.

"Hello, the Osgood's," he answered.

"Rich, it's me, Dad. Look I want to talk to you man-to-man. Can you meet me today over at Joe Jost's about one?"

"Ah, yeah, sure."

"If you get there before I do, try and grab a booth up front. I don't really like sitting at the bar."

"Yeah. See you at one."

As he crossed the kitchen to return to the sink, he saw Mr. Riley, who his dad called 'Sarge' but he didn't feel it was his place to use his nickname so it was always Mr. Riley, pushing the lawnmower over the grass. He watched the unusual way he moved his left leg, sort of dragging it behind him, rather than throwing it out in front of the other leg. Rickey knew that was because that was not his real leg but rather a wooden replacement with a leather hinge at the knee. He had lost his leg out in the Pacific at a place called Guadalcanal.

As Rickey watched him move the mower back and forth, he could almost hear his father telling him the story. Mr. Riley had been one of the first to enlist after Pearl Harbor. December eighth actually, the day after. He enlisted with the Marines and by the next August he was part of the invasion group that landed on Guadalcanal to take it back from the Japs and secure the airstrip. The Japs were out-numbered and surprised by the attack but did not surrender; they fought back like wounded animals. One of them shot him right in the left leg, blowing it in half. He was luckier than some and his life was saved by an Ensign on a battleship that was laying off shore in support of the invasion. But he lost the leg and with that got an immediate transfer back to the Mainland and a discharge order.

But he refused the discharge and convinced the powers that be that he could still serve as a rifle instructor. So he spent the rest of the war 40 miles down the coast at Camp Pendleton teaching thousands of recruits how to use the M-1. When they discharged him, his rank was Gunnery Sergeant, shortened to 'Sarge' by his father.

Thinking about Mr. Riley and what he had lost and how he still wanted to help his country made Rickey feel proud, yet small. Proud to know him, the man that tended their yard, and small for his own doubt over serving. No matter what anyone says about their beliefs or all the reasons, Rickey felt that somewhere deep inside of them all was a fear of being killed or maimed like Mr. Riley. He knew it was in him, and it was a fear that ran deep.

55

Stepping into Joe Jost's was like stepping back into the '20's. A full-length wooden bar ran along the left side of the narrow entry room, while small booths filled the right side. Between the booths and the bar stools was just enough room to pass. Unless it was filled with customers and Joe Jost's was always filled with customers. A large moose head hung on the far wall just over the entry to the back room where the pool players whiled away the their afternoons. Rickey had spent many afternoons in that smoke-filled room shooting pool and drinking beer with his buddies. Even though all of them were well under the legal drinking age, the bartender would gladly fill Tommy's order when he went to fetch the next round for them. Tommy not only carried himself much older than his 17 years, but he looked like he was 35. No one ever carded Tommy. So naturally he was a popular fellow.

As Rickey entered the door he saw that nothing had changed; that was one of the things he liked about it. The smoke-filled air, the camaraderie that seemed to fill the room as the crowd chatted amongst themselves, the moose head dust, the spider webs which hung from the top of the bar. This was a safe and comfortable place, and the smile from the bartender when you walked in affirmed it.

He saw that Bailey had gotten there first and had taken the last booth next to the back wall. It offered the most privacy in a place where privacy was not to be found. Rickey slipped into the booth nodding a "hello" to his father and noticing that two beers had been placed on the table along with the standard Joe Jost's Special; a red basket filled with straight pretzels topped with a polish sausage cut length-wise, stuffed with a slice of dill pickle around which a slice of cheese was wrapped, all wedged between two pieces of rye bread covered in tart mustard. Nothing tasted better than a Special washed down by a cold *Pabst Blue Ribbon* beer; and nobody's beer was colder than Joe Jost's.

Rickey quickly dug into the sandwich and finished it in three bites; washing it down with half the beer.

"Wow, you must be hungry. Want another?"

"Please, and a couple of their pickled eggs."

Bailey eased himself out of the booth, elbowed his way through the crowd and caught the bartender's eye. He placed Rickey's order and ordered two more beers and a couple of eggs. He thought, *What was I thinking? A Special each and a beer? I guess I wasn't thinking.* But he had been thinking a lot about so many different things, but all with a common nucleus: Rich and how he could help his son.

With one egg and half a beer each left, Rickey finally spoke up, asking, "OK, tell me why we are here."

"For the Specials, why else?" his father half joked. "They are good, but I wanted to talk to you away from your mother and in a place where I don't think we'll be overheard. And no damned music to distract us."

Rickey just nodded. With that, Bailey continued.

"Look, son, I know what you're facing and how difficult a decision it is for you. No matter what you decide, the direction of your life is forever changed. I've done some research and made some calls to old buddies of mine from the service. Afraid that didn't do much good, as they tell me the National Guard is full up and there is a waiting list, and they say it doesn't matter cause only Congressmen's kids get in now. Same for the Coast Guard; full up.

So I did some research on the four other branches; interesting stuff. By far, the safest is the Navy, and less than 15 percent of their available forces are assigned to Vietnam. The Army is the most dangerous with the Marines not far behind. The Air Force looked pretty good and the advantage to them is they have a large selection of tech training that you can do. You know, stuff like being an air traffic controller, that you can use once you are out."

Bailey sat back and looked at Rickey who hadn't said a word nor had his facial expression changed but Bailey was sure he was listening. Rickey took a small sip of his beer, fingered his shark tooth for a moment and said, "So, you want me to go?"

"Ah, no. That's not what I am saying. I am saying you have choices and on one side of the table, these are your choices. Then we have to look at the other side of the table and try and figure what is best for you."

"Do we have to do this now? I really need a break from all of it. I just want to go off and find some waves and a beach where I can cook some fish over a fire and stare at the stars. All of this is just so much bullshit." Rickey could feel anger rising in his voice and didn't want his dad to think he was angry with him. He quickly added, "Look, dad, I appreciate your concern and taking the time to look into this stuff, but can you understand how overwhelming it is?"

"Yes," Bailey replied, but his voice had an edge to it. "Yes. I can understand that but I also understand some other things. And that's why I wanted to have this conversation away from your mother. Son, don't get me wrong, but we, your mother and I, although we love you, and because we love you, we have done you a great disservice. We have let you slide for the last ten years. Maybe it started after your mother lost the baby back in '58. Or maybe it started when we realized we weren't going to have any more children and you were it.

"We wanted to make life good for you and for you to love us and for all of us to feel like a family. Everything we did, we did because we love you so much. But we have coddled you. We didn't get on you for your C's in high school. We knew you could have done much better but we didn't force you to do the work. We never forced you to look down the road and choose a college or a career. We bought you your first car and paid for the insurance. We knew you ditched school to go to the beach but we let it slide."

He paused. "Damn, I need another beer. You?"

Rickey nodded.

By then the lunch crowd had thinned out and the early outers from the offices hadn't come in yet, so Bailey quickly brought two fresh beers back to their table.

"Do you understand what I am saying?"

"Yes," Rickey replied, "and it's something I've known for awhile. Well, if not known, at least thought about. I knew what other kids were doing, they were working while I was goofing off. I knew that. And I know what you're saying. I need to grow up, be a man, and face this shit head on."

He looked down at the table, and put an errant pretzel stick back in the basket. He paused some more but his father didn't speak.

"And look, dad, I know myself. I don't react well to being pushed. Not that I think you are pushing me, far from it. I know how you are too. You like to get to the heart of things. Get the facts, read the books, identify the possibilities and get on with it. I know, and I know it's probably worked well for you. But I'm not you. I need to get to a place where I can see things clearly. And most times, that's some place quiet, alone, and it comes to me; the way to go.

"Now I don't have as much experience as you; how could I? But I have to tell you after Linda and I broke up I was a mess. I didn't have any idea of what I wanted to do, how I wanted to do it, or why I was even living. I felt so hollowed out inside. Now you may think that was foolish, and maybe it was. But that's how I felt. And the only way I could deal with it was to get some quiet time. And let me add right here how pissed I was that I couldn't take my van and head down to Mexico and camp out for a week or two. No, I had to stay here and take those bullshit courses at that half-baked college. I did the right thing. But it wasn't right for me. And trying to decide this shit right now isn't the right thing either. So what I am going to do is pack the van, head south for awhile, and try to sort things out."

With that, he finished his beer and put the glass gently down on the table. He looked at his father and his father looked back. Finally Bailey said, "OK, maybe we can talk again when you get back."

"No maybe about it."

56

Bobby was anxious. His father had told him to be at his office at 10:00 AM. The tone in his voice had said "sharp." Bobby was inclined to do what his father asked, as recently, in fact, since the episode at the Pacific Dining Car, his father had seemed to move away from him. Fewer orders, which was nice, but less trust and less of him helping with the old man's business. In fact, just the other day he suggested that Bobby take a summer's clerkship with one of LA's biggest firms. At first he thought his father was testing his loyalty but now he was pretty sure his old man wanted him out of the office. It was a quarter to eleven and he was getting a little pissed that he was left cooling his heels.

At first he opened a file and read it, then pretended to take some notes. *This stuff was pablum,* he thought. A rear-ender with $5,000 in meds; the old man's office doesn't take this crap. Maybe it was somebody's mother and he was doing her a favor. But before calling the lawyer for the defendant, he better find out the whole back story.

He tried to look busy as he didn't put it beyond his father to hide a camera to record how he reacted to being kept waiting. So he pulled some papers from his briefcase, hidden between which was last month's issue of *Barely Legal*, a porn magazine he had damned near become addicted to. He spent some time turning the pages but they started to get to him and he realized if he continued he would have to do what he always did; but he couldn't do that here. So he tucked it back into the briefcase and instead flipped through the latest issue of the *California Bar Journal*. He liked to read the back section with the names of the lawyers recently disbarred.

Just before eleven, the Master himself breezed into the office and nodding to Bobby said, "I want you to look at something." No good morning, no sorry I'm late, no nothing. It put Bobby on edge.

As he said that, he reached into his desk and pulled out a thin folder. He flipped it in Bobby's direction and said, "See anyone you know?"

Bobby slowly opened the folder, half fearing his father had pictures with that hooker he had picked up on Hollywood Boulevard a few nights ago. It wasn't that; but something that frightened him even more.

"That's South Point and that's Bobby Kennedy. It looks like the kitchen of the Ambassador Hotel right before Kennedy was killed. Where the hell did you get these?"

"That's none of your business. I recognized the kid from the Rita Rains photos but I wanted you to confirm it. Thanks. Now hand them back."

"No, wait one God damned minute. I need to know how you got these and if Rickey is in danger."

"You don't need to know but you want to know. Christ, make a proper argument. OK, I'll tell you but if I ever find out you told anyone about this, you'll meet a guy who makes Raul from the Dining Car look like a house pet. Understand?"

"Ah, maybe you shouldn't tell me. Let's just let it pass. Yes, that's Rickey Osgood, ah, Richard."

"OK, I'll tell you this much. The photos are just photos floating around the open market. No big deal. They were sent to me because the Secret Service got your boy's name and because they couldn't ID the guy in the photo and wanted to know if I knew who it was."

"Well, how did they get his name, and why you?"

"Simple, at events like this, they take down all the license plate numbers they can. They ran his name and it bounced against the Fort Lewis log. My name was on the reporting roll for Fort Lewis."

"So now what?" Bobby asked, sliding the folder back across the desk, wanting to be rid of it as quickly as possible.

"I give them the ID. They probably will want to talk to him. See if he has any information they can use at trial. No big deal. No need to worry about him."

"Trial. Who in the hell would ever take that case to trial? Fifty eye witnesses, one who took the hot gun right out of his hand. Hundreds of photos all showing the same thing. Sirhan Sirhan did it. What is there to try?"

"Bobby, you know I love you. But if you are going to pursue a legal career, do corporate work, or give opinions on bond offerings; you will never make it as a top flight litigator. You just don't have the ability to see behind the picture. Forget the full picture, what you need to look at and know is not only the picture, but what is behind the picture. What led up to the picture being taken? Who benefits if X wins, who wins if Z loses or vice versa. You always have to look at where the money goes or who gets the benefit of any event turning one way or the other.

"Let me explain it to you. These three assassinations are tied together. Maybe by some great plot, though I doubt it. But they are tied together in the public's mind. And I will grant you, the government has done a piss poor job in explaining them. So questions start, conspiracies are seen where none exist, people start questioning the very basis of our government. So the government needs to respond."

He had been standing but now moved and sat behind his desk, hands folded in front of him. Bobby felt compelled to sit in one of the client chairs and face his father.

"Let's face it, the killing of Oswald by Ruby was just too damned convenient. It appears that someone thought dead men can tell no tales and had him taken out. They must have had something damned strong on Ruby to get him to do it. Maybe he did do it on his own. But what is important is that questions remain.

"Then we have James Earl Ray. Who can argue with a defendant pleading guilty? Especially when they didn't offer any real deal. Not a bad tactic but because Ray was Ray, questions remained that the confession couldn't kill.

"Now we have Sirhan. Caught dead to right. Plenty of evidence against him, including a confession. But no. The powers that be want a trial. They want a trial so bad that if on the first day of trial Sirhan motions to withdraw his not guilty plea and pleads guilty and will stipulate to the death penalty, Judge Walker won't accept it. We must have a trial. Now I have never heard of a judge insisting on a trial when the defendant wants to plead guilty and will accept the maximum sentence. I would bet that could happen here.

"Put on a whole show and demonstrate to everyone this is on the up and up. Pretty smart. They get a big name attorney, Grant Cooper, who has that Hollywood shine on him to defend Sirhan. So what we will get is a long trial that every night will be on TV with more and more evidence coming out against Sirhan. Like a dripping faucet; drip, drip, drip, more and more

156

evidence until everyone is sick of it and well convinced he did it and did it alone."

Bobby sat slumped in his chair. His dad laid it out perfectly clear, but he never would have seen that on his own. *Maybe the old man is right and corporate is where I belong.*

"Wow, fuck me! Now that you laid it out it makes perfect sense. And by cleaning up the last case they kinda help clean up the other two. Brilliant," he paused for a second and then said, "Dad, I think I will give Latham a call. I think I might be better suited for corporate."

"Let me call Paul Weiss first and test the waters. Dave Walters, the managing partner and I play over at Wilshire sometimes."

"Thanks."

57

Before his chat with Bailey, going south was just a playful thought in the back of his mind. But now he knew that he had no real alternative. He needed to get away. Away to a place of quiet and peace and long tubes where he could find that connection to the clarity he so wanted. South now was like a mantra in his brain. It blocked out all other thoughts and desires. He knew he had to go now, and go alone.

He wanted to take Rusty but his parents convinced him that his best friend was just too old to make such a trip. He patted Rusty on the head and whispered to him, "I'll be back soon. You take care of mom and dad." With that and a lump in his throat, he walked out the door and headed for the van.

He had stocked it the night before with provisions for a few weeks; three boards, two cases of beer; five paperback books and a tablet to write notes to himself about what he saw and what he thought. At the last minute he asked his father if he could borrow his camera so he could capture on film some of the places he'd visit. Now on the floor of the van next to him was the camera bag holding the *Nikon* body, 55mm and 30mm lenses and ten rolls of film. Kicking around in the back of his head was the idea that he could write a diary-like account of his trek along with some shots of the beaches, waves and people he would meet along the way. He liked the idea as now he had a purpose and wasn't just running away.

His first night would be at Rosarito Beach, which they all called Rosie's, just south of the border. Then he had no real plan other than to wander south to Cabo San Lucas and then decide what to do after that. He wanted no schedule, no demands and most of all, no problems. Just the Ying of the Road and the Yang of the Sea. The Taoist philosophy appealed to him; keeping things in balance, and in harmony.

After ten days he found himself just north of Cabo San Lucas in a small village that called itself Todos Santo. Not more than 300 people lived there scratching a living from the sea and the parched land. They lived simple and quiet lives far removed from the cares of the people in the big cities up North. They had never heard of Vietnam, let alone the war. They didn't care about the big election up North even if they knew it would happen in a few months. Their concerns were if there would be enough rainfall to refill the wells and if when the small boats went out to sea they would come back, and come back with enough fish to feed everyone.

Rickey had found a spot a few hundred yards north of the village on a rising sand berm which gave him a good view of the sea as well as the beach. He had been camped there for a few days when she first walked up to the van. He had been eating breakfast under the pull-out tarp on the passenger side of the van. The tarp ran the length of the van and was held up by two poles on each end. This created a shaded living space where he had set up a small table and three small chairs and a cooler which he often used as a foot rest.

"Good morning," she said in perfect English, which surprised him as all he had heard here before was Spanish.

"Good morning," he replied putting the spoon down and starting to stand up. "How are you this morning?"

"Good. Got any coffee?"

"Sure. I'll trade it for a name."

"Susan, Susan Tanner from New York."

"Well, Susan Tanner from New York," Rickey said as he handed her the coffee, "you are a long way from home."

"Home is where your heart is. Or at least that's what I've heard."

"Well, where is your heart?" he paused then added, "right now."

"Right here. Where else could it be?"

And that was the beginning of a six week trip which would take them across the Baja Peninsula to La Paz and then by ferry to Mazatlan and then down the Mexican mainland hitting every good surfing spot until they reached Puerto Escondito south of Acapulco. The surf at Puerto Escondito, which the Americans call Pete's, was some of the best in the world. They called it the Mexican Pipeline comparing it to the famous surf of Hawaii. With breaks both left and right, it was both unique and challenging.

They had been camped on a ridgeline above Pete's for a few days when Rickey was hit with reality in the form of a former school mate, a guy they called Smacks. He was called this because every time he caught a wave and dropped in, he would smack his hands together in excitement.

"Hey, Smacks, how they hanging?"

Smacks broke out a big smile and wrapped his long well-muscled arms around Rickey. At 6'3" and 200 pounds he smothered Rickey in his hug. "Hey bro, so good to see you, man. What the fuck you been up to?"

"Taking a little time out. Drove down the Baja and then worked my way here. But I think this is the end of the line. I'm getting low on dinero and hell, it's mid-August."

"Well I might be able to help you with that dinero thing if you are heading back to Longo Congo. Drop off a little package for me. No big deal."

"Really, you're bringing weed up?"

"Look, let's not talk here. Why don't I come by your van tonight and we can have a few beers and catch up and I'll lay it out for ya?"

"Yeah, cool. Why don't you come around six and we'll have some dinner for you?"

"We? Not traveling alone?"

"Started out that way, but met her outside of Cabo. No worries, she's cool."

"Man, I know that. She's with you. See you at six."

As Smacks walked away Rickey didn't give a second thought to the weed, but thoughts he had pushed aside for almost two months came crashing down; Vietnam, the draft, and Bobby Kennedy with a hole in his head.

58

He was a few hundred clicks north of Acapulco when it hit him. He was alone for the first time in months. The low level roar of the little air-cooled engine filled the van with a white noise that he had now associated with travel and new experiences. The van constantly swaying was another reminder that he was underway; moving on to that next chapter in his life. He knew this one would close in a few days, and he also knew that he hadn't taken care of the business that had prompted the trip in the first place. *But hey*, he thought to himself, *Susan had a lot to do with that*. And she had, but he also knew that he had used her as an excuse so as not to deal with his problems. He did not want to talk to her about them as he hadn't wanted to spoil their time together. Their interlude of sun, sea and sex was wonderful and he didn't want the war, the draft or Bobby Kennedy's blood to stain that. *Package and put it away*, he told himself. It was a special slice of life to be remembered.

As he'd lived it, he knew it was just that; a passage in time that would not last. She was great fun, a pretty fair surfer, a wonderful lover and a fair cook. But best of all, they got along together; they fit. Rickey saw that, he knew that the casual way they moved together was unique. But he didn't love her. That feeling he had for both Marsha and Linda just didn't happen for him; and he suspected it didn't happen for her either.

As he drove that long ribbon of highway north, with the fuzz-ridden Mexican music barely audible over the engine noise and the hot air blazing into his face from the downed side window, he flashed back to the scene outside his van just three nights ago.

Rickey had built a fire in the small bar-b-que and its glow lit the area under the tarp with a smoky yellow haze. Smacks had left after outlining the basic arrangement if Rickey wanted to carry some product back home. He would pay him $500 to move twenty bricks. He explained that each brick was a kilo; 2.2 pounds and would take up the space of a single shoe; about a size nine.

Smacks would give $250 now and $250 on the other end. The way it worked, Smacks explained, is he had this special tool which pumped the grass into a really small package then they vacuum-packed it and triple sealed it. They would hide it in various parts of the van. Rickey remembered Smacks asking if he had a water tank in the van. "Yeah, holds about ten gallons."

"Great, we can stash most of it in there. If the cops check it, it will still pump out water. We will leave some space between the bricks. They are sealed so they won't get wet. We'll find a place for the rest."

Then he continued on, "Once you get to Long Beach you will call a number I will give you and thirty minutes later you park the van behind Bob's Big Boy on Bellflower. Leave the keys on the driver's visor. Go in get a burger, whatever. Kill about 45 minutes at least. The van will be in the same spot, the $250 will be on the visor with the keys."

They agreed Rickey would think about it overnight and let him know in the morning. Susan hadn't said a word during the discussion but now piped up, "You going to do it?"

"I'm not sure but the money sure is good, and I have to make that drive anyway."

"I'm glad you said I as I guess you know I can't go with you."

"You mean the weed?"

"No Rickey, I mean I can't go back to the States with you. This has been fun but we both knew it wasn't going to last. Besides, I like living down here. I like being away from all the noise, the traffic, the TV's, but mostly I like the people down here better than the people up there. Those folks, jerking her head toward the north, are all about making money and seeing who has more stuff. No thanks. I prefer being down here with people who are more interested in the sun, and stars, and the sea than who is who at the country club and who just got divorced, and who is cheating on whom. I grew up with that shit and I don't want it ever again. And please don't tell me LA's not like that."

"No, I couldn't say that. But you're right, this has been fun but it's time for me to head home."

She smiled at him, and came over to where he was seated and extended a hand. He took it, and followed her into bed.

It was a pleasant memory and he let it play over and over in his mind as the miles rolled on under his wheels.

And as the miles clicked off, Rickey began to think about those things he had pushed aside for so long. Last night before going to sleep, he had re-read his father's letter by the dim light of the candle he had lit and set on the stovetop. That was his third reading of the letter and he had to smile at his father's approach. There were pages with graphs and pie charts and any number of things to explain why one branch of the service was better than another. He knew his dad always thought the answer was in the numbers. You just had to look at them the right way and they would explain everything.

But it wasn't which branch, that was clear to Rickey. The Navy was where he would go, if he was going. It was the safest, the cleanest, had the best food and he could travel. Yes, the Navy was the ticket. He would never go into the Army or Marines. Death before dishonor and all that bullshit; who is to say what is dishonor but we all damn well sure know what death is. No, the Navy is where he would fit best. But Christ, four years is a long time; four years ago I was 16 and in 11th grade and that seems like a lifetime ago.

But the bigger question was to go at all.

The Mexican landscape rolled by unnoticed as he continued his meditation. He asked himself, *Are you really against the war or is it more like you are afraid of it?* He knew the reasons to be against the war and could recite them off the top of his head. But somehow they seemed shallow and contrived compared to the sacrifice Mr. Riley made or those of his classmates. Maybe Harris is right, work within the system rather than run. But running had several advantages: like staying alive and being free. But one huge disadvantage: he would never see his parents again, and that would destroy his mother. He couldn't do that. He wouldn't do that. *No, the Navy is the smart play, and who knows, maybe I will like it.*

And as he approached the checkpoint at the border, he thought, *Hell, it may all be moot.*

59

Bobby was a bit winded after climbing the two flights of stairs from the lower parking garage. His hand twitched as it reached to open the door to his father's office. Just as he touched the knob, a voice he didn't recognize boomed out, "Fuck you, Raymond! After all they've done for you, you're telling me you won't help them? I don't want to be the messenger that delivers that note to them. Christ, are you crazy?"

In a calm and deliberate voice, Bobby's father replied, "Jason, it's not a question of wanting to, I just don't know anything more which would help them. I have told you all I know about that kid...what's his silly name? Southpaw or some damn thing. I just have no further information about him. Last I heard, he was down in Mexico chasing waves and pussy."

"Now see, that's a new piece of information."

"I already told you he was in Mexico, traveling around in his camper."

"No, the pussy part. Anyone you know? Have a name?"

"For Christ's sake...I was just making a generalization. Everyone his age is chasing pussy. No, I have no idea if he caught any. A name; give me a break."

"No, you should give yourself a break, Raymond, because just as fast as you built this firm with the help of our friends, you could lose it."

"Oh, so now you are threatening me? Come on! They all know I appreciate the support they have given us over the years. But don't forget, I've done a lot for them, too."

"Exactly, Ray. That's what I am talking about. Now they need a little help from you."

"What is it that you want from me?"

"It's not what I want, Ray. Please remember I'm on your side. It's what they want."

"And, what exactly is that...and no bullshit about information. What do they want?"

"You know, they want the kid, Rickey. They feel they need to, well, you know, get more information."

"Now you are bullshitting. They have all the information they need... hell, all that there is. He's a not-too-bright, weed-smoking surfer, who couldn't maintain his student deferment status at a shit-bird JC, and now is going to be inducted tomorrow morning downtown. You know where he lives, what he drives, where his parents live and work, where he works; hell, you even know his favorite places to surf. What the fuck else do you want? It's not information, that's for damned sure."

"Look, that's what they tell me. But, I've been around and so have you. We both know they want the kid in a room. They want to sweat him for what he saw that night."

"And, then?"

"Hey, I am not on that committee. My job is to bring him in. Period. Then I am done. You're done when you help me bring him in. Pretty fucking simple."

"OK, what is it exactly you want me to do?"

"Well, we think we have a good chance to grab him at the Induction Center after he does the swearing in thing. Our intel is he has applied to the Navy and they have given him the OK to join. What's going to happen is that after he is sworn in, the officer in charge will take him to a separate room isolated from the others. Then he will be told that the Navy has rejected his application because of his smoking weed, and he is being sent to Fort Lewis that afternoon, as he has been assigned to an Army platoon for training, and he can call his parents and tell them where he is going."

"So, they are going to DB-1 him?"

"I don't think so. I think they will take him to a secure location and find out what he saw that night."

"And, then?"

"Who knows? But if I was to hazard a guess, it would be something like a DB-1 situation; or a training accident."

"OK, but you haven't told me exactly what you want me to do."

"All they want from you is the assurance that if we miss him tomorrow at the Induction Center, you will help us bring him in."

"And how would I do that?"

"Have your son arrange to meet him. They met before, as you know. Hell, they had breakfast together the day before all this shit started. The kid trusts your boy. If he called him and said meet me at the what-the-fuck-ever, the kid would come. We take him there. It's safe, it's clean. Not as good as the Induction Center, but it's doable. And, we are working on a tight timeline."

"OK, I will talk to Bobby. I am sure it won't be a problem. But I can't let him know the back-story. I will have to come up with something but I know Bobby will be OK with it if he thinks no harm will come to the kid. Otherwise, I can't guarantee it."

"I don't give a shit how you do it. Just do it."

"Fine. But maybe if you jackasses don't fail tomorrow, I won't have to do anything. So, good luck. Now, I need to get back to my real job."

"OK, Ray. I'm sure all this will be just fine. See you later."

Bobby stood frozen at the door in a trance. He knew his father sometimes played the ball out of bounds, but he had no idea he was in this deep. *Christ, and now he's pulling me in. Bobby, you fool, he has been pulling you in for years. What about that whole Rita Rains Rancho Park deal? Sober up, son, you've been played and he will continue to play you for as long as it suits him.* "Well, fuck that!" He muttered under his breath, "two can play that game."

Quickly, he fled down the stairs and jumped into the *Healey*. Turning out of the parking lot onto Sunset heading west, he thought, *Right, but he plays chess, and I play checkers.*

60

Christ, these old neighborhoods get really dark with all of the low hanging trees, he thought, as he slipped the *Healey* in neutral and coasted the last block and a half toward the Osgood's home. He could see Rickey's van out front, which pleased him to no end; he had been fearful that Rickey might be somewhere else, somewhere where he couldn't find him. But, he was here, and Bobby relaxed as he turned off the headlights 50 yards from the van.

He shut the engine off and sat for a moment, listening to the silence of the street. No dogs barking, no traffic, no TV's, no radios playing the latest hits, nothing but the crickets and they would hardly cover any sounds he would make. Looking around, all the homes were dark except for a few front porch lights, and none showed any signs of life. *What are you afraid of dipshit? You're leaving a note for a friend. No crime here. No one cares. Just get on with it.*

Carefully, he opened the *Healey*'s door and walked quietly across the darkened street to the van. Good old Rickey - the door was again open and he slipped the note under the mat, leaving just enough showing so that he would notice it.

He started the *Healey* and slowly drove away, somehow feeling like a thief. He knew what he was doing was the right thing. South Point did not deserve what his father's friends had in store for him. Yet, the sense of guilt and betrayal toward his father clung to him like a bad smell and with each breath, his sense of anxiousness increased.

Even with the top down and the chilly fall air blasting him as he roared north on the San Diego Freeway, he couldn't escape the feeling that he had done something wrong. Not only had he betrayed his father, but put himself in harm's way in a major way. If his father's friends ever had the slightest thought that he had helped Rickey, they would most likely kill him. The mere thought caused his hands to tremble and once he almost lost control of the car.

"This has to stop!" he screamed to himself over the sound of the wind and the roar of the trucks. *God damn, think like your old man, not some pussy. Outthink the motherfuckers. Out game them. Hell, how hard can it be, if they are worrying about picking up a twenty year old kid who is half-stoned most of the time? What would Ray do?*

The sign for Olympic Boulevard snapped him into the present. *Hell, I've been driving on autopilot this whole fucking way. Christ, did I get lucky.* He downshifted and exited at Olympic and headed to Chasen's. *Some of Maude's chili and a few drinks should clear my head and help me focus,* he thought, as he ran the red light at Westwood.

Maude Chasen greeted him warmly and asked about his mother and father as she led him to a small booth adjacent to the far end of the bar. He liked this booth; one she had given him many times before. It afforded him a bit of privacy, while at the same time giving him a clear view of most of the bar and part of the smaller dining room.

He scanned the room to see if there were any familiar faces or friends. To his relief, he saw no one who would feel obliged to come over and chat. He was in no mood for chatting with anyone. Even that pretty blonde at the end of the bar; he knew she was a small player in the movies but he couldn't put a name to her face. *Ah! but what a face. Maybe some other night but not tonight. No, tonight was for planning.*

Walter brought him his *Dimple*-on-the-rocks without him asking. Walter knew what he liked, and asked as he placed the drink in from of him, "Steak or chili tonight?"

"Chili, please, Walter, with a small side salad." And with that Bobby was alone, in a crowd with his thoughts.

As he sipped the *Dimple*, he saw Peter Lawford across the bar from the small dining room. *What a handsome man,* he thought to himself as his eyes wandered over the crowd. *What was that movie he had been in? The one in Vegas with Sinatra and Dean Martin. Oh yeah, 'Oceans 11.' They stole a bundle of money only to lose it when they tried to move it out of town in a coffin. Smart plan until the wife decided to cremate the remains instead of shipping them back to wherever the fuck they came from. Deception had been the basis of their scheme: make things appear not as they are, but as you want them to be.*

The seed of a plan began to form in Bobby's brain. The key would be deception too. Make them think Rickey is in one place, or heading for one place, while in fact, he was going elsewhere.

As he finished the second *Dimple* and wiped the last bit of chili from the bowl with a piece of sour dough bread; he had a plan.

The start would be rough, and it would only get rougher from there. Now, he had to convince Rickey.

61

After being back for a few days, Rickey with his parents sat down after dinner around the large dining room table. The dishes had been cleared but the glasses remained each with something waiting to be sipped. Rickey looked at his parents and said, "First, thanks for being so understanding and letting me go down to Mexico and sort through things. Also thanks for sending me that money, it really, really helped and I want to repay you now." Pulling his wallet off his hip, Rickey carefully took five twenty dollar bills out and handed them to his father. Bailey didn't reach for them and instead said, "No, Rich, we were happy to do it. There is no need to repay us. We're just glad you had a good time and were able to work out what you want to do."

"Well, I think the best thing is the Navy. I have an appointment tomorrow with the recruiter and what they tell me, I will still have to go to the Induction Center but they will give me some papers and that will be that. I'll know more after I meet with them."

Maggie spoke for the first time, "Let me understand this. First you go to the Navy and meet with them. If that works out then you go to the Induction Center the next day?"

"Yeah, mom, that's right."

"And the Navy is going to give you some papers which will tell the people at the Induction Center you're going into the Navy?

"Right."

"But you won't be in the Navy yet, right? It's you saying you will go and the Navy saying they will take you. Right?"

"Well, I guess. I mean I guess they do this all the time. It sounded easy. But I'll know more in the morning."

"OK but I want you to call us at the office right after you meet them. OK?"

"Yeah, sure mom."

The next morning Rickey drove to the Navy's recruiting office just off Atlantic on 3rd Avenue and met with two recruiters who explained things more fully but it all sounded like it ended up in the same place. After he went to the Induction Center he would report here, either that afternoon or the next day. At that time, he would be sworn into the service and given orders to report. They estimated that he would be ordered to report sometime around the middle of November but they had no idea where he would go for his basic training. They gave him some forms to fill out and a green sheet of paper and told him to show that to the officer in charge at the Induction Center.

He called his folks as he promised and then drove promptly to the beach. He knew that by now the on-shore breeze had destroyed any surf there was, but he just wanted to sit on his board and watch the waves roll in. It might be one of his last chances for a long while.

62

The next morning he felt really good and relaxed. For the first time in a long while the weight of "The Decision" had lifted and he felt a freedom he thought he had lost. That feeling didn't last long.

As he got into the van to head out to the Induction Center he saw an envelope corner sticking out from under the coco mat. "What is this?" he asked as he reached down and picked up the plain white envelope with a large R written across the front. He tore it open and pulled out a single sheet of white paper with handwriting on it and he began to read:

> *Burn this once you have read it. I mean it. And don't tell anyone, no one, about it. I can't tell you everything but you could be in grave danger. There is this program the government has for punishing war protesters. It's called BD-1. In a nutshell, they take you from the Induction Center and fly you to Vietnam. They put you in a platoon and send you out into the jungle on a Search and Destroy mission; generally on point. Life expectancy is less than an hour. They have your name because of the thing with Rita Rains at Rancho Park. They have a photo of you near Kennedy when he was shot. The FBI or Secret Service is looking for you as are the people from Fort Lewis, and it's not just to talk. Not sure going into the Induction Center today is a good idea.*
> *Good luck, and burn this.*

Rickey's hands were shaking violently as he put the letter on the seat next to him. A wave of nausea hit him and tossed his morning coffee up into his throat. He was able to gag it back down. He felt himself start to slide into a deep depression. He began pounding the wheel with both hands and shouting, "God damn!" into the morning air.

Slowly he regained some sense of composure, and started the van. He got on the 405 north on auto pilot for he wasn't really driving but moving through traffic as if guided by some invisible hand. Off the 405 to the Harbor north, off on 6th and across to Center. He had planned out the route on the Thomas Guide Map the night before. That seemed ages ago now. He was right back where he had been before but now there was a very steep downside. He was frightened and could smell his own fear.

He parked one block south of the Induction Center and walked up two blocks before he found a pay phone. He dialed his father's office, praying to God Almighty that he was there and not busy. His mother answered, "Insurance office, good morning."

"Mom, it's me. I need to talk to dad right now."

"Rickey, he is with a client..."

Rickey cut her off, "No mom, I have to talk with him right now. This is urgent."

"You're scaring me."

"Well, I'm scared so I'm sorry but I have to talk to dad."

The phone went silent and Rickey was afraid he had lost the connection. He checked the dimes and quarters in his fist, just as his dad came on the line. "Rich, what the hell is going on? Your mother is as white as a sheet."

"Dad, I don't know but I wanna read you something. I found it in my van this morning. Please just listen," and he began to read the note.

His father was stone silent until he finished. "Fort Lewis, are you sure, not Louis like the city but Lewis? Oh, OK, just wanted to be clear. Well that sounds crazy, the American government doesn't just grab people off the streets and whisk them out of the country. We have courts and rights, that's third world stuff, not here in America. Do you know who wrote it?"

"Well it's not signed but I have a guess."

"Who?"

"This guy named Bobby, I forget his full name, but his dad is some big shot lawyer to the stars and super well connected. He was the one with Rita Rains when she changed her story about that night I hit the cop at the park. I don't know for a fact it's him but I think it is."

"Does he have any reason to jerk you around?"

"I don't think so. I think he and Marsha may have had something going on at some point, I really don't know. I saw him back in June and it was all cool between us. We had breakfast together before Kennedy's speech at Long Beach State. I don't think this is a prank. He told me to burn it; twice. Sounds like he's afraid someone might find out he warned me."

"Well I don't know. But I think if you do what you were going to do, join the Navy, they would have no reason to screw with you. Look, you were never a big protester. You had that thing at Rancho Park but hell that was almost a year and a half ago. I don't think anyone cares. And the Kennedy thing, if they really wanted you they would have come to the house and asked us. No, I think you're fine. But you have to do what you are comfortable with and what you think is right. Your mom and I will stand behind whatever decision you make. OK? I got a client waiting."

"Yeah sure, dad, and thanks. I feel much better." As he hung up he could hear the coins drop into the box and he felt like dropping down a hole, too.

He looked at his watch: 7:15. Almost two hours before he had to report. He decided to walk around a bit and maybe find a place to get some coffee. He wanted to wash the taste of bile out of his mouth and no amount of cigarettes seemed to be doing the job.

Time passed without him knowing it and now it was 8:50. Gut check time. He had been standing in this same side street, an alley really, for awhile now; that he knew. He still did not have a plan. Something deep inside him screamed not to go into the Induction Center. Yes the war was wrong, there was no debate on that, and joining the Navy was supporting the war any way you sliced it. But running would kill his mother; well maybe if she thought he was running from possible assassins rather than just running to protest. Maybe that would help her. But still he would have to disappear. How could he do that? "Fuck, fuck, fuck," he screamed silently to himself.

He reached for another smoke but found only an empty pack. *Ah*, he thought, *there's another pack in the van.* He walked out of the side street and toward his van. He looked around and smiled. It was a beautiful morning, no guys in black jumpsuits lurking about, no one looking at him weird. No, just another nice day in LA. He was going to get his smokes, walk back up the hill and go into the Induction Center and tell them he was signed up for the Navy. He felt good, he felt strong.

He opened the big side door on the van and reached in and grabbed the pack off the shelf under the stove. As he turned, a voice said, "Hey Rickey." He turned further and all he could see was a black towel being pushed against his face. He smelled the overpowering scent of violets and then everything went black.

63

"Hey amigo, wake up." The voice came to Rickey from far away and it had a slight Mexican sound to it. He tried to open his eyes but his eyelids felt like they weighed two tons. Slowly, he was able to open them, but everything was out of focus; large round balls of color with soft edges.

Again, the voice spoke to him, "Jefe, wake the fuck up!" And he felt ice cold water hit his face. It had the desired effect, as all at once, his vision cleared and his eyes were wide open. *What the fuck?* he thought, "Where am I?"

"East LA. Ever been east of downtown before, homie?"

"Ah, no, don't think so. Why am I here? Who are you guys, anyway?" Rickey blurted out after casting a look around the room which was filled with a crew of about ten, all of whom looked like they'd seen the inside of a prison at one time or the other.

"Fuck we know. Roberto asked us to escort you to a safe place. And Roberto is a friend, so we did. Don't worry, amigo, you're among friends. No one here wants to hurt you...except maybe Skinny over there," nodding to a guy who buried the chair he was sitting in with his bulk. "But fuck, Skinny wants to hurt everyone, right Skinny?"

Rickey looked over toward Skinny but there was no reaction; just a blank stare. Rickey took a deep breath and looked over the room. *What the fuck have I gotten myself into? And who the hell is Roberto?* "Where is my van, and do you have a smoke?"

"It's right outside, out in back, and yeah...Ice, give the man a smoke."

They sat in silence which seemed to Rickey to last forever but according to the clock behind the sofa, was only twenty minutes before Bobby came blowing into the room. He was carrying three cases of beer and had a few bottles stacked on top of them; he was winded from the climb up the stairs from the street.

In a breathy voice, he said, "Greetings, one and all. I see you found my friend. Gracias! Man, thank you my friend for this favor. I know it was last minute, but it was so important. Here, I brought a few things for your crew and this, too." Bobby handed a thin brown envelope to a guy he called J-man and with that, turned to Rickey.

"How you doing, man?" He asked it like Rickey had just come off the dance floor, not like a man who had just been kidnapped off a public street.

"What the fuck, Bobby? You tell me. What is this about? Who are these guys and why did they grab me? I'm missing my time at the Induction Center which means I'm screwed. They might not let me join the Navy now, and I'll get stuck in the God-damned Army!" Rickey was shaking as he let loose on Bobby and if his hands weren't tied behind him, he would have reached out and torn Bobby's face off.

Bobby calmly took his abuse and when Rickey seemed spent, Bobby put his hands on Rickey's shoulders and said simply, "You were never going into the Navy. They had other plans for you."

He said this so calmly and yet with such conviction, Rickey immediately relaxed and slumped down into the armchair. After a few seconds, he looked up at Bobby and said, "Kennedy?" Bobby nodded and from that moment on, Rickey knew his life was changed forever.

64

They were seated in the back booth of El Gato, a dumpy Mexican restaurant in the heart of East LA, which was famous for its green corn tamales. The remains of lunch were spread out on the table between them and each clung to his bottle of beer like it was an anchoring post.

"This is some heavy shit, Bobby. You sure it's true?"

"Man, like I said, I stood just outside my father's office door and I could hear every damned word. Why would I make it up? Do you know how risky this is for me? If a word of this leaks out and gets back to my father's associates...fuck, I'm probably dead."

"Who are these guys, these friends of your father's? I mean, who the hell is your father?"

"Well, my dad is a very well respected lawyer whose clients are all very respectable. He belongs to all the best clubs and knows the Governor on a first name basis. But he comes from a town back East where, let's just say there is a certain mob influence. He grew up there. He trained in a small law firm there which had special clients. They got to know him. And after awhile, they saw a bright kid who they could trust so they helped him get started. I don't know if it was their idea or his to come out to LA but that's where he landed and started his own practice which, in a very short time, had some big named clients. I don't know how they are connected to the Kennedy shooting, either one for that matter, but I do know they have some interest in it. Maybe not for themselves but as a favor or maybe on their own or maybe together with someone else. But the why doesn't matter. What matters is they are involved and that's all there is to it."

"Sorry, man, I didn't mean to doubt you. But it all sounds so off the wall. Why would they go to all the trouble over me? I don't know jack shit. I didn't see anything. Maybe I should just go talk to them...tell them what I know and that will be that."

Bobby looked around and then spoke so softly Rickey could barely hear him. "Dude, they will do things to you that will make you tell them what they want to hear even if it isn't true. You dig me? And if there is anything you are holding back, they will get that and then start digging for more. You walk in there and say X, Y and Z, they will want the rest of the alphabet before they are done. No, that's not a plan unless you've got a death wish."

Rickey's legs were sweaty and sticking to the cheap vinyl seat covers. He felt seasick and unstable. But most of all, he felt scared. "So what is the plan? Do you have a plan? But before you lay out your brilliant plan, tell me why you are doing this. We hardly know each other."

Bobby shifted in his seat and looked for the waitress. "I'll be right back," he said, as he got up and left to find the waitress, another beer, and the restroom, but not necessarily in that order. He was buying time.

Bobby sat two fresh beers on the table which had been cleared while he was gone. "Good question. I am not sure there is one answer. But, I do know this: you do not deserve what they have in mind for you, regardless of what you may have seen. I am tired of watching my father use his influence to hurt people who have done nothing to hurt anyone. I am sick of watching the powerful fucks in this city get away with murder while guys like you get screwed for doing nothing wrong. And, I know Marsha loved you. She never loved me, but that didn't stop me from wanting her. So, if I can help you, I am helping her, and that's a big deal to me. I don't know if that answers your question. I am not sure if I have a single simple answer; it's mixed together. But, bottom line, I like you and I don't want to see you get hurt."

Rickey looked up at Bobby, who had never sat down while he spoke, and simply said, "Thank you, man," then hung his head and reached for the pack of *Luckys* across the table.

Bobby sat down, and took a long pull from his *Budweiser* long neck bottle and felt the icy beer flow all the way past his throat and into his gut. "Here's my idea; tell me what you think."

65

They walked out of El Gato into the harsh glare of the low setting sun fighting its way through the smog. The whole scene had an other-worldly feeling about it, or maybe it was just Rickey's imagination.

"Look, now that they haven't picked you up at the Induction Center, my old man will be looking for me, so I had better check in."

"Yeah, cool. I think I will head up to Malibu and spend the night. Figure things out. Your plan is a good one, but I need to sort through the details like where to go first, north or south, and like you said, get a new ID or just go with my own. I need to punch those things together. Say, man, thanks for your help and stay cool."

With that, Rickey walked toward his van and never looked back at Bobby. He hoped he would never see him again. He pulled out of the parking lot and drove across the median and entered the 10 Freeway west; he would drive until he saw the sea.

He came out of the tunnel where the freeway meets Coast Highway in Santa Monica just as the sun was burying itself in the Pacific Ocean. As he drove north past the large homes on the beach, he thought of his parents and how worried they must be. He had promised to call hours ago. He pulled into the Safeway parking lot at Sunset and Coast Highway and saw the long line of pay phones along the south wall; he would need some change.

"Dad, it's me, Rickey. Dad, don't say a thing, just listen. That note I read to you this morning, well, it was true. I am free at the moment but I don't know if they have your phone tapped or not. I need to see you. Go to a pay phone and call me on this number, 213-555-1711. I'll be waiting." As Rickey hung up, he scanned the parking lot, looking for who knows what. It was to become a habit, even though it never seemed to satisfy his anxiety.

As he waited, he thought about his options, which were basically three. Leave the country, which meant Canada or Mexico, stay and hide in plain sight, or get caught and hope to come out of it OK. The third option, at least according to Bobby, was not worth considering; they most likely would kill him. So, Canada/Mexico or stay and hide in plain sight. But how could he hide in plain sight? He would have to totally change who he was, where he lived, what he loved. Basically start over. Move to the Midwest and live on a farm, or go to Green Bay and just stay indoors ten months of the year. Hide in front of the TV. No thanks. If he was going to go, then go where he could still be himself. What was the point if they robbed him of *Him*; he might as well be dead.

Before he could go any further, the jarring ring of the phone snapped him back to the now. "Ah, yeah, Dad? OK, good. Look, this is a very bad situation and I need to see you and work out a solution. I will explain all the details when you get here, but please bring some money with you. Yeah, I know the banks are closed, but even a fifty would help and we can deal with the rest of it later. Yeah, I understand. I'm at Sunset and Pacific Coast Highway, at the Safeway. OK, right, I know where that is, Sunset and the 405, the Holiday Inn. I will be there by 8:00. And, ah, thanks, Dad."

As he sat in the van outside the Holiday Inn, he listened to Tim Buckley singing a song called *Wings*, which had a line, 'and one day, the questions die and on wings of chance, you fly.' Rickey felt they played that song just for him. It was a low watt station out of Santa Monica Junior College; a station he couldn't get in Long Beach. They played other artists whom he hadn't heard of and all of them had a distinct style and all were mellow. Mellow was what Rickey needed right now.

Headlamps flashed across the driveway and Rickey recognized the *Buick* and eased the van in behind it to follow his father. They climbed up the hills along Mandeville Canyon until his father abruptly turned off of Sunset onto a small street without lights. Slowly, they crawled up the canyon until they turned into a large driveway which fronted a house that hung suspended over the side of the hill. The lights of LA spread across the horizon like a blanket of stars and the air smelled of eucalyptus trees and night blooming jasmine. For some reason, Rickey felt special just being there; he could imagine what the people who lived here must feel.

His father stepped out of the *Buick* with a set of keys in his right hand and a large grocery bag held high in his left and nodded to Rickey. For a moment, Rickey was too stunned to react. *What is going on here?* But quickly he recovered and grabbed the brown bag from his father and said, "Thanks for coming. I know it's a long way."

"Of course I was coming. The only problem I had was preventing your mother from coming too. She is very worried and upset and has been praying since you called. I haven't even told her about the letter. I just told her there was some SNAFU with the Navy and we needed to work it out. No sense in making her more upset."

"Whose house?"

"A friend of mine from the war. He's in DC right now; said I could use it tonight if I wanted."

Rickey nodded but something didn't quite ring true. *How had Bailey gotten the keys before getting to the house. Fuck it,* he thought, *I need him and he is here. What else matters?*

Bailey opened the front door and found the light switch without any problem. The interior of the house was even more impressive than the outside. The front door opened onto a raised platform. The main floor expanded across a good 60 feet to a wall of glass which framed the City of the Angels in a spectacular display of lights. Rickey imagined that in the morning they could see the ocean too. Impressive, and a reminder of what people with money and power could have.

Bailey went into the kitchen and started pulling items out of the shopping bag and arranging them on the counter. The second thing out of the bag was an expensive bottle of whiskey. "A gift for our host." Bailey added quickly, "We are stuck with *Miller's High Life*. I thought the name suited our surroundings."

Rickey chuckled at his father's attempt at humor, but it had its desired effect; the room seemed lighter than moments before. Bailey pulled two beers from the six pack and put the rest into the refrigerator along with some cold cuts and fruit. *He must think we will be here awhile,* Rickey mused to himself. *But, hey, why not?*

Bailey took a seat in a big recliner, leaned back and gave Rickey a serious look and said, "OK, tell me all of it."

He paused, trying to figure out where to start and then decided to start at the beginning; with finding the note under the mat. *Hard to believe that was this morning,* he thought to himself; *feels like a long time ago.*

He told Bailey everything he could remember about the day. For the most part, his father sat and nodded, taking an occasional sip of beer and listening without saying much. A few times, he asked something be repeated or for Rickey to rephrase it, but for the most part, he just listened.

Rickey was exhausted and felt he couldn't talk anymore when his father dropped the bomb on him. "OK, Rich, now tell me what you really saw at the Ambassador that night. All of it."

Rickey just froze. *How the hell did he know he had held back some critical details? How could he know that? Fuck me!*

"I need to go to the can first. I'll be right back." He had no idea where the bathrooms were, so blindly took the first hallway he found and luckily just there on the left was a small service bath. He barely got the door shut before the dry heaves started. Over and over again until his sides ached and his mouth was dry. Finally, he got control of himself, and held his hands under the water and scooped up some to splash on his face and wet his lips.

What is going on here? Well, dude, you either trust your dad or you don't. Christ, Rickey, get a hold of yourself. It's Bailey, your father. Climb down off the walls and have him help you figure out what to do next. "OK, OK," he muttered as he opened the door and headed toward the kitchen for another beer.

Rickey sat and stared out at the lights of the city and it made him feel very small and unimportant. But, apparently, some people thought he was very important; and that scared him.

"OK, so I remember all the stuff you told me before. About going up there alone, being in the ballroom, the noise, the beer, the pretty girl. I've got the picture there, but I want you to tell me every single thing you can remember from the time you entered the pantry downstairs. Every detail, Rich, tell me everything."

"Well, it was hot and crowded, but not at first. At first, it was basically empty, I mean when she took me down there. But right after, the room started to fill up, and I was pushed aside. I was being pushed by the crowd against a big concrete post and I was afraid of getting crushed, so I ducked under this big table that was there, and came up on the other side. As soon as I came up and turned around, I realized I was right behind Bobby Kennedy. His back was to me, but I knew it was him. He was reaching out, shaking hands with someone when I was pushed hard from behind; this caused me to bend over the top of the table. I remember clearly, because I was afraid my nose was going to smash into the tabletop. I turned my head to the right and I saw...I saw...Oh! man, this is hard. I saw a gun in the hand of a white guy. He was right handed and the gun's barrel was about an inch from the back of Bobby's head, by his right ear. Man, it's like it's in slow motion in my brain. I can see his hand sticking out from a pale pink shirt, which was covered by a dark blue jacket. The gun looked small in his hand. His fingers wrapped all the way around it. I saw a gold ring that was oval shaped with a dark stone in the center of it with the letter C and on the side, I saw a '53' engraved. While I am watching this, I am hearing shots being fired. Pop, Pop, Pop, Pop. But then, there is a cracking sound, different than all the others. The man next to me must have pulled the trigger. One shot. And I saw Bobby's head jerk forward. The clearest thing I remember is that stream of blood squirting out of his head. God, it was awful."

He looked at his father but couldn't say another word. His palms were dripping sweat and he could feel the dampness soaking through his shirt. He was spent.

Bailey didn't say a word for a very long time. Then, all he said was, "Shit."

66

Rickey awoke to the sun shining in his face. He was in the same chair he had been sitting in when he told Bailey about the Bobby Kennedy killing. He forced himself out of the chair, and it seemed every one of his joints cracked or popped as he straightened up. *Christ, I feel like shit. Where am I?* Then it all came back to him. *Where I am is on the fucking run from some insane guys who are connected to the government. Nowhere to hide but I can run, and that's what I am going to do.* For some reason, this came as an epiphany to him. All day yesterday, he fought the idea like it was the plague; now it seemed not only simple, but the only sensible thing to do. Just get lost; leave no tracks behind.

He heard Bailey in the shower and suddenly he could almost feel the hot water tingling his skin and immediately that sounded like the best idea in the world. He had no idea where he could find another bathroom but figured a house this size had plenty.

Two showers and 30 minutes later, Rickey walked into the kitchen to find Bailey sitting in the breakfast nook drinking coffee. He nodded at Rickey and jerked his head toward the stove to indicate there was coffee waiting for him.

As he lowered himself into the breakfast nook, his knee joints creaking, Rickey looked at his father, and asked, "Shit. Really? Shit? That's all you have to say?"

"Well, what do you want me to say, Rich? You want me to sugar coat it and tell you everything will be just fine? Pamper you some more? Pretend that your ass isn't on the line and all we have to do is be quiet and everything will be roses? Is that what you want?" His voice was raising with each additional question, and his face was getting redder and redder.

"No, I don't expect that. I just was surprised by your response, that's all."

"Really? I will tell you what my reaction should have been. I should have torn you a new one for lying to me. And don't say you didn't lie. I asked you to tell me what happened and you withheld the most important piece of information. Why would you do that? Are you just stupid? Or has all that weed you smoke so clouded your brain that you can't think straight?"

Rickey was now nearly in tears. His hands were shaking and there was a break in his voice when he spoke. "I don't know. I guess I thought if I just kept it to myself that no one would know and it would be alright. I should have told you, I know that. But, reliving that moment is hard, really hard."

"Do you know why these people are looking for you? Do you understand why they must find you and kill you? And don't think for a second, they won't. They don't give a damn about what you know. All they care about is that you don't tell anyone. Dead people tell no tales, as the saying goes. Do you understand why it is so important to them to find you?"

"Ah, well cuz I saw someone shoot Bobby Kennedy?"

"No, Rich. Everyone knows Bobby got shot. But the official version, like JFK and Martin Luther King, Jr., is that Bobby was shot by a lone gunman. Just one crazy person acting alone. What you saw means there was a second gunman. It blows their whole story apart. And they have been selling the lone gunman story since Dallas; they can't change stories now. If their story fails, it calls into question the official version of the two other killings. In fact, it basically confirms what people already suspect. The entire credibility of the government turns on the lone gunman theory. That's why they want you dead."

"So, what do we do?"

"You said your friend Bobby had a plan. What is that?"

"Well, first of all, I don't know that I can trust him. Yeah, he yarded me out of the scene at the Induction Center. But, I'm not sure why. I asked him, point blank, and basically, he said he likes me. So, he's going to put his ass on the line because he likes me? Doesn't make sense. There are two ways to look at it. One, he does like me and thinks his father and his associates are over-reacting and they should just leave me alone to smoke and surf and drift along. Don't! I know that's what you think and I know other people think the same thing. And, maybe it's true.

Or Bobby is angling to make himself more important by just helping his father, but either way, helping dodge the set-up at the Induction Center puts the ball in his court. If he delivers me, he's a big man with his father, which I know is super important to him, and maybe he gains some respect from his father's friends. Who knows? But I do know that if he comes looking for me then it's not out of the kindness of his heart and his great concern for me."

"Well said, and well thought, Rich." Bailey had decided he needed to lighten up on Rickey or the poor boy might break. "So, what was his plan?"

"Pretty simple, really. Either leave the country or stay and hide in plain sight, as he called it. He really didn't have any specifics but he said it was based on deception. Make them think one thing while doing something else."

"Well, that's not a bad idea, but that's not a plan. We just need to put some meat on those bones. Speaking of meat, how about we head down the hill and find a place for breakfast?"

"Great idea. I'm starving."

67

They sat in a red vinyl booth at Rae's, a coffee shop made famous because it was open all night and the Hollywood types would drop in after a night of drinking, or doing whatever was currently the 'in' thing to do. Ricky fingered his coffee cup and adjusted the silverware before beginning to speak. Even now he was still nervous sharing with Bailey all that he knew.

"He gave me a number to call. It's one of those services. He said to just say 'Mr. South called' and to leave a number where I could be reached. He said the number should be a pay phone, and he would call me back within 30 minutes regardless of the hour."

"Well, it could be a set up. You call, they know by the directory where the pay phone is located, and the send the boys in to pick you up. But that only works if you're here locally. If you're more than a few hours away, I doubt they could scramble a team out quick enough to find you. Maybe we should test it."

"How?"

"Simple. We give some kid five dollars to make the call, but we give them a pay phone twenty miles away. We stake it out, and if they show up, we know Bobby's not your friend. If no one shows up, but the phone rings, then Bobby might be OK, but we would still have to be careful. Remember, if he is really your friend in all of this, he is a great asset because he could provide information as to what they are doing. Having someone on the inside is always the best intel. So we don't want to dismiss Bobby out of hand. What we want to do is test him."

Bailey continued after a brief pause and a scan around the restaurant. "I also think we should head him in the wrong direction. Just because he might be your friend today, doesn't mean he won't change his mind or have it changed for him."

"And, how do we do that?"

"Well, your common link is Marsha. And if he is getting pressure, or even just on his own, my guess is, he will contact her and ask if she knows where you are. You trust Marsha, Rich?"

"Absolutely."

"With your life?"

"Yes."

"OK then. What we do is get hold of her, and tell her to tell Bobby where you are. Except, you will be somewhere else."

"You mean lie to Marsha?"

"Well, yes and no. You could tell her where you will really be and have her tell Bobby something else. Or lie to her and have her pass the lie on to Bobby. Obviously, the former is riskier than the other, but it's up to you."

"I don't want to lie to Marsha."

"But, will she be willing to lie to Bobby? How much do you know about their relationship and their feelings toward one another? It's a gamble, and it's not one I see as worth taking. Look, Rich, even if she finds out later that you lied to her, you certainly had a damned good reason. Someone was trying to find you to kill you and you were trying to stay alive. If she doesn't understand that, then really, you are better off without her."

"I know. Man up. Put soft feelings aside and deal with the hard core reality of staying alive. You're right, Dad, and keep reminding me until I get it right."

"OK, I am going to call your Mom. See Rich, even she understands. We worked it out that I would call only during even hours and then I would let it ring just twice and hang up. Our code for 'Love You and we are alright.' You must know how much she wants to hear your voice and mine and have everything explained to her. But she will put aside her feelings and her needs to protect you. She understands that sometimes life requires hard choices. I hope you do, too."

"OK, but one more thing. If we want Bobby as an insider, do we still want to lie to him about where I am?"

"Yes, long before we can treat him as a reliable insider, we will need to test him. If we tell him you are in Mexico and we hear that there are people in Mexico looking for you, then we can't trust him. But if we tell him you will be in a specific place in Mexico, like one of those surf spots you really like, and no one comes around, then maybe we can trust Bobby. But not until we test him a number of times."

"Got it. Go call mom."

68

His father's call wasn't unexpected, but it still caught Bobby off guard; he thought it would take a week and it had only been three days.

"Oh, hi, dad. What's up?"

"Hey, I haven't seen you in awhile. How about dinner tonight?"

"At the house?"

"Nah. Let's leave your mother to her flower show at the Riviera. How about meeting at the Jonathan Club at eight o'clock? I have some depositions that will run late. I hope the hour isn't too late for you."

"No, that's fine. See you at eight."

The fucking Jonathan Club, Bobby thought. *Worst food in the city and the biggest bunch of back-slapping assholes around.* But, if you were or wanted to be a 'power broker' in LA, membership was a must.

Before the phone rang, Bobby was looking over a map of Mexico. *Large fucking country, but he will stick to the coast and only the places where the surf is good,* he thought to himself. *The kid isn't too bright.* He whispered to himself, "He will go where he's been before."

The night air was crisp but Bobby had put the top down on the Healey and the chill refreshed him as he drove across town.

Bobby was always amused by the entry to the Jonathan Club. It was a non-descript staircase, off of a busy downtown street, which also featured a cut-rate clothing store and at least one X-rated bookstore. *Yep, real high-tone. Makes me want to join,* he thought, as he climbed the concrete steps leading to the heavy bronze door with the club's name engraved on a small placard just to the right of the door.

Whereas, at the Wilshire Country Club or Riviera, the greeter always recognized him and welcomed him warmly; here, there was always a problem with him being admitted.

"I am sorry, sir, but your father hasn't arrived yet. Could you please wait there in the lounge?"

What he called a lounge was three straight-backed chairs pushed off into a corner just off the staircase, partially blocking the entry to the restroom.

"No, I will not sit in the fucking toilet waiting for my father. We happen to have a firm membership, and I am a member of the firm. Would you care to see my card? When my father arrives, tell him I am in the bar, and I am telling them to put my first Pinch on your tab."

With that, Bobby turned his back to the greeter and headed for the bar. He ordered a *Dimple*, but put it on the firm's account. He was still a bit steamed when his father arrived.

"What, Curtis didn't kiss your ass? Oh, poor baby."

"Look, he knows me. How many times have I been here? What's that dipshit think...this is some cool place and I need to sneak in? I hate this place. The food is terrible, and the drinks are watered down. Why the hell do you continue to come here?"

"Well, you are right. The food is pretty bad. But places like this, you need to be seen. It's that simple. Everything in this town, like all other towns, gets done based on relationships. The people you know and who know you. It's a mutual exchange of favors and influence. For example, that guy over there, in the sharkskin suit with the gold chain; he doesn't know anything about how to arrange a meeting with an SEC committee member. But, I do. So, we rub elbows and if he happens to need to meet with the SEC or one of his friends does, or they are getting some heat from it, they come to see me. If I have a client who needs to quietly go into rehab outside the country, I would give Gino a call. He would take care of it. See, that's why we come here. Not for the veal."

"Yeah, I get it. And it sucks."

"It pays the bills. Let's get a table."

Bobby was into his third *Dimple* when Raymond finally got around to why they were there. Bobby knew from the moment he got the call, it was about Rickey, but he enjoyed watching his father perform and pretend that he was oh, so interested in Bobby's possible job at Latham and if he should trade the *Healey* in on a new *Porsche*. *Damn, he is good,* Bobby thought, even he was half convinced that Ray gave a good God damn.

"Ah, Bobby, look, I've got a situation that I think could benefit both of us. They are in pre-production over at Paramount on a surfing movie and they are looking for a technical expert. Someone who really knows the sport and will give them good advice, so it doesn't come off as another *Gidget* picture. I thought your friend Rickey might be able to help out. There might even be a part in it for him."

"Well, I'm not sure what he's up to right now. I haven't spoken with him since we had breakfast in Long Beach the day before RFK was shot. I can make some calls and see if I can rustle him up. Sounds like something right up his alley."

"Can you do that for me? I would like to tell Paramount that I have someone lined up for a meeting by next week. Monday or Tuesday."

"Sure. Can't imagine how that could hurt."

"Say, whatever happened to that gal you were dating? Marsha, wasn't it? She seemed different than the others. Your mother and I got the feeling that you had some strong feelings for her."

"I did, but she didn't. She's in Vermont, last I heard, but it's been some time."

"Vermont? Left Berkeley for Vermont? That doesn't seem like a career move."

"Well, dad, some people put happiness before career."

69

The view from the house in the morning was all Rickey had imagined the night before. Although the low-lying fog mellowed out the lowlands, the large expanse of the Pacific was stunning.

"Christ! This is some place. But, dad, don't tell me this is a friend's home who is away in DC. No one lives here. There are no clothes in the closets, or personal touches anywhere. It's like...Ah, I'm not sure, but it sure isn't someone's home."

"Yeah, you're right. But it was, not that long ago. It belonged to a fellow who started back in the '50's a private security firm. He did real well with it. About two years ago, he and his wife were killed in a plane crash; he was the pilot. And, what was so unlike him, he left no will. So there is this huge fight among the relatives as to who will get what. An unknown daughter appeared last year, claiming she was the product of a liaison between her mother, a former employee of the company, and the Director. I mean, Mr. Gabriel; everyone called him the Director. So, my old buddy from the war, is now running the show. He mentioned this place to me once, and when you called yesterday, I immediately thought of it as a perfect safe house. Kit was kind enough to offer it to me when I called."

"Well, that is what it is today. A safe house. But I can't stay here forever. We need to come up with a plan."

"Well, I've given it a lot of thought over the last 24 hours, and I discussed it with your mother just a bit ago. I think there is only one real option: Canada."

"Oh, shit. It's freezing up there and there is no surf."

"Exactly." Bailey moved from the barstool he had been sitting on to a large recliner which commanded one corner of the great room. He turned toward the view of LA tumbling down the hill into the flatlands of Culver City and then racing to the sea where its chaos ended and the indigo blue of the Pacific took over. He didn't say a thing for quite awhile and Rickey began to get nervous, fearing his father had had enough of his immature approach to life, and was ready to abandon him.

Finally, in a very low voice, Bailey began to speak, and as he spoke, not only the seriousness of his tone, but the words themselves, struck Rickey a hammer's blow.

"They will look for you where you have been. At my home, at my office, at my favorite place to eat, where you surfed, where you worked, where you made love to some girl on the beach; don't, son, don't fall into a repetitive pattern. That's what people do. They are scared, so they want something familiar, something reassuring. That's a death warrant. If I can give you one piece of advice, it would be this: be unpredictable. Change everything about yourself - from what you wear, to what you smoke, to how you think about yourself. Truly, Rich, you are on your own, and you need to create a new 'Rickey.' And no one but you can do that. Now, here's why Canada is a good idea."

70

The view no longer interested Rickey nor made him feel special. Four long days in the house had made him stir-crazy and he just wanted to do something. Go to Canada, go to Mexico, go to New Zealand or Denmark; they had discussed them all and more, and Rickey was sick of it. He knew his father meant well, but there was a point when too much study, too much talk, just dulled you down. Make a choice, and go for it. If it doesn't work out, then find another way.

His father came into the room and started to suggest that perhaps the best thing to do would be to look into Australia, as they had surfing, and, for the most part, a warm climate.

Rickey nodded at the idea, but then, without really knowing what he was doing, said, "Fine. How about one of the African countries, or how about Russia? They would probably love to hear my story. Wait! I think there may be some countries in Asia that you haven't looked into yet. We better hide out here for another month or so, so you can research every God damned country in the world. And you know what? You still couldn't decide. I love you, Dad, but Jesus Christ, at some point you have to make a decision. And, I've made mine. You were right about Canada three days ago. They will think I went to Mexico for the warmth, the surf and the weed. They will scope out the best surfing spots and spread some money around and, sooner or later, they would find me. So, if for no other reason, Canada is good, it will buy me time. And I truly believe that is what I need more than anything; time. Enough time passes and no one will give a shit about what I saw or didn't see."

Bailey stood there, taken aback at first, but the more Rickey spoke, the more comfortable he became. It was what he had been hoping for since this nightmare began; for Rickey to make up his own mind. He was the one who would have to live it, not him, not Maggie, but Rickey. So it damn well needed to be his choice. "Great. I'm glad you decided. Now, we just need to fill in the details."

The sun was setting out over the ocean and the TV rumbled on in the background, the election results. The polls would close out West in about an hour and it looked like the western states would decide it. George Wallace had swept the South, taking away from Nixon states he had hoped to win. But he was doing well throughout the Midwest and the Rust Belt states. Humphrey won the old stand-by Democratic states, but according to the exit polls, was losing in the West, including California, with its 40 Electoral college votes.

"Looks like Nixon will be the next President," Rickey said to his father, who was in the kitchen dividing up some take-away Chinese food he had just brought up the hill. "Yeah, most likely. People want a change, or maybe they want to go back to the '50's. The '50's were a pretty good time for Americans. Jobs were plentiful, everyone was settling in after the war, there was a good feeling that everything was on track. Then that damn war came and everything seemed to go sideways. I don't know, maybe it started with the JFK killing. Nothing seemed quite right after that. But trust me, sooner or later, the people will see that Nixon is not a man to be trusted. Dick Nixon is all about Dick Nixon."

He carried the two plates of food on one arm and had two bottles of beer gripped in his other hand. He motioned for Rickey to take a seat at the end of the bar so they could face the TV while they ate.

"Look, I am sorry about the van. I know you really loved that car, but we had no choice."

"No, I know that. They will be looking for it and it stands out, that's for sure. But, getting only $1500 for it hurt."

"Well, yes, but what could we expect? A dealer is going to lowball you, he knows you want the money right now. Plus, Rich, for a van less than a year old, it had a lot of miles on it."

"Alright. So, are you going out tomorrow and get me some nice American sedan which will blend right into the scenery? Maybe something in a nice tan?"

"No, wise guy, no car at all. Not until you get to Canada. I want something with their plates, not California plates. Besides, it's a hell of a drive from here. No, you are going to fly, well at least part of the way."

"Really? Cool. I've never been on a jet before. So how am I going and where am I going?"

"OK, tomorrow is Wednesday. We are going shopping for clothes and other things you might need. Thursday, your mother is going to meet us at our friend's house in Redondo Beach so we can all be together for a few hours. Then on Friday, you will fly up to Seattle. There is an airport shuttle bus that goes from the Seattle airport to a place called Anacortes.

"Saturday morning there is a ferry that goes to Vancouver Island out of Anacortes. It will be packed with tourists who are going for the day or overnight. Canadian immigration is pretty lax about coming into the country as they know damned near all the people are headed back to the States that day or the next. You will have to show your passport, but generally they don't even stamp it. The ferry lands in a small town called Sidney and there are buses into Victoria, the biggest town on the island. You can hang out there or cross over to the mainland. There are numerous ferries running back and forth. As it's all inside Canada, there are no check points, so there should be, with any luck, no record of you entering Canada. Even if our *friends* make a request, it should come back negative."

Rickey sat back as the TV showed a big map of the United States, but he hardly noticed; as he got caught up in Bailey's detailed plan. It made good sense and didn't seem that difficult to do. Perhaps he was going to be OK. Yet, he still had some housekeeping to do.

71

The wind blew his hair back into his face as he stood on the foredeck of the SOUTHERN, a car ferry carrying him to a new life. He was restless, and truth be told, a bit scared. This wasn't a three week trip to Mexico; this was damned near forever, and a commitment he would have otherwise liked to have passed up. *Too soon*, he thought to himself. Sure, there was a time to move out of his room at his parents' house, and to be on his own, but this seemed more like he was being forced to fly. *So, get some wings, you pussy. This is what you are doing, and that is that.*

He pushed those thoughts aside and returned to his earlier thoughts of Marsha. Speaking to her from a pay phone in the back bar of Chez Jay's in Santa Monica felt not only unreal, but fake. He got the strong impression she was just telling him everything was fine and she was happy there with Charles, but something didn't ring true. And, of course, what he was telling her was total bullshit. Man, he hated to lie to her, but he knew he had to, anything else was too risky. He could hear himself now, standing here in the cold wind, under a grey sky, saying, "Mars, I need to get away for awhile. This thing with the draft is all fucked up. I think if I just go to Mexico for six months, then I can get my 2S renewed. I went and saw some guys and they had me change my draft board to one up in Venice Beach. What? Yeah, I had to get an address up there but they had it all figured out. So in about three weeks, my file should go up there and about six weeks after that, I will ask for a re-hearing. These guys have a lawyer who sorta lays it all out for you. You just follow his script and they think I should get back my 2S. Nah, they say it doesn't matter if I am in school or not. It's I guess, a question if the Long Beach Board made a mistake in not letting me make it up over the Summer. See, what they are telling me is, the rules say 15 units a semester or 28 units a calendar year. So, if I had gone in the Summer, I could have gotten the 28. Yeah, I know. I didn't go, and that's part of the problem. But, for now, Mexico looks good; looking forward to it.

"Tell me, Mars, what are you looking forward to?" He waited quite awhile, listening to the silence before saying, "Hey, look, if that old friend of yours, you know, that Bobby guy. Yeah, him. If he calls or asks about me, just tell him the truth. I owe him a solid and tell him I won't forget it. And, Mars, I need a favor. If he does call or come around, send a postcard to my mom saying, 'Snowing still.' Yeah, that's all. Just that, nothing else."

His thoughts were interrupted by the blast of the ferry's horn signaling that they were about to dock and he left Marsha in his thoughts the same way he left her on the phone that day: without a good-bye; just a "Later."

He was reminded of the special on lemmings he saw on TV years ago. When too many lemmings are pushed together, they go crazy and will jump off a cliff to certain death rather than stay penned up. The crowd in front of Rickey looked, to him, like a bunch of lemmings, right before they decide to jump. The reds, and blues, and greens of the parkas all pushing and shoving to get off the ferry. The crowd and the crowding was overwhelming, so Rickey just wandered aft to the back of the ferry and watched as the crowd slowly thinned out. As he made his way down the gangplank, it shifted under his weight, nearly causing him to fall. Catching his balance, he crossed to the weather-beaten office which housed Customs and Immigration. He slowly made his way up the bare, wooden steps and crossed the deck with its green paint worn thin from many travelers' boots. He sighed loudly, as he pulled open the door, not from its weight which was considerable, but from the fear raging in his belly that he would be arrested or just taken away. An officer in a heavily pressed white shirt with epaulettes on the shoulders and little gold stripes decorating them, smiled broadly and said, "Welcome to Canada. Customs is on the left if you have anything to declare. If not, you can just pass on through to the door on the right." He said this as he waved Rickey through, never asking for his passport even though Rickey was clutching it tightly in his right fist. Rickey mumbled a, "Thank you," and headed for the exit door.

Swinging it open and walking out onto the broad porch, he took in what he assumed was the downtown of Sidney. A tree-lined street which wound its way up a small hill going east and down the same hill to the waterfront to the west. As it was called Main Street, Rickey decided it must be, but there wasn't much to look at, just a few small shops and the police station.

Just past the police station, Rickey spied the familiar logo of *Blatz* beer; Canada's finest, displayed under a larger sign with a halo and in script inside the halo, Smiley's; it flashed in a secret code, urging Rickey in. But Rickey needed no urging; the chill of the breeze coming off the sound was enough to push him indoors. And, Smiley's looked as good a place as any.

72

Once, Smiley's had been painted a bright blue, but too many winters and too many rains had washed it out to a pale blue, which in places faded almost to a denim as the grey wood showed through the surface. But the front door must have received some attention recently, as its bright yellow paint looked fresh and said, 'welcome stranger.' He opened the door and experienced, for the first of many times, that blast of warm, moist air that rushes out to greet you and pull you into the shelter of a welcoming and cozy room. He thought, *no matter how long I am here, I will never get used to the cold.* But that warm rush was to become to Rickey a feeling of security and shelter.

Smiley's had a full bar running along the length of the west wall which was on Rickey's right as he stood in the doorway absorbing the sights and sounds. But the bar, rather than stopping at the back wall, curved around and continued the full length of the back wall. Behind the bar was a series of lockers and shelves framing the deep-set mirrors which reflected the images of the hundreds of bottles of liquor from all over the world, each with its own story to tell. Rickey had never seen such a huge collection of liquor and couldn't imagine that all of the bottles had been used. *Many just must be for show,* he thought. To his left was a small bandstand which led to a hallway where he imagined the restrooms hid. There were tables and chairs scattered in no particular fashion in the center of the room and their clutter gave the place a relaxed and homey feel. Rickey slung his duffle off his shoulder and wandered his way to the bar, trying not to knock over any of the lightly framed chairs which laid out in front of him like a mine field. He felt like a stranger in a strange land, although the Neil Diamond song, 'Solitary Man', blasting from the jukebox was familiar and its message reinforced his feelings of being alone.

"We're not open yet. 11:30 on Saturdays," the unseen voice said from somewhere behind the wall of the bar off to Rickey's right. "But you're welcome to sit for a spell to warm up. That wind today has a lot of Alaska in it."

"Ah, thanks," Rickey replied to the disembodied voice. "I think I will. But just for a moment, if that's OK."

"I just said it was," she shot back, with a bit of sarcasm in her voice. She had come through a small passageway between the two bars, which Rickey hadn't been able to see before. So to have her there, right in front of him, was a bit of a surprise.

"Oh, wow! There you are. Didn't see you before."

"That's because I was out back getting ready to open. But now that you are here, I guess I am open," she said it in a way that made Rickey think she was talking about more than the bar.

She was tall, with long, willowy legs which were encased in very tight blue jeans. The jeans were tucked into cowboy boots with fancy stitching on the sides and a silver half-moon which covered most of the toe. *Perhaps it's the boots which make her so tall. Need to get her out of them*, he mused to himself. She turned half-wiping the bar top behind her. Rickey wasn't sure if she was showing herself to him or simply wiping the bar; either way, the view was great. She turned back and he noticed she was wearing a black leotard top under an open lumberjack's shirt of vivid plaid. He couldn't help but notice her small, but well-rounded breasts, pressing against the leotard top. She knew he was checking her out, and she didn't seem to mind; in fact, she seemed to be enjoying their little pantomime. She smiled and shook her blonde hair which cascaded down her back well past her shoulders. It was thick and had that fullness that only God's natural curls can have. Her blue eyes sparkled and held onto him as she spoke, "OK, stranger, I'm Sandy. What do they call you?"

"Ah, Rick -- Richard Rhodes, but everyone calls me Dusty."

"You say that like you're not sure about it."

"Well, to tell you the truth, I'm exhausted. Just came up from LA. Hitchhiked. Took 42 hours and I haven't eaten or slept for the last 16, so excuse me if I'm a little foggy."

Her face softened immediately and a large smile spread across her lips, exposing perfect teeth but with a slight gap between the upper center; something Rickey found immediately attractive. "Well, you've come to the right place. My special today is Mexican pollo soup with corn, carrots, onions... hell, anything I can find, I toss in. I don't know how Mexican it is, but people like it. Perfect for a day like today. Can I get some for you?"

"Sounds great. Do you have a cold beer to go with that?"

"Lots of 'em," she said, flipping her head to the left, indicating a tallboy cooler tucked behind the end of the far bar. "We're famous for our zillion beers. Help yourself." And, with that, she disappeared behind the bar as quickly as she had appeared. But Rickey could feel her presence still lingering in the room.

73

The lunch crowd had thinned out at Ma Maison and only a few customers lingered over their mid-day cocktails or coffee. However, in a booth tucked into a corner, three men sat engaged in earnest conversation, apparently uninterested in their drinks which sat in front of them with the ice all but melted. Normally their waiter, Jimmy, would have approached and asked if everything was OK, but not this afternoon; he could tell from the tone of their voices there was some serious tension at the table. So he busied himself just out of earshot but near enough they could hail them if they wanted anything more than their privacy.

"Listen, Raymond, Bobby...I'm only the messenger. Personally, I don't give a shit if you never find the kid. But they have given me the assignment to work with you and to take back to them what you have, what you don't have, and what your plan is. All I am hearing is what you don't have. So, one for three in the majors is a great average, but here, it sucks. They won't accept it. So you damn well should give me something more or the shit will come down. No threat. Just what I know."

Bobby sat between his father and the man who had introduced himself simply as Anthony. He spoke with a soft New York accent and was dressed in very expensive clothes, but due to the style, looked out of place in the new hot spot in LA; where the stars come out at night. Or so said its ad in the *LA Times*. And, apparently, during the day too, as Bobby noticed Orson Wells at a table which was on an elevated platform in the front of the house, and Lee Marvin drinking at the bar with Robert Wagner and a third man he didn't recognize. As Anthony spoke, Bobby twisted the swizzle sticks into knots and then untied them. He did this without thinking that someone could take it as a sign of disrespect. But that's exactly how Anthony took it.

Without seeming to move, his left hand flashed out and collapsed over Bobby's right index finger and with a simple jerk, broke his finger at the joint.

"Don't say a word. Don't scream out. Just sit there, punk. You think I came all the way across country to listen to your whining and have you sit here and ignore me? Fuck you! If you want to be able to wipe your ass tonight, you'd better start telling me where this Rickey is and how I can find him. Understand?"

Bobby fought back the tears and looked to his father for some type of support, but Raymond seemed, at the moment, to be totally enchanted by the dessert menu. "Damn, that hurts," he mumbled to himself, *but I have to give this goon something or he will break my other fingers. Christ, how did I get myself into this mess?*

Bobby started to talk, but his voice was broken. He actually wanted to speak words but his jaw just wouldn't open to allow him to inhale. He mumbled a few grunts and choking sounds but could only nod his head at Anthony, hopefully to make him understand that he was compliant. Anthony leveled a hard stare then broke out into a big smile. "Kid, no hard feelings. I thought you were dissing me by playing with your whatever that thing is called. OK, I've got a short fuse. Sorry. We good?"

Bobby nodded in reply. And slowly leaned back in his seat. "Anthony, if I knew more, I would tell you. We are on the same side. I called his ex-girlfriend and she told me he told her he was going to Mexico. He planned to do basically what he did earlier this year. Just go down the coast and end up in La Paz then cross over to the mainland. I knew he spoke once of wanting to go to Costa Rica, so maybe he just continued driving south. I also checked with some of his local buddies, a guy, Sticks, and another guy named Riley, and they both said they heard he was in Mexico."

"Why then can't we find his sorry ass? There is no trace of him or his van. No credit card charges, but that's OK, he would know he would leave a paper trail...but no park receipts, no gas receipts, no sightings and we have people looking for him. Would this Marsha lie to you?"

"Don't think so. Rickey told her I did him a solid without saying what I did. So I think Rickey told her the truth and she in turn told me what she knew."

It suddenly dawned on Raymond what had transpired. When he first heard that Marsha had sent Rickey's mother a University of Vermont postcard with the simple inscription, 'Still snowing,' he didn't give it a second thought. Former girlfriend, maybe she and mom were close and she was just reaching out during the holidays with a note. And, in Vermont in November, 'still snowing' would be just a statement like 'I am fine,' or 'wish you were here.' But now Raymond understood its real meaning. It meant, 'They are still looking for Rickey.'

So, the kid had Marsha send a signal to Bobby that they were still looking for him. Smart play. So he has tied Bobby to Rickey's escape plan. If they find that out, Bobby becomes a liability and he is as good as dead. I wonder what the solid was Bobby did for him. Or maybe that was just more of Bobby's bullshit. You never know with that kid.

Quietly Raymond added his thoughts to the dialogue. "Because that's what he wants you to think. It's a misdirection play. I didn't think he was smart enough to come up with that, or maybe he has some help. But that's what it is."

"Marsha wouldn't lie to me. Or if she did, I would know it," Bobby insisted with his voice getting louder.

Raymond turned partially to face his son, "Oh! Bobby, sweet Bobby. He lied to her, you idiot. He knew you, with your head so full of yourself, would think she would never lie to you, or with your God-like powers would know instantly if she was lying. So he simply fed her the line he wanted you to get. He knew you would call her because it was the easy thing to do and you always do what's easy. Look, Anthony, I haven't paid much attention to this situation because I thought it was handled, and to be frank, I think it's a big waste of time. But next week is Christmas and my guess is our little friend will make contact with his parents. Somehow. And I will put some people on it and get you what we get forthwith. Hopefully by New Year's we can have this bullshit wrapped up and get back to making money. Christ, what a clusterfuck!" By the time he finished, his face was bright red, and his left hand was shaking involuntarily but with force.

Anthony looked around and caught Jimmy's eye and made a circle with his finger in the air. Jimmy knew the universal sign for, we are done here, bring us the tab. Then Anthony slowly turned to Raymond and the very way he shifted his body sent a clear message to Bobby that he didn't consider him part of the conversation any longer; nor the enterprise. "OK, Raymond. I will take that back and tell them I will contact you after the holidays." He stood up and slightly bowed toward Raymond and turned and walked away.

Raymond looked at his son, who was sunken down into the booth, holding his hands between his thighs and rocking back and forth in a trance-like state, while emitting a low groan. Pathetic was the only word Raymond could think of to describe Bobby at that moment. He was totally defeated, reduced to a childlike state. He needed to get him out of the country for awhile, if for nothing else but his own peace of mind; he couldn't solve this problem if he was constantly worried about Bobby. He finally spoke, "It's OK, son. Let's get you over to Cedars and have them look at that hand."

74

"Damn, that was good," Rickey said, pulling the last bit of the soup out of the bowl with a chunk of homemade sourdough bread.

"Glad you liked it. I get $3.75 for a bowl. And 75 cents for the beer." As she said this, she had a teasing tone in her voice which Rickey didn't pick up on. "Ah, shit. Don't think I wasn't gonna pay. I have some money right here, and he pulled out a large roll of Canadian bills.

"What'd ya do, sell your car at the border?" she teased him some more, delighting in the fact that Rickey didn't catch onto the continued ribbing.

"Ah, no. I sold it in LA."

"Why?"

Rickey didn't have a quick reply for that, so she stepped on his pause and said, "Because you needed the cash to live on while you sort out how you're going to live up here with the Army on your ass. Right?"

"Well, yeah." *Damn, I wish it was just the Army,* he thought, but he knew he could never tell her or anyone else the full story. *So letting her think I'm a draft dodger is better than I am a witness to history, and injustice.* "Well, yeah, something like that," he mumbled, half hoping she couldn't hear him.

She didn't press, and instead, turned the conversation to more practical matters. "So, where you staying?"

"Staying? I just walked off the ferry into your fine establishment. I have no idea what's available or how much it costs." As he said that, he felt a great fatigue pass over him and a huge yawn distorted his face. With a loud, "Ah ha," he shook his head back and forth, literally trying to throw the cobwebs out of his head. "Oh, hell. Pardon me. Sorry, I don't know what came over me."

"You're tired, silly boy. Here, come with me," and she extended her hand for him to take.

He looked up into her eyes and saw a kindness there and he felt an old familiar rush. He took her hand as she led him out of the kitchen, where they had been sitting, back out into the bar. He panicked for a moment thinking she was taking him to the front door to toss him out. But his momentary fear fled when she turned and headed for the long hallway toward the bathrooms. There was an alcove just before the entry door to the women's restroom and it was marked simply, 'Employees.' Sandy fished a key out of her front pocket and quickly unlocked the door. As Rickey stepped into the room, he saw it was a small room with a single window on the wall to his left. There was a queen-sized bed pushed against the back wall which occupied most of the floor space with just a little walking room on the sides. It had the sad smell of old sex, cigarette smoke, and cheap perfume. It was lit by a single bare bulb hanging from the ceiling on a snake-like cord that swayed slightly, as if there was a breeze pushing against it; but there was no breeze in this room, nor had there been any for a very long time.

"Ah, home sweet home," she said as she spread her arms out and spun around. "Like it?" she asked with a twinkle in her eyes.

"Christ, when does Anthony Perkins show up?"

"Oh, cute. So, you think this is the Bates Motel? No, you're wrong. This is more like the *House of Usher*, but as she said it a huge smile broke out across her face, causing dimples in her cheeks. "So, why don't you lie down and take a nap? It will be slow this morning, but around two o'clock, we will start to get pretty rowdy with the start of the hockey game."

"Hockey?"

"Yes, hockey. You are now in Canada and we love our hockey. So you'd better learn to love it too." With that she spun once more for effect, shutting the door behind her as she left.

Wow, thought Rickey. *Quite a girl. But, hockey? No fucking way.* He stretched out on the bed after a half-hearted attempt to make it. He laid on his back, looking at the ceiling and watching the lamp sway. *Man, what have I gotten myself into?* But before he could answer himself, he passed out.

He awoke with his tongue pasted to the roof of his mouth and a foul smell on his breath. *Where am I?* was his first thought, followed by a brief wave of panic until he realized that the roar he was hearing was the bar crowd reacting to the hockey game on the TV. He needed to piss badly and just as badly, needed a drink of water. He remembered the restrooms next door and swung his long legs over the side of the bed. The floor felt sticky under his feet and he wondered why. Then it occurred to him that when he came in here, he had his shoes on; now he was barefoot. So someone had undressed him while he slept. Instinctively, he checked his left hip pocket and felt the reassuring bulk of his wallet. *Good. Can't afford to lose my stash. I've already lost enough,* he thought. *Christmas is next week and I can't even speak with my parents or Marsha.* But then again, maybe he could.

75

"Irish, I am Raymond McKnight. Oh, why thank you. Very kind of you to say that. Look, Ed Davis said you might be able to help me find a witness I need for an up coming trial. We think he may have left the LA area or maybe even the state. OK, you know where my office is in Beverly Hills? Yes, that's right. On Beverly Drive between Wilshire and Olympic. Say 3:30 this afternoon? Great! And thanks for making time for me."

He looked across his desk to Bobby, sitting in the client's chair with his casted hand propped up on his knee. "They say he is very good. Has a million contacts and an encyclopedic mind. We'll get him on this this afternoon and hopefully he will give us something to pass on to Anthony. God damn it, Bobby, you better hope so, or your ass is in deep trouble. Do you understand me? Do you get it? You just sit there with this wet puppy dog look on your face, like it will all go away after Santa comes next week. Well, unless he's got that kid in his sleigh, it's not going away until one of two things happen. They find him and get what they want out of him. Or they decide he no longer matters because the trial will seal off all questions. Either way, they still think you are a dipshit and that you let them down. What were you thinking with that lame-ass attempt to find him? Or were you thinking? Or maybe you didn't want to find him; feeling sorry for him. Was that it?" He tried to read his son, sitting there, slumped in the chair, devoid of expression or concern.

"Well, what was the solid you did for him?" And, as he asked, Raymond searched Bobby's face and body for any sign which would lead him to under-standing what his son had done. "Come on now, Bobby. I'm here trying to help clean up this mess. Give me a little help, will you?"

Bobby just looked at him with baleful eyes, but for one second, a flash of contempt flicked in his face and Raymond's watchful eye caught it. Every-one has a tell, the old card players told him that when he was just a kid play-ing straight poker in the back of the law office on Friday late afternoons.

Everyone. Find the tell, you will find the lie or the bluff or maybe the excitement; but it will be the key to what they are holding. He never forgot that bit of advice and had used it well over the years. Now he was using it on his own son.

"Oh, Jesus! I got it. Oh, Bobby, how stupid could you be? You didn't want them to get him; you wanted to deliver him to them so you would be the big hero and earn some respect from them. So, can you bring him in now?"

Bobby just shook his head and stared back at his father.

"Do you know where he is hiding?"

Again, Bobby just shook his head.

"OK, why don't you just tell me what went down and we will figure a way out of this together?"

Bobby leveled his own stare back at his father and said, "What the fuck difference would it make? Rickey's gone and I do not know where he is. What I did or didn't do is irrelevant."

"No it is not. It will give me the background facts and help me shape the story I give them. Look, I've got a pretty good idea already. I was just hoping you would trust me. But, here's what I think: You got some guys to grab him before he went into the Induction Center. Then you told him some bullshit story about how he was going to get killed and he was better off hiding out with you. But you turned your back and he just disappeared. Isn't that about what happened? You sprung him from the arms of the Army so you could later turn him in. What'd ya think? They would make you a made man? Give you a crew? Or hire you to replace me? Oh, Bobby, whatever am I going to tell your mother?" *The boy is just stupid. It happens; smart people have stupid kids.* "So what the fuck should I do with you now? If they figure out what you did, or one of the boneheads that helped you talks, you're dead...period, end of story. And they might just kill me and your mother, thinking that we helped you. Or just as added punishment for you, kill us first, in front of you, then pull you apart behind two trucks and dump all of us in a hole in the desert. Gotta say, Bobby, I knew you were a fuck up, but I never thought you'd get us killed. How did I not see this earlier?"

"Probably because you spend too many afternoons in Room 312 of the Beverly Hills Hotel with that blonde. Hell, I doubt she's even seen her 21st birthday. I've got a file; with photos. It's with a lawyer friend of mine and if two Mondays in a row go by without him hearing from me personally, then he drops them in the mail. Yes, them. There are two files. One addressed to mother, naturally. The other to the girl's father. You know him of course, don't you, dad? The head of Paramount. One of your best friends; isn't he, dad? Jack Avery. Don't you guys golf every Saturday at Wilshire? Didn't you and mom go with them to Aspen last winter; shared a villa together, as I recall. Oh, yeah, he's going to be real pleased with you.

"And, dad, you know that girl you brought in for that three-some that time, oh, yes, you remember. That one. Well, she's only 15. I know she looks a lot older, but her birth certificate says 1954, and in this state, that is rape... good for 30 years. What...you'll be 78 before you get out. Well, I am sure with all of your influence, you can pull a shorter sentence or get an early release. Hell, you're such a great trial lawyer, maybe you can get a not guilty verdict, but they would still pull your law license. Then where the fuck would you be? Garage attendant at Bullocks in Westwood, or maybe you can move to another state and change your name and get a job at a McDonalds. Yeah, I'd say...your future isn't looking too bright. And, by the way, in mom's little package of joy, there're copies of all the offshore accounts, just so her lawyer doesn't have to spend a lot of time and money trying to find them."

Bobby, by now, was standing in front of his father's desk, leaning over it with both hands placed firmly on the desktop. The venom in his voice revealed years of hatred and feelings of disgust. The sweat ran down his forehead and dripped off the end of his nose, leaving big, fat splashes on the desktop. He knew toward the end he was spitting out the words. A madman unchained was how he saw himself at the moment, and he hoped his father saw it, too. "Just too God damned many, 'Oh! Bobbys!' Too many, 'you're stupids' and 'how much did I waste on your education?' Too many times you looked at me with disgust, like I couldn't even carry your bag around Wilshire; like I would hand you a driver instead of a putter. You have always treated me as a retard, as if I couldn't think and make good rational choices. Well, maybe you're right that I'm not as quick as you...but, oh! baby, has the hare now caught the fox. How does it feel, motherfucker?"

One of Raymond McKnight's strengths was his composure. Even if appearing upset on the surface, down below, he was calculating, figuring the angles, and developing a story he could sell. Often, he acted angry for effect; as rarely was he actually truly upset. So, Bobby was not surprised to watch his father absorb his rage with a placid look on his face and his lips loosely drawn in a partial smile. Bobby knew his old man was a pro at the poker face. But he was surprised at how calm he sounded when he spoke.

"Well, this motherfucker feels just fine, Bobby. Will Chapman called me as soon as you left his office. He may not know what's in those packages, but he knows who they are addressed to, and Will is no stupid man. He knew immediately it had something to do with me, and so he called. I told him to just hang onto them, but he suggested that he burn them. He said he really didn't want the responsibility and the burden of keeping them. Or, he said I could come and get them. But Will's a good lawyer and I trust his advice; so he burned them that very evening." He rocked back in his chair with a giant shit-eating smile on his face and the warm feeling of castrating his son.

Bobby leaned back away from the desk and stretched out to his full height. He shook his shoulders, then his arm, trying to get the blood moving again. He ran his good hand through his hair, trying to comb it over, out of his eyes. He smiled slightly, and then said in a quiet, calm voice, "Well, Dad, that is disappointing. I thought Will had more respect for the attorney-client relationship. Funny...he didn't return my fee. But it really doesn't matter since I gave copies of those same files to four different storefront lawyers in Lawndale, and Highland Park, in Bellflower or was that Paramount? I know one was in Long Beach, or was that Lakewood? All those little towns seem the same to me. They each have the same instructions and you will never find all of them." He stood there for a moment and then said, "How am I doing, dad? Am I learning the game?"

76

The air in the bar was thick with smoke and the smell of the over-heated crowd. From what Rickey could tell, every move by any one of the players in red, resulted in loud cheering or shouting of various swear words with 'BMF' often sworn or chanted by the crowd. *Well, one way to spend a Saturday afternoon,* Rickey thought as he tried to find Sandy through the press of the fans. As he turned around, he bumped into the first of many wannabe Hells Angels types he would see spread out across the bar. This fellow was flying the colors of the Death Vikings and was dressed in an open sleeveless *Levi* jacket decorated with the club's name in bright blues and reds across his back in the form of a large D with a large V overlaying the D. Beneath the logo was a simple tombstone with 'Death Vikings' inscribed. Naturally, that was all in grey and black.

Tattooed on the side of his neck, SONNY was inscribed in the club's colors. Covering his lower half, he was wearing *Levi* jeans, held up by a thick black belt with a heavy chrome chain clipped to it on his right side and a large chrome skull served as the buckle. Work boots caked with grease covered his huge feet. Rickey was staring at his feet when he first heard, "What the fuck?" being roared at him out of a mouth with several broken teeth showing behind the thick black beard. It was then Rickey realized in bumping this human time-bomb, he had caused him to spill the beer all down his chest, where it was now laying, glistening in the dull light on his mat of chest hair. Rickey quickly looked up and said, "Hey, watch where you're going. You gonna drink beer, walk and watch the match all at the same time, then sometimes, shit happens. But, fuck, it's only beer; not like you wasted good Irish whisky." The stranger squinted his eyes even tighter together and peered down at Rickey, who was now facing him and staring up into his ugly face, and thinking to himself, *Christ, that is one big and ugly SOB, and look at the number of knife scars on his face. This is one bad dude.*

At that moment, someone in red must have scored as the room exploded in cheers, whistling, shouting and most of all, foot pounding to a mythic beat, which caused all of them to stand on their left foot and pound their right foot into the floor as if they were trying to stomp a hole in it. Rickey could feel the building shake from the force and wondered if they would all be crushed under the roof when it collapsed. But he also recognized an opportunity and slipped away into the crowd of cheering hockey fans.

He finally saw Sandy behind the bar, pulling beer into large jugs with a big smile on her face. He guessed she had witnessed his encounter with Mr. Death Viking. He smiled back at her, and shrugged his shoulders as if saying, "No big deal." Only a few weeks later, he would find out what a big deal it had been.

He moved through the crowd, being careful not to bump into anyone else, which was damned near impossible. So he tried avoiding the really big guys in full road warrior costume. Finally, he reached the bar and ducking under the lowered leaf which joined the two bars together, he found an oasis of empty space and solitude amongst the chaos of the game. She turned to him and said, "This is just a regular season game. Wait until the playoffs." He didn't know how to respond so he just smiled and shook his head. "You'll get used to it."

"I doubt it. Here, let me help you with those." She had ten of the large pitchers lined up along the bar and was beginning to deliver them to tables. "No, you'll just spill more than you get to them. Just pull me another eight pitchers and I'll be right back." And, without another word, she left Rickey facing six different taps without a clue which one was the right one. *Ah, to heck with it! Just start pouring.* Just then he saw a slender hand with perfectly manicured nails reach across the bar and slap the *Blatz* tap. He looked up and she smiled and said, "It's always *Blatz* on Saturdays. Two for one."

"Ah, thanks for the heads up," and he started filling pitchers as fast as he could. It was a lot like frying taco shells; develop a pace and just stay in rhythm with it. He had three taps going at once and had the eight pitchers filled by the time Sandy returned. She nodded and said, "Nine more." So he did nine more; and ten more after that, and he continued pulling beers until the game ended and the crowd thinned out.

They were sitting back in the kitchen, having been relieved of their chores by the arrival of the evening shift. Rickey was sitting on the edge of the counter with his feet dangling above the floor. Sandy was pushed back into the corner of a large, overstuffed chair with her legs curled up under her, and a large cup of tea balanced on the arm of the chair. Rickey kept looking at it, waiting for it to tumble to the floor, but it never did; as if held in place by some magical power she held over it.

"So, I asked you before, but you fell asleep on me. Have a place to stay?"

"No, not really. Thought I would find a motel for a few days. I think I'll go over to Vancouver and see if I can find a camper van, something I can stay in for awhile."

"Well, that's cool. But you can come up to the house tonight if you want; we have a spare room and you're welcome to it."

"You own a house?"

"Why, think I'm too young to own a house? Only old people can own houses? Is that it?" She did so like to tease him, and watch as he tried to figure out the right reaction.

"Ah, no. Well, yeah, sort of. I'm...it's pretty cool that you've been able to buy a house so soon. I mean, that's a good thing." He knew it was a pathetic reply, but it was the best he could do at the moment. He looked down at his feet as he said it, trying to convey an apology without saying the word, sorry.

"Well, thanks, I guess. But, you're right. I didn't buy it. It was given to me and my brother by my grandpa, Willis. He came out here from Maine to avoid the harsh winters and bought some land and farmed it for 50 years. He died about three years ago and left the house to Wiley and me. He also left us the farm and this bar. He let us decide who took what, but it wasn't really a decision. Wiley always loved farming and started riding in the tractor with grandpa when he was about five. Me? I've always hated dirt. Never liked the feel of it. So, it was a pretty easy choice. I took the bar and Wiley took the farm. Of course, it pissed off our parents as they thought all of it should have gone to them, 'since my mom was grandpa's only child."

"Wow! So, you got a damned good business and a house; you're set for life. Me? I've got shit, so I guess I'd better find some work and start making some money."

"What kind of work do you do?"

"Ah, well, the only real job I've ever had was frying tacos."

"Great! We have a Taco Tuesday Night every week. Bring 'em in for some real South of the Border tacos."

"Hmmm...well, I only know how to fry the shells."

"Really? They never let you graduate to filling the shells or making the salsa? Damn, you're lucky you are so cute. Let's get up to the house."

77

Bobby sat in the *Healey* on a side street off of Vine in Hollywood, watching the rain hit the windshield and roll down the glass. He knew he had played his father, but he also knew that his father was a master of untying the knot. Bobby had figured that by setting up the blackmail scheme, it was forcing his father to protect him from Anthony and whoever Anthony's friends might be. But it could also spur his father into killing him. What he hadn't figured, when he first came up with the play, was the receiving end. For any pass play to be completed, not only does the quarterback have to read the defense correctly, then deliver the ball to the receiver on target, but the receiver has to catch it, hold on to it, and not let the defender take it away from him.

Well, he had read the defense right, and tossed a perfect strike, but would it be caught? His guess was his father's first move would be to have his mother take a long trip just after the holidays. His second move would be to bribe someone in the Paramount mailroom to not deliver a particular package. That he had covered, by having it sent to Mr. Avery's home. But now it dawned on him that mailmen could be bribed just as easily as Paramount employees; maybe easier. So the upshot of his brilliant game plan was to convince his father that he was a rat, and a rat of the first order.

Bobby knew the offshore stuff was way over the top as it affected not only his parents' personal monies, but also some of the clients. His dad would not forgive that. Ratting to his mother, that was a different thing. That might cost him some money, or hell, maybe even a divorce, but not the wrath of some grease-ball from Kansas City. Bobby secretly felt his mother already knew about the cheating but maybe not this blonde, just one of the many others. Certain half-truths and spilled secrets many people can live with if it keeps their lives on track. But when it will cost them millions, they want revenge.

He shifted in the seat, trying to relieve the tension. *Where was she? It's already ten minutes after and she said two o'clock.* Just as he reached to turn on the wiper motor, the side door rattled open and she stepped in, dripping water off the rim of her hat. Working in the rain was a street girl's problem she hadn't had a few years ago when she worked the bars of the finest hotels in the city. But she'd had an out of town salesman die on her in the middle of the act at the Beverly Wilshire and she made a career mistake: she called 911, hoping to save him, but instead made herself a witness. After that, none of the finer hotels in the city and some of the not so fine would let her work their bars or conventions. So she had two choices: work in a house for some pimp, or go free-lance on her own in the streets. Windy liked her freedom; that was one of the reasons she had chosen the profession, so the choice hadn't been hard to make. But on days like today the thought of a nice big bed under a broad roof and dry sheets made her second guess her choice.

"Sorry I'm late. A bus splashed me over on Iverson and I had to go home and change. Fucker saw me standing there and gunned it just to make sure he got all of me. I think that silk dress will be ruined by the gas and oil in the water. But, hey, I know you've got problems of your own. What can Windy do to help?" As she said this, she reached over and rubbed Bobby's shoulder in a manner imitating a massage.

"That's nice, but what I need today is a classic tension reliever."

"Here? Are you fucking kidding me? There's no room. What am I supposed to do with that thing? It's right in the way."

Bobby reached over and shifted the lever to third gear to give her a bit more room, and said, "You've done it before."

"Yeah, but that was with the top down, on a sunny day, out in the middle of nowhere without anyone around. Hell, the tourist buses roll right past here. I ain't playing to no audience, honey."

"OK, how about an extra 50; will that cover it? I just don't have all day."

"Classic or Royale?"

"Let's go Royale," and with that, she took off her hat and placed it on the small jump seat in the back alongside her oversized purse. Bobby, ever the gentleman, had already undone his belt and loosened the zipper on his fly. As she reached in to help him with the last bit, he leaned back and watched the rain splash onto the windshield. He wished Windy had similar answers to his other problems.

78

The Christmas tree filled the foyer of their house. It had to be 25 feet tall and had been decorated by professional tree trimmers. *Who,* Bobby thought, *would have such a job? Maybe someone who only wants to work two weeks a year,* he replied to himself. The base of the tree was filled with presents; large and small boxes, all colorfully wrapped and he checked that they all had name tags on them. Uncle Ernie got something in a large red and gold box, while Aunt Millie got a small, but beautifully wrapped box. He looked for something with his name on it, but knew he would never find anything under the tree. They were all fakes; just props to give the display of Christmas cheer his father wanted to convey to their guests during the holiday season. And there were many. Parties for the clients, parties for the hope-they-will-be clients, parties for the staff, and a party, too, at Hanukkah, and last but always the most lavish, the Christmas Eve afternoon party for the politicians and their hangers-on. Bobby attended all of them and acted the good, loving son, just home for the holidays from his last semester in law school up North. Truth be told, he hadn't attended a class all year and had decided to skip the midterm exams which were coming up in a few weeks. They would certainly toss him out after that, regardless of how much money his father threw at them. He wasn't ready to be a lawyer; not yet, anyway. His first objective was to stay alive, and his first task in that regard was to find Rickey. As soon as this holiday bullshit was over, he was heading north; he would find him and deliver him to Anthony. *Fuck it. Some live and others die,* he whispered to himself, as he turned to walk upstairs to make some calls.

It was Christmas morning, a time the McKnights spent alone. After all the parties and occasions, it was nice to simply sit in the family room and have Helen bring them their drinks, and small bites which she served from a silver tray; it was the same ritual every year for as long as Bobby could remember. In his adult years, it was always a bit uncomfortable. Just the three of them, sitting there with some Christmas music playing low and the lights twinkling around them. The mammoth tree was out of sight, so each year, his mother decorated a small tree on one of the end tables. It wasn't a real tree, but one of those green metal ones with the lights already attached. She would plug it in, put some tinsel on it, spread some powered sugar around the base and say a Christmas wish. That made it Christmas for his mother. That and the expensive present she would get from her husband. The more guilty he felt, the better the gift. She had become quite good at judging the number of affairs he'd had during the year, by the size of the gift.

Bobby accepted a Bloody Mary from Helen but passed on the finger food. He was already eyeballing the large envelope with his mother's name on it which sat on the coffee table right in front of him. He would bet the *Healey* it contained plane tickets or something even more elaborate; mom was going on a trip. He was not surprised then when she opened it, his father said, "I wish I was going with you, sweetheart, but I have the Global United trial scheduled for mid-month. But, there are two tickets in there; take whomever you want. Just not that new tennis pro down at the club." He said it as a joke, but it fell flat. "Oh, my God, Raymond...a trip to the South Pacific. How wonderful! You've known I've wanted to do this very trip for so long. Look, honey," she said, turning toward Bobby, "Hawaii, Tahiti, Fiji, and then New Zealand. Oh, Raymond, thank you so much. Who should I take with me?"

Me, Bobby thought to himself; *at least I would be out of harm's way.* "Mrs. Avery might be a good choice," he said, as he looked at his father, with a smirk on his face. "If she's not available, maybe her daughter. She's a lovely girl."

His father just smiled broadly at him and said, "Honey, whoever you chose, I'm sure you will have a great time. Now, who wants some eggnog?"

79

Rickey wasn't thinking about Christmas when he walked up the stairs of Sandy's house. There were many of them, reaching from the ill-defined walkway to the large porch which ran the full width of the house. The porch was covered in decorations; small trees fully filled with lights, ornaments, and snow flocking, garlands reaching from the low hanging roof and winding around the posts which supported it, and large wrapped boxes, suggesting presents waiting to be opened. He was surprised, and turned to Sandy and said, "Wow, you guys must really like Christmas."

"It's my brother, he just loves Christmas. This is all his doing. Wait until you see inside," as she said this, she rolled her eyes as if to say her brother was a bit crazy.

It was a Winter wonderland inside the old farm house. The foyer and the rest of the downstairs living area was decorated in the most elaborate fashion, with what appeared to be icicles hanging everywhere. Rickey had no idea what they were made from, but they shattered the light like a prism and colors danced all over the room. As Rickey walked through them, he was amazed at the riot of colors and the ever-changing shapes and textures of light. Rickey had never thought of light having texture, but here, he could feel the light and colors emitting from the icicles and actually thought for a moment, he could smell it. He quickly realized the smell was not from the icicles, but from the kitchen at the back of the house where someone was cooking a lamb stew. He suddenly realized how hungry he was, and how at home he felt in this very different environment.

"Dinner?" she asked, turning toward him.

"Absolutely," he replied, as he took her hand and locked his eyes on hers. Then, quietly said, "Thank you," with a gentle squeeze to her hand, and a soft stroke to her free arm. She smiled shyly and still holding his hand, turned and walked away. She led him through the dining room which was decked out as a Santa's workshop, then down a short hallway into the kitchen, warm and rich with cooking smells. "Wiley, this is Dusty. Dusty, Wiley." The two stared at each other awkwardly for a moment, until Wiley, wiping his hands on a long white apron, extended a hand and said, "Welcome. Here, have a seat," gesturing to one of the chairs at the small table tucked into an alcove which formed a semi-breakfast nook.

"Ah, thanks. Wow, this place is something. Sandy says you've done all the, ah, ah, decorating."

"Yes, that be me. I just get carried away. I think this year more than before, but, hey, I love doing it," as he spoke, he turned back toward the stove to stir the stew and then checked the oven, where bread was baking. "Any minute now, and it should be ready. Let's say 10 minutes?"

"OK, I'm going to take Dusty up and show him his room. He's going to stay with us until he gets himself sorted out. That's cool, right?"

"Of course, sis. Always cool."

Immediately Rickey was struck by a flash of jealousy. *She's done this before. He wasn't special?* Then, as quickly as it had come on, it faded. *So what if she had?* He had no claim on her. *What's wrong with me? Tired, insecure, lonely and a bit homesick. Oh, yeah, horny. Other than that, not much at the moment,* he thought. But he had forgotten the most important factor in his life right then: fear. The fear of being caught and killed.

80

"Well, thank you, Irish, for coming in on New Year's Eve. I know most folks want to relax today to be ready for tonight. But sometimes, in our business, we can't look at the calendar."

"It's no problem, Mr. McKnight. Happy to help. Hope what I've got so far is a help."

"Well, let me hear it, and we will see." Raymond McKnight was posturing himself at his professional best. Sitting erect behind his spotlessly clean desk, hands folded in front of him and with an earnest and eager look on his face. The fear he had felt just a few minutes ago on the phone with Anthony had faded back into the recesses of his consciousness. Now, he was all lawyer, ready to hear his investigator give him the facts he needed to win.

"First, he sold the van. Over in Glendale to a dealer. Didn't get the best price for it. So that tells me, he had to dump it. Didn't have time to hang around and advertise it and get his best price. Which, in turn, tells me that he knows someone is looking for him and he has some money so he could take a hit on the sale of the van. There is no record of him or his parents buying another car, so we figure if he left he either used public transportation or got a ride. I checked with the airlines and the bus companies, and there is no record of him buying a ticket. But you know, if he just flew or traveled within the US, they don't push the ID thing. I think he went north to Canada. And my guess is, he stayed on the west coast. Toronto is far away and really cold, and in Montreal, they speak French and he doesn't. He has enough to deal with, so why complicate things with a foreign language problem? Except for BC, the rest of Canada is a huge wasteland. So my guess is British Columbia... and in BC, you got Vancouver and Vancouver Island. The big city versus island life; my first choice would be the island. On the island, you've got the city of Victoria or a bunch of small towns. To get there, he has to go by ferry or float plane. Float planes are all by charter and there is no record with any of the companies of anyone fitting his description, arriving by one of their planes. So, if he is there, he went over on a ferry.

"From the US, the ferry is out of Anacortes, Washington, and it arrives at the port of Sidney, a small town without much going on. From Canada, the ferry goes to Victoria, a much bigger locale. But to do that, he would first have to enter Canada and possibly clear immigration twice. Why take the risk? Besides, the immigration folks at Sidney have a rep of not looking too closely at the paperwork. So he could have gone into Canada at Sidney and there would be no record of it. So, my guess is, he landed at Sidney but probably wandered toward Victoria, hoping to get lost in the crowds."

"OK, but can you find him?"

"Anyone can be found, it's just a matter of resources. You can put 15 guys on it and probably find him; or one guy and he might find him, too. It's the same old story. How valuable is this witness to your case? But, understand, I personally won't go and look for him. I stay in LA. I have some contacts up there and would be happy to call them and maybe you want to hire them, that's up to you. I've written this all up in a report," he said, pointing to a manila file folder he pulled from his leather briefcase and laid on the desk in front of Raymond.

There was a prolonged silence before Raymond McKnight spoke. "Well, Irish, you are as thorough as Ed Davis said you would be. I agree with your conclusion and think we should start our search on Vancouver Island. Please make your calls and let's see what your friends say. I am not sure the kid has money. His parents certainly don't. They live a very modest life and we couldn't find any trace of cash the kid might have. I think he was just scared and dumped the van for what he could get. And, if he lives simply, that money could last him for some time. But, I still think he will have to get a job and all he knows how to do is to make taco shells."

With that, Raymond stood up and extended his hand across the desk and asked, "Is there an interim bill in the folder?"

"No, I always bill at the end of the case. And as you've asked me to make some calls and do some follow-up work, we will keep our file open. You'll pay me soon enough," he added, with a large smile, as he shook Raymond's hand firmly.

Bobby sat in the *Healey* in the parking lot across from his father's law firm's lot. Being New Year's Eve, it was empty except for Raymond's *Cadillac* and a non-descript white sedan which could have once been a police car. Bobby sat, knowing his father had to get down to Long beach by five o'clock to see his mother off on her cruise to paradise. He figured correctly that the office would be closed and had expected Raymond to be at his room at the Beverly Wilshire with the newest blonde he had corralled. He was somewhat surprised when he pulled into the firm's lot to find not only his father there, but someone else, too. So, he decided to sit and wait and to find out who the mystery guest might be; he knew the wait wouldn't be long.

And, he was right. Within five minutes, a large fellow with wispy reddish colored hair came lumbering down the stairs from the office to the parking lot. He carried a briefcase in one hand, but it looked like something for a child, compared to the hand that held it. The longer Bobby looked, the more he realized this man was huge, certainly six foot four and 300 pounds; maybe more. He had the look of someone who could handle himself, but not the look of a criminal. *No, more like a private dick,* Bobby thought to himself. *So, the old man's hired some private help; he must be getting pretty worried.* A large smile crossed his face, knowing he was causing his father some grief, and he nodded to himself, *a briefcase...maybe he did a report.*

Twenty-four hours later, Irish's report sat on the passenger's seat as Bobby drove off the ferry into Sidney. Although the windows were steamed up and his breath clouded the interior, he saw the sign for Victoria and followed the arrow pointing to the highway. Just off the highway, on a small feeder road was a bar with a bright yellow door and a flashing sign saying, Smiley's. He drove right past it, without even noticing it.

81

The three of them sat around the table, each feeling full, warm and satisfied with the dinner Wiley had prepared. Sandy stood saying, "Relax. I'll clean up. You two get to know each other." With that, she took Rickey's bowl, bread plate, knife and spoon, and whisked them away with a professional flourish. Wiley was leaning back in the cane chair with just two legs on the floor; he slowly rocked back and forth as he rolled a tight, thin joint. As he was tightening up the joint and slowly wetting the paper with the thinnest bit of spit, he eyed Rickey and said, "So, what do you do? Or really, what did you do down in the States before you came up here?" There was a slight accusing tone in his voice, as if he disapproved of the Americans who fled to Canada, rather than kill in Vietnam.

"Well, I was in school until a few months ago. I traveled a bit, and, you know, worked here and there." Rickey was very awkward with his reply and somewhat defensive that Wiley would ask him personal questions. Then it occurred to him, *he was sitting in the man's house, eating his food, and there was a good chance he would be sleeping with his sister tonight, so, yeah, he could ask him whatever the hell he wanted.* These thoughts sped through his brain just as Wiley rocked forward dropping two legs of the chair hard on the floor with a cracking sound that was reminiscent of a small caliber gun going off. It startled Rickey and he jumped a bit.

"Whoa! Hold on there, Lone Ranger, everything's cool. I was just asking to pass some time." Holding the joint out to Rickey, he asked, "You smoke?"

Rickey nodded and took the joint and picked up a small *Bic* lighter off the table and lit the long, flat tail and took a deep breath. He felt the warm air hit his lungs and the blessed chemical hit his blood. "Damn, that is good stuff. I'm so used to smoking Mexican ragweed. This shit rocks." He handed the joint back to Wiley, who after a quick toke, handed it to Sandy, who had just come back to the table. She took a long hit and handed it to Rickey saying, "It damn well should be. It takes up four of our 10 acres. But then again, it produces about 99 percent of the income from the farm."

Rickey was stunned. The 'Christmas man' was both a grower and a dealer. "Well, I can see why. This is primo stuff. You should get top dollar for it."

Wiley leaned back again and looked at his sister as if some type of secret code passed between the two, and said, "Yes, we should. And we do. But the locals either grow their own, not as good as this generally, still a decent smoke, or they just don't have the money to meet our price. The folks in Seattle do, and we were selling a fair amount down there each month but..."

A long silence followed, and although Wiley looked at Sandy a few times for help, she didn't say a word. Apparently this was a path Wiley had to walk alone.

"Well, to tell you the truth," he finally said, "we lost our boatman. He, well...ah, well, how can I put this?"

Just then, Sandy interrupted and said, "The guy was a fucking stoner. He ran Whisper up on Pull Point and tore the bottom out of her. Our grandfather built that boat back in the '30's and ran fresh fruit and vegetables to Victoria and sometimes over to Vancouver in it. And that little shit just left her there to get pounded by the tide and of course, ruined the whole load." Her eyes were blazing and her skin was flush, and Rickey could tell this was a major sore point between them. "How many times did I ask you to get him off the boat? I know he was your best friend in high school and he wasn't a total fuck up in high school. Yeah, he was fucked up back then, but in a mellow way. The last few years, he has been out of control."

Wiley, still laying back in the chair, but now so much further, Rickey thought he would surely fall, or the weed gave him the power to levitate. "Sis, for Christ's sake, I've heard it already. You were right. I was stupid. I made a mistake. I'm sorry. I will fix it."

"Yeah, you've been saying that for six weeks and if this goes on, we won't have a Seattle market. And, without a Seattle market, you can't buy me out so I can get out of here. So, yeah, I'm being a bitch, but I have good reason."

"Never said you didn't," Wiley retorted, but without much vigor.

"Well, I know how to fix broken surfboards. Maybe I can look at it tomorrow and see what can be done." Rickey said this, knowing full well he had never fixed anything in his life. If his board got a ding on it, he simply took it to the shop and they fixed it and sent his dad the bill. But he felt he had to say something. He liked them both and didn't like seeing them argue with one another. "Yeah, in the morning, I can see what I can do. But now, I gotta get some sleep; I'm whacked."

82

Not every day, in fact, very few days during the Winter, does Vancouver Island get the Banana Belt weather her sisters just south experience much more frequently. But those days are glorious, with the sun breaking through the grey sky and the forever rain stopping long enough for the roadways and fields to dry out. Everyone on the island feels reborn on those days. Rickey, having spent all of twenty hours on the island, awoke and thought nothing of it. But Sandy had been up for over an hour and had opened the windows to the bedroom, letting the summer-like air blow through. She stood there, wearing nothing but the cup of coffee she held in her right hand. The morning light pouring through the window, highlighted her hair into a golden mane and played soft shadows on her skin, making her small breasts stand out and making her legs seem even longer than they were.

"Well, it's about time," she said, handing him the coffee cup and now facing him so her hair hung over her face like a mask; a beautiful mask of mystery. "Really. What time is it? Doesn't seem that late."

"Oh, you will learn. When we get BB weather, you get your ass up and enjoy it because who knows when it will be back."

"BB? What's that?"

"See, we sit on the edge of a jet stream flow or some type of wind pattern that makes those islands just south of us sometimes tropical...yeah, swear to God, tropical. But the flow stays just south of us, so most of the winter we are buried in grey and cold and drizzle, well, you know, you were here yesterday. But sometimes, the Gods are gracious and move the line just north so we get it too. It's called the Banana Belt...we just refer to it as the BB."

"OK, good to know."

"And this means it's a perfect day to go look at Whisper and see what we can do with her. I hope it's something we can fix. I looked in the newspaper for something similar and, Jesus, they want like five to six grand just for a 27 footer. And it won't haul our load. Whisper is 35 feet and can carry a lot. Grandpa knew what he was doing. I don't know if we could even find a boat like her, let alone afford it." There was an anxiety in her voice and a plea that went unspoken. She was telling Rickey he held the key to her happiness and her future.

Two hours later, they were standing in a shed which was covered with green moss. And while today was a dry day, most of the days before, hadn't been. The only reason Whisper wasn't full of water was the huge gaping hole torn in her bottom. Grass and sand showed through her hull, while small creatures scampered both under and through her.

"Jesus, half that side is gone!" Rickey blurted out involuntarily. What had he signed up for? Without knowing anything about boat building, he knew that simple fiberglass and some resin wouldn't fix Whisper. No, most of her right side needs to be reconstructed. But how?

"Yeah, no shit. But the good news is, those folks who own this land, they got her out of the water fairly quickly. They are from California, too, and while Joe doesn't know much about boat engines, he knew enough to call his father, who gave him a list of things to do to it to save it."

"Well, that was damn nice of him. I'm sure the sooner it was done, the better the engine will be."

"OK, but not that nice. Joe and his girlfriend or wife, I don't know what their deal is, they own a small health food store in town and they buy from Wiley their fruits and vegetables. Often they can't pay, so Wiley fronts them and sometimes, I think just gives it to them. Joe's like you; dodging the draft."

"Oh, really?" Rickey turned away from Sandy and looked again at the breached hull of the Whisper. As he stood there, he could see how she had been built. There were pieces of wood cut about an inch and a half wide and about two and a half deep. He could still see the saw marks on the wood which seemed to form Whisper's shape. Then there were long planks, like three-quarters inch by four inches which ran the full length of the boat. Rickey could count eight of those planks missing or torn apart by the bottom colliding with Pull Point. *So, they made a web then connected them with the planks. I can see that.*

"You know, maybe we can cut away that wood that is damaged then get new wood and nail it to the old one and then get some planks to cover the hole. What'd ya think?"

"I think we need to move the boat from here closer to our farm and I think we need to go to the library and see if there is a book that can help us."

"Fuck an A! Good idea." Rickey said it with a big smile, thinking he would get out from under fixing it. He was wrong.

83

"OK, Irish. I think we've got what we need. A kid about twenty, surfer by calling, well-built, not too bright, but a decent young man who decided to split rather than testify in some trial. Irish, do you think I'm stupid? There is no trial. The kid is a draft dodger. Christ, there are hundreds of them here. But because they are Americans, they tend to hang out with other Americans. If he is on our island, my guys will find him. Right, I got that. Find him, tail him, and report back. We won't touch him, my orders will be clear. I promise. OK, and hey, thanks for the referral. Beverly Hills lawyer, eh? Right, bill him hard but fair."

Fair my ass, thought Jake Bishop to himself. *Fifteen grand should be about right for one of those tight-ass lawyers in LA. How hard can it be to find some kid away from home for the first time? I will talk to Annette, the head telephone operator on the island. All off-island calls have to go through her office. It's Christmas. I'll just slip something special into her gift basket and ask her to tell me about the calls for Southern California; how many can there be during the next ten days? I mean, this is the holidays...call home to mommy. But before I do that, I'm gonna send a retainer invoice; let's test the waters with $5,000. I don't want to front anything, especially the hunt money. The Death Vikings are perfect for this job, but they will want $50 a day per guy and a bonus for finding him. Say 15 guys, that's $750 a day for let's say, three days max. So about $2300 and a $500 bonus. So $2800. The retainer will cover that plus some for me. The rest will just go straight into the retirement account.*

He moved from his desk to the smaller one across the room where the typewriter sat. He typed out a retainer invoice and addressed it to Raymond McKnight. He figured he would get to work once the monies came in. Little did he know he was giving Rickey some breathing room for ten days.

As Jake was thinking of how he would spend the 15k, Rickey was at the library looking at books on boat repair and design. *This is cool stuff,* he thought, as he flipped the pages and looked at the illustrations. *I need to get a few of these and study them back at the house.*

He hadn't given it a second thought as he approached the librarian seated at the check-out aisle. "Hi, I would like to check these out for a few days."

"Great. Do you have your card?"

"No."

"Well, if you have a driver's license, I can get you a card."

"Ah, no, well, I have a California driver's license. Would you like to see it?"

"Not really. I need something from here. How about your apartment lease, or even a utility bill...that will do."

Rickey felt a pain in his chest and a fleeting numbness in his left arm. "Ah, sorry, but I just moved here and I don't have any of that stuff. Look, I have money. How about I just buy them from you?"

"Sir, this is a community lending library, not a bookstore. We don't sell books. So, if you don't have any proper ID, then I am sorry, but you cannot check out...what is this? *Broken Boat Repair* and *Boat Repair Fundamentals.* Sorry."

Rickey flipped the hard front cover open on both books and pulled the card showing how often it was checked out. "Well, maybe you should sell them, as this one was last checked out in May of '66, and this one, hell, March of '59. You think if I take these there will be a big rush? All of the island will come in here, screaming at you, 'Where is Boat Rebuilding' like they will die without it? Come on, give me a break. I will bring them back in two days. I just want to show them to Sandy and maybe together we can fix Whisper."

"Oh, you with Sandy? Sandy of Smiley's?"

"Yes."

"Take the damn books. Keep them as long as you need. Tell her we'll see her Saturday for the hockey game."

Rickey walked out of the library feeling like a member of the community. But another member had just stepped out of the shadows of the Anchor Bar. He wore the colors of the Death Vikings and immediately recognized Rickey as the guy who had spilled beer all over his colors and his chest. *Motherfucker!* he swore under his breath. *Figures a pussy like him would be coming out of the library.*

84

"Hey, Sandy, look at this," Rickey said as he pushed a book of boat designs across the table. "It looks just like Whisper."

Sandy studied the drawing and the few photographs of boats built to the design called a Down East Lobster Fisherman. "Yep. Looks like her. Grandpa always called her a Down East boat, but I never knew what that meant. Says here they were designed for the lobster fishery in Maine, and the area they fished was called Down East. So that all makes sense. Perfect design for hauling traps. Low free-board aft, with flat, wide decks for storing the traps or food racks like we used. Yes, nice little work boat. If she was working."

"She will be soon. I promise. Another week and we should be ready to test her."

"Learn the terms, you land-lubber! It's called a sea trial," she said laughably, as she was genuinely happy. Not only with the progress on Whisper, but with Rickey. He was the first man she had met in a long while who was both sincere and loving. *Perhaps,* she thought, *he could be the one.*

One grey day followed another and none of them motivated Rickey to get working. But Sandy was motivation enough as she pressed Rickey to get to work on one hand, then seduced him in the bedroom with favors on the other. Rickey was inspired to get Whisper sailing again and was putting in 12 to 14 hours a day working in the small barn behind the house where they had moved her. While not ideal, it had power and a portable diesel heater, which he had lit all the time. After studying the books, Rickey figured the best way to repair her was to duplicate the parts he could salvage and then make patterns from them for the missing parts. By changing the size ever so slightly, he should get the progression from forward to aft close enough; it was getting the shape right of what they called the *frames.* If they were close enough, then the outside planks should attach to them to form the hull and keep the water out. He had to re-cut the pieces many times to get the fit he needed and then lay them up against the old frames and fit the new ones in. This, he learned, was called *sistering*. As the very lower frames and upper frames were still there, he simply had to make new pieces to attach them to bridge the gap where the rocks had ripped a hole through. Once the frames were in place, the job was nearly done. Laying and fitting the planks didn't take a lot of time. However, he had to caulk each seam and that did take time, not only to fill the seam with the cotton and the sealant, but to let it dry enough so the whole boat could be painted.

Rickey was off on his estimate of how long it would take to finish her, but by mid-January, she rested on her trailer, ready to taste salt water again. It was a BB day when, with the help of several friends, they launched her off of Dutch Point and started the engine on the first swing. As she bobbed on her mooring, Rickey stood on shore and was, for the first time in a long time, pleased with himself. The fear, confusion and anxiousness of the fall and winter months was starting to fade as he became more and more comfortable in his new life. His thoughts of his old friends, the waves they had ridden together, the places he had visited, his van, even Taco Time, became less and less frequent as the days wore on. The only memory from the past which didn't fade, but weirdly grew more intense, was Marsha. Almost every day, he saw her face before him; so close, so real. It was an image he couldn't shake. And, he felt guilty of having such thoughts, with Sandy's arms wrapped around him tight, and her lips close to his ear. *What's was wrong with me?* he'd asked himself, time and time again.

85

The Death Vikings had two bars they called home. The Anchor Inn and The Sixes. The booze was cheaper at the Anchor Inn but the food was better at The Sixes; so where they landed, depended on what they were doing. They always went to Smiley's for the hockey games, no bar had as many girls there for the games as Smiley's. But tonight, they were in the back room of The Anchor, having pushed the pool tables to one side to make a meeting area. The tables tonight were used to stack the coolers of beer on, along with plates filled with sandwiches and bags of chips. A single table had been set up in the middle of the room and chairs had been haphazardly set out in front of it. This wasn't one of their monthly meetings where they discussed road trips, membership issues or other club matters; tonight, they were guests of their old friend, Jacob, who from time to time, employed them for various tasks. Tonight was one of those times.

"I know that little motherfucker. He spilled beer all over me at a hockey game a few weeks back. He ran and got away from me in the crowd or I would have broken his face." Sonny's arms were shaking with rage, recalling the incident and his lips were white.

"Really, Sonny, you know him?" Jacob said, tapping on the photo of Rickey and Rita Rains. "You know where to find him?"

"I can find him," Sonny shot back, acting as if Jacob was challenging his manhood.

"OK, where?"

"Around."

"Sonny, don't jack me off. Either you know where the motherfucker is or you don't. It's OK. I expected that we would have to look for him and that's why you guys are here. Here's the deal. I need this dirtball eyeballed as soon as possible but not longer than three days. You'll all get paid for three days, $150, plus a $500 bonus to whoever eyeballs him first. But that's as far as it goes. We eyeball him and then track him, but we don't move on him. That's the way it is. You move on him, no bonus, and maybe a bunch of shit from the guys paying the tab. Understood? Good. So, Sonny, got any ideas where we can find him?"

"Yeah, well sort of. I saw him coming out of the library last week. He had some books, so let me go talk to the gal there and see what she can tell us."

"Alright. I knew you boys were good for this job. Find this mother-fucker and call me immediately. I don't care if you need to take a piss first or if you're in the middle of a blow job. You see him, you call me. Right? OK, let's have some beers."

86

The next day, Sonny made a beeline for the library; he was hell-bent to get the beer spiller SOB and the $500 bonus. Sonny was about as out of place in a library as a turd on a dinner plate. As he entered, all eyes moved over to gaze at the brute and then quickly shifted back to their books for fear that he might notice them. He eyeballed the young woman sitting at a desk which had a small plastic plaque which read 'RESEARCH.' She was not the mousey type Sonny expected to find there. She was attractive, dressed in a pleated wool skirt with a matching light top which showed she was a woman but not much more. Her hair was pulled back into a French roll and a silver chain hung from her neck.

Sonny approached the desk where she was seated and looked directly into her eyes. Sonny's only real way of communication was through intimidation so he naturally fell into that role. As he stared at her, he said in a low baritone, "I need to find the pretty boy."

"Excuse me, but I don't understand. You're looking for a book on *Pretty Boy* Floyd, the gangster from the 1930's?"

"Hell, no! There was a guy here a few days ago, came out carrying some books. He's like this tall," Sonny said, as he pointed to his shoulder. About 150 pounds with brown hair and a pretty face. The kinda face a broad like you would like. Ya had to have seen him."

"Sir, this is the research section. We help people find source materials, and reference items to facilitate their research. We are not the missing persons department."

"Listen, bitch. Me and my boys will come back tonight and burn this shithole to the fucking ground. Then we might just come over to your place for a party. So tell me where I can find him; you gave him books so you must know him."

Monica, the librarian who actually dealt with Rickey, was standing within earshot of their conversation but behind a column which separated English and French literature. *Shit, I know who he wants, but if I say anything, they will know I just gave them to him and didn't check them out properly. They will fire me.* She looked over at Julia and could see she was very frightened, and she blurted out, "Hey, I think I know who you want!" She said it loud enough to raise all the heads in the library.

"Yeah, what's his name?"

"Not sure, but I could check the log for check-outs a few days back. I don't remember his name, but maybe by looking at the list, I will. But I know he is a friend of Sandy. You know, the gal that owns Smiley's, the bar by the dock." By now, her voice was just a quiver and she was starting to feel faint.

"Yeah, sure. That's where I first saw him." And with that, he turned and walked back out the front door without as much as a thanks.

87

"Well, now that you fixed her, you wanna run her?" Wiley was sitting hunched over on a tree stump, smoking a cigarette, looking out to Whisper, gently rolling in the wake of a passing boat. The late afternoon sun washed the water and the boat in a soft, hazy glow, making the entire scene magic-like and a bit surreal.

Rickey sat on the hood of the truck, feeling the warmth of the engine radiate up into his legs and butt. It felt good, in a place where he was always cold. *Oh, for Mexico, and some sunshine,* he thought. "Well, I've never run a boat before, but I guess I can figure it out. The trick is not to hit the rocks, right?"

"More than that. It can be tricky. Look, I've lined up a delivery for tomorrow night. We meet here in the afternoon and load the boat. The racks are full of produce, but under the fruits and veggies, I have the weed packaged into kilo bricks. We move about 50 kilos at a time. So, we have about 25 to 30 racks on deck."

"OK, I got that part. Sounds simple enough."

"It is. We do all the packing at the farm. Then we move Whisper over to the public dock and load her. We leave here about five. It's about 45 miles but we motor at about seven knots, so without currents or anything, it would be about six and one-half hours. But there are currents, and tidal flows and winds. So generally, we figure five knots average or about eight hours. Depending on the trip, sometimes we stop at Lopez Island until about five in the morning so we are coming into La Connor or Anacortes around seven with the sun up. Other times, we just go straight."

"What makes the difference?" By now, Rickey had moved off the hood and was walking around the dirt lot, which was the parking lot for the small marina. He stopped and pulled a *Lucky* out of the breast pocket of his *Pend-*

leton wool shirt Sandy had gotten him as a surprise. It seemed he wore it all the time now; never able to feel warm.

"Who we are delivering to. The boys in La Conner have a house with a dock, so we just go there. But the Seattle guys have to drive up and so we have to time it so we get to the public dock in Anacortes at about the same time."

"OK. So you want me here tomorrow at what? Four?"

"Let's make it three. We have a bunch of stuff to go over. Kind of a check out of you and the boat. Remember to bring your passport. And, you'll need to go over to Wells Supply and get some gear."

"Gear? What'd ya mean?"

"Sailor's gear. Foulies, hat, gloves, boots, rigging knife, just a bunch of stuff. Just ask Jimmy, he'll know what you need. And have Sandy make us a lunch up along with some coffee and shit. OK?"

"Yeah. No problem. Anything in particular ya like?"

"She knows. She packed for these trips before." He said it in such a way as to say to Rickey, "You, dude, aren't as special as you think." Then he nodded at Rickey and walked over to the truck and with a jerk of his head, told Rickey to get in; time to go.

88

"OK, I give up!" Bobby was in a corner booth of the Dangle Club at three in the afternoon, having chosen it simply because it was open and he was tired of walking around downtown Victoria. The place was actually nicer than he thought it would be. After walking a few steps down a short foyer, the club opened up like a peeled orange. There was a stage with the 'must have' pole in the center and a short catwalk out into the first few rows of tables; both were brightly lit and cast the rest of the club into a sanctuary of darkness. Bobby could see booths lining the walls and quickly maneuvered his way through the sea of tables to secure a booth for himself. Having spent the entire morning looking for Rickey at hostels, hotels and flop-houses, which attracted American ex-pats, his legs ached and his feet hurt so much it was hard to stand. What was worse, he had come up with nothing; no one had seen him or heard of anyone matching his description. "The son-of-a-bitch just vanished," he complained to the waitress, as she placed his first drink of the day in front of him.

"Who did? Or were you just talking to yourself? I do it all the time," she said giggling, at the last bit.

"Oh, hell, I'm sorry. Yeah, I was talking to myself. I am just very upset that I need to find this witness for a trial in LA and I just can't seem to get a line on him. Maybe he's just not here. Hell, maybe he's just not on the island."

He pushed himself back further into the booth and now he could get a better look at her. She was about five foot six and slender with full breasts that were made fuller by the push and shove of the red and silver uniform she was wearing. A silver nametag was positioned on her left chest just below her collar bone. She had small feet encased in silver low-rise pumps and black nylon pantyhose that disappeared into the fringe running around the bottom of the uniform.

The tag claimed her name was Rene. She had soft blue eyes, pale pink lips and her light blonde hair was pulled up off her neck and tucked behind her ears; small stud earrings with pale red stones framed her very pleasant face.

"What's his name?" she said, through a brilliant smile.

"Rickey. Rickey South Point. Well, South Point isn't his last name, it's like a nickname someone hung on him 'cause he surfs. Or did awhile back. Don't imagine there's too much surfing up here," as he said it, he felt his resolve wane even further. "Here's a guy who loves to surf. Hell, lives to surf. Why would he come to a place where he can't. Makes no sense. He's probably in Hawaii. We never considered that."

"A surfer? You mean like a guy who rides waves?"

"Yes, honey, a guy who rides waves. I know it's not much up here in freeze-your-ass-off-country, but it's pretty popular in a lot of places around the world."

"I know that!" she snapped. "I've seen it on *Wide World of Sports* many times. Buzz Edwards and Rickey Dent. They ride those really big waves. And there are guys who have made a lot of money off of surfing, like Hobby Alter and Dewey Weber. So don't think I don't know about surfing, because I do."

"Ah, yeah, you seem to know more about it than I do. I'm just looking for a guy." Bobby then tried to recover by turning up his charm machine and smiling and said, "In fact, I bet with your knowledge of surfing and the local scene, you could help me find him. There would be a nice something for you if you did."

"So, tell me about him," she said, as she glanced around the club to make sure her manager wasn't going to bust her for not working the room, but he was nowhere to be seen. Besides, at this hour, there were two college kids at the bar, and Sammy, a regular, over in booth four, where he spent most of his afternoons. Two *Jim Beams* and a three dollar tip; everyday as long as she gave him a good view of her tits when she brought him the second drink.

So, Bobby told Rene, as she called herself at the club, all he could remember about South Point Rickey and his likes, dislikes, and the way he had lived the first twenty years of his life. He even mentioned Marsha and their relationship and how he felt Rickey could never let that go, even with her being with another man. Rene sat quietly and listened, and when Bobby finally paused and then said, "Now you know what I know."

She didn't say a word for a good two minutes, which seemed much longer, and made Bobby uncomfortable, but he resolved to wait. His father had taught him, there are times when you shut up and let the witness fill the empty air. So, he waited. She took a short breath, while she absentmindedly ran a hand down the seam on the neckline of her uniform; up and down in a motion that had Bobby in a trance.

"Well, from all you've told me, I think you are looking in the wrong place. He wouldn't come to the city. Everything you've told me about him tells me he wants it simple, quiet, peaceful, and above all else, a place where he feels in control. No one feels in control with thousands of other people swimming around them. My guess, if he is here, on this island, then he found a spot in the countryside. And, as you've said, he was never a real motivated guy, more laid back than most, which from Southern California, is saying a lot about how laid back he is. I think he's somewhere near where he got off the ferry. I'd start looking in Sidney. You said he was good looking. I'd bet he found some girl to take him in right after he arrived. He's living with her and there is no way to trace him because he has no address, phone number or utility bill which could give him away. And, if he has gone to that much trouble, he's no witness; he's a fugitive. Either you're with the US Government or some bounty hunter."

Bobby sat there stunned. After he composed himself, he said, "Neither. I am his friend and you are right. He is on the run. I must say, that was really impressive. It sounded so professional. So well reasoned. What's your story, Rene?"

"I am a graduate student at the university. I have a BA from McGill University in Behavioral Science and currently I am working on my Masters in the same field. So, why do I work here? First, the money is great. Yeah, the afternoon shift sucks until five, but from five to seven, it rocks. I come in at eleven and work until seven, five days a week. I make about $200 a week. If and when I finish my Masters, and if and when I can secure a teaching position, I might make $150 a week. But, it's also a lab of human behavior. You see it all in here. And, it's real. People living out their lives as they choose; no pretense. Of course, some play roles, but the role-playing is part of their real life experience. It's a goldmine for research."

Bobby just sat there and finally said, "Well, Rene, it's been a pleasure, but I think I'm heading over to Sidney now." And, with that, he dropped a twenty dollar bill on the table and walked out into the late afternoon sun. "Why," he said to himself, "do I always feel I am playing catch up?"

89

The motion of the boat pleased Rickey. It was different than surfing, but in some ways the same; connected to the water, to the sea. He felt at home and comfortable as they left Vancouver Island and crossed the water to San Juan Island. He looked at the map, or rather, the chart, as Wiley had called it, and saw they really only had to go through two open bodies of water; the rest was just navigating along islands or around them. But Wiley explained they were at most risk close to land, not offshore. He was a good teacher, calm and deliberate with his explanations. Safer because out in open water there was a lot less to hit, and the cops, or harbor patrol, tended to stay close to shore. Sometimes they would see a naval vessel out in open water, but they didn't care about what some small fishing boat was doing. They were on the lookout for Commies. As he said the last line, Wiley laughed and gave a snort while shaking his head, as if to say, "Dumb motherfuckers."

After about 45 minutes out in the middle of the channel between Vancouver and San Juan Island, Wiley throttled back the engine and brought Whisper to a stop. He left the wheel and walked back to the stern of the boat and leaned over. When he came back up, he held in his hand, the curved wood piece that said "Sidney, BC" on it. He placed it in a small cubby-hole next to the aft deck where it was hidden by one of the racks. Then, he went back forward, near the wheel, and dropped the maple leaf and raised the US flag.

Rickey didn't say a word, but in a bit after they had returned to their seven knot march across the channel, Wiley said, "You always do that. When we leave Sidney, the people know us and know we are a local boat. We do deliveries to Victoria at random times but frequently enough so when they see us, they think we are a Canadian boat and there is no need for us to go to customs or immigration. If we get stopped, it will be on the US side. I have two sets of papers for Whisper; one US, one Canadian. Whoever stops you, you show them the right paperwork. It's kept up there in the wheel house behind the autopilot. You have a US passport, so if we get stopped by the US guys, then you are the captain and I am just a friend getting a lift to the US. If by some cosmic fuck-up, we would be stopped by the Canadians, I would be captain and you would be a hitchhiker getting a ride home. Cool? You got it?"

"Yes, I've got it. Have you ever been stopped? How long have you been doing this? No, wait, it's not my business. I'm sorry."

"No, it is your business because next week, you make the trip alone. And you are taking a risk. A big risk. So you have a right to know. No, we have never been stopped. We have been doing it for three years. The first year, it was once every several months. I was still learning how to grow and harvest the product; then I had to learn how to process it for the market. Then I had to find buyers who wouldn't rip us off. It took awhile. Before the accident, we were doing a run to the US once every two weeks; once a month for each customer. Our deal is that they have to buy 50 kilos for us to make a run. They pay us $560 a brick, about $15 an ounce. They sell it for $20 a half ounce, or about $1400 a brick. So there is good money in it for them. Of course, they have a lot of risk selling retail, they have to deal with a lot of people. My guess is they have a limited group they sell to and these folks in turn, split the bags into quarters or just double the price. The clubs in Seattle are getting $50 for a half ounce and they move a lot of it. Our risk is pretty small really, but we do take precautions. So, always change the hail port board and the ensign. OK? All good?"

"Yeah, good. Very good," Rickey replied, but what he was thinking was, *Where's my end? After all, 50 kilos at $560 is $28,000 a trip. Holy shit! Twice a month - that's over 50k a month. No wonder Sandy was pissed with the layoff. So, what do I get? Ten percent, 3k, 5k, what?* As they motored throughout the night, Rickey continued to think about the money and what he could do with it and about getting a piece of it. He decided the best play was no play. Sit back and wait and see what they do. I mean, hell, in 30 days, he should know if he's a rich man or not. Christ, in three months, he could make enough to buy a house on the beach in Hawaii and have enough to live off of forever. *This 'on the run thing' is working out pretty good,* he thought.

That night, they made the trip

to La Connor. The next night to Anacortes. By the third night, Rickey was skippering the boat on his own. "I know it's a lot to do in a short period of time," Wiley explained, "but in order to keep our market, we have to do it. And, I've added a third port of call, Oak Harbor, as I don't want to be seen in Anacortes too often. It's for our same guys. Just a different drop off point." Wiley was standing among the racks that held the product and the covered goods, trying to convince Rickey that eight trips in the next ten days was both doable and had to be done. As he spoke, he gestured with his arms, and at times reminded Rickey of one of those TV preachers selling religion by the donation in the middle of the night. Finally Rickey had heard enough and put his hands up in the universal sign of 'surrender' and pleaded, "Enough! Enough already. I'll do it. But aren't we getting greedy? You're talking about doing like, over 200k in the next two weeks; seems like overkill to me."

"No, what it is, is just breaking even for the time we missed." Wiley moved from behind the racks and now was standing in front of Rickey. He looked Rickey hard in the eyes and said in a flat tone, "It's what Sandy wants." He didn't say anything for a moment, then shifted his stance so he was more relaxed and spoke in a softer voice, "Look, Sandy is hell bent and determined to get off the island. She is tired of the cold, the grey, the bar, its customers, the list goes on and on. We agreed sometime back that we would do two runs a month...about 50k and put it into a buy-out fund. When it got to one million dollars, Sandy would take it and I would get the ranch and the bar, along with the house. I like it here and I want to stay." He said it so matter-of- factly, that Rickey took it as gospel. "Wow! One million. That's a lot of money. I guess she wants some pretty fancy stuff."

"No, not really. She's 26, so she has about 60 years to live, so that's not even 20k a year. Now I know, 20k sounds like a lot, but trust me, by 2005, it won't be. Of course, she can invest it and make it last longer and she will work, too. Just don't get to thinking she's rich because she won't be; but she will be free of here."

And so for the next two weeks, Rickey ran the boat nearly every day regardless of the weather. He began to notice the shifting of the tide by the light on the water and how it reflected differently than a few minutes before. He could sense the change in pressure as a front began to form. He could tell from the motion of the boat, the sound of the prop as it bit into the water, and the strength of the current, where along their cruise they were. He felt at home on the boat, like he once felt on his board. He had made the transition from a guy who drove a boat to a boatman, to a seaman, to a sailor. He was now in all respects, a waterman.

90

The moon had left the sky dark and the heavy cloud cover made the sea seem bleak. Whisper's diesel engine was purring softly, pushing them along at a stately six knots. Just off Lopez Island, Rickey noticed the knot/log meter drop to four and a half knots, and the helm start to jerk as the autopilot fought to maintain their course. *Cross-current,* was Rickey's immediate thought, then just as swift, *no, flood tide.* He remembered checking his tide tables before leaving Sidney and the tide turned there at 11:57 but because of the distance they had come, it would hit Compass Point on Lopez Island later. Glancing at his watch, he saw it was 12:34; *so that was about right,* he thought, as he reached to disengage the autopilot and hand-steer until they cleared the race caused by the tide striking the point. Just as his hand touched the helm, the sky lit up with bright lights. Orange and blue lights flashed, and a voice commanded him to heave-to. Rickey pulled the throttle back and brought Whisper to a halt; however, the tide continued to carry her toward the shore. The voice again commanded him to stop, but this time, it was more stringent and harsh. It occurred to Rickey that the only way he could obey was to disobey. So, he re-engaged the gear shifter but left the throttle alone and turned Whisper into the tide. He was attempting to hold station by idling into the current, and after several attempts, found the right spot with the throttle and she just sat there rolling in the swell.

The bright lights blinded Rickey, so he couldn't read the identification on the vessel which had hailed him. He was pretty sure it was US Customs or the local Harbor Patrol; either way, it was the United States he was dealing with and the real possibility that they held a warrant for his arrest. Rather, for the arrest of Richard Osgood, as tonight, his passport and California driver's license said he was Richard William Rhodes. The disembodied voice again boomed at him: "All persons on board move to the starboard rail and put your hands above your head while facing us." Rickey did as he was told, but the blazing lights caused him to turn away as the lights made his eyes burn. "Only you aboard?" the voice boomed. "Yes, sir," Rickey answered, summing up all the authority in his voice he could muster, hoping to appear calm and unconcerned. In reality, the sweat was pouring down the crease of his back and pooling at his waistband and he was afraid it would next break out on his forehead; his underarms were rank,. But it didn't, and he was able to stand at the rail with his hands in the air and while terrified, project an air of indifference.

The night went dark again, except for the single round glow of a hand-held flashlight which jerked with the boat's movement. Slowly, Rickey's vision returned, and he could make out in large letters, HARBOR PATROL; he breathed a sigh of relief as they were locals and according to Wiley, much more cool than the Feds. But cops were cops, and he needed to be calm, professional and respectful. *Easier said than done,* he thought to himself as the patrol boat pulled up alongside and the man on the forward end of the cockpit tossed a line around one of Whisper's mid-ship cleats and pulled the two boats together. He then went aft and attached another line, causing the two sterns to be pulled together. Then he went around resetting the fenders tied to his boat with small lines, so as to provide a cushion between the two hulls.

As Rickey watched the officer tie off the two boats, he thought about the procedure he and Wiley had worked out. He had already switched the hailing port board out so that it now read Friday Harbor, and the US flag snapped in the breeze. The US boat documentation was in the wheelhouse and he hoped that would ally their suspicions that he was trying to enter US waters from a foreign port but even US boats could be smuggling materials into the country or carrying contraband between US ports. He knew just because they bought his story of being a US boat, he wasn't home free.

His ID was what worried him. He flashed back to that day, which seemed so long ago, but was merely weeks. His father gave him the name of a guy in downtown LA who worked at a commercial printing plant, who, for a price, would provide Rickey with a US passport and a California driver's license. The plant was huge and took up a full city block; the roar of the presses was something Rickey had never heard before and it reminded him of a commercial jet airliner taking off. Stanley was the man's name and Rickey met him in a small office right on the main floor of the plant; all out in the open. Rickey was surprised thinking they would meet in one of the many flop-house hotels in the area; but Stanley's motto was to hide in plain sight. And, who was Rickey to argue with success? Stanley told him he had been doing this since after World War II. The US government had trained him as a forger once they discovered his talent for art. He spent the war in a comfortable office in Washington, D.C., creating Nazi officer's papers, war orders, supplies requests, and other fake documents to confuse and disrupt the German war effort. It was rewarding work and he was safe. After the war, he continued to create documents for a small, select clientele as a way to provide for his always growing family.

Rickey remembered the feel of the passport when Stanley first handed it to him; it felt real. And, looking at it closely, you could not tell it hadn't been issued by the State Department; the details were exact. The California driver's license was equally good. But Rickey still worried that somehow these cops would question them. And, of course, a close inspection of the produce racks would reveal more than tomatoes and greens. If they discovered the weed, he was toast. Those thoughts bounced off one another as he stood in the chilly wind awaiting his fate.

"You can put your hands down but keep them where I can see them. OK?"

"Absolutely, officer," Rickey replied, as he slowly lowered his hands and placed them on the rail. He could see the fellow who had tied them up was young. Maybe in his middle twenties, with short hair, like a military cut, which caused his ears to look large as they protruded from beneath his hat, which he wore low and forward on his head. He was about six feet tall and looked to be in good shape, and sported a thin, wispy mustache under a large potato-like nose. He looked up from tying the mid-ship line and said, "Good evening, sir. May we come aboard?" Rickey was surprised. *They were asking for permission? What if he said no?* he wondered. "Sure, come aboard. The aft deck is pretty full, so watch your step."

As the young officer, Morgan, by his nametag, came aboard, the older, heavier-set one sat behind the wheel, pointing the flashlight this way and that. He never spoke a word to Rickey, or moved from his seat behind the helm.

"Papers?"

"In the wheelhouse, in the drawer behind the helm."

"Any weapons?"

"No, sir."

Morgan removed the documentation papers from the drawer and unfolded them. Holding them up to the dim light provided by a single 12 volt lamp in the wheelhouse, he turned the pages slowly. Rickey thought he could see his lips move as he read the paperwork, spelling out the dates and names.

"Looks good," he shouted to his partner. "I think I've seen you up in Friday Harbor before. You docked there?"

Rickey froze for a second, not sure what the best answer would be. "Well, to tell the truth, that place is a little expensive for us. We have a small dock we use just north, down on the channel side. Mr. Nelson lets us use it and we give him some of the fruits and vegetables we bring down from up island. But, we're in and out of Friday a lot."

"Yeah, the marinas are getting really expensive. My father-in-law is paying a dollar a foot a month to dock his *Chris Craft* 40 over in La Conner. Can you believe that? But, hell, he can afford it; he's a lawyer."

Rickey wasn't sure how to reply, so he simply stood there, nodding slightly as Officer Morgan continued to talk. Finally, he asked, "and what do you have there?" jerking his head toward the racks across the aft deck.

"Fruits and vegetables for the La Conner Farmer's Market. We come over every few weeks. It depends on what they order." Morgan nodded, and said, "Oh, yeah, my wife loves going there. Good stuff. Better than the markets. God, you get a peach at Safeway and it's like a rock. No flavor, no nothing."

Rickey, starting to feel comfortable, started walking to the aft deck toward the produce racks. Just after he turned and moved, a booming voice rang out, "Freeze or I will shoot!" Rickey was stunned and stopped mid-step, then held up his hands in a gesture that said, "Hey, no problem."

"Ah, sorry. I was just going to get Officer Morgan a peach."

"Just stay where you are and do what you are told."

"Yes, sir."

Morgan slowly walked over to Rickey and said, "Sorry, kid. He's a bit of a hard-ass. Ex-Marine, and all that."

"Hey, Roger, paperwork is in order and everything looks good. Anything else?"

"Nah, if you're satisfied, then let's go."

Those were the sweetest words Rickey had ever heard and he felt the tension rush out of his body like someone pulled a plug.

And, they never checked his ID. *How sweet!* he thought, as he pushed the throttle up and Whisper gained speed.

91

"Do you want to tell me who you really are?" Sandy was obviously pissed and the anger in her voice almost blurred her words beyond recognition. She was standing in the dining room of the house, which now no longer was Santa's workshop, but once again a conventional dining room of an old farmhouse. The large oak table could sit eight in the framed chairs that circled it; one was a captain's chair which changed the symmetry of the scene, giving it a lopsided feel. In the center of the table was a hand-tossed clay bowl of bright colors filled with the greenest apples to be found anywhere. A circular light fixture hung down from the ceiling directly over the table, and the light from it now made Sandy's rage clearly visible. She stood no more than three feet away from him, but the distance between them was continental.

Rickey wasn't sure why she was so upset. He always thought she understood he was on the lam and the name he gave her that first night was not the name he was born with. *And, there was more than anger going on here,* he thought. *She's afraid. But of what?*

"Please, honey, calm down. I will explain everything to you but I need for you to relax. OK? Can you do that?"

She just stared at him and after awhile, slowly nodded her head.

"Great. Then, here, have a seat," he said as he pulled one of the straight-backed chairs and turned it toward her. "How about a drink before we start? I could use one."

Again, she just nodded, but Rickey could tell the rage was still in her; the slight trembling of her lips gave away the calm she was trying to project. He arranged two short highball glasses in front of her and sat a bottle of *Remy Martin* down between them. He hoped the brandy would have a calming effect on her; hell, on both of them.

"Yes, I will tell you my real name, and everything about me. All I ask is that you listen and understand I never meant to hurt you, or cause you any harm." And, with that, Rickey began to recount to her how he came to be sitting in her dining room, drinking her brandy. She sat silently as he told his tale and never asked a question. "And, that is the truth. I never wanted to deceive you, but I needed to keep what I know to myself; it's simply safer that way." He sat back and looked at her and noticed the anger seemed to have left her and been replaced with an empathy of understanding. She reached out and took his hand in hers and said very softly, "They were here looking for you."

While surprised at how quickly they had found him, Rickey wasn't stunned. "What did they look like?"

"Look like?"

"Yeah, look like. What kinda vibe did you get off them?"

"I don't know. Older. White. Probably American." Her voice had a whiney, reedy quality to it Rickey hadn't heard before.

"What was their hair like? Their haircuts?"

"Oh, well, one was, I don't know, about five feet nine and kinda average build, the other was taller and heavier."

Rickey was starting lose patience with her but then realized she was badly frightened and wasn't clear-headed. "OK, honey, that's good," he replied in a smooth, calm voice. "There were just two of them?"

"Yes, just the two. They came into the house and asked for a Richard Osgood. I said I didn't know anyone by that name. Then they said, how about a Rickey, you know a Rickey, and I said no. Then they asked me if I knew the guy in a picture and they showed me a picture of you and that actress, Rita something-or-other. By now, I was getting scared, as they kept moving closer to me and the one guy kept raising his voice. I said, yeah, I knew the guy in the photo...you...I meant, what else could I say? They asked where you were and I said out on the boat making a delivery and would be back tomorrow."

"Good. You did good. Now, take a breath and try and picture them standing here. Now focus on their haircuts. What do you see?"

"Well, the taller guy had a kinda shaggy cut with little curls just over his ears. And the other guy, his hair was very black and slicked back, ya know, kinda like he put something on it. Oh, yeah, he had a small gold cross hanging over his tie."

"Really! Well, they weren't Feds then; they were the other guys."

92

Each of them laid on their backs, the sweat dripping off their bodies. The sheet beneath them was drenched and was cold and clammy against their skin. Rickey was breathing hard but noticed Sandy was not; *How can that be?* he questioned himself. They had only moments before, finished the most physical sex Rickey had ever known. For nearly an hour, they clawed at one another at what sometimes felt like a rage and at other times, felt like the quiet before the storm. Her nails had bitten into his back and shoulders, while her piercing screams caused him to feel both fear of hurting her and a weird sense of power. Her long legs wrapped around him and crushed him into her; he had to fight to break free some room so his hips could once again pound against hers. It was violent, it was sweet, it was caring and it was brutal all at the same time; he had never experienced anything like it.

The room was dark except for the glow of twenty or so candles circling the bed. In the softness of their light, Rickey watched her breathe slowly, steadily, and in a peaceful rhythm. *My God, she is something,* he thought. He hated the idea of letting her go and yet he knew it would be impossible for them to leave together. She needed to buy out her brother and that required at least another year of produce runs. And, what could he offer her? He had some money, but not much, no home, no place to go, no family and not even a real name. He had to do this alone; but maybe someday they would meet again.

Sandy rolled over on her side and reached out and touched him with a small, "Ahhh" sound. "Baby, what was that? My God, I've never felt like that before."

"Me neither," he mumbled under his breath. "Me neither."

There was silence between them for a very long time, until Rickey, with a small cough to break the spell said, "I think it was good-bye."

"Yes, I had the same thought. I've tried to figure some way for me to go with you, I mean, I know you can't stay here, so it's on me to go with you. But I just can't see it. I know this is going to be so hard for you; cutting everyone off, leaving everything you've known behind, in the past and out of reach. You won't be able to ever touch it again. Gone means gone and I'm sorry, but I don't believe in ghosts."

He rolled over to face her and tears were running down his face. He reached out and she came into his arms and they embraced and melted into one. For the first time with her, he felt that unconditional love he had only felt twice before. They held each other as they rocked gently to the sound of the wind beating against the windows; a slow, constant rhythm which led them into sleep.

Rickey awoke to the sun in his eyes and Sandy sitting on the edge of the bed fully dressed with a cup of coffee in her hand. She handed him the coffee and in a flat, matter of fact voice, asked, "Do you have a plan?"

He nodded yes.

"Good. Let's get to it, but we have to include Wiley."

93

Bobby was very pleased with himself as he placed the call to his father's office. He had found Rickey and after much self-examination, decided to tell his father first rather than taking it to Anthony directly. He was hopeful his father would give him credit. "Hi, Dad. How's Mom? Great. She having a good time? That's wonderful news. Well, I have some more news for you. I found Rickey. He's up on Vancouver Island in a small town called Sidney. He's living with a woman who owns a local bar. Not sure what kind of work he is doing, but he's gone a lot. But, yeah, it's him and he is there."

"Well, son, that's nice, but it's a day late and a dollar short, as are most things with you," Raymond snarled back into the phone. "My guys found him three days ago and just this afternoon Anthony called to give the green light to pick him up and bring him back to the States. But, thanks, I will let them know that you called, and made an effort, even if it was only half-assed. Maybe they will take it as a gesture of respect and forget all your fuck-ups. I gotta go now." Raymond all but slammed the phone down, already calculating the odds of Bobby telling Rickey the boys were coming for him. *Maybe I should have them grab him and hold him until this thing is wrapped up.* He pondered the advantages and disadvantages of that tactic as he absentmindedly drew circles on a notepad.

Bobby was frozen on the other end of the line. Not from the chill of the wind blowing outside the booth but from the fear that his father might turn him over to Anthony. *He damned well could do that, and I would disappear.* The fear choked the words in his throat and sweat broke out along his belt line; he could taste the sourness of his own breath. This was fear of the rankest kind; fear of your imagination.

He slowly replaced the phone in its holder and opened the booth's door. The morning breeze slapped his face like an Ali short-right, and actually cleared his head. He remembered his packages safely tucked away with four members of the California Bar, who for a fee, would follow a client's instructions to the T. He could call them, or one of them, and have them mail the files. But he wasn't sure if he was ready to bring Armageddon down on his father, and of course, change his mother's life forever, not to mention, his own. *Nah*, he thought, as he walked to his car. *Let's hold off on that, at least for awhile.*

As he slid behind the wheel of the rental car and closed the door, cutting off the chill from the wind, he thought, *Should I tell Rickey the goons are about to grab him?* An inner voice said to him, *Why would you do that? How does that help you?* "It doesn't," he said out loud. "Not at all." He turned the key and started the engine. It would be a short drive back to Victoria. Rene would start her shift in two hours.

94

"So, your name is Rickey, not Dusty or Richard or Rhodes, or was there some other name I've forgotten?" The tone in Wiley's voice was one of both distain and anger. He was facing Rickey with Sandy on his left, the two of them a team united. Rickey sat off to their right with one leg dangling off the stern of Whisper wishing for the world he was somewhere else. The smell of Wiley's cigarette was actually pleasant to Rickey as it was familiar. Everything else seemed so unreal.

"What kinda shit have you gotten us into? Our whole operation is in jeopardy. I mean, Jesus Christ, my sister takes you in, we give you a home, we feed you, hell, we even cut you in our operation and this is how you thank us? What an asshole!" Wiley cut a look at Sandy that said, "and it's all your fault too." Then he turned and walked across the aft deck, pulled a beer out of the ice chest which laid against the port transom, slammed the lid down and muttered under his breath, "motherfucker." As he stood there the drops of ice off the beer pooled on the decks leaving dark spots. Rickey thought they looked like blood and imagined his own blood puddling on the deck until it ran out of the scuppers into the sea.

Then everything went quiet. You could hear only the soft sounds of the waves slapping Whisper's hull and the sounds of the gulls chasing each other on the far side of the inlet. They were anchored just off shore about three miles from the house. Wiley had insisted they move Whisper off the dock and he refused to speak to either of them while inside the house. As Whisper gently tugged on her anchor line, the quiet of the late afternoon surrounded them, and the feeling of anger amongst them slowly ebbed.

They sat there in the fading light, each in turn lighting a cigarette, taking a deep pull and not saying a word. A good twenty minutes passed when Sandy finally said, "I am as angry as you Wiley, and probably as scared as you are Rickey, but the truth of the matter is, we are all in this together and need to come up with a plan which will make whoever is looking for Dusty or Rickey go away and stay away." Rickey glanced at her but said nothing, and Wiley just nodded and took a long pull on his *PBR*, before muttering, "Fuck."

"I hear ya, sis. Sitting here pissed off isn't going to solve our problem and it sure as hell won't make those sons o' bitches go away. So what do we do?"

"I die." Rickey said it so softly that Sandy didn't even hear it and Wiley's only response was, "What?" It was clear he had heard Rickey, as his tone was challenging and his hand tightened around the empty beer can so tight as to crush it. The collapsing sound it made crashed like a bass note at a symphony's end, and lingered in the air like an exclamation point.

Rickey swung his right leg up and over the port side rail and stood up. Feeling more sure of himself than he had in hours, he repeated himself, but now with the full voice of a tenor striking just the right note said, "I die. It's that simple. No one looks for a dead man."

"And just how do you do that?" Sandy asked with a tone that reeked of sarcasm. "Shoot yourself on the outbound ferry?"

"No he is right," Wiley said quickly before Rickey had a chance to respond. "That's the best way to end this thing quickly. But we need to do it right. No loose ends. Just gone without a trace but in a believable way."

Rickey looked out across the inlet to the narrows where the tidal rip was always the strongest. "I fall off the boat and the current carries me out to sea."

"No, I don't like that. Why would you fall off the boat?" Sandy asked raising her hands in the universal sign of, *What, are you stupid*? "No, that won't fly."

"Yeah, but if the boat has an accident and he's swept overboard, that will sell," Wiley said, looking at Rickey, half-wishing he was dead already.

"OK, but why would he have an accident? I mean, how would we explain it?" Sandy asked as her fingers drummed the rail and her eyes flickered between Rickey and Wiley seeking a response but at the same time afraid of what it might mean.

"Simple." Rickey now spoke up after feeling like the child at the table while the adults decide where he was going to go to middle school. "When we load the boat for our run to Anacortes we leave a tool bag next to the autopilot. That causes the pilot to steer the wrong course which will put us on Pull Point when the tide is at full ebb. We will slam into Ginger Rock and the theory will be that I was pitched out of the boat and carried out with the tide. We will have some torn fabric from my jacket on the rail and they will hopefully find my cap or something adrift down stream. But we will have to damage Whisper...I don't see any way around that." His voice trailed off leaving the thought hanging in the air. No one wanted to own it, but they all recognized the reality of it.

"No," Wiley interjected quickly, "we need something more dramatic than that. How about we arrange it so it looks like you were lying in the bunk when she hits. You're thrown out of the bunk and smash your head on the corner of the sea chest. Head injuries bleed heavily. We make sure there is a lot of blood on the chest and a trail of it up to the aft deck. Bloody hand prints on the rail will make it look like you staggered on deck, were tossed into the rail, lost your balance and fell in. Once in the water there is no way to get back onboard; the topsides are too high. But a few smear marks on the hull will make it look like you tried." Wiley fished a cigarette out of his breast pocket and lit it with his lighter; in the darkness the flame made his face look ghoulish. His eyes locked on his sister's as she quietly nodded her head. After a few moments he turned and looked across the deck, "Well, that's how you die Rickey, or Dusty or South Point or whatever the hell your name is."

Rickey just sat there in the darkness, feeling more alone than any time during his life. The darkness could shield him, but it couldn't protect him from what the future held. He stood and nodded in Wiley's direction, "You're right. Sounds convincing even without a body."

"So what we need is a dark night with a strong tide. Let me check the almanac and see what we have coming up. Wiley took a long drag on his cigarette and looked out over the horizon which was quickly turning the afternoon sun into a pale yellow haze as it sunk into the western sea. He shook his head, as if trying to clear it and then turned and looked directly at Rickey. "Or we could simply turn you over to the Feds...it's just a phone call." His voice was flat, and his tone was steady but there was a slight stutter in his voice which gave away the anger he was feeling. "Then I don't get my boat all fucked up."

"Our boat," Sandy spat out like an epithet. "It's our boat, Wiley, and I will not turn Rickey or anyone else over to those war-loving sons of bitches.

And you agreed with me, remember? Besides we can fix the boat; we did it before."

"Ah, sorry sis. I didn't mean to upset you. I was just pointing out to this guy that there are choices..." and his voice trailed off. A silence filled the boat just as the darkest of the night descended and the only sound was the rushing of the water against the hull.

Finally Rickey spoke up, knowing it was his job to patch the breach and give them both a way to carry on. "I agree, Wiley, I should be gone. Then come back and make sure some of the locals see me, then do our Houdini act. They will have to believe I was on the boat or the whole thing collapses."

"Alright, let's get you to Oak Island tonight. Take the bus into Seattle and get lost for a few days. Then call the bar and say you're from Pacific Fish Company and you have the crab cakes we ordered. If we say 'great' then you say 'when would you like them delivered' and we will tell you the date we've picked for you to return to the island. Cool?"

"Yeah, cool."

"Sandy, you agree?"

"Yeah, I, hell, I don't know what else to do so that sounds good." She looked over at Rickey and smiled and he knew that she would help him, yet she had lost her feelings for him. He could taste the bile in the back of his throat rise, and he choked it back down. Long afterward he could still taste its bitterness.

95

As Rickey stepped off Whisper, Wiley silently pushed her into reverse and eased her away from the dock. A thick fog hung over Oak Island and the inlet and where Wiley dropped Rickey was dark except for the small lights that ran along the outside rail of the dock, and each of those glowed with a halo of dim yellow light. They reminded Rickey of the front porch of Sandy's house that first night they met and a pang of regret seared through him. She had chosen not to make the trip over to Oak Island with them, instead said her good-byes at the bar while washing glasses. Both of them knew he would be back in Sidney, if only briefly, before his fatal accident, but it still felt like good-bye, and it left Rickey hollowed out.

As he stretched to reach the dock, his foot partially slipped. Regaining his balance he turned and nodded to Wiley, who touched his finger to his cap in a gesture of farewell. Rickey watched Whisper quickly disappear into the fog and the darkness. All that remained was the dim glow of her green nav light and that too within minutes faded. It was as if his past was dissolving in the morning mist along with Whisper. It was time to create his future.

He knew from the map of Oak Island that he had a 40 minute walk from the inlet where Wiley had dropped him off to the public dock were at 7:00 AM he could get a ferry into Seattle. As he walked he pondered his situation. The ID in his wallet said Richard William Rhodes, but he knew nothing of this person or even if there was such a person. While he was confident that the ID would pass inspection, he wasn't sure it would pass investigation. He needed a new ID, so if his background information was checked it would pass muster. *But how the hell will I get that?* he thought to himself. He knew he didn't know, but he thought he knew someone who would: his dad.

When he left for Canada, Bailey told him that he had installed an additional phone line in the office. No one would ever use that line, but if Rickey really needed to reach them he was to call during business hours and let it ring seven times, then hang up. After 30 seconds had passed he was to call back; either he or Rickey's mom would answer. While he had been tempted to call before, he never did as his father had made it clear this was a survival tool, not something to use for reassurance or out of loneliness. He had the number on a carefully folded piece of paper, tucked into the back of his wallet hidden between some old photos of Rusty when she was a puppy. When he reached Seattle he would call.

Not sure what he was expecting, he had assumed a ferry would be of a certain size like the one he had come over on to Sidney. This was about the size of Whisper and luckily there were only five other passengers this morning or he would have to sit up on the bridge with the skipper, a kid even younger than Rickey. As the other passengers pressed forward to board, Rickey stood back and looked the Idle Time over. The decks were wet from the morning fog, and dew caused her bright red wheelhouse to appear dark brown in the dim morning light. She was about 35 feet and built of wood, most likely before the war, and she had been built as a work boat not as a pleasure craft. A small cuddy cabin forward, a long open deck starting midships and running uninterrupted aft, with a steering station up one level where currently her young skipper looked down watching everyone board.

A stout and solid little vessel built for a purpose, and here she was all these years later still working, still plying the waters of Puget Sound, still earning her keep; a testament to her builder's integrity. Rickey thought of Whisper and while he knew he had to damage her in order to make his escape, it pained him and he often thought there must be a better way; but he hadn't come up with it yet.

There were two bench seats running along each side of the after deck, but the other passengers had grabbed those and had stacked their luggage on the remaining seats. He quickly figured out it was all one family led by a big burly woman wrapped in a dark grey all-weather coat, who looked right at him with a hard stare, which seemed to challenge him to say something. He glanced away and saw the engine box had a clear space on the starboard side and thought, *Perfect, I'll be nice and warm while they freeze their asses off.* He glanced back at the woman and smiled while slipping onto his seat.

The low rumble of the engines signaled they were underway and soon the chill of the morning cut Rickey's face like a razor; smooth but with an edge. He could smell the sweet oily smell of the diesel exhaust as it mixed with the sea water. That combined with the greasy smell coming from the tinfoil carton that the oldest child was holding flush with his chin as he quickly shoveled the contents into his mouth made him a bit queasy. In that moment Rickey flashed back to a memory of elementary school and a kid they'd called "The Shovel" because he ate just like that. Rickey was filled for a moment with a warm secure feeling remembering the days before the Induction Center, before his flight for life had begun, back when he was just South Point Rickey.

A blast from the boat's fog horn as it entered the main channel to Seattle brought him back to reality like a slap in the face. No more South Point Rickey, no more Dusty Rhodes; he had to become someone else, some real but fictional someone who lived and breathed but could never show up to spoil his identity, someone of character with a good education so he could have a reasonable future, but most of all, someone he could live with. He had to create himself. But first he had to decide what he wanted to be. While he wanted to give himself an education, it needed to be in something more theoretical than practical. He couldn't give himself a degree in engineering because he might have to produce something; he would have the same problem with any vocational skill. So he thought to himself, *it needs to be something where I can bullshit my way, but still something I know something about. Sports. I know water sports. I can surf. I can drive a boat. I can swim and dive. How hard can it be to learn how to fish or sail? Plus, it's outdoors and there is where I want to be.* Slowly he rolled the idea around and the longer he did, the better it felt. "So exactly how am I going to do this? What do I need?" he muttered to himself, no fear of being overheard as wind off the water ripped the words off his lips almost as he spoke them.

His thoughts were interrupted as the Idle Hour slowed and then stopped even though they were still in the middle of the channel. The skipper lowered himself down the ladder from the bridge and spoke loudly to try and overcome the noise from the engine. "Folks, this here is the Ballard locks. We need to go through them in order to get into the lake. This will take us a few minutes and it will be about another twenty minutes until we dock, so just relax and please keep your hands inside the boat as we pass through the locks. As the water level in the channel is about seven feet lower than the lake this morning, we will be riding the water up. What will happen is the lock keepers will close the lock gates and then pump water into the lock, and the water will rise, taking our boat with it. Once we get to the same level as the lake, they will open the gates and we will motor on in. There is nothing to worry about. These gentlemen have done this a thousand times. OK. No questions? Great. Looks like the sun is trying to peak out so enjoy it and we will be on our way shortly."

Yep, I could do this, Rickey thought. *I wonder what you need to qualify, like to have been the Navy or something. I need to look into it...and a lot of other stuff, too. Damn, there is so much I don't know.* With that he turned to watch the lock keepers pull the heavy lines to bring Idle Hour alongside the lock's walls to start her journey into the lake. As he watched, he thought, *Lock keeper looks like a pretty boring job. I need something more engaging, something more challenging.*

96

As the Idle Hour nudged into her slip at the far end of Lake Washington, Rickey stood and gaped at the sight of downtown Seattle. He had never seen a big city that brought her commerce and bustle right down to the water's edge. Los Angeles was big, but her downtown ended miles from the sea. Even San Diego's business district ended blocks from the bay. But here the building and parking lots, the shops and stores crowded each other right down to the water's edge. And reigning above them all was the Space Needle, a tower or a building built as a tower, depending on your point of view, which was constructed for the World's Fair in 1962 and had remained a Seattle landmark ever since. Rickey remembered reading about it when he was fourteen and thinking how modern and progressive it was. It symbolized America was on the cutting edge of space exploration. *Funny,* he thought, *It still has a modern look all these years later. I need to go up in it.*

The Idle Hour was tied to the very last slip at the end of a long wooden dock which looked like the last time it had had serious maintenance was before World War II. It sagged a bit toward the water, and its rough wooden planks were not something you wanted to walk barefoot on. Fishing boats, power cruisers, sailboats of various sizes and condition were in single finger slips which ran off the main walkway dock on both sides. The pier ran for about 200 feet then made a jog to the right, and then straightened out for another 400 feet so the boats out on the end were moored well into the lake. He noted the tidal marking on the concrete wall which served as a buttress to the shore, and realized that only shallow draft vessels could be moored inside as the tide would fall and leave a deeper draft vessel aground twice a day.

Just as he was looking at the tidal marks on the wall and musing about the groundings at low tide, he heard a "Hey watch it, will ya?" Startled, he turned quickly just avoiding an old man struggling under the weight of a huge anchor. "Here, let me help you with that," Rickey volunteered and quickly dropped his duffle and grabbed one of the flukes of the anchor. Its weight quickly bent him over and it took him a second to regain his balance. "Wow! This mother weighs," he said without much thought.

"Hell yes it does!" the old man replied, "That's why I want it off my boat. Here, just set it here and I'll get a cart to move it over to Slim's Treasured Lady, he's giving me 50 bucks for it." Rickey was afraid to set the anchor down fearing it would plunge right through the dock but his arms were screaming and he welcomed the chance to unload the burden. Once both men rested their ends on the dock, they began to speak at once. "Hi, I'm..." But Rickey was over struck by the old man's powerful baritone. "Captain Jack Peterson. Glad to meet ya."

"Yeah, likewise, the same." Rickey got out, just as the old man reached for his hand and gave it a powerful squeeze. "Wow, that's quite a grip you've got there for...I mean, well, you know."

"Yeah, I know...for an old man. That's what ya meant, right? And I get it, but pulling trawl lines for 50 years will give you a grip no matter...but it won't keep that old ticker going, or that's what they tell me."

"Hell, they ran enough tests so I guess they got it right. And whenever I walk up to Clancy's for a pint, damn, I can barely breathe. So something ain't right. But that won't stop me from walking up to Clancy's. Been doing it every night at five for as long as I can remember."

"Nah, what will stop me is living in Portland with my daughter and her kids. Just too far a drive for a pint." The old man chuckled under his breath at his little joke. "Yeah, too damn far. I'll just have to find me a Clancy's down there."

"So, you're moving then? Leaving Seattle? How long have you been here?"

"My whole damn life. Born up there in the Heights. Daddy was a lawyer, but that wasn't the life I wanted. So at 14, I quit school and took a job on the Daisy, a small long-line boat out of Ballard. Started fishing, and just stopped last week. Did my last trip on Don Jenkins' Party Girl, a 42 foot *Hatteras*. Old Don likes drinking more than fishing so he hires me to run the boat while he and his buddies drink and tell lies, and every so often, pull on their rods. Good trip, too. Got four good-sized snapper and two salmon;

everybody had fish to take home to momma. I took some too, and shared it with some of the guys; we had ourselves a little bar-b-que - sorta a last trip party. It was nice. They gave me this." He pulled a whale-boned knife from his pocket and it had his name, Captain Jack, carved into the handle.

"Nice. And thoughtful." Rickey didn't really know what to say and felt a little awkward, not sure what to make of the old man's rambling.

"Ah, yes and no. Nice knife, but now every time I pull it, I have to think of those damn bastards." A huge smile crept across his face and he gave Rickey's shoulder a light punch. "Hey, how about a quick drink and I'll show ya my little boat, Carol."

Rickey shrugged and thought, *Why the hell not, what else have I got to do? And, this guy's a trip.* "Great, which one is she?"

97

"Well, here she is," Captain Jack said, with a slight catch in his voice. "My sweet Carol. Named her after my wife, God rest her soul. Never a better woman walked this earth."

Rickey wasn't sure what to say, so he simply stood and looked at the old sailboat with its yellow hull and tan decks. After a few moments, he said, "What is she? I mean, what design?"

"Ah, that's a good question. When I got her back in '44, I was told that she had been built up in Port Townsend by a fellow named Jake Thompson and was designed by Bill Garden, Sr., his-self. But then around '59, I was burning some paint off her bottom and found a bronze plaque that said she was a Carol ketch designed by John Hanna, the fellow who did the Tahiti ketch, and built by Jake Thompson in 1939 over at Fellows Yard down in LA.

"I always reckoned that was the true story. And I like the idea she was a Carol ketch and named Carol. Here, come aboard and looks around," he said as he stepped onto the aft rail which formed part of the cockpit.

What Rickey noticed immediately was the Carol did not roll down under Captain Jack's weight; she was as steady as a rock. This was new to him, as Whisper was what they called *tender*, which simply meant that any weight on her rail or change of weight below would cause her to lean, not a lot, but enough to cause you to shift your weight or stumble.

Rickey deliberately put his full weight on the cap rail to see if she would tip under it, but not an inch did she move. *Wow*, Rickey thought to himself, *What a steady little boat. Bet she'd be good in a seaway.*

Captain Jack motioned him below and Rickey immediately noticed the boat was spotlessly clean and looked like it had been stripped of any possessions, with the sole exception of the fifth of *Old Overholt* standing like a lonely soldier on the scarred oak countertop.

Captain Jack grabbed the bottle, took a short pull and then offered it to Rickey. The liquor burned his throat and brought tears to his eyes. "Holy shit! What is this stuff?" he blurted out. "Sure as hell isn't like any whisky I've ever had."

Captain Jack stood there, a sly smile spreading across his face and was working hard to keep from laughing at Rickey. "Yesiree, sonny boy, that's no store bought whisky. That's homemade by my buddy on the Sea-Siren; 120 proof but it does keep the blood moving on those night watches. Here, have another pull, you'll get used to it."

Rickey eyed the bottle with suspicion but took it and pulled another few ounces of the dark brown fluid into his mouth and swallowed hard. This time the bite wasn't as bad and the flavor of the whisky started to come though. "Hey, that wasn't too bad. In fact, I think I kinda like it."

"There ya go, boy. I knew you was OK the minute you stopped to help me. Not many folks these days take the time to help one another along. I appreciate it...really do. Shows me that you youngsters have more to ya than just growing out your hair and playing loud music." With that he took another sip from the bottle and pointed toward the bow of the boat.

"Ya see, right up there in the fo'c'sle, you've got yourself a nice bunk for sleeping. Then right over here is the galley, outfitted with a wood burning stove which on cold nights also works as a heater, and a small ice box...that there is a pump for fresh water and the other one is for sea water, but here on the lake, it's fresh water too. And over here, you have a little table for eating and a sofa for sitting and reading."

Rickey looked around and thought back to his *VW* bus and how comfortable he'd been in it while on the road in Mexico. But this was even better. Not only was it bigger and more comfortable but it sailed and the wind could take you places. Places far, far away from the Feds, the Army, from Bobby and his gangster friends; far away from all the forces pressing down on him. His imagination ran wild, swinging from Mexico to the South Pacific, to Alaska. *The whole world was yours for the taking,* he thought, and for a moment, he saw Sandy standing next to him as they sailed into some remote anchorages. "But no, no, that would never work."

"What wouldn't work?" Captain Jack asked, not realizing Rickey was talking to himself. But his question had the effect of bringing Rickey back to the present and face to face with his situation.

"Oh, nothing. I was just..." his voice trailed off, leaving his unfinished thought hanging in the air.

"Ah, I know what you were thinking. I've seen that look on so many greenhorns over the years. That look of wonder after the realization that you can jump on a small ship like the Carol, and make no mistake about it, she is a small ship, not some toy like those boys outta the yacht club sailing on Sundays, and boom...be gone, leaving all the shit your life has become in your wake. Yesiree, I've seen that look many a time. But ya know what? I've known only a few people to cast off these dock lines and go. Me included. Nope, the shore-side ties are sometimes just too strong to be broken. Unless of course, you're on the run, then that's a different story. You on the run, son?"

98

The smell of onions frying on the grill from the hamburger stand at the top of the pier washed over Rickey and reminded him he hadn't eaten since yesterday afternoon. The roughness of the deck under his feet somehow felt like gravel. There was a low roaring sound in his ears, like when he would turn at the bottom of a twenty foot wave. His senses were on high alert, yet his mind was spinning. *Why would he say that? What did I say to make him think that? What should I say now?* These thoughts and a fear like panic gripped him as he stood frozen, unable to flee or respond. He wobbled slightly as if being blown by the wind.

Captain Jack took him by the elbow and slowly steered him toward the mid-ship settee and he sat down slowly as if he was deflating. Rickey sat there quietly for a few minutes then raised his head and looked Captain Jack square in the eye and said in a voice not more than a whisper, "How did you know?"

"Know? I know nothin'. Never have. You wanna tell me, fine, if not, well that's fine, too." He sat down on the opposite facing settee, grabbing the handrail to steady himself all the while still looking into Rickey's eyes. He slowly rubbed the three-day old stubble on his chin as he rocked back and forth, letting the silence do its job.

Finally Rickey straightened up, arching his back to try to release the tension which had built up there, took a deep breath, and sighed, "Sweet Jesus. Yes, yes I am on the run. Have been for a while now but they damn near grabbed me up in Sidney, and I had to go, but I'm not sure..." His words were tumbling out of his mouth like water out of a fire hose; all rush and emotion but hard to understand.

Captain Jack reached over to the galley where the bottle and fruit jar glasses stood like centurions waiting for the call of duty. He poured a full measure into a glass and without getting up, handed it to Rickey and with a nod said, "Drink up...and tell me about it."

By the time he'd finished, the sunlight was coming in from the other side of the boat. Little lasers of lights streaming in through the round bronze port lights casting a warm yellow light throughout the cabin and making it feel like a confessional. Safe, intimate, and yet, soul searching. The boat smelled a little musty inside, reminding Rickey of his grandmother's house; another safe place. He felt relieved and content but on edge for having told a total stranger his darkest secrets.

"Well, young man, that's quite a tale you've just spun but it sounds like to me you have only half a plan. Getting away from anything, or anyone, is a two-step process; the getting gone and the stayin' gone. Sounds to me like you got the gettin' gone down real good. But how you gonna stay gone?"

"Well, I think I have to, if I want to stay alive. And, I want to stay alive," Rickey responded, startled by the forcefulness of his reply. In that moment, the haze and uncertainty which had engulfed him since hearing about the men hassling Sandy lifted like the morning fog and a fresh resolve flooded him. It surged through him like a primal force and he realized his teeth were clenched and his hands knotted into fists as if ready to strike a blow against an unseen foe.

"I reckon so. From what you said those boys sound as serious as a heart attack. But a wantin' to and doin' are two different things. How you plannin' to stay gone? Whatcha gonna do for money? For a place to live? For ID? I mean, hells bells, they want a picture of yourself to go to the toilet nowadays. How you gonna get some paper? You thought about this stuff?"

"Hell yes, it's damn near all I've thought about for weeks. And I'm not sure about a lot of it. Money? Work. At what? I don't know. All I've done is surf and then run Whisper on pot runs over to the US. Kinda limited skill set. But, I'll find something."

"Yeah, but they will ask for a social security card. You got one to give 'em? Now ain't like when I was your age. You talked your way into a job and you worked. No one asked shit, because no one cared. Nowadays the government wants to keep tabs on everyone so they can take their money I guess, but whatever is their reason, there will be questions and you need the answers. I do know of one place where they don't ask too many questions and a man is judged by the cut of his jib, not somethin' wrote on no paper. Where it's more important how he pulls a trawl than where he's from."

"Really? Where's that?"

Captain Jack jerked his head out over his right shoulder as he half-turned his body, "Out there. On the water. In the boats, no one cares about the man next to him except can he pull his weight and bring in the catch. Ya see, they all share in the catch. A piece goes to the boat, a piece for expenses, then the rest is split up among the crew. The bigger the catch, the better everyone does. So a greenie who fucks up, well it ain't just his share that gets dinged but everyone else's too. So you can see why the other guys get pissed; you've taken food off their tables. But they ain't gonna ask you for no papers, or no fancy resume. Nah, they'll look at your hands to see if yuz worked at all, and look ya in the eye to judge ya. They like ya, they give ya a spot. If not they give ya an excuse."

"So what you are saying is, I should look for a fishing job, a job on a fishing boat? Where do you look? I'm guessing in the paper like other jobs or is there a hall or place where they put up cards? I mean, how do you know which boats need help?"

"You are a green one, ain't ya? Christ, son, you go and ask. You walk the docks and look over the boats. Stay away from the ones that're real rusty or dirty lookin'...dem ones will always have trouble. Broken this or that, bad crew, a drunk for a captain, but worst of all, they won't make ya any money. Look for the boat that looks like its together. The lines are tidy and the nets are piled nice and straight, the paint is good and the rim around the stack is black but clean black, not soot or grey streaks...sure sign of trouble if they's there. Then go talk to the captain. Be honest. Yuz green but have some boatin' experience but most of all ya listen and is a hard worker. And you be judgin' him while he's a-judgin' you. You don't need to jump on the first boat that comes along. Like a woman; be choosey."

Rickey again caught the pungent smell of frying onions and realized he was starving. He didn't want to be rude and just leave the Carol but he was unsure of how to gracefully depart. Then without thinking, he blurted out, "Damn, look at the time. I've kept you from Clancy's."

"Oh, I know, but Clancy's is 'bout friendship as well as a wee nip. And I think I've had both here with you this afternoon. But just the same, maybe we should amble up the hill and grab somethin' to eat. What's it? Tuesday? He'll have the snapper off the Fairy Queen for sure. Let's go. Best damn snapper you ever had."

And with that, Captain Jack grabbed a handrail fitted to the side of the cabin, steadied himself and in one sweeping motion, slid back the hatch to reveal a black and inky sky with little dots of lights, which made the sky seem even darker. But to Rickey, it looked like the dawning of a new day.

99

There was a small fireplace off to the left of the door when you walked into Clancy's but it couldn't account for the heat that hit Rickey's face as he followed Captain Jack in. Immediately, the heat overwhelmed him, and stood in stark contrast to the knife-like wind that had been cutting him only moments before. He started stripping off his jacket before the door closed behind him.

It must be all these people, he thought to himself as he scanned the bar and small cafe which was packed with large men with rough hands and sunburned faces. Many had shed their jackets and some their outer shirts, revealing the stark demarcations between their bright red forearms and their pale biceps which gave away their Norwegian heritage. But even a crowd this size packed as it was into a small place, could not generate the humid breathtaking heat that seemed to come in waves. The sour smell of old beer mixed with the smell of fish added to the general atmosphere of an old waterfront bar. A bar that had been serving fishermen for generations with beer so cold it numbed your teeth and chowder so thick you could eat it with a fork. This was no nouveau-fern bar, nor was it even like Smiley's which was a party bar for the working class. No, this was a fisherman's bar, where the whisky was drunk straight, and wine was reserved for the occasional wife or girlfriend who happened by.

Rickey pulled on Captain Jack's collar to get his attention, as he was like a last term mayor at the Fourth of July parade; everyone wanted to say 'hi' to Captain Jack. "Where are we going?" Rickey half-shouted into Captain Jack's ear, "and why is it so damn hot in here?"

"We's going to the back bar. I'm lookin' for Red Anderson off the Flying Genny. He owes me five bucks from back in '59 and I want to git it before I move. Fucker has been avoidin' me for awhile now." With that, Captain Jack pushed through a double set of doors that had an elaborate sign above which read, Davey Jones' Locker.

Once Rickey stepped into the back bar, it was like he was entering a different world. It was dark, cool, and except for Dean Martin singing something in Italian, very quiet. Rickey's eyes quickly focused and he noticed a long copper-topped bar along the east wall and maybe ten to 12 tables filling the west side of the room. The far back wall was all glass and looked out onto the lake which in the darkness was sparkling with the lights of small boats and ferries making their way. It was peaceful and Rickey liked it immediately.

Captain Jack sat on a stool at the bar and pulled one out for Rickey. "Here son, set yourself down for a moment and tell Eddie here what yuz having while I go and try and find Red."

Eddie smiled at Rickey and said, "So you're a friend of Captain Jack's. What can I bring ya?" Rickey was startled by being left alone and still off balance from the contrast between the two rooms.

"Ah, a beer I guess. Whatever you have on draft, please."

"One draft *Pabst* for my polite new friend. By the way, what should we call you?"

"Oh, I'm Rickey but everyone calls me South Point." No sooner were the words out of his mouth did he realize his mistake and dread flowed through him like a tidal wave. *Jesus Christ, what did I just do? You idiot!*

"South Point, now that's a handle we don't hear much around here. Why they call you that?"

So he noticed, damn. Just tell him the truth, about your name, nothing else, a small voice in the back of his said. "Ah, it's nothing. Just the way I ride a surfboard. Just a name some kid gave me one day and it stuck. Tell you the truth, I prefer Rick. But it's OK. Call me whatever you want. I'll still call you Eddie."

A big smile broke across Eddie's face. "You, kid, I like you. I think you will fit right in around here." And with that, he turned and pulled a perfect pour of *Pabst Blue Ribbon* into a tall stemmed glass and handed it over to Rickey. It felt cool and inviting in his hand. "Welcome to Clancy's. First one's on the house." And he turned away to tend to a fellow at the far end of the bar who was tapping his empty glass with a ballpoint pen.

Rickey sat alone for a few minutes replaying his screw-up in his head. He had to be more careful. Just about the time he drained the last bit of beer from the glass, Captain Jack slid onto the stool next to him. "Find Red?" Rickey asked.

"Hell yes, but he sez he don't owe me no fiver, that it's the other way around. I owe him. I got ta thinkin' and maybe he's right. So we shook and agreed we was even. Good thing, too, as I was asking him a favor, and it's best to ask if you are all even in tradin' favors."

"Really. Never thought of it that way. But I get what you're saying. What favor did you need?" Soon as he said it, he thought, *What is wrong with you tonight? You don't ask that of a guy you just met.* "Ah, sorry. That just kinda slipped out. It's none of my business."

"Well, yeah, it is sorta your business. See, I'm heading down to Portland on the early train and I'm trying to find someone to look after Carol for me. Ya know, check the lines and the bilge. If a storm comes a brewing, to do what needs to be done to make her safe. But all my buddies are too old or too busy or too drunk to be trusted. And I was thinkin' that maybe you'd look after her for me, now just for awhile, but if yuz so inclined, then yuz need some work. So I asked Red if he might have somethin' for ya or knew someone with an empty berth."

Rickey was stunned and not sure he understood the old man correctly. "Captain Jack, are you saying you want me to stay on the Carol and look after her?"

"Well, yes. Why, you don't like the idea? I know she's no fancy-dancy yacht but she warm and dry and has made me a good home for some twenty odd years now."

"Jesus no! I am overwhelmed that you would trust her to me. Even just on the dock. I know how important she is to you and you just met me today, and after hearing my story, I didn't think anyone would trust me."

"Well, I does, and that's all I gotta say on the subject." He looked down the bar to catch Eddie's eye, and made a circling motion with his hand. "Two more," he whispered.

100

"So, you're Rickey?" Red was sitting behind a large wooden desk with a thick glass top which reflected the overhead ceiling lights causing Rickey to squint.

"Ah, yes. Captain Jack told me to come and see you. You might have some work for me."

"Yeah, old Jack told me your story, lad, and I must say, it's quite a tale. Now, now, don't get all twisted up over him telling me. Your secret is safe with me. In fact, Jack had no choice cuz what he was askin' was a lot, and I needed to know why. But I get it. Been theres myself. Fucking government always there to hassle ya, but never there when you needs some help. Yeah, I get it, so you not be worryin' now. I ain't sharing your story with no one, cuz no one needs to know. They just need to know they're doing old Red here a favor and that's all there is to it."

Rickey was standing as Red spoke, but now he felt a little vertigo and grabbed the back of a chair facing Red's desk. To hide his feeling, he quickly slid around the chair and sat down. "I'm sorry, I don't understand. Captain Jack said to see you, ah, to see if you had any work I could do or knew anyone that needed a hand. It sounds like more than that."

"Well, hell yes. Jack's no half-trawl kinda guy. He may sit on the rail for awhile but when he decides to go, then he goes like nobody else. Lookey, son, Jack and I go back to '27 when we met on the deck of the old schooner, Arlene, laying off Vancouver Island awaitin' for the small boats to bring the whisky out. It was late December and so damn cold ya couldn't feel yer feet. But even worse, was the fog. So thick ya couldn't see the man next to ya on the rail. I was standing there having myself a smoke and Jack walked right into me, causin' me cigarette to fall into the water. Well, this upset me a might and I starts to cuss the blind bugger out. But before I could start, Jack's all, 'I'm sorry. Didn't see ya, mate. Here, have one o' mine. I'm Jack Peterson of Seattle.' Well, I tell ya, son, I thought to me-self, *Here's a gentleman.* All from then on, it was always Gentleman Jack. Yeah, we go back a long ways, Jack and me. And I sees what Jack sees in ya."

"Really, what is that? I just know he's a damn nice guy and has really treated me well."

"It ain't like Jack to talk about it, and most folks don't even know, but he had a son once. They called him Windale, after Jack's dad, who I heard was a fancy lawyer up on the hill back in the day. We was running whisky right up to the day old FDR said we could drink again. It was good money and a few of us did OK. Jack, he took his money and bought the Annabelle. She was a 40 tonner and ran long line. Me, I saw the money in booze so I bought this joint off Clancy who'd decided to move to California. It was all before the war. We was all single and having a hell of a time. People don't talk about it much but there was a window of a time between the real hard times of the Depression and the war when things was really good. At least up here, for us folks. Well, Jack was doin' pretty good and he meets Carol Jenkins, right here in this bar, and before ya could say 'Nice to meet ya,' they was married. And sure as shit, bout nine months later, little Windale was born. Man, oh man was Jackie proud. He'd march around the bar showing little Win, that's what they called him; Win, like he was a prize bull. Well, anyway, the war came and Jackie up an volunteered for the Navy...figured he know how to drive a boat and they could probably use that. While Jackie was out in the Pacific, I think it was '43 or '44, little Win was at his grandma's house and he fell outta a tree. Died right there. Jackie and Carol had another child after the war, Jenny. She lives down in Portland. But they never had another son. And I think that's what Jackie sees in you; that other son he never had."

Rickey sat there quietly listening to Red and when he had finished, Rickey realized that he hadn't moved the entire time and his left leg had fallen asleep. "Wow, really? Well, all I know is that he is a good man, and he said I should trust you and do what you say."

"Well, give me a day or two and I will have somethin' for ya. OK?"

"More than OK. Thanks a lot! And if there's anything I can do for you, just let me know." With that Rickey stood up, but felt unsteady as his left leg was still asleep. He withdrew his right hand from the pocket of his coat and extended it to Red who took it and squeezing it firmly said, "Be careful son, be careful."

Rickey turned and crossed the darkened bar, and out into the chill of the night. He felt things might be moving into his direction.

101

The surge from the morning ferry rolled Carol to her side and woke Rickey with a start. He was momentarily confused as to where he was but quickly the fog lifted as he recognized the deck beams just over his head. He realized his ears and hands were cold but the rest of him was toasty warm under a pile of comforters and blankets. So he quickly pulled the covers up over his head and tucked his hands between his legs.

He hesitated to get up, knowing the cabin would be cold and the cabin sole freezing to his feet. So he laid there thinking of what had passed and what he needed to do to stay free. "First thing, I need to get back up to Sidney and put Rickey to bed," he said out loud, his own voice waking him out of his sleepiness. He had been putting off the phone call to Sandy and Wiley, ashamed for the troubles he had caused them and enjoying the freedom the job as a deckhand on the Jennie J gave him. It had been only two weeks since he had left Sidney but it seemed like a lifetime ago; so many changes, so many new faces, so much he wanted to tell Sandy but was afraid she wouldn't care. The fear of the disappointment, he realized, was what had kept him from making the call. "Damn it, I'll do it today," he said out loud, as if that would make it so.

As he had thought, the cabin sole was like ice on his feet and his hands shook from the cold as he tried to light the *Dickerson* diesel heater. He could taste the pungent smell of the long-tipped match as he struck it against the striker and reached into the black well of the heater to light the burner. Slowly the burner grabbed the flame and spread it's blue-yellow glow across the deep basin of the heater and quickly he could feel the heat starting to radiate. He cupped his hands in front of the burner and nearly dropped the match. He stood there for a moment and let the heat wash over him and fill the small cabin with warmth. *Christ, I miss Mexico*, he thought, as he stood there with his hands nearly burned and his butt freezing.

He moved quickly across to the galley and grasped the teakettle from out of the sink. As the bronze handle pumped up and down, he could feel the coldness of the water filling the kettle but knew in a few minutes, it would be warm enough for him to wash his face and get the sleep out of his eyes. He would wait for mid-day to use the shower up on the main dock as there would be fewer people and much more hot water then. *Yes, after he showered, he would call Sandy,* he thought to himself. "Today is the day," he said out loud, checking himself in the small mirror and then giving himself a brief salute.

102

As he stepped off the ferry, the late afternoon sun was just above the hilltop leaving the small town of Sidney in a soft pink light. The electric blue *Blatz* sign was still flashing its welcome from Sandy's bar. He paused for a moment at the head of the dock and wondered if he should go into Smiley's; would he be welcomed? Should he be seen by the local townsfolk? Were the bikers still looking for him? How about the other guys? He scanned the horizon and saw nothing of concern but he was concerned and confused. *Christ,* he thought, *How'd it all get so fucked up? All I ever wanted to do was ride some tubes and hang out with my friends.* Just then a strong hand clamped down on his elbow and turned him around.

"So, you made it? She said that you'd called and would be coming over today. I've been watching the ferries all day looking for you." The scowl on Wiley's face could not have been uglier and from his breath, Rickey could tell he had been drinking.

"Yeah, I made it. Now let go of my arm." After a pause, Rickey lowered his head to be closer to Wiley's ear. "Wiley, you don't wanna fuck with me. I've got nothing to lose." And with that, he jerked his arm away. They exchanged hard stares before Wiley looked away and said, "She won't be seeing you. You broke her heart, you know. So don't go looking for her. I've sent her away. You and I will handle this and then you're gone. Right?"

"Whatever you say, Wiley, and I know I broke her heart...and mine, too. This isn't easy shit for any of us." He gave Wiley another hard stare and then stepped back. He looked down at his work boots covered in fish scales, shook his head slowly and then looked up at Wiley and said, "Thank you, you've been real solid."

Wiley looked over Rickey's shoulder into the setting pink sky, slowly rolled his head from side to side and said, "Fuck it, let's go get a beer."

The country western song hit Rickey before they even opened the front door. Once inside, Rickey didn't know if he was in a bar or on a jet runway. The crowd noise was one constant roar while the music bounced off of him in waves leaving him feeling a bit off-balance. He followed Wiley to a booth in the far back reaches of the main room. There was a small reserved sign on it so he knew this was part of Wiley's plan. Rickey slid into the booth, sitting across from Wiley but not sure he would be able to hear him over the band.

His eyes roamed over the room but there was no one he knew nor anyone who looked familiar. He reached into his breast pocket and pulled out a pack of *Lucky*'s and offered one to Wiley who just waved him off. Rickey lit the cigarette and took a long drag, blowing the smoke up toward the ceiling. Just then a waitress, who Rickey had seen around put down a small galvanized bucket with six beers in ice and said, "They said it was on the house," smiling at Wiley as she said it. Wiley handed her a five dollar bill and said, "Thanks Wanda. Oh, and Wanda, this is Rick. Rick, Wanda." They exchanged smiles and Wanda turned and elbowed herself through the crowd and was quickly swallowed by it.

They both reached for the same beer at the same time but Rickey pulled his hand back quicker and said, "No, after you, amigo." They banged the bottles together and each took a long pull. Rickey watched the water from the cold bottle puddle on the tabletop and it reminded him of the afternoon on the Whisper when they had come up with the plan for him to disappear. But his reverie was broken when Wiley shouted, apparently not for the first time, his name. He came back into the moment and mumbled an apology.

"I brought you here for a reason. I want you to be seen. It's important that people can say they just saw you the other day. Get it?"

"Makes sense."

"So, what I want you to do is get out of the booth, go find a girl, dance, order drinks, just put them on my tab. The girls are instructed that anything you order comes to me. Have a good time, and make sure you're seen. OK?"

"Ah, sure, Wiley, whatever you say. I just want to play this out and get on down the road."

"And once you're gone, you stay gone. If you ever try to contact my sister, or come back here looking for her, I will put you down like a rabid dog." Wiley had slid partway down the booth and now loomed over Rickey so that his beer and cigarette breath added an additional menace to the tone of his words.

"Man, I get it. I will be gone and stay gone. Trust me." As he spoke, he leaned into Wiley and reached out for his hand. Wiley slowly grabbed Rickey's hand and they shook as though it were a blood oath.

After a moment, Wiley reached into his pocket and fished out a key ring with the number six carved into an old fishing float. The Blue Bell. It's yours for the next three days. It's paid for. And Jackie is an old friend, so don't give him any shit. I've spread the story that you and Sandy split up and that you'll be crashing at the Bell until you find a place, so don't make me a liar. Go look at some cabins or apartments or something and chase some gals. Make a name for yourself." With that, Wiley dropped the key on the table and whispered over his shoulders, "Tomorrow, the Purple Cat at three, we need to talk."

Rickey picked up the room key and slowly stuffed it into the front pocket of his jeans. To do that, he had to arch his back getting his butt off his seat, leaving him half hanging in the air. "Hey handsome, I can help you with that, if you want." She was about 25 with long blonde hair that curled around her pretty face and covered part of the red plaid shirt she was wearing. Her smile was large and friendly, her eyes blue like the Pacific sky, and her perfume spoke of promises unkept. "I'm Cindy."

Rickey paused, trying to remember what name he was using at the moment. "Ah, Richard, but everyone calls me Dusty. So call me Dusty."

"Dusty it is. So what're we drinking cowboy?"

103

The Purple Cat was Sidney's fine dining restaurant, a place for a wedding dinner or an anniversary celebration, not your Tuesday night quick-eats place before going home or back to the office. It was both elegant and understated, conveying an air of respectability to itself and to its patrons. Rickey thought it was an odd place to meet Wiley until he realized it was empty and would stay empty for the rest of the day as it was a Monday.

He saw Wiley's jeep parked off to the side of the road near the back of the restaurant which Rickey assumed was where deliveries were made. He was right. Wiley was leaning back against a sign that said, 'Morning Deliveries Only.' He nodded to Rickey and pointed to the step just across the porch from him. "Grab a seat. We have a bunch of stuff to go over, so pay attention. No drifting away like you sometimes do. There has been a change of plans. Well, not really a change, but more like a refinement. I want you to know Sandy spent hours coming up with this shit and I damn well expect you to listen and agree to do it her way. If not, I'm telling you right now, we will walk away and you are on your own. Understand?"

"Fair enough. What's the plan? I still die?"

"Yeah, you still die. It's just the way the accident occurs is different, more detailed, more refined. OK, here's the gig. Like we talked about before, you take Whisper out on a delivery run, but instead of going to Anacortes, your destination is Greenfield which takes you down the Baker Inlet and across to the Sound. About a half mile past the mouth of the inlet there is a sandbar which splits the inlet into two separate channels. The channel on the port side is narrower and shallower than the one on the right, so most traffic bears to the west and takes the bigger channel. The sandbar is marked by a single yellow marker right off its northern point. Wednesday night, it will not be there. You will run Whisper onto the bar, hard. Let's say at six knots. It's soft sand, so she will heel over to her portside and this will cause you to fall across the cockpit, striking your head on the roof support, knocking you out, and of course, causing you to fall into the water.

"Wednesday night at 2140 hours, the tide will be ebbing at its peak. I've seen it at two to three knots at times. So what you will do is get some blood, you know, cut yourself somewhere, smear it on the pole and some on the deck and some on the rail. Try and leave a bloody handprint on the deck or hull side, like you were trying to climb back on. The current will carry you down the mouth of the inlet. About 200 yards down the stream the channel narrows to about 50 feet. I'm going to tie a line across the channel and you will need to grab it and pull yourself ashore. Once you are on shore, untie the line from your side and let it drift out into the flow. I'll get it when I come back to rescue Whisper. There will be a hard dinghy with an outboard about 40 feet from where you will land. There will be dry clothes in a bag. Try, if you can, to lose your Whisper cap and maybe even the jacket. See if they can't get downstream and tangled into the brush.

"You'll take the dingy to the game warden's dock. They're never there at night. There will be a '56 *Ford* station wagon parked at the far end of the lot. Keys will be under the visor. I bought it from an old farmer out in Gainesville and he didn't care about ID for the title. He just wanted the $500 I gave him, so it's still in his name. Just dump it in the city and walk away. You got all this? I know it's a lot to absorb all at once."

"Yeah, I got it. The rope you're going to use...does it float?"

"Yeah, it's the polypro but I got it in black rather than the yellow. Harder for you to see, but also harder for anyone else. I'll rig it Wednesday evening."

"Thanks, man. Look, I gotta good job. I'll send you some money for the car and the repairs to Whisper."

"No, no you won't. After today, I don't want to see you, hear from you, or have anything to do with you. I'm doing this for Sandy. As far as I'm concerned, you're just another flake from California who is nothing but trouble. Adios! Motherfucker!"

Wiley spat the last few words out with a venom Rickey had never heard before but he understood. He had brought nothing but turmoil and heartbreak to them since he came into their lives. *Hell*, he thought to himself, *I'd want me gone, too.*

Wiley turned and walked away. But Rickey couldn't help but think, *there goes the best friend I've ever had.*

104

The throttle quivered under Rickey's hand as he eased Whisper off the dock. The sun was setting over the hilltops casting a pink hue over the island. He had four hours to reach the Baker Inlet which was less than twenty miles away. Plenty of time to reach the place where he would stop being South Point Rickey and become Richard Lee Connelly for the rest of his life.

As Whisper slipped along at six knots, and the pinkness faded from the sky being replaced by the inky blue of a moonless night, he thought back on all that had happened to him and all he had lost; and all that he had gained.

What grieved him most was the thought that there was a real chance he would never see his parents again. The mere passing thought of that cut into his heart and he could physically feel the pain in his chest. He knew he lost his innocence but had gained a healthy distrust of certain people and their motives. He had lost the camaraderie of his surfing buddies but had gained the friendship of Captain Jack and Red. He had traded the quiet routine at Taco Time for the raucous life of hauling trawl and hoisting nets aboard the Jennie J. He had lost the groove of surfing shore breaks in the morning but had replaced it with afternoon sails on Carol out on Lake Washington. The peacefulness of sailing compared favorably with the tranquility of surfing.

Much of what he had lost had been replaced by something equally good or in some cases better. He pondered if that really wasn't the secret of life that Captain Jack had prodded him to think about. Nothing in life is as certain as change, and with any change, something is lost. Perhaps the key to a rewarding life is with each change and loss, finding something to replace it; hopefully something even more precious and rewarding.

As the twilight faded, he reached down and turned on his navigation lights; the small red and green lights mounted on the bow and the white light on Whisper's stern. Against the blackness of the night, the lights would shine brightly and alert any other vessel of his presence. More importantly, tonight it would fix Whisper's route when investigators tried to determine the circumstances of the fatal boating accident. He was hopeful that at least a few people would remember the little lobster boat moving steadily down the channel with its lights twinkling off the water.

While Wiley hadn't told him to, yesterday afternoon he had borrowed a car and driven down to Baker Inlet to get a feel for the land and what he was facing once he was in the water. Standing on the shore just downstream from the inlet, he was shocked at how fast the water flowed and how many large boulders lined the shore. He knew he was in for a rough ride and the threat of dying in those icy waters was real. It gave him pause and for a moment he thought, *there must be a better way.* But that thought quickly disappeared as he heard Wiley's voice telling him that they would walk away from him unless he followed Sandy's plan. He had no choice; into the icy waters he had to go.

A soft thump against the hull pulled him back to reality and made him realize that the autopilot had allowed Whisper to drift off course. He quickly moved to the helm and corrected his course, and in so doing, saw the large white boulders on the distant shore which marked the dividing line between Canada and the United States. From there, he knew had about one hour left to go. He checked his watch and it read 8:25 PM or 2025 hours; he had exactly one hour and fifteen minutes to reach Baker Inlet. He double checked his chart, marking off the Inlet to Whisper with a pair of dividers; 3.25 nautical miles. He pulled back on the throttle, slowing Whisper to about 3.5 knots. He knew the tide had already started its ebb and that would give him a little boost. He re-engaged the autopilot and began to prepare himself.

He pulled the small gym bag off the bunk in the cuddy cabin and sat it under the light by the helm. He pulled the syringe and a long needle out of the bag and placed them on the small shelf next to the helm which also doubled as the chart table. After fixing the needle into the syringe, he cleaned it with rubbing alcohol from the eye dropper bottle and returned the bottle to the gym bag. He checked his course and scanned the horizon for other traffic and feeling sure he was clear of any hazard, he removed his jacket and rolled up the sleeve of his over-shirt. He immediately felt the bite of the night chill and involuntarily shook like he had been hit by an electrical current. He steadied himself and slowly pressed the needle into the vein just under his elbow. He pulled back on the plunger, sucking his dark red blood into the tube of the syringe. Once it was full, he unscrewed the cap off a half-pint of *Old Crow* and injected the blood into the empty bottle. He continued to pull blood out of his arm and inject it into the old whisky bottle until it was about half full. He tightened the cap on the bottle and placed it in the breast pocket of his shirt. He quickly put his jacket back on as by then his hands were shaking from the cold and the sight of his own blood.

He reached into the gym bag and pulled out a small waterproof flashlight, some plastic wrap and tape to waterproof his wallet, and a *Snickers* bar. With that he rechecked the bottom of the gym bag for the three pound lead weight he had placed in it, and then with a swift sweep of his arm, tossed the bag and its contents into the sea. He rechecked his course and saw the horizon was clear.

After visiting Baker Inlet yesterday, he realized he could well drown. But wearing a life jacket was out of the question so he decided to use a rubber fender. As they are filled with air even a small two footer should give him enough flotation to keep his head above water.

He went below into the cuddy cabin and retrieved the fender, and while there took a moment to wrap up his wallet. Upon coming back on deck, he felt he was as prepared as he could be and now it was just a matter of waiting to get to the inlet.

Five hundred yards from the sandbar was the entrance to Baker Inlet. It was so named as on the western shore there was a small cottage that a baker once owned and sold bread and cakes to the passersby. Rickey spotted the cottage when he was about 200 yards away from it but he could not see the sandbar nor the dividing of the channel. He continued to motor slowly along but knew he had to increase his speed to six or seven knots well before the sandbar to make the accident look real. He was about 50 yards from the cottage when he was able to see the channel on the right open up. But he was only able to do that because there had been a flash of light on the water, as if a vessel was approaching him at high speed. This caused him to panic momentarily, realizing they might see his "accident" and come to his rescue. But the panic quickly left him as he realized there was another vessel but it was going down channel just like he was, and would be over the horizon in a matter of minutes.

Now he was even with the cottage and had to increase his speed but before that he had to smear the blood in strategic places throughout the cockpit and he was running out of time. Quickly, he opened the small whisky bottle and poured some blood into his hand then rubbed it on the rail supporting the cockpit roof at about head height. Then he repeated the procedure on the side deck and cockpit rail. He reached over, nearly dipping his elbow into the water to leave a smeared handprint on the hull. Then he tossed the bottle into the water.

He returned to the helm, disengaged the autopilot and directed the bow of Whisper right at a clump of trees on the left side of the island. As he steered with his clean hand, he pushed the throttle forward to gain speed by using the elbow of his other arm. Whisper's bow lifted as her speed increased and the roar of her engine became pronounced. Rickey could feel her rise up and speed across the small wavelets crossing her bow. Then without warning, he was violently thrown forward. He heard his rib crack against the wheel as his head struck the compass and he was pitched to port as Whisper rolled heavily on her side. Rickey could hear the screaming of the engine as the prop spun free and felt the whole boat shake violently as the prop dug into the sandbank, killing the engine. For a moment it was totally quiet then Whisper let out a groan as she rolled further onto her port side causing a few frames to break.

Now the deck was at an acute angle and Rickey, still half-dazed, had a hard time pulling himself upright. He was only able to do so by wrapping the helm with his right hand and using all of his strength to pull himself up high enough to get his feet underneath his butt and push himself upright. His hand, still coated with blood, slipped several times but he finally managed to gain his balance. He knew he had left blood on the helm but he had no time to clean it off as water was coming in over the port side and he had to get overboard. He was hopeful that no one would notice the blood on the helm and if they did, just think he cut himself when the boat hit the reef. He knew it could be a problem but there was nothing he could do about it now.

When he let go of the helm, he was immediately tossed into the cockpit rail, smashing another rib. He had no control of his body as gravity and the motion of the boat controlled his every movement. His brain was screaming at him to get over the side, but he knew he needed the fender. He looked around for it and at first could not find it. Panic again flooded through him.

He had left it next to the helm but it wasn't there, or at least he couldn't see it as he was pinned down to the deck up against the hull's side. He knew he had to stand up and get over the side but it was impossible for his feet to get a grip on the deck with the boat pitched at such an angle. He tried again and again but each time his feet simply slipped on the deck, dropping him back down onto his butt.

He knew it had been only seconds since Whisper hit the reef but it seemed like hours. Everything slowed down and yet at the same time seemed to speed right by him. As he sat there thinking how he could pry himself off the deck, a wave came over the rail and dumped its icy coldness all over him. It was as if a lightning bolt had struck and the panic hit him again. But this time, the panic caused him to react by literally jumping off the deck, grabbing the cockpit railing in his left hand and push-pulling himself into a half upright position. As he did this he saw the fender wedged into the lifeline, sitting there as if to say, 'what's keeping ya?' He grabbed it and with a second strong pull, freed it from the lifeline and tucked it under his arm. Without a second thought, he pushed himself over the rail and into the water. He was quickly swept away as the current fought him for the fender. He clung to it like his life depended on it; because it did.

Whisper quickly became a shadow with two lights. One green not quite directly above the red one. As he looked at the lights he realized how quickly he was moving downstream and he needed to find the rope Wiley had strung across the channel. As he had that thought his left leg struck something taut and hard. He realized it was the rope and lunged for it. As he did, the fender popped out of his arms and leaped airborne downstream. His fingers grazed the rope but slipped off. He lunged for it again; but missed.

He felt everything slow down and then realized the rope was cutting into his stomach and all he had to do was reach down and grab it.

With his fingers digging into the hard plastic rope, he started to pull himself toward shore. It was much harder than he ever thought it would be and he soon realized that pulling with his arms alone would not get the job done. So he wrapped each leg around the rope and bent himself into a U shape. Then he would straighten himself out, using his legs to push himself along. Of course his shoes slipped on the plastic rope allowing him to gain just inches at a time. Slowly he made his way into shallow water, banging his knee into a rock in the process. He tried to stand up but the rip of the tide pushed him sideways and down. He continued to inch closer to shore until he finally reached a spot where the water just pooled. He slowly stood up and untangling himself from the shoreline rope, looked around. He pulled out the flashlight and scanned the darkness for the rubber dinghy, and he quickly saw it about 40 feet away. A great sense of relief washed over him.

He stood behind the old *Ford* wagon trying to find a bit of shelter from the chilling wind. He stripped of all his clothes and pulled a towel out of the bag Wiley had left for him. His skin felt tender under the towel and when he passed it over his ribs, there were bolts of shooting pain. "I fucked up something," he said to himself, "but it's a small price to pay for freedom."

As he opened the door of the *Ford*, it screeched, breaking the silence of the night startling him. "Boy, oh boy! Are you ever edgy tonight," he said out loud, trying to calm his fractured nerves. The overhead light came on with the door opening and there on the seat was a half pint of *Old Crow* with a note saying, GOOD LUCK.

It was laying on a dark blue navy pea coat. There was a note pinned to the collar.

"Travel far, and travel well my dear one. -S"

As he moved the coat to get in, he felt something shift inside of it. He ran his hands down the outside of the jacket and felt a rectangle near the breast pocket. He tried to reach in, but his fingers were shaking uncontrollably from the chill of the sea. He rubbed his hands together to warm them and after a few seconds was able to reach in and pull out a banded packet of hundred dollar bills. The tears welled up and he choked back a sigh. *She did care after all.* A broad smile stretched across his face and he glowed with relief.

Rickey then slipped behind the wheel and in the same motion picked up the bottle. He reached up and pulled the column shifter down then up finding reverse. He released the footbrake and eased the wagon down the incline and out of the parking spot. He pulled the column down to first gear, feeling the pain in his ribs; then he stopped. Taking the cap off the *Old Crow*, he took a long pull then said, "Thank you, God." He eased off the clutch and the wagon's lights cut a path across the tree-lined lot. He was heading home.

105

It was another Thursday morning no different than the 17 other Thursdays that had followed one another in silent procession since Bailey had hugged his son for the last time on the overlook to Laurel Canyon. The dust particles danced in the late afternoon light which poured through the front porch casting a pale yellow hue across the room. Maggie sat at her desk addressing envelopes containing renewal notices while Rusty laid across the cable rug in front of her desk sleeping the afternoon away. Ever since Rickey left, they'd brought Rusty to the office each morning, more for their reassurance than his. There was a quiet comfort having him there, a gentle reminder of better times.

Bailey came through the door from his office, obviously upset over the call he had just received from a client who had cancelled his line of business after having just read an article in the local paper which identified Rickey as a draft dodger and wanted by the FBI for failing to report for induction into the United States Army. His call wasn't the first, nor would it be the last.

But before he could say a word, a phone rang. It wasn't the business phone, but the phone he called Rickey's hotline. Rickey was to reach out to him only if he was in grave danger or needed information that he couldn't get anywhere else.

The phone was buried under a stack of files on the shelf under the front windows. They were both startled to hear it as they had decided that their son was gone to them, at least until the crazy war ended. Bailey turned to his wife, wide-eyed, quickly having purged his anger, and said, "Probably a wrong number or one of those ad calls." But before she could reply the phone stopped ringing. They both stared at the pile of files like it was the Oracle at Delphi and didn't say a word. Then it rang again and Bailey bolted out of his stupor and charged across the room, casting aside the file that only moments ago had been so important. He pushed his hand into the stack of files fumbling for the receiver. Having found it, he quickly raised it to his ear and said, "Yes?"

"Hi, dad," was all Rickey could say as he felt he was about to burst out in tears. Bailey spun around and nodded his head up and down letting his wife know that it was indeed Rickey.

"Rickey, are you all right? Where are you? Do you know that the FBI had the papers print an article calling you a fugitive from justice? Do you need money?" The questions tumbled out of Bailey, one after another, until Rickey finally interrupted.

"Dad, dad, please slow down. Please just listen. Promise me you will just listen. I know you have a lot of questions but I don't have a lot of time and I need to tell you and mom something. OK? Will you just listen?"

Bailey had calmed himself down and fighting his emotions with all of his willpower, softly answered, "Of course, son. I'll be quiet."

"Dad, tomorrow or the next day someone will call you, or come to the house and tell you I am dead."

"What?" Bailey shouted into the phone. "Dead? What the hell are you talking about?"

"Dad, please just listen and don't interrupt me. OK? Please?"

"I'm sorry. I will try. Go on."

And with that, Rickey laid out the events of the night before on Whisper and the plan to fake his death. He spoke calmly, even though inside his emotions were raging and he felt at any moment he would throw up. He had to make them understand that his only chance for a life, was death.

After a few minutes, Bailey said, "Yes, son, I understand and I agree. I will explain it to your mother and I am sure she will understand too. I love you. We both love you. Be safe." He slowly placed the handset back into the cradle and turned to his wife.

"Honey, we need to plan a memorial service."

106

Although it was only eleven o'clock in the morning, Bobby was already seated at what had become his booth. It was in the back of the room far from the stage and was semicircular in shape allowing him the illusion of privacy. For more than two weeks he had come every morning to have a breakfast of Bloody Mary's and scrambled eggs. The eggs weren't on the menu, actually nothing was at that hour, but Bobby had worked a deal with the kitchen help trading eggs for some first-class weed.

But he wasn't there for the eggs or the ambience. No, he was there to see Rene, whose new shift started at eleven every weekday. Most days she brought his eggs out at about eleven-thirty and sat and chatted with him while she sipped coffee. There really wasn't much for her to do until the lunch crowd started coming in just before noon. They had fallen into a routine of chatting about current events and the efforts of the local hockey team, the Otters. Bobby enjoyed his time with her and still was trying to get up the courage to ask her for a date. It puzzled him as he had never hesitated before. See a girl, ask her out. That had been his motto; his playbook all the way back to high school.

Yet, here he sat day after day staring at her large breasts and totally mesmerized. But time was running out as his father was becoming more adamant that he return to LA.

Like most mornings, Rene came out of the kitchen and across the bar holding his second Bloody Mary and his plate of eggs and toast. She smiled sweetly as she approached and said in a husky voice, "Good morning, good looking. How are we today?" as she placed the food and drink in front of him.

"Good as gold. Well, maybe silver. But damn good. And you?"

"Well, pretty good, but coming in, I heard on the local news that there was a boating accident last night up by Baker Inlet and they can't find anyone onboard."

"Really? That sounds awful. Why would somebody be out there last night? The weather was freezing. Boating at night? Maybe fishermen?"

"No, they said it was a boat bringing fruits and vegetables down to the Farmer's Market at O'Connor. It was Canadian. From Sidney."

"What? Sidney? Are you sure?"

"That's what they said. Weren't you looking for somebody up that way? A witness or something?"

Bobby's brain was spinning with possibilities but what he knew was a concrete fact: he had to get to Sidney fast. "Ah, yeah, I was but that's all over now. Tell you the truth, I was getting ready to go back to LA tomorrow but wanted to see you one more time." He picked up the Bloody Mary and tipped it in her direction and drained the glass. Before she responded, Bobby stood up, peeled a hundred dollar bill off his flash-stash and placed it on the table. He leaned over and kissed her on the cheek, turned and headed toward the sunlight streaming from the front door. *Ah! What could have been,* he thought to himself.

He had been driving for three hours by the time he reached Sidney and his back ached, his shirt stuck to his chest and he could smell himself. He needed a drink, a shower and a shave; just in that order.

The billboard promised large rooms with water views, a bar and a good restaurant at a modest price, all at the Wharf Hotel. "Perfect!" he muttered under his breath*, but I don't need any water views. Had enough of that since I've been here. Give me Beverly Hills any day.*

He turned off the side road and was immediately in the parking lot for the Wharf Hotel, *Home of the All you can eat Fish Fry every Wednesday night.* He parked and pulled his *Hartman* bag from the trunk. Bobby liked nice things and also things which impressed people. He knew a *Hartman* bag would do that and give him instant status. He felt good about himself walking into the Wharf Hotel; he knew Rickey was the person in the boat. Now he just needed to verify it.

After a long, hot shower, a second drink from the small bar they had set up for him in his room, he stretched out on the bed and thought, *How am I going to prove it was Rickey, and is he, in fact dead?* He knew Rickey was dead. He was certain. He just had to prove it.

Outfitted in a fresh shirt and pressed pants, Bobby looked over himself in the full-length mirror. *No, a jacket is needed.* So he pulled a blue blazer from his bag, pressing out the fold marks with his hands. *That's better. You look professional but still hip.* He knew the no socks with loafers was the latest *GQ* tip for being casual while still dressing semiformal. He liked the look and felt confident as he walked down the curved staircase to the reception area below. The Oak Room bar was off to the left and was the type of bar Bobby craved. Dark, old world, quiet. Meant for serious drinkers who wanted a shield from the world. It was small, with an unlit fireplace on the back wall. There were a half dozen leather over-stuffed chairs in the middle of the room and an oak bar which ran the entire length of the western wall. There were two open stools at the bar and Bobby took one, nodding to the elderly gentleman on his left as he sat down. "Double *Haig & Haig*, neat, please," he said as the barman approached. Upon hearing Bobby's order, he spun on his heels and walked to the far end of the bar and reached up to the top shelf and pulled down the dimpled bottle.

"Here you go, sir. That will be $3.75 unless you with to charge it to your room."

"Thank you. Yes, please charge it to Suite 101." As he said this, he reached out for the drink with a twenty dollar bill between his fingers. "Say, I understand you've had a bit of excitement up here today. I was in Vancouver and they said someone died in a boating accident. I had an old college roommate who moved up to this area and I was sure hoping it wasn't him. But where would I go to find out?"

The barman eyed the $20 casually and placed both hands on the oak bar top. "Well, I guess the best place would be the Police Station, it's just down the road about half a mile on the left. But somehow I don't think you're the kind of guy who goes to the cops too often. Tell you what. Stop finger-playing the $20 and push it over here and I'll tell you what I know and where you can go to get the straight scoop."

Bobby unwound the $20 from his fingers and pushed it across the bar top where the bartender quickly palmed it.

"OK, this is what I heard at the cafe this morning. Some rescue guys were in there and I heard them say that a lobster-style boat had hit the sandbar at the Baker Inlet and there was blood everywhere but no one around. They think the driver was knocked out, hitting his head on something and fell into the water. Best they can tell, it was around ten last night when the tide was flooding out. If so, the boy is headin' to Japan."

"Well, what makes you think it was a boy?"

"Well, boy or man, I don't know, but it was the Whisper and I saw Sandy this morning in town and Wiley brought in some greens for the kitchen about two hours ago. So it wasn't them. It was probably that guy who has been staying with them and running the boat some. He is young. That's why I said 'boy.'"

"Where can I find this Sandy or Wiley?"

"Sandy runs Smiley's, the bar up by the dock. Big blue building with a yellow door. Can't miss it."

"Ah, thanks, man. I think I'll go up there and see them." He drained the drink in one pull and headed for his car. Thinking to himself, *what a light pour.*

107

Bobby pulled on the big yellow door but it wouldn't open. *Closed at six in the evening. That's not right*, he thought just as a voice came around the corner.

"Can I help you?"

Bobby was surprised but quickly turned in the direction of what he knew was a female. But when he completed his turn, he was taken aback by the beautiful woman standing at the bottom of the porch with one foot on the first step. She was wearing tight jeans tucked into boots which nearly reached her knees. The Dylan song of *Boots of Spanish Leather* immediately flashed through his mind. She had on a long-sleeved shirt with a leather vest fully buttoned and a piece of lace wrapped around her throat. The late evening sun made her glow, looking like an angel to Bobby.

"Ah, yes. I'm Bobby McKnight. I'm from LA. Well, actually Berkeley, that's where I'm going to school at the moment, but my parents, they live in LA. Actually, Beverly Hills.

"I'm sorry. I must sound like an idiot. The bartender down at the Oak Room said maybe you might know something about the boating accident that happened here last night. He said it was your boat. I mean, I don't know if that's true but that's what he said."

Sandy stood there in the fading light, looking at this guy with his city clothes, and no socks, and wondering, *What the hell is this?* "Yes, it was our boat. My brother's and mine. We own Green Fields Farm and ship vegetables and stuff down to the States sometimes. Our farmhand was driving the boat last night. May I ask; what is it to you?"

"Ah, yeah, sure. See, at school, I have this friend, Marsha, and she had this friend, Rickey, and we met and discussed the war with Rickey and how some felt it was better to come up here than go to Vietnam. I heard awhile ago that Rickey had come up here and I was going to look him up while I was up here looking for a witness in a case my father has going to trial in LA. I thought I would see how he was doing. I only met him a few times but I liked him. A surfer kinda guy, but still cool. Then I heard about this accident and I don't know, I just had a bad feeling and if it was Rickey, well, I wanted to call Marsha before she heard it on the news or something."

"Oh, I see. Well, our hand was named Dusty, Dusty Rhodes. Yeah, I know but we are all stuck with the names our parents gave us. Oh, by the way, I'm Sandy."

"They call me Bobby but my parents stuck me with Robert." He gave a lopsided grin as he said it. "Say, could I show you a picture of my friend, Rickey? Maybe you've seen him around and then I could go find him."

"Sure."

"It's in my car. Can you wait a minute?"

"I'm not going anywhere."

Bobby pulled out the six by ten inch glossy of Rickey with Rita Rains and handed it to Sandy. "That's him. Know him?"

Sandy's hand trembled slightly but she held her gaze on the photo. "Wow, with Rita Rains. Your friends travel in fast company."

"Well, not really. He just helped her out of a jam at an anti-war demonstration. It's not like they're good friends. It was just a picture I happen to have."

Sandy nodded. "That's Dusty. I thought that name was phony. What was his real name?"

"Ah, Rickey or really, Richard. I mean, his birth name is Richard Wilson Osgood, but everyone called him South Point Rickey or South Point... due to the way he surfed."

"Well, what can I tell you? Rickey, South Point, or Dusty - he sure did destroy our boat. Not to mention the $600 of produce and goods. It's gonna hurt us. So what are you going to do? He's gone."

"What do you mean, gone?"

"The police called me about twenty minutes ago and said they were calling off the search. They figured the accident took place at about ten last night. After eighteen hours, there is no point in searching anymore. If he is in the water, he drowned or froze to death. Most likely the current took him out into the straits. There's no coming back from that."

"Oh, my God! You mean he's dead? There is no chance he came ashore and is holed up somewhere?"

"Not likely. The shore there is very rugged and the water flow at that time of night was very strong. I mean, miracles happen, but generally not. I'm sad. I liked him. He was a good worker and helped my brother out a lot. But he wrecked our boat and that is going to really hurt. Look, I gotta go. Sorry to be the bearer of bad news but it's hard on all of us."

"Hey, I know. Man, I am not looking forward to calling Marsha. Even though she moved to Vermont and lives with a guy there, I know it will hit her hard. Well, thanks for the news, I guess. I am sorry about your friend."

He moved toward her and held out his hand for her to shake it, and she reached out and gave him a light brush and said, "He wasn't my friend. He was a guy who worked for us."

108

Rickey placed the handset back in the holder and stepped out of the booth in the foyer of the Space Needle. He noticed his hand shook slightly as he removed it from the phone. He was shaken; both by the emotional impact of speaking with his parents and the finality of it all. It was as if he had been playing a role, Rickey on the run, but now it hit him; this was reality, this was his life. He was alone in the world with a false name, and a false sense of being. He started down the hill to the docks wondering what he had done to deserve this fate other than being in the wrong place at the wrong time. Not once, but twice.

The wind came off the lake with a knife-like chill as the grey clouds assembled on the horizon like an invading army. The sky was grey and the mood threatening. *Time to get home*, he thought, *and quick*. He picked up the pace but the rain and the howling wind overcame him when he was only halfway down the hill. The rain came down in sheets but in an almost horizontal pitch, nearly blinding him. It was all he could do to make out the outline of the door to the Jib and Tackle through the watery mess. He dodged under the partial shelter cast by the bar's awning and jerked open the door. The madness of the street was immediately replaced by the smooth sounds of Art Baker's trumpet and the warmth of the cast iron potbelly stove which sat in the middle of the main room radiating not only heat but that sweet smell of burning oak. Rickey immediately relaxed and felt the tension from the phone call drift away.

He looked over the room but didn't see anyone he knew, so he made his way to the bar and found an empty stool near the entrance to the kitchen. He waved at the bartender and pointed to the taps, indicating he wanted a *PBR* on draft. The fresh-faced barkeep nodded affirmatively and wiping her hands on a towel, walked toward the taps.

She placed the pale yellow brew with its white cap of foam in front of him and said, "Thirty-five cents or three for a dollar. Special today because of the weather." She said this with a half-smirk, half-smile as if to say, "the weather here always sucks , so every day is Special Day."

Rickey nodded and placed a dollar on the bar top but didn't reply. A woman's presence behind a bar was becoming more common but still was an unusual sight. He immediately thought of Sandy, and remorse and longing quickly flooded through him, as once again, he realized how much he had lost.

He was starting a downward spiral into self-pity when a voice intruded, cutting off his thoughts and bringing him back into the presence of the warm bar. "Honey, put a shot of *Old Crow* with that. This boy looks like he needs a pick-me-up." He felt a heavy hand fall upon his right shoulder, and the warmth of another being press into his back. "How ya doin', son? I was down on the boat when I sees ya walking down the hill looking like ya was comin' back from a funeral. Then, bang, the weather broke and I knows the Jib was the only shelter on that side of the street. So I decided to come up and join ya. That's OK, ain't it, son?"

"Captain Jack! Hell yes! It's always a good time to see you. How's Portland?"

"Boring as shit. But it's good to be there to help out my daughter with her babies. She has her hands full. So I make 'em breakfast and clean up, do a little around the house while they's at school, and then walk down to the bus stop and walk 'em home around three every afternoon. Like standing watch. You do it because it has to be done but half the time ya'd rather be somewheres else. Today's a holiday so I jumped the train and come up here to see ya and the rest of the fools. So tell me son, was that you I read about in the paper?"

Rickey was stunned. He wasn't surprised that a small boating accident had made the papers in Portland but that it had done it so fast. Christ, it hadn't been 36 hours and already the papers have it. "Shit, already?" he said, turning to look directly into Captain Jack's face. "Really?"

"Well, whatcha expect? People love boating accident stories. Why, I never done figured out. But they do. And the missing body thing, well that makes it even more interesting...people love a mystery. Yeah, it's in the papers and my guess, it'll be on the telly by tonight. Son, you'll be famous for a day or two."

"God damn it," Rickey said in a heavy whisper but wanting to scream it out at the top of his lungs. "When just when, will I get a break?" he swore to himself. "When?" Then it hit him, Captain Jack was his break. "There's no holiday today, is there?"

"Well, ya got me there. Always said ya was right quick. Nah, when I saw the small story in the Portland paper this morning, I knew I needed to come up here and warn ya. Hell, maybe help ya somehow. But I think we should gut us another round and go back into the lounge where there ain't so many people. Right now, my friend, people...well, they's your enemy."

As crowded as the front room was, the lounge was empty. The reason for this became clear to Rickey the moment he stepped through the double doors which separated the two rooms. No heat. "Christ, it's cold in here. Can't we go down to the boat?"

"Well, not unless you wants to walk through 30 knots of freezing rain. This system will take about twenty minutes to blow through. Follow me, we'll go into Cory's office. He won't mind. I don't think he used it much since he started seeing that widowed gal over in Ballard. Most afternoons he's over at her place doing whatever."

Rickey followed Captain Jack through the lounge and into a room that was built like a funnel. The entryway was not even three feet wide and was about ten feet long. Then the main room of twenty by twenty opened up exposing a seven walled, all glass view of the lake. The impression was the lake was right there to touch, and there was nothing between you and the sea. Most people's reaction was 'Wow!' and Rickey's was the same. "Man, what a view. Looks like the rain has stopped."

"Yeah, it's nice, but we need to talk, so grab a seat. And look out over Queen Anne's. See how dem clouds are all stacked up? That means the wind done shift and soon the weather will be comin' outta there. It ain't done by a longshot. Sit, sit. Enough of this chitchat."

"Rick, remember when we first met, I told you there's gettin' gone and there's stayin' gone? OK, so you got yourself gone but how you fixin' to stay gone?"

Rickey stared off, looking at the lake for the longest time, almost as if he hadn't heard Captain Jack's question. But Captain Jack knew he had and also knew there were times when silence was a better prompter than words.

Finally Rickey said, "Well, I thought I had already. Here on the dock, fishing with Jennie J, my new name, living on Carol, in Seattle where I've never lived before, no one other than you and Red know the real story. I figured I would just blend in and become Richard Lee Connelly. Just live quietly and blend in."

"Well, that's one way. And it might work. But ya gotta major problem. Ya still got the same face. And I ain't no girly-man but I can see it's a very handsome face and a face that gets remembered, specially by the ladies. Whatcha gonna do 'bout that face? Rickey, my boy, you are only a few hundred miles from Vancouver Island. It ain't that far. People come back and forth all the time. What happens if someone sees ya and remembers ya as that guy what died; but didn't? Ya don't think they wouldn't run off to the first newspaper that give 'em 50 bucks and tell 'em what they saw?"

Rickey nodded as Captain Jack spoke, realizing everything he was saying was true but dreading the idea of leaving his new found home. *Life on the run. Him and 'The Fugitive.' Christ.*

"And not to beat you up but those two who owned the boat, what's their names?"

"Sandy and Wiley."

"They know where you is. Right? You done told them about me and the Carol and the fishing and all of it. Right?"

"Right." Rickey sighed, feeling like a fool when it was all tossed out in the harsh light of Captain Jack's glare. "But I trust them. They helped me. They wouldn't tell anybody. Why would they?"

"Well, let me ask ya this. Them boys that was looking for ya...was ya afraid of 'em?"

"Well, yeah."

"Why? Ya think they was gonna hurt ya? Well, if they was gonna hurt ya, why won't they hurt Sandy? And if they really hurt her, you don't think she'll tell 'em what they want to know? And even if you think she'll stand up to the pain, I can damn sure tell ya that Wiley won't let 'em hurt his sis to protect your sorry ass. No God damn way! No sir."

"Shit, I thought once I was dead they would stop looking."

"Maybe they will. But if there is a one percent chance, they'll keep comin' then ya gots to be where no one knows ya and no one can find ya. Even if they figure out you're not dead, they still have to find ya. You have a small window of time to slip into the mystic and disappear. And that's right now."

Rickey stared at his hands and then out the windows which showed nothing but a blue-white haze with sunlight streaks through it. "Well, I guess I could get another van and head south to Mexico or Costa Rica or fly to Hawaii. I'm not going anywhere cold, no way. Yeah, I could do that. That would be cool."

"Well, that's one way, but there is a slight problem. They know you surf...you're a surfer. So if you are looking for a surfer where ya gonna look? Come on Rick, those are the three places above the equator where they would look first. I don't think you are taking this seriously enough. There are many places that don't fit into your past. That is where you have to go."

Captain Jack got up from behind the big blonde desk where he had been sitting and flung a finger toward the far glass wall and said, "There's a globe of the world over there. Go take a gander at it and see if you can come up with somethin'. I'm gonna get that pretty little bar gal to make us some drinks. Pick a place before I get back."

Rickey sat momentarily stunned by the force of Captain Jack's words; never had he given him an order before. After a few minutes, he got up from the lounge chair where he had been sitting and wandered over to the far side of the room where a large globe sat on a three foot stand. There was a cord with a thumb switch hanging from one side of the stand and Rickey flipped it and the whole world came alive in a bright white glow. The land was various shades of brown; light tan to dark purple brown. The sea, shades of blue; aqua to deep royal blue. Rickey never realized how much of the Earth was water. "My God, most of it's water; amazing," he spoke to no one but himself.

But he heard Captain Jack, "Yes it is. And it's a highway that you can travel and leave not a trace."

Rickey turned and looked at Captain Jack and instantly understood. "The Carol?"

"I always said you was a sharp one. Yes, the Carol. Take her and take her here," he said as he pointed to that vast blue expanse between South

America and New Zealand labeled 'South Pacific.' Look at all dem islands. You could spend a lifetime and never see all of 'em."

Rickey didn't know what to say. He understood the rightness of the Captain's thinking but the idea of sailing a small boat across such a vast sea caused him to feel a queasiness in his stomach and fear in the rest of him.

"Don't worry, son. I will start out with you. Git ya on down to San Diego or maybe Cabo. By then you will know alls ya need to know. In?" As he said this, he held out his hand to Rickey.

Rickey paused, then reached out, took the Captain's hand and said, "In!"

109

It was dark now as Bobby walked back to his car. The new moon hadn't started to form and the cloud cover blocked out the stars. But the big Smiley's' sign flashing its yellow neon welcome creating an almost psychedelic effect on the rock pathway.

"Not a friend," he mumbled to himself. *Now that's odd to say about the dead. Of course, she seemed terribly bitter over losing the boat and the produce. But, still, to say that about someone who worked for you is kinda cold.*

"Yeah, but how would dad see it?" he said out loud as he opened the door and the interior light blinded him with its brightness. *Yeah, what would the old man make of that comment? What was he always saying, like some kind of mantra? Oh yeah, 'Things may not be what they seem.' Maybe I need to check this out a bit further. Make sure that boy is gone. Damn straight, look at it hard, talk to the cops, go look at the accident scene, take some photographs, do a real investigation then call Raymond. Make it complete.*

He started the rented *Buick*, flipped on the lights and backed out of Smiley's with a deep resolve to complete a job and make his father proud. On the short drive back to the Wharf Hotel, he ran through all the things he was to cover tomorrow so he could give specific details to his father as to how Rickey died or maybe didn't.

There was a good sized crowd at the Wharf Hotel when he arrived. So much so, he had to park in a sub-lot half a block away. This bruised Bobby's ego as he felt that a guy who rents a suite, and mind you, not just any suite, but the best suite they offered, shouldn't have to schlep back from parking.

He heard the music before he climbed the front porch steps and immediately thought of Lawrence Welk, a TV performer who was very popular with the silver-headed set and Republicans. *Oh! Christ! I can't listen to that shit all night.* And it only got worse as he opened the main doors and entered the reception area. It was a full-blown dance party straight out of the 1940's.

The only thing missing was Benny Goodman. His heart sank as he realized the band was directly below his room, and any chance for a quiet night planning tomorrow's endeavors was out of the question. Then he noticed the doors to the Oak Room were closed. *Oh, please God, give me an oasis of quiet and good whisky.*

He was not disappointed. As soon as the heavy oak door closed behind him, all he heard was the mutter of polite conversation and the tinkling of glasses being washed by the bartender. In the dim light, he saw half a dozen people spread out in the overstuffed chairs and a few solos at the bar. He made his way to the bar and nodded to the bartender.

"Usual?" he replied.

"Please."

"A double?"

"Of course."

Bobby was impressed as this was not the bartender who he had the exchange with earlier but rather a younger version and blonde rather than dark. *So, I guess I made an impression*, he thought smugly to himself.

"What's your name?" Bobby asked as the barkeep placed a bowl of warm nuts in front of him along with the double *Dimple*.

"Really? My name? Same as it say on the jacket. Ross."

"Oh, shit. I didn't see that. Pretty stupid I guess, but that music sorta messed up my mind. Hi, I'm Bobby," he said as he extended his hand. "Glad to meet you."

"Likewise," Ross said as he moved away toward the far end of the bar.

While Bobby sipped his whisky and picked at the nuts, Ross quietly lifted a phone to his ear and spoke softly, "We have a player, if you're interested. Good. Normal split, right? OK, then what, twenty minutes? I'll hit him with another double before you get here." And with that, quietly replaced the handset into its cradle.

Bobby was thinking about dinner when Ross slid another double *Dimple* in front of him and said, "Here's one on the house. Sorry about the music but they do it once a month like clockwork. Fills the dining room but don't do shit for me in here. Anyway, enjoy. If there is anything you need, just let me know."

"Well, damn. That's really nice of you. Thanks, Ross."

Bobby hadn't had two sips from the second drink when she came into the room. She quickly adjusted to the dim lighting and spotted Bobby over at the bar. *Who else could it be? No socks, oh, Jesus, save me.*

She took a seat at the bar two seats to Bobby's left and didn't glance in his direction. She knew his type even before she lit her first cigarette. *Watch,* she said to herself, *when I order my white wine, he will offer to pay for it, then pretend he can't hear my response and then will slide over and sit next to me.*

But he surprised her. "Ross, five dollars if you know what this lovely young lady likes to drink, and if you're right, put it on my tab. But if you're wrong, you pay. We on?"

"Well, can I ask her a couple of questions first because I've never met her before?"

"Of course. I might be a gambler, but I'm a fair man."

"OK then. Miss, do you prefer wine or liquor?"

"Wine."

"Do you prefer baseball or football?"

"Well, that's different. Hmmm? Football."

"Alright," Bobby injected, "You said a couple and that means two."

"Right on, so it does." And after a pause said, "The lady's drink is a champagne cocktail."

"How did you know that?" she asked with a sense of real surprise in her voice.

"It's my job. Stem glass?"

"Please." Then turning to Bobby, "Wow, that was something, and kinda fun. Hi, I'm Janice," she said as she extended her hand which Bobby noticed was ring-free and nicely manicured.

"Well, hello Janice, I'm Bobby McKnight. I've come up from Beverly Hills on a case we have going to trial soon. What do you do?"

The sunlight streamed into Suite 101 and hit Bobby like a freight train. *Christ, how many of those double Dimples did I have?* He swung his legs over the side of the bed and looked around. His head was swimming and his stomach was in revolt. The dead, nasty taste of too many cigarettes coated his tongue and he smelled like an ashtray. He tried to focus but his vision was fuzzy and the room looked like giant puffballs.

He could tell his suite was empty even with his impaired vision. As he fell back groaning, his head hit something out of place. He reached back, rising up just a bit, which caused his head to spin. It was a note written on the room service menu. "Morning sweetie. You were great. I hope you had as much fun as I did. I found the $500 in the suitcase, which I knew you were good for." At the bottom of the note was a little heart and a big J.

"Oh, fuck!" he moaned out loud. "$500...how can I ever expense that?" In that moment he realized he didn't have enough cash to pay the hotel bill. "Ahhh..." But he didn't finish either his thought or his curse; instead he fell back to sleep.

It was four in the afternoon when Bobby finally woke up, but he only did because someone was pounding on the door.

"What, God damn it?" he shouted at the door, half hoping the tone in his voice would make the intruder go away. But the response was to bang even louder. "All right, all right. I'm coming. Relax yourself."

He pulled a sheet around him and shuffled across the marble floor nearly tripping over the Persian rug which guarded the vestibule.

The banging had stopped by the time Bobby opened the door with, "What the fuck do you want?"

He was confronted by a short man with the manners of an English butler. "Well, sir, our first concern was your safety. Are you alright?"

After being assured he was fine, just a little hung-over, the man continued. "Excellent, sir. I'm Mr. Jenkins, the house manager and we had you scheduled to leave by one this afternoon and now it's after four."

"Oh, I'm sorry. I thought I would stay another day. Is that a problem?"

"Well, sir, this is festival weekend and we are quite booked."

"Ah, well, can we make some arrangement? I really don't want to move."

"Yes, sir, arrangements are always welcomed. What did you have in mind?"

"How about I pay double for the room for tonight? Would that do it?"

"Perhaps so, sir, if the room handled the paperwork, but sadly it doesn't."

Bobby stifled a laugh and said, "Of course. That's not what I meant. What I meant was, I pay for the room and if you would take care of the formalities, I would pay you, you personally, an equal sum. Fair enough?"

"Quite, sir. I will make the adjustment once I've received your payment."

"Ah, look, I just got up. Can you come back in an hour after I've gotten showered and dressed. Say 5:30?"

"Of course, sir. I will be back at 5:30 with the necessary paperwork."

Bobby slowly closed the door and let the sheet fall to the floor. As it did, he caught a whiff of himself and almost gagged. "To the shower, now," he shouted, as if he needed someone to tell him what to do.

Sitting in the middle of the room with an ice pack on his head, he was trying to remember what had happened last night and why he felt like something was missing. Something he was scheduled to do. Through the foggy haze of memory of Janice's perfume, it hit. It hit him so hard he dropped the ice bag and jumped from the chair. "Shit, shit, shit!" he repeated over and over again. He was scheduled to call his father at five o'clock and now it was 5:15. In fifteen minutes the butler would be by for his pound of flesh and he had no news for his dad or money for Mr. Jenkins. "Shit, shit, shit!"

OK, call dad and make up some bullshit and when Jenkins shows up, show him the phone and tell him you are on long distance and will come down to the front desk in half an hour. Make like it's important legal business, and he is preventing justice from being done.

"Yes, dad. I am 100 percent certain he died in the boating accident. As I explained to you, I interviewed the Chief of Police and he confirmed the details of the accident. His crew took samples of the blood on the boat and compared it to blood Dusty, err, Rickey, had given during some blood drive they had here back in January. Same type, A negative, which like only three percent of the population have.

"They found a jacket he was wearing when he left the dock in Sidney tangled in some bushes down river from where the boat went around. I spoke to this gal, Sandy, who owned the boat and the farm where he worked and she confirmed he was on the boat alone when it left Sidney. In fact, she saw him leave the dock wearing the jacket they found.

"And she told me he showed up here right around the time Rickey split. I showed her the picture of him with Rita Rains and she ID'd the guy in the picture as her employee, Dusty Rhodes, aka Rickey.

"I got copies of the police report and for $25, I got the desk sergeant to let me look at the whole file. Everything points to an accident where he went overboard and was carried out to sea.

"I hiked out to the scene and the boat is a wreck; it's in pieces. And it's in the middle of nowhere; there was no one to help him. He's gone. Man, I know it was him, and he's dead. What else do you want?

"OK, I can do that. A death certificate. It might take me awhile as he was American but living in Canada and the accident was less than a mile from the border. You know, jurisdictional jazz.

"I'm mailing to you the newspaper piece from this afternoon's edition. It's pretty complete and they are saying it was an American, Richard Osgood, living in Canada under the alias Dusty Rhodes, and they are saying he is dead. If it's good enough for the *Seattle Sun Times*, it should be good enough for the Kansas City Boy's Club.

"I know, I know. Sorry. I was just hoping that you would think I did a good job. That's all. I will get the death certificate but it will take a few days. So I will need you to wire me more money. Ah, yeah, $300 will be enough. Please send it to the Wharf Hotel, they can convert it for me.

"OK, thanks, dad," he said into a dead line.

Bobby slumped into the chair exhausted. He realized that he had sweated through the fresh clothes he had put on and now would need to shower and change again.

Then go sweet talk the butler.

110

Raymond McKnight sat at his huge wood desk and looked at the vanity wall behind him. The pictures of himself with the cream of LA: the movie stars and politicians, the celebrities, the famous and the infamous. There he was at the center of every photo; not a bit player but a star in the never-ending soap opera of LA's social scene.

But as he gazed over his success, a nagging thought continued to circle in his brain. *Was Bobby telling him the truth? Had he done what he said he had done, or was it more of Bobby's hot air?* He knew he had delayed for about as long as he could with reporting to his clients, but he also knew the damaging consequences that could come about if his report was anything less than accurate.

Assume the worst, he thought, *assume Bobby did nothing but read the newspaper. So what? The article*, he guessed, *would be as Bobby reported and how could Kansas City bitch if he didn't have anything more than the police and the major regional newspaper?* "They might, but they wouldn't do anything about it."

"Who wouldn't?" his secretary asked, coming into his office without his noticing.

"What? Oh, nothing. Just going over some thoughts for the Gladstone deposition next week. Say, do me a favor, call our friend over at the *Times* and see if he can pull a story out of the Seattle paper about a boating accident. Happened yesterday or the day before. If he can pull it, send a messenger to get it." With that, he waved his hand which she understood, after all the years with him, meant, 'That's all. Please go.'

"Sure, I will call Tim right now. Thought you might like to know that fellow, Irish, called. Should I get him on the line?"

"Ah, yes, please. Thanks, Helen."

Raymond McKnight rolled his chair back from his huge desk and walked over to the windows fronting Beverly Drive. From there he could look west to the small patch of the Pacific just peaking out as a small soft blue smudge. In the opposite direction, he could see downtown with the phallic City Hall building dominating the skyline but he knew plans were afoot to build not one but two large towers nearby. Soon commerce would over-shadow government as the dominate force in LA. *Much as it should*, he thought. More importantly, he needed to figure out how he could represent one of the developers. The fees and potential bribes could be huge. *Yeah, if I could tear off a piece of that, maybe I could walk away from all this crap. Get a boat and fish all day long.*

His reverie was broken by Helen's voice, "Irish is on the line."

He quickly stepped back to his desk, snatched up the phone, and spoke. "Irish, my, my, how good to hear from you. I was just thinking this morning I needed to give you a call. You know you've never billed me for the work you did on the Rita Rains thing and that kid."

"Well, as I told you before, I only bill when the case is over and I'm ready to close the file. And I'm getting close."

"OK, how can I help you?"

"Well, it's not so much you helping me, but me helping you. My guys up North, well they have been keeping a loose eye on that kid, Rickey some-thing or other, and bingo, the other day, he ups and goes and gets himself killed."

"You think he's dead?"

"Well now, my guy up there, he did a pretty thorough job. Talked to cops, checked out the accident scene, talked to the rescue guys and he thinks so."

"What do you think?"

"Look, it was clear, this kid was on the run. And there was something about it that always struck me as more than just dodging the draft. I mean, most guys I've tracked down for that don't change their names. Hell, some of them parade it around, think it will help them get laid. This kid changed his name before he got up there. And he got some damn good paper. He was hiding from someone besides the Army. And now he's dead. I don't know, maybe, maybe not. But all circumstances point to it."

"So you think he is?"

"Let me put it this way: I have no reason to believe he is not."

"Can I repeat you on that?"

"Yeah, sure. I just find it a little too convenient, ya know? But, hey, what do I know?"

"Can you send me a final report confirming your conclusion that he is dead and died in that boat accident?"

"Like I said, I have no reason to doubt it."

"Great. Thanks for the call, Irish. I appreciate it. Please send me that invoice so I can get you paid. Take care."

By now, Raymond McKnight was back sitting in his chair, rocking slowly back and forth. *Well, maybe Bobby wasn't bullshitting me after all. Maybe the boy is growing up.*

*   *   *   *   *

"He's dead," Raymond McKnight said quietly into the phone. He was standing alongside his desk, alone in the large office, watching the traffic crawl along. He delivered the message in a solemn tone, as he was saddened by thought of the young man's death; a death he helped cause.

"Who? Who's dead?"

"The witness for the upcoming trial. He died up North. He won't be able to testify." Raymond said it in his most lawyerly tone, as if they had just lost a key element in their case, and hoped Anthony would pick up on the hint.

"What? Come again; he's dead? Oh, that's terrible. How did it happen?"

"Well, I just received, by Special Delivery, from our investigator up North, a clipping from the local newspaper. It reads:

> *March 7, 1969, Victoria, B.C. The local authorities released their report this afternoon of a boating accident which apparently occurred during the evening hours of March 6th. The vessel, Whisper, a 35 foot lobster-style boat delivering fruits and produce to O'Connor Market on Thursday, March 6th, encountered some type of problem during the voyage from its home port of Sidney. She was found aground off Baker Inlet, a mile and a half from Point Richmond. It appeared to investigators that she ran aground while traveling at about*

seven knots, which caused the cargo to shift. They think when the cargo shifted, it struck the skipper, Richard Wilson Osgood, also known as Rickey, most likely in the head, as there was blood on the starboard rail, and he fell overboard. He was known to wear a heavy pea coat jacket while operating the boat; experts say the jacket would become soaked with water, causing him to drown. They say even if he got the jacket off, it is unlikely he could have survived the freezing water for more than a few minutes. They estimate the outward tidal flow at 3.5 knots when the accident occurred and assumed the body was carried out to sea.

The marine patrol notified the parents, who live in Southern California. No local services were announced.

"So, it seems our investigation is over," Raymond said, while listening to the breathing patterns of Anthony on the other end of the line.

"What if it was staged? How do we know if he's really dead?" He asked this in a dead, flat monotone and, it seemed, without real interest if Rickey was dead or alive.

Choking on a short cough, Raymond answered in his best lawyer voice, "For the purposes of the trial, it makes no difference. And, really, for any other purpose it makes no significant difference as someone who fakes their death and then comes back to tell some tale; he would have no credibility. Few are going to believe a man who has been living a lie. So, he's gone, one way or another, he is no longer a concern to our case. I recommend we close that part of the file and pay off the invoices."

"Right. Do it." And the line went dead in Raymond's hand. *And thank you for a job well done,* he thought to himself. "Fucking clients," he muttered as he re-cradled the phone.

111

Rickey stood on the bluff at Laguna Beach and watched as his family and friends gathered on the beach below for his memorial service. It was early April and the always chilly waters of the Pacific were now downright cold. But he saw some of his old pals slide their boards into the water and carry baskets of flowers out into the surf in spite of the cold. The sky was a hazy grey and off the horizon, dark clouds formed, telling him later there would be rain, and lots of it.

He had the collar on his Navy issued pea coat turned up, in part, to hide the end of the wig he was wearing, and to act as a shield for the lower part of his face. He wore a red turtleneck sweater under the coat, and a pair of heavy grey corduroy pants with *Clarks* desert boots. Inside the boots, there were two inch lifts added to change his height. The pea coat was a size too large to add to his bulk and make his overall appearance bigger, bulkier than his true skeletal frame. The pea coat was oversized for another reason too: inside the silk lining, he had sewn five packs of $100 bills, which he now fingered through the lining as he watched the service below. The $20,000 gave him a feeling of strength and security, while the people on the beach reminded him of all he had lost.

Yet, he was more than mindful of what he had. Just a few short miles down the road, in San Diego, Carol was safely tied to a dock with Captain Jack aboard. He was taking the day to bring fresh stores on board, fill her tanks, and make any last minute repairs before they headed off to Mexico in the morning. Captain Jack could have come with Rickey, but he knew some voyages you have to do alone. Rickey was aware of Captain Jack's wisdom in this regard and counted it another of his blessings.

Captain Jack had proved to be a true friend in word, counsel and deed. He had, as he said he would, slipped the Carol out of her marina on Lake Washington and sailed her alone to Port Townsend. After their chat at the

Jib and Tackle, they had agreed Rickey should leave Seattle and simply move from town to town around the sound until he could meet up with Captain Jack in Port Townsend a few weeks later. Captain Jack's story would be he was moving the Carol down to Portland because as much as he loved his grandkids, he loved his peace and quiet more. Besides, he missed the Carol and boat life.

The sail from Port Townsend to San Diego took three weeks with stops in San Francisco and Santa Barbara. But for Rickey, it was a lifetime. He went from the greenest hand who couldn't steer the course, to having the confidence now to continue on his own after Cabo San Lucas in Mexico. This was yet another thing he had that he lacked before: the feeling of having his own legs. That he could face life on his terms and without the help of his mother and father. He could march to the beat of his own drummer. He remembered reading that somewhere some time ago. Then, he wasn't sure what it meant, but he was today.

As Rickey looked down on Shaw's Cove, his heart swelled at the sight of so many of his friends turning out to say farewell. Although just dots, he could make out his mother and father moving through the crowd, stopping now and then to shake hands and chat. It moved him that so many people cared. Yes, he had a lot to be thankful for.

Not the least of which was the ID he carried in his wallet and the passport in the breast pocket of his pea coat. That was Red's contribution to the endeavor. Red explained to him how he scoured the obituary files of the *Seattle Sun Times*, looking for a white male infant who died within days, weeks or even months of his birth, during the Summer or Fall of 1948. The death notice often contained the name of the hospital where the child had been born.

Eddie explained that the hospital was where the birth certificate would be issued, and there where they could get a copy of it. There are no state or federal requirements to obtain birth certificates and therefore hospitals just make them up to suit their needs or fancies. All that is required to get one is five dollars and a return self-addressed envelope. Once you have the birth certificate, it could be used to secure a social security card, and with that combo, a passport. Red had explained in detail what he had done, and warned Rickey to remember how to do it just in case he had to do it himself someday.

Red had done all that, and now, tucked away in Rickey's wallet was a brand new license issued by the State of California to Richard Lee Connelly, DOB, July 17, 1948, 8811 Pacific Coast Highway, Laguna Beach, California. He was back, but he knew he couldn't stay in Southern California; too great a chance he might be recognized. But before he could go, he had to stay for his memorial.

He watched the flowers drift out to sea and the group gather around a small fire that had been started in a pit. Each person took a candle and lit it from the dancing flames, then moved to be part of a large circle. His father was the last in line, and as he stepped into the circle, all the others raised their candles into the wind, which quickly extinguished them. He couldn't hear them but saw a person playing a guitar and assumed they were all singing a song of good-bye. He couldn't hold back his tears as they streamed down his face and fell past his quivering lips. He could taste the salt in his mouth; which made him cry even more. As he watched the crowd below break up, he slowly regained his composure, wiping his face with his hand and wiping it on the jacket. He gulped large swallows of sea air and steadied himself.

He took one last look from the bluff and out to sea. Way out, he could see a small bunch of flowers being carried out past the surf line and into the blue waters of the Pacific. He watched his parents separate from the crowd and walk up Coast Highway to the north, where his father's favorite *Buick* was parked. He watched as Marsha walked in the other direction to the bright red Mustang her mother had bought her as a high school graduation present. *Oh, the memories they'd made in that car that summer.* He was pleased to see she was alone and knew that was a cruel thought but it pleased him just the same. He watched as the rest of the crowd moved off the beach and headed to their cars and vans to continue on with their lives.

He turned and started down the back side of the cliff, with the setting sun on his back and long shadows extending out in front of him, for he, too, had to continue on with his life.

He sat behind the wheel with so many cross emotions pummeling his heart. He reached into the breast pocket of his shirt and fished out a pack of *Luckys*. Lighting one, he took a deep drag while looking at Sandy's picture; she was standing on the deck of the Whisper, waving back to him. It caused him to smile.

Before his emotions overwhelmed him, he turned the key and listened to the engine roar. A few seconds later the radio came alive with the Beach Boys singing, "Help Me Rhonda." *Damn straight*, he thought as he headed down the cliff to Coast Highway and south to San Diego, where Carol and Captain Jack were waiting.

112

Captain Jack stood at the tiller, holding it steady against the soft push of the ebbing tide. He watched as Rickey, on the bow, slowly paid out the anchor line and heard him call out, "100 feet."

"Perfect. We's in twenty feet of water so that's five to one. Just right. Tie her off and attach the snubber. We should set back just right."

Neither Captain Jack nor Rickey were too worried that Spring morning about swinging as there was only one other vessel anchored off the beach of the sleepy fishing village of Cabo San Lucas, which everyone just called Cabo. It was at the tip of the Baja Peninsula and about as isolated from mainland Mexico as possible. But it had access to Baja 1, the main highway which ran right up to San Diego where the demand for fish never ended. So while a quaint village, it had a commercial heart and the new dirt strip airfield was bringing in gringos who fished for sport, rather than to feed their families. There was change in the air, but it was the slow change associated with the lower latitude lifestyle.

The fish cannery was off their left with its pier jutting out into the aqua blue water of the bay. There was one boat tied there this morning off-loading its small catch. No mechanized equipment here to move the fish from the boat to the pier. No, it was manpower, and manpower alone. From the Carol, you could see the men on deck, dark brown skin shining from sweat, bent over filling canvas buckets with fish, attaching them to the line swinging off the ship's boom, and hear the grunting of the deckhands as they pulled the line hoisting the bucket in the air and then with the smoothness of a dance step, swinging it out over the dock and dropping it into the waiting cart. Every 30 seconds, with the whop sound of the bucket hitting the cart's bottom, the count man chanted, "Gracias Dios!" as he counted the buckets in the cart. Once the cart was full, its driver would snap a long pole with a bit of string on the end of it around the donkey's ears. That was his signal to start moving the load over to the covered shed where they would dump the fish onto the conveyor for its journey into the plant where it would be de-scaled, de-boned, de-skinned, canned, and cooked. A new can came off the line every 15 seconds making the work both hard and frenzied. But no one complained as the wages of 25 cents an hour American was the best you could get in this little dusty village 1000 miles from San Diego.

Rickey and Captain Jack had just brought the Carol down those 1000 miles without stopping in nine days. Now, standing on the deck and watching the small waves break against the sand, they were both excited and exhausted. The village was a small assembly of cabins cobbled together from whatever materials the locals could find. Here and there, scattered amongst them, were concrete block houses of the most primitive kind. Yet, because of the cannery, the wide dirt road, which was the main street, was anchored on one side by a sentinel-like procession of black power poles which brought the magic of the twentieth century to their lives.

Some of the houses were clustered near the beach but that was mostly the fishermen who needed to have their homes close to the water so they could fill and launch their pongas easily. Other professions placed their cabins where they worked. The ranchers, on the outer edges next to the open land where their cattle and goats could roam. The shopkeepers, near the main road, and the simple homeowner, more toward the center of town, away from the dust of the road and the smell of the cannery.

Rickey stood on the bow and looked into the rising morning sun and began to pick out the various structures against the glare. The sky was a royal blue that defined the silky white clouds with a clear, hard edge. The chill of the night was wearing off quickly and he could feel the warmth of the sun through his poncho. He fingered the edge of the front of the old grey shirt which he hadn't worn in quite awhile. Last night with the wind picking up, he had reached blindly into his duffle for something warm; out the poncho had come. As he fingered the edge of the pocket, his hand instinctively slipped in and he immediately felt paper tucked into the deepest fold. He was surprised and curious at the same time and pulled the paper out. He carefully unfolded it and like a slowly revealing dream, he read its words: YOU ARE ORDERED TO REPORT... He read no further as there was no need. There had been days when he read it over and over again, but not this morning, as he knew all too well what the words said and what they meant. There in his hand, was the beginning of the end of his life.

But standing on the deck of the Carol with the morning sun shining down and the gulls soaring overhead, he felt it hadn't been the beginning of the end, but rather, the prologue of the beginning. He tucked the notice back into the poncho and turned and yelled to Captain Jack, "Damn, it's pretty here." Captain Jack just nodded back. "Think we can get some breakfast ashore?"

Captain Jack just rolled his shoulders and pointed to some smoke coming from a house near the beach with a small fence around it. "We can try."

Half an hour later they were seated at a round table which had the words *AT&T* Cable printed across its diameter. It clearly had been one of the cable spools which carried all those miles of wire which linked this outpost of a village to the rest of the world. The chairs were really stools made from smaller spools nailed together to get the right height. The dark brown *Indio* bottles were so cold, the condensation ran off them leaving deep black rings on the spool tops. The rings reminded Rickey of the Olympic Games which had occurred the Summer before and the strife which had been caused by Tommy Smith raising his fist over his head while on the victory stand. How far and away it all seemed.

"Huevos Rancheros?" the elderly lady standing next to Rickey asked. Not knowing what she was asking, he politely nodded his head and watched as she lifted out of the black iron skillet, two eggs with the most golden yolks Rickey had ever seen. The eggs were resting on a layer of brown beans which was supported by a piece of corn tortilla. Once she placed it on Rickey's plate, she poured a reddish chunky sauce over all of it. Rickey looked it in wonder, never having seen anything like it. He pointed to the sauce and the lady said, "Salsa. Salsa rojo," and smiled as she backed away from the table.

Captain Jack, with an amused look on his face, smiled and raising his beer said, "To many more mystery meals in your travels." They both took a bite and their smiles got wider.

As they sat there in their post-meal stupor, a tall weather-beaten gringo walked into the small front room of Senora Cortez' home, which also served as her restaurant every morning. He had to duck to clear the doorway and as he straightened himself up, he noticed Rickey and Captain Jack. "Hell-o," his voice boomed across the room. "Finally some new faces in town." In two strides, he covered the distance from the front door to their table, and as he approached, he extended his hand. "Howdy there, strangers, I'm Willis. Come down here back in '56 and sorta stayed. Figured it was better than those winters in Minnesota. And I think I figured right. Where ya' all from?"

Captain Jack stood and shook the stranger's hand and said, "Nice to meet ya, Willis. We just sailed our little boat in here this mornin' and are trying to shake some of the salt off. This here is Richard," pointing to Rickey.

Rickey, who was still seated and feeling a bit foolish, just nodded and quickly added, "Grab a stool and join us."

"Well, don't mind if I do as I don't get a lot of chance to talk to new folks and especially fellows on a sailboat."

"Louisa, tres *Patrons,* por favor, con limon."

Captain Jack had a puzzled look on his face. Rickey, who had spent some time in Mexico knew Willis had just ordered three tequila shooters, and good stuff, too; *Patron.*

She sat the tray down in the middle of the table and three empty double shot glasses framed the square bottle on three sides. A silver bowl had quarters of lime spilling over its top, and another silver bowl held some rough looking salt.

"Amigos," Willis said, "this we do every once in awhile to greet newcomers to our little village. It's a simple ceremony but you must do it right to get the best taste of the liquor and the lime. Here, let me show you."

He reached over and poured the pale golden brown liquor into each of the shot glasses. He picked up a slice of lime and rubbed it on the backside of his left hand, and then grabbed some salt and tossed it onto the damp lime spot causing some particles to cling to his skin and others to fall to the floor. He took the small glass and poured it down his throat, and once finished, slammed the glass on the spool top. He then quickly picked up a lime wedge, licked some salt off the back of his hand, then took a hard bite into the lime wedge. It was all done very quickly and without wasted motion.

"Ahhh, damn that's good. Welcome to Cabo. Now your turn."

Captain Jack and Rickey each drank down the burning liquid then soothed the fire with the lime. After several times around the table, Willis leaned back and with a sigh said, "Now I know it don't look like much right now, but this place is gonna be a goldmine someday.

"Now Rickey, don't ya all be lookin' at me like that. Captain Jack knows what I'm saying. You've seen it, ain't ya?"

Captain Jack just smiled and nodded as by now he was feeling the soft edges of reality that the *Patron* caused and was drifting between this room, and a hazy memory of long ago.

Willis took that as an answer and continued, "Look, right now our main attractions are the wreck of the Inari Maru ten feet off the beach there, the girls over at the Riding Club, and fishing. But man, I can just feel it. Someday this place will be full of bars, and hotels, and houses...it will be packed with Americanos looking for fun, booze and sex on the cheap. No matter what happens, this place will always be cheaper than LA. Many will come here to party. And let's face it, things are more easy going here, so you can cut loose and not worry about it. A little kiss of cash and everything is alright. Besides, we've got beautiful beaches. Americanos love beaches."

"Oh, for sure, for sure. The land I'm buying is for my daughter or her kids, not for me. Just buy it and sit on it and bingo, the years go by and you have a small fortune without doing a damn thing. Lookey here, stuff is going from $20 to $90 an acre. I've got four acres off the bluff there backing up to the main road I paid $300 for last year. Another twenty acres up back next to the airstrip. I paid $500 for that only 'cause everyone knows that strip is gonna get paved real soon. Now I ain't braggin', I'm just suggestin' ya all think about it. If ya' all are interested, come see me, I'll help ya out."

"As we were coming to shore this morning, I was thinking that that spot about 200 yards down the beach would be a perfect spot for a surf camp. Build a small lot for campers to park on, and some lean-to's for the back packers. Maybe give some lessons or sell some gear. Funny, I was just thinkin' that this morning."

"Well, you can't buy beachfront land unless you are a Mexican but you can lease it for 99 years, which even for you, should be long enough." Willis said this with a slight chuckle and then stood up. "Well, boys, thanks for the chat and I'm sure I'll see ya before ya leave." He reached over the table and shook both their hands, then turned and walked out the door ducking slightly as he passed through it.

Rickey realized he was paying for the drinks.

113

They stood to the side of the dirt airstrip but it was hard to tell where the strip ended and the side began. The wind whipped small clouds of dust, and caused their collars to flap and strike the sides of their faces. Captain Jack stood with one foot resting on his old grey duffle while Rickey sat on the one piece of hard luggage Captain Jack carried. They were quiet in these last minutes together; minutes they both realized might well be their last. Rickey pulled a pack of *Lucky*s out of the side pocket of his windbreaker and offered them to Captain Jack. He took the pack and shook one loose and put it to his lips to drag it out of the pack. He handed the pack back to Rickey while at the same time palming the *Zippo* lighter from Rickey's hand. As he bent over to shield the flame from the wind he said, "Yuz gonna be fine. Yes, got a damn good little ship under ya, and yuz become a damn good sailor. Yep, nothin' to worry about."

He turned and looked Rickey straight in the eyes as he said, "Nothin at all. Hear me, boy?"

"Ahhh, yeah, yes sir. And I'm not worried. That HO249 for figuring the sun sights is confusing but I've got the worksheets you made for me, and I think I can work it out."

"Now remember the most important thing when yuz taking a sun sight with that sextant, is to hold the sextant steady and get yer timing right. Just a few seconds can make ya miles off. Use yer compass and yer common sense and you'll be OK. He reached out and patted Rickey's shoulder as both of them worked hard to push back their emotions.

As if on cue, the single prop, six seat *Cessna* touched down twenty feet in front of them, kicking up a huge cloud of dust, momentarily turning their world into a hazy brown caldron of dirt and exhaust fumes. The cloud passed as quickly as it came, clearing just in time to see the *Cessna* spin around and head right back toward them. A tall lanky guy opened the cockpit door on the portside and stuck his head out and shouted over the engine, "San Carlos?"

Captain Jack replied, "No, San Diego."

"Same thing. We just gotta few stops first. Let me get some fuel and then we're gonna get going, coming in I saw a front forming out over the ocean. No big thing but I would like to be on the other side of the Sea of Cortez before it hits. I'll be right back." And with that, he throttled up and slowly drove the *Cessna* off in the direction of the small tin shack they had driven past coming in.

"Well," Captain Jack started out, before he could get the second word out, his shoulders began to shake and his hands went into a violent spasm. He shook his head as if trying to clear it and at the same time, get control of his thoughts. He started again, "Ahhh, Rickey..." But again just could not get any further words out, and shook his head in frustration.

"Jack, Jack. I know and I get it. You've been the best friend anyone could have asked for. I love you like I love my parents. They gave me life, but you've given me the freedom to live that life. I will never forget you or all of your kindnesses." They embraced and hugged for what seemed like an awfully long time. Then they broke apart but still held each other's hands. Tears were streaming down Rickey's cheeks but he didn't want to let go of Captain Jack's hand to wipe them away.

The spell was broken when a young boy came and pulled Captain Jack's duffle away. He could barely lift it off the ground and staggered as he walked the 50 feet to where the *Cessna* was parked.

"Well, that's it. I'm off. Back to the grandkids and afternoons in the park. You, my friend, have a great adventure, and kiss a few of those Tahitian women for me."

Rickey held out his hand and Captain Jack took it and they shook but it was more than a handshake; it was an embrace of father and son. "Thank you, Jack. Wherever the Carol and I go, you will be with us."

The roar of the *Cessna*'s engine washed out any further words. They nodded to each other, and Captain Jack turned and walked to the plane. He never looked back.

It wasn't a long walk back to the center of town but for Rickey, it seemed endless. His thoughts rolled back to the last eighteen months and all that had occurred. And here he was, alone, a thousand miles from his family, staring at thousands of miles of open ocean and endless days alone, but free and able to shape his own destiny. His emotions were a swirl of anxiety, hope, gladness, fear, and relief. He was conflicted but not confused. He knew his freedom depended upon his anonymity. And freedom took second place to nothing. You were either free or you were trapped.

He walked steadily and with a purpose as he knew whatever happened would be his choice. He thought of a line from the Moody Blues song, 'Nights in White Satin' - it always struck him as so true:

> "just what you want to be,
> you will be in the end..."

The music from the El Paso Bar filtered out the swinging door entrance and broke off Rickey's singing of the Blue's song in his head. Although it was soft and melodic, he had heard it called *romantica* by the locals; it tore through his own song and cast those thoughts aside. Instead it made him think of Sandy, and Marsha, and Linda, and those women who had left scars upon his heart. It was sad but at the same time with a touch of nostalgia. He knew he had truly loved each of them and now he only hoped there would be another special woman in his future. Having tasted that fruit, he was hungry for it again. With all of the assuredness of youth, he knew he would.

He coughed and realized the dust and the dryness was caking his mouth and throat, and the music was calling him to hear more. He reached into his pocket and felt the roughness of the twenty pesos coins; he counted them. *One hundred pesos. More than enough for a beer or maybe two,* he thought. *Let's grab a cold Indio before going back to the Carol.* "Why not?" he said to himself. "Why the hell not?"

The bar was cool compared to the heat outside and dim compared to the brightness of the street. There were a few Mexicans sitting around two tables playing a card game Rickey didn't know. The stools at the bar stood open waiting for customers to fill them and the bartender stood quietly with a bar towel over his shoulder like a shepherd watching over his flock. The band had paused between songs and the only constant sound was the overhead fan as it stirred the dry, dusty air.

Rickey crossed the floor to one of the open stools while looking at the bartender. Then he heard a voice call out:

"Hey, South Point."

- - - THE END - - -

Acknowledgements

My heartfelt thanks to the many people who helped me shape this tale with their input and comments. However, there are two who deserve special mention.

The patience, guidance and instruction of Sally Alexander of Maryland not only made me a better writer but made this story so much more readable. And without the nimble fingers and critical eye of Victoria Jones of Arizona the manuscript never would have been completed. To both of them I am so very grateful.

I also want to acknowledge the men and women of my generation who faced the same difficult choice that Rickey faced regarding the war. Some chose to resist. Others chose to serve. For all of us, it was life defining. Thankfully no one has to make that choice any longer.

Robert M. Granafei

About The Author

Robert M. Granafei is an Admiralty attorney from Southern California. In his early fifties, he retired and redefined himself as a charter boat captain in the Caribbean. This is his first novel and it is based on his experiences in the 1960's while attending UC, Berkeley.